Mia Sheridan

ISBN: 9781731153500

COVER ARTIST: MIA SHERIDAN
FONT DESIGNER: JUAN CASCO,
WWW.JUANCASCO.NET
(ROMANCE FATAL SERIF)

To Fred, who always has the best advice.

PROLOGUE

Jonah's whistle echoed off the marble walls as he strode purposefully down the empty courthouse hall. Glancing at the domed ceiling, he inhaled deeply, appreciating the timeless smell of law and order. *God, I love it here,* he mused, satisfaction filling his chest.

He'd been coming to the Orleans Parish Criminal District Court since he was just a boy, trailing behind his father and hoping someday to be looked at in the same way others had eyed his dad—with respect, but also laced with a hint of fear.

"If others don't fear you a little, son, you're not doing it right." Of course, his dad applied that same theory to his parenting as well. If anyone ruled his home with an iron fist, it was Edward Chamberlain.

"Have a good day, Mr. Chamberlain," said the blonde attorney in the pencil skirt as she passed through the metal detector. She was entering on the other side and looked over her shoulder as she passed, running her eyes quickly down his body and biting her full bottom lip. She'd been sending him *come hither* signals for weeks, and although he'd been too busy to indulge in extracurricular activities, as soon as this case was over, he was going to take her up on her "offer." The thought of peeling that conservative suit off her shapely body and finding out what she wore beneath caused a pleasant twitch between his legs.

He jogged down the stone steps outside, swinging his leather briefcase by his side. *The world is my goddamned oyster,* he thought with a grin.

Applegate, Knowles, and Fennimore was less than a mile from the courthouse and he chose to walk, whistling again—that damn song that had been stuck in his head since Palmer Applegate's retirement party two days before.

Palmer was the senior of all the senior partners at the firm, who, by the way, wasn't anywhere *close* to a jolly good fellow. The old guy was a "Stodgy, Lifeless Bore," but Jonah supposed a tune by that name might not have gone over quite so well at an honorary event. In any case, he would now be boring his new trophy wife on a full-time basis rather than the rest of the employees at the firm Jonah had been hired at six months ago.

The prestigious law firm occupied the entire top two floors of the brick building Jonah entered, whistling a few bars yet again as the door swung shut behind him.

That nobody can deny!

The elevator ascended smoothly, dinging as the doors slid open.

"Good afternoon, sir," his secretary, Iris, greeted.

"Iris. Any—" His words cut off abruptly when the man sitting in a chair in the small waiting room to his left stood. *Justin.*

"Sir, I told this gentleman your schedule was packed but—"

Jonah gave her a nod, concealing a grimace. "It's okay, Iris. This is my brother, Justin."

"Oh," Iris said. "I didn't realize . . ."

It spoke to how little anyone at the firm really knew him—though he spent the majority of his time there—that they didn't know Justin Chamberlain was his brother. Justin was a lawyer as well, though the law firm Justin worked for was in a far different zip code, and from what Jonah could tell, took on more pro bono cases than paid clients. It was a wonder they could afford office space at all.

He gripped his brother's hand, smiling as they shook. "What's up, bro? Long time no see."

Justin gave him a thin smile. "Do you have a minute?"

"Not really—"

"It's important." Justin shoved a hand through his dark brown hair, exposing the Chamberlain widow's peak before his hair flopped over his forehead again.

Jonah glanced pointedly at his Rolex as Justin continued. "I've been calling you for weeks now. I even stopped by your apartment a couple of times."

Jonah sighed. He'd received the messages. He just hadn't had time to call his brother back. What the hell could be that important anyway?

He signaled Justin to follow him to his office down the hall. "I've been slammed. You know I'm in the middle of this big case. I'm preparing to cross-examine the victim tomorrow. This could be—"

"That's what I want to talk to you about." Justin shut Jonah's door, and Jonah felt a moment of pride as he watched his brother take in the small but luxurious office with a glimpse of the New Orleans skyline out the window. But when he turned his eyes back to Jonah, Justin's expression was grim.

"Don't do this, Jonah."

"Do what exactly?"

"This case." He shook his head, his bleeding heart making his eyes glisten in a way that made Jonah want to roll his eyes. "Murray Ridgley committed this crime and you know it."

Jonah leaned back against the wall, crossing his arms. "The partners took on his case because they believe in his innocence, Justin. True, it doesn't look good. The circumstantial evidence is . . . extensive. But he deserves a fair trial and good representation just like any other citizen."

"I'm not arguing with that. All I'm saying is let someone else talk to the news cameras from here on out. Let someone *else* cross-examine the victim. I know you, Jonah. You're a damn good attorney. You'll crush her if that's your aim. But please don't, I beg you. Don't be tied to this. Don't have this case be the one you're remembered for. This is not something you want to hang your legacy on."

"Jesus, listen to yourself. Are you telling me not to *win?*" In the last few weeks, he'd become the face of this case—the partners had designed it that way and he hadn't needed to ask why. He was handsome, and he had the smile of a golden boy. Women liked looking at him; men respected him. *The jury trusted him.*

"I'm telling you not to be like Dad."

That stopped Jonah like a punch to the gut. He knew that Justin, being the oldest, had taken the brunt of the discipline in their house. The lion's share of the pressure Edward Chamberlain pressed upon his sons had landed on Justin's shoulders. As a little boy, Jonah had watched and learned. He knew what brought about his father's wrath and what gained his approval, and he strove always for the latter.

"Dad wasn't all bad."

"Is anyone?"

Good question.

Maybe Murray Ridgley if he had in fact committed the crime. Jonah had plenty of doubts himself. And he had this notion that there was something the partners weren't telling him. But he had no proof of that, just some whisperings behind closed doors as he'd walked past.

And this case . . . this case was the one that could catapult him to the next level. If he impressed the partners, it could literally *make* his career.

One of the junior partners was taking Applegate's vacancy, but one of the other two remaining original partners, Knowles, was practically a walking corpse. In the next couple of years, he'd retire or die, and if Jonah played his cards right, he could make junior partner and then partner thereafter. *Partner!* Even his dad hadn't made junior partner until he was thirty.

Jonah had worked his ass off to graduate college in two and a half years, had attended an accelerated law school program, passed the bar on the first try, and had received a job offer at one of the most prestigious firms in New Orleans immediately after that. He was on the fast track. He couldn't afford a stumble.

Jonah met his brother's gaze. "Dad was *respected.*"

Justin's eyes narrowed. "Dad was a sonofabitch who cared about power far more than he cared about *people.* He ruined lives as easily as he buttered toast. That's not you, Jonah. I'm your brother. I know—"

"All right, listen, I appreciate this whole do-gooder speech, but let me assure you that my conscience is perfectly clear where my job is concerned. Murray Ridgley may very well have committed this crime." *Murray Ridgley may very well be a monster.* "But I'm *not* going to ask to be removed from his case. It would ruin me."

Justin studied his brother for long moments before moving his eyes away again, toward the picturesque view. "I just have a feeling . . . you're choosing a path here, Jonah." He looked at him again, and this time Jonah detected sadness in his brother's eyes before he gave him a small smile. "Quitting this case . . . you're right, it would probably mean your career at this firm was over, but you always have a job with me."

Jonah chuckled. "Fighting injustice for little more than pocket change? That's *your* calling."

Justin released a laugh that contained more breath than levity. "I could use a little help. There's a lot of injustice in the world, bro."

"Some might say it's worthless to try to fight against it."

"Some might."

As he looked at the person he loved most in the world, something pressed on his chest, some weightiness he wasn't sure how to explain. A feeling that— His phone rang, breaking the strange sort of trance that had descended upon Jonah. "I really gotta get back to work. Can we talk later?"

Justin nodded, his smile sad again as he moved past Jonah. He laid a hand on his brother's shoulder. "Sure, Jonah. Let's talk later." And with that, he turned and walked out of Jonah's office, shutting the door behind him.

The phone continued to ring, but Jonah didn't answer it. Instead, he walked to the window and stared out at the sweltering summer day, that feeling returning to his chest again—pressing. *I miss my brother,* Jonah realized. He *had* been avoiding him. But after this case was over, he would make it a point to see Justin more often.

Absentmindedly, Jonah brought his hand to the place where his heart lay and massaged lightly.

You're choosing a path here, Jonah.

But he'd already chosen it. There was nothing to be done now.

Two weeks later, as Jonah lay in a pool of spreading blood, the charred smell of his mutilated flesh heavy and rancid in his nostrils, his brother's words would come back to him, flowing lazily through his mind like the misty wisps of a forgotten dream.

You're choosing a path. Let's talk later.

But there would be no talking to his brother later.

His brother was dead.

The screaming dimmed enough for Jonah to register the high-pitched expulsion of air rasping from his smoke-drenched lungs.

He was whistling again.

Only this time, there was no tune.

CHAPTER ONE

Present Day

"Extend your arm. Clara, you are supposed to look like a swan but you look like a duck. Begin again." The music came to a sudden halt and there was a collective—though quiet—groan from the other dancers. Heat rose in Clara's face as she noticed the disdainful glares shot in her direction. Being the new girl in the New Orleans Ballet was proving to be everything she'd feared. And more.

"Yes, Madame Fournier." Clara returned to her mark, positioning her body as the music began again. *I am a swan. I am a swan,* she chanted in her mind.

The problem was, despite her focus on a gracefully extended arm, Clara *felt* like a duck. One very much out of water.

As practice ended and the other dancers began gathering their things, Clara walked to her duffle bag, putting her foot on the bench and untying the silken ribbons of her pointe shoes.

"A girl I know went to the Goddard School with her," Belinda Baker whispered from behind Clara, clearly referring to *her*. "She was the recipient of that Dance For Life Scholarship, otherwise she never would have gotten in." Clara swung her duffle bag over her shoulder, glancing back at Belinda, who obviously hadn't realized she was there, her eyes widening in surprise as their gazes met. Clara turned and quickly walked out of the theater.

It was true what Belinda had said: Clara's father had sacrificed in every way possible so she could follow her dream of becoming a professional ballerina. But he never could have afforded that school without assistance. Clara was *proud* of that scholarship, and she wouldn't let a couple of gossipy girls make her feel differently.

Still, thoughts of her father caused that familiar ache to take center stage in her chest and she had to force herself not to tear up. Her recent move to New Orleans had been hard, the fact that her reception in the ballet had been less than . . . *warm* only compounded that hardship, and this feeling of *melancholy* seemed to be her constant companion.

She spotted the bus rounding the corner and speed-walked to make it to the bus stop a block away, fumbling for her phone. "Thanks," she said breathlessly as she scanned her mobile ticket, and the bus driver gave her a wide, welcoming smile. She smiled back, grateful for what felt like a little sunshine on a cloudy day.

Thirty minutes later, she stepped off the air-conditioned bus, the heat hitting her and causing a physical jolt. If she were living a story, the New Orleans summer heat would be a character all its own. A large, corpulent fellow with sleepy eyes and steamy breath. Intense and all-consuming.

A lock of blonde hair fell loose from her bun and Clara tucked it behind her ear, as the smell of something savory and delicious met her nose, wafting from the house on the corner and distracting her from the mugginess. *Comfort food.* What was it about almost all the Louisiana cuisine she'd sampled that seemed to minister not only to the palate but to the soul?

The smooth, plaintive sound of a saxophone from an open window somewhere nearby wound through the tree branches and seemed to penetrate Clara's skin.

Is there anything lonelier than the distant sound of a singular instrument floating on the wind? she mused.

But then another sound joined that lonesome melody—a sweet, rich voice accompanying the notes, weaving, growing louder, clearer. The music—both distant and close by and yet somehow still a seamless duet—filled Clara, causing her skin to feel charged and her heart to lighten. She knew that voice. It sounded like smoke mixed with molasses and so often carried hymns along the street where Clara lived.

The voice halted. "Well hello, darlin'."

Clara smiled even before she looked up at Mrs. Guillot rocking in her rocking chair at the end of the block where Clara rented a small garden apartment.

"You looked so deep in thought I hardly wanted to disturb you," the old woman said with a smile.

Clara opened Mrs. Guillot's black, wrought iron gate and slipped inside, climbing the brick steps and sitting on the second wooden rocking chair that usually sat empty. "Just going over the moves from practice today."

"Ah. How is it going with the other swans?"

"All right. I just wish . . . " What did she wish? That they didn't act so petty? That she'd make a friend? Feel more accepted and not as if she were being judged and found lacking? Clara shook her head. "I wish I knew at least one person here. Starting from scratch is harder than I imagined it would be."

Mrs. Guillot smiled kindly. "Well, you do know one person. You know me."

"Oh, Mrs. Guillot, I didn't mean—"

"Nonsense, child." She laughed. "I know what you meant. I was only teasing you. A young woman like yourself needs other young people. You'll find them. Don't you worry your pretty little head now."

Clara released a breath. "I know. And that will be nice. But I'm grateful for you too." It was true. Mrs. Guillot had been so kind to Clara since she'd moved to New Orleans two months before, offering up her knowledge about the city, giving her directions when she needed them, and sitting and chatting when Clara had a few minutes now and again.

"I know, darlin'." She paused. "How's your dad? Have you spoken to him?"

A stab of pain pricked at Clara's insides as she shook her head. "I wish. His moments of clarity are so few and far between now."

Mrs. Guillot studied Clara for a moment, her gaze filled with the sincere sympathy of someone who knew the pain of loss. Of course she did. How many times had Mrs. Guillot grieved in her lifetime? "Well now, sweet thing, that's two wishes. Go give one of them to Angelina."

"Angelina?"

"Mm-hmm. You've been in New Orleans for a couple of months now. You haven't heard of the weeping wall?"

The weeping wall. A strange tremble went down Clara's spine. "No. Where is it?"

"Why, it's at Windisle Plantation."

Windisle Plantation. Clara took the duffle bag from her lap and placed it on the ground next to her chair, leaning forward slightly. "Will you tell me about it, Mrs. Guillot?"

Mrs. Guillot's gaze moved away from Clara, out to the ancient magnolia tree that grew in the yard next door, its giant white blossoms and glossy green leaves shimmering in the last rays of the summer sun.

She settled herself back in her chair, the old wood squeaking as her eyes met Clara's once more. "It's a sugar plantation that was built more than two hundred years ago." Clara realized she was holding her breath. She released it slowly so as not to distract Mrs. Guillot from her story. "Oh, some call it sacred. And some call it cursed. But everyone does agree that it's haunted."

Mrs. Guillot's brown, gnarled hands gripped the arms of the rocking chair, the wedding ring she still wore glinting in the final vestiges of daylight. "You see, darlin', a young woman named Angelina Loreaux, broken-hearted by her lover's betrayal, took her own life in the rose garden, and that is where her restless spirit lingers still, along with the ghost of the man who rejected her, denied eternal peace by the tragic results of his worldly actions." Mrs. Guillot smiled ruefully. "Though I've always thought if such a thing were true—if people are destined to haunt the earth because of their selfish human choices—why, there wouldn't be any souls in heaven at all." Mrs. Guillot's lips tipped, and internally, Clara agreed. No, in that case, she suspected heaven would be quite empty.

"What a heartbreaking story."

Mrs. Guillot nodded solemnly. "Oh yes."

"Who was she? Angelina, I mean. Was she the daughter of the plantation owner?"

"Well, yes. Robert Chamberlain was his name. But she was also the daughter of Mama Loreaux, a kitchen slave who bore his illegitimate daughter. Mama Loreaux was a striking woman with dark, perceptive eyes, they say, and known among her fellow slaves to practice a West African form of voodoo passed down by her mother and her grandmother. She used herbs and charms to provide relief from every ailment under the sun. Their daughter, Angelina Loreaux, was a beautiful, spirited child, beloved by her mother *and* her father. It's said that Robert Chamberlain was enchanted by his little girl and would rock her on his knee on the front porch of the plantation house . . . much to the chagrin of his wife and legitimate children, who tolerated Angelina though not much more."

Intrigued, Clara tilted her head in wonder, soaking in every word of the story. *How utterly tragic.* It stole her breath.

"Angelina grew up in the Chamberlain kitchen under the careful watch of her mother, charming her own family of slaves and visitors to the plantation alike. Quick to laugh, possessing kindness as warm as sunshine, a spirit as delicate as the wings of a hummingbird, and the rare beauty of an exotic flower, she was very easy to love. Or so it's been said."

"Where does all this information come from, Mrs. Guillot?"

"Oh, the other slaves who lived at Windisle, I imagine. It's been passed down through generations. Why, my own grandmother told me the story of Angelina Loreaux and John Whitfield when I was knee-high to a mosquito." She laughed, the sound melodic and sweet.

"Anyway, the way the story goes, when Angelina was seventeen, she met John Whitfield, a young southern soldier from an extremely wealthy family, who was at the plantation. They spent only a short time together but John became enchanted by the beautiful Angelina." Mrs. Guillot frowned. "It's said they both fell in love, but I find it hard to believe due to what occurred later."

"He betrayed her," Clara whispered. "And she took her own life."

"Yes." Mrs. Guillot nodded. "But before that, they became lovers in secret."

In secret. Of course, Clara thought. What a completely different world they lived in. Her own problems, her own sadness suddenly seemed . . . well, not minor exactly. But how terrible would it be to fall deeply in love with someone and have to keep it hidden like a shameful secret? It would be unbearable, wouldn't it? "How did he betray her?" Clara asked, almost afraid to know.

"Well, oh I guess it'd be in 1860 or '61, John was called to serve in the Civil War. He left Angelina, making promises to return to her. Angelina waited, loving him unendingly, her pure and tender heart filled with hope for the future they'd somehow create together. She must have been a dreamer, that one." Mrs. Guillot looked thoughtful for a moment. "Perhaps it seemed to her that she'd finally found a place to belong in a world where she felt part of nothing at all." Mrs. Guillot smiled. "But that's just my own supposing."

"It makes sense," Clara murmured.

Mrs. Guillot frowned. "However, John's heart was not as true, and he sent a note through his family telling Angelina he no longer loved her, and she should forget him as he'd already begun to forget her."

She started to rock again, the squeaking of the chair breaking the silence that had descended upon the street. The saxophone player had put away his instrument at some point and Clara hadn't even noticed. "Angelina was shattered and she fled to the rose garden. It was there, the place where she'd first met her beloved, that she took one of her father's razors to her wrists."

Clara gasped, sorrow flooding her heart, though she'd already been told the outcome.

Mrs. Guillot nodded as if she'd perfectly understood Clara's small intake of breath. "Yes, I know. Mama Loreaux found her daughter, and they say her keening cry of horror carried on the wind to every corner of Windisle Plantation and far beyond. She held her daughter's sweet head in her arms and cursed the love that had taken her precious girl, calling to the spirits that John *never* find true love, in this life or the next."

Mrs. Guillot sighed. "John came home from the war and lived alone until his death, indeed never finding love at all. He was rarely seen in public, and it was said he suffered frequent flashbacks from the war. He contracted tuberculosis in his late thirties and died of the disease shortly thereafter."

Good! Clara was tempted to say. But she didn't. It seemed wrong to curse someone who was already dead. *And* already cursed.

They were both silent for several moments as Clara let the story filter through her mind. She felt somehow taken over by the sad tale, as if it had not only piqued her interest but had wrapped itself around her bones, her very being. "How is the weeping wall tied to the story? And why do people make wishes there?"

Mrs. Guillot's deeply lined forehead lowered in thought. "From what I remember, it's believed that John and Angelina's spirits wander the rose garden, even still, unable to find rest, unable to find peace, always seeking the thing that will free them of the burden of their earthly sins. The locals believe that Angelina, somehow tangled up in the curse in a way no one truly knows, will grant a wish to those who slip one through the cracks in the wall surrounding Windisle."

Mrs. Guillot smiled. "Angelina grants wishes, they say, to encourage more people to come, hoping that one special someone will be able to solve the riddle and break the curse."

"What riddle?"

Mrs. Guillot frowned again. "Well now, I don't think I remember exactly how the riddle goes, but I do believe it was spoken by a voodoo priestess at some time or another. You could ask Dory Dupre at the neighborhood library. She'd probably remember or be able to look it up for you."

Clara smiled, happy to be given a direction in which to learn more about the mystery. "I will. Do you know why it's called the weeping wall?"

"It's said that the wall weeps tears for the heartbreak and tragedy that came to pass behind it, for the spirits still trapped within. Now I don't know about that as the few times I've been there, I never witnessed it, but it's said that it will only stop weeping when John and Angelina's spirits are set free."

"Who lives there now, Mrs. Guillot?"

"I don't believe anyone does. It's been empty for years."

Clara's thoughts were interrupted by the squeak of the gate as it opened. An old man holding a cane walked through, removing his hat and smiling bashfully up at Mrs. Guillot. "Bernice, fine evening, isn't it?"

Clara glanced over at Mrs. Guillot, and though her skin was a beautifully deep mahogany, she swore there was a blush glowing on her wrinkled cheeks.

"Harry."

Harry glanced at Clara, inclining his head. "I didn't realize you had company. I was just on my evening stroll and thought I'd drop in and say hi."

Clara stood, grabbing her bag. "Actually, I really should go. I have an early morning." She leaned over and kissed Mrs. Guillot's cheek, her papery skin as soft as velvet. "Thank you so much for telling me the story."

"I don't have a lot left, but I'm full to the brim with stories." Mrs. Guillot laughed. "You go slip a wish or two through the cracks in that wall," she said softly. "And say hi to Angelina for me."

Clara nodded and shot a grin over her shoulder as she walked down the steps. "I will."

"Oh and Clara dear," Mrs. Guillot called. "I'll have some more of that homemade liniment for you next time you stop by."

Clara suppressed a grimace, smiling back at the sweet old woman. "Thank you, Mrs. Guillot." She nodded at Harry as she moved past him, noting that he was looking pretty dapper in his pressed shirt and fedora for a simple evening walk. "Have a good evening, you two."

****

That Sunday, Clara woke up bright and early and walked the ten blocks to the library.

She'd been turning over the story of Windisle in her mind ever since Mrs. Guillot had told her about it several days before. Clara had become captivated—perhaps even a little obsessed—with the tale of heartbreak and misery that had occurred more than a hundred and fifty years before. She thought about it as she rode the bus to and from the ballet, she thought about it as she drifted off to sleep at night, and she even thought about it as she danced, the whispers of the other ballerinas becoming mere background noise.

She was no longer distracted by them, her mind instead focused inward on a beautiful girl who had a smile like the sunshine and a spirit as delicate as a hummingbird's wings. What had her life been like? Had it been filled with suffering even before the betrayal that caused her to take her own life? And what dark secrets lay behind that wall?

Perhaps the intensity of Clara's focus on the legend had as much to do with her loneliness that summer as with the intrigue of the tale. But she also felt this strange *pull* inside whenever she thought of Windisle. *Whatever* the reason, she wanted to know *more.*

The small library was dim and quiet, and as Clara entered she paused, inhaling deeply of the unmistakable smell of old books—aged paper and souls cast in ink.

There were a few people browsing the shelves quietly, but even on a Sunday, the space was mostly empty. Clara spotted an older woman with a cart next to her re-shelving books and walked to where she was. "Excuse me?"

The tiny old woman turned, smiling. She looked to be in her nineties at least, a pair of glasses hanging on a chain around her neck, her poof of white hair a startling contrast to her rich brown skin. "May I help you?"

"Are you Dory Dupre?"

"I am."

"Oh good." Clara smiled, extending her hand. "I'm Clara Campbell. Mrs. Guillot suggested I should come speak to you."

"Oh, how is Bernice?"

Clara's smile grew. "She's very good."

"Wonderful to hear. Now what subject did you want to speak to me about?"

"Windisle Plantation."

A shadow moved across Ms. Dupre's face, her wrinkles seeming to tighten for a brief moment. She shook her head. "Tragic tale."

"Yes," Clara breathed. "Mrs. Guillot told me what she knew, but she wasn't able to answer all my questions."

"Ah. Follow me. I'll see if I can fill in some blanks."

Clara followed the elderly librarian to a round table near the checkout counter, and they both sat down. "May I ask why you're interested in Windisle, dear?"

Clara glanced to the side, considering the question. "Truthfully, Ms. Dupre, I'm not entirely sure. Mrs. Guillot told me the story, and I can't seem to get it out of my mind."

"I don't blame you. It's an intriguing story. And so much mystery." She smiled. "And who knows, maybe you'll be the one to solve the riddle and set Angelina free. Do you believe in curses, dear?"

Clara laughed softly. "I don't know that I believe in curses, but I'd love to hear the riddle if you remember it."

"Oh, I remember it well. I heard it spoken in person by the voodoo priestess herself."

Clara's eyes widened in surprise. "You did?"

"Oh yes. It was first said at a party held at Windisle Manor in 1934. Now, that was back when the Chamberlain family still occupied it and threw lavish soirees. I was only fourteen but my sister got me a job working for the catering company at that gathering. Prentiss Chamberlain and his wife, Dixie, asked an old, blind voodoo priestess to attend." She paused. "From what I knew, the Chamberlain family never did put much stock in the belief that ghosts roamed their property—though there were always rumors that guests to the house reported seeing ghostly apparitions, especially near the rose garden. But in any case, Prentiss and Dixie Chamberlain were happy enough to use the legend as entertainment, and for that reason, the priestess was invited."

Ms. Dupre looked off behind Clara, her gaze growing distant as she looked into the past. "The priestess sat in a red velvet chair and the crowd of partygoers gathered, the entire room growing silent. I watched from a doorway off to the side, practically holding my breath. There was this . . . feeling in the room. I remember it well, though I still find it difficult to explain. A . . . heaviness, something pressing. The priestess—I can still see her closing her milky eyes as she spoke—confirmed that indeed the spirits of John and Angelina haunted the grounds, specifically the garden where they both roamed, blind to the presence of the other."

"How sad," Clara whispered. Although she supposed it was better that Angelina not have to wander eternally with a man who broke her heart.

Ms. Dupre nodded. "A party guest asked about the curse Mama Loreaux had cast, and the priestess said that indeed it was true and that *such* a curse could be broken by one thing and one thing alone." Her pause was full, weighty as she met Clara's eyes. "By a drop of Angelina's blood being brought to the light."

By a drop of Angelina's blood being brought to the light. Clara let the words slip around her. "No one has any idea what it means?"

Ms. Dupre shook her head. "No one, including the priestess, who insisted the spirits didn't always reveal their secrets, even to her."

Clara turned that over in her mind, committing the line to memory.

They spoke for a few more minutes, Clara telling Ms. Dupre the gist of what Mrs. Guillot had imparted about the legend. Ms. Dupre couldn't offer anything more in the way of information, but pointed Clara to the computers where she said she might find something about the house itself, and the family who had once occupied it.

Clara thanked Ms. Dupre warmly just as a woman approached the desk to check out a stack of books.

Seated at the computer, Clara did a search of both the plantation and the family, scrolling through the articles she found, making a few notes on the small pieces of loose paper provided at each of the three stations.

Windisle Manor, a Greek Revival-style home, was built in the early eighteen hundreds on a one-thousand-acre sugar plantation owned by the Chamberlain family. Before the Civil War, Windisle Plantation owned over a hundred slaves, most of whom toiled in the sugarcane fields, but some of whom worked in the manor.

"Mama Loreaux," Clara whispered softly, picturing the striking woman with the knowing eyes Mrs. Guillot had described. She could see her now, watching from a window as Robert Chamberlain rocked her little girl on his knee and his family looked on with disdain. What had that been like for her? *How had she felt?*

Coming from a working class, single-parent household, Clara had experienced her share of scathing judgment from the haughty rich girls at the ballet schools she'd attended, and it had made her feel uncomfortable. But it wasn't twenty-four hours a day. And not everyone participated. She couldn't fathom the nasty, open barbs of vitriol that'd be thrown her way if—for most anyway—it wasn't frowned upon to criticize those considered beneath you.

Clara focused her mind back on the information in front of her. Unlike many of the other plantations in the area that had been passed on to the Historic Preservation Society and opened to the public, the Chamberlain family still owned Windisle, and it remained a private residence. Eager to get their hands on this great piece of American history, the Historic Preservation Society had made many offers to the family and had received just as many rejections. *Interesting,* Clara thought, wondering why the family had no interest in preserving the estate.

She got lost in her search, lost in the history on the screen in front of her, and before she knew it, the large clock on the wall told her several hours had passed, while her stomach told her—loudly—she'd missed lunch.

Ms. Dupre was speaking to a library patron on the other side of the room and Clara gave her a small wave before heading outside where the sky lay soft and blue against a fiery sun.

As she walked home, she admired the old, quaint homes along the street, painted in bright hues, embellished with ornate architectural details: scrolling corbels, hand-carved columns, formal molding, and large transom windows. Many of them had fallen to disrepair, the railings loose and sagging, flowering vines and bushes mixed with weeds overtaking the tiny yards, grand wooden doors cracked and faded. But even those homes still held beauty, and Clara felt a tug at her heart for all things in the great wide world that had been loved before and waited patiently to be loved again.

As she turned onto her street, Windisle Manor rose in her mind, the way it'd been depicted in the photos she'd seen: grand, striking . . . endless sugarcane fields fanned out around it.

She'd found several articles in the society pages from decades past, referencing parties and events held at the manor. Guests of those gatherings had praised the condition and beauty of the house and grounds, and the pictures offered proof of its grandeur. But in recent years, nothing whatsoever appeared in print regarding the plantation.

From what Clara could gather, there was no one living there—at least no one whose heart was still beating.

CHAPTER TWO

"Hello, Mrs. Lovett? This is Clara."

"Oh hello, Clara dear. How's New Orleans? How are you settling in?"

"It's good. I'm settling in just fine." Clara put a smile in her voice, determined to sound positive, even if she wasn't truly settled. *Yet.*

"I'm so glad to hear it."

"How is he today, Mrs. Lovett?"

There was a short pause before Mrs. Lovett answered, and her voice was lower than it'd been just a moment ago. "He had a bit of an episode yesterday." When Clara began to cut in, Mrs. Lovett steamed ahead. "Oh, nothing major. He got a bit aggravated and threw his lunch tray. We gave him a sedative to calm him down and he's still sleeping."

Clara's heart sank. She'd been hoping to speak to her dad, if only for a moment, just to hear his voice. Tears pricked her eyes. "Was he lucid at all yesterday?"

"Not yesterday, dear." Clara could hear the regret in her words. She knew how much the sweet older nurse would have liked to give her good news. Clara had grown close to her in the time she'd spent in the care facility with her dad before she'd left for New Orleans.

"Will you call me later tonight if his condition changes?"

"Of course I will."

They spoke for another minute and then said goodbye. Clara put her phone slowly back in her purse, a singular tear rolling down her cheek. She swiped at it, taking in a big, shaky breath. She was homesick—lonely—and she would have missed her father even under the best of circumstances. But to know that he was fading away day by day and she was so far away was like a knife carving into her heart.

Soon he'd be gone and she'd have missed the last few precious moments with him while his mind was still clear, while he still knew she was there. When the fog lifted, now and again, did he wonder where she was? Did he wonder why she'd deserted him when he needed her the most? Or did he recall that he'd told her to go? "Oh, Dad," she whispered into the emptiness of her apartment.

Clara stood from the chair in her tiny kitchen, grabbing her purse. She needed air. She needed to escape the four walls closing in on her. Dancing helped her remember why she was here, helped her remember the willing sacrifices her father had made. But it was her day off, and anyway, her body needed the rest. She wished she had—

The thought cut off abruptly as she stepped out into the sultry New Orleans day, the word *wish* bouncing through her mind. She pulled out her phone and searched for Windisle Plantation, easily finding the address. A few minutes after that, an Uber was pulling up to the curb and she was on her way to the weeping wall.

Twenty minutes later when she stepped out of the car, the day had grown slightly breezy, the moving air feeling wonderful across her heated skin. Clara sighed with pleasure, breathing in the sweet, ripe scents of summer and enjoying the reprieve from the sweltering weather of the past few weeks.

Above her, the sky was cast in various shades of gray, the clouds ringed in a silvery glow. It looked as if there was going to be a summer storm. A flock of birds swept through the sparkling mist, one falling out of formation and trailing alone for a heartbeat before the rest of the group turned back, gathering their lost member, the whole of their pattern complete once more.

For a minute, Clara simply stood on the side of the narrow street, no cars in sight. She was surprised to find the street deserted. She'd pictured at least a few other people standing at the wall, wish in hand. She began walking toward the stone structure across from her, happy she'd chosen a day when she had the place to herself.

Clara wrapped her arms around her waist as she approached what she knew must be the weeping wall. It was an eight-foot-high stone structure ending in dense woods and high reedy grass near the edge of the Mississippi River on one side and the beginning of what had once been the sugar crops on the other, now a tangle of overgrowth.

The middle of the wall formed an open arch, barricaded by an iron gate. Wild roses spiraled through the bars, creating a thick tangle of green leaves, heavily thorned vines, and vibrant crimson flowers. There was something both lush and savage about it, and that strange chill—part fear, part excitement—skittered down her spine.

For a moment she simply stared, in awe of its size and that she was finally in front of the very thing she'd spent weeks pondering. If it were true that the wall wept, it wasn't weeping today. The stone was dry, its color reminding her of the sky above with its various hues of pewter and sterling. Thin slivers of platinum light shone through the cracks where mortar had broken away, the spots through which a wish could be slipped.

I wish . . .

I wish . . .

It was as if the whispers, the hopes . . . the prayers, still hung on the wind, suspended somehow as if they, too, were ghostly spirits forever trapped in the air surrounding this haunted place.

"Get a grip, Clara," she murmured to herself. She'd always been drawn to stories. She loved learning the tales of the dance productions she was a part of. The romance and the heartache always fueled her creativity and helped her *become* the character. It was another reason, she supposed, that she was so drawn to the legend of Windisle, of Angelina Loreaux and her tragic tale.

But ghosts? Curses? She didn't *necessarily* believe in any of that, although she didn't dismiss it entirely either. But, in any case, it was the story at the *heart* of it all that intrigued her the most. And *this* was where it had all begun.

She approached tentatively, wonder mixing with breathless sadness. Placing her shaky hands upon the wall and leaning forward, she rested her cheek on the solid structure, her mind filled with hazy imaginings of what had happened beyond it.

The wall protected the house and the land from potentially harmful forces outside, but who had protected those contained within? Suddenly, Clara was completely overwhelmed by the knowledge that such harrowing anguish—not just Angelina's, but the slaves who had lived their lives there as well—had been experienced so close to the very spot where she now stood.

She wondered if their blood and their sweat was still mixed in the soil of the weed-ridden sugarcane fields and felt so full of grief she thought she might weep. She remembered crying as a little girl over a sad story she'd overheard on the news. Her father had wiped her tears and told her she couldn't always cry for the world or she'd be crying all the time.

"But, Daddy," she'd said, "if I don't let my tears out, won't I drown inside?"

And that's how Clara felt, standing before that wall . . . her heart drowning slowly.

She slipped her wish out of her pocket—the one she'd written in the Uber on the ride there, pausing at the soft sound of movement on the other side, a small animal perhaps, or maybe just plants rustling in the breeze. Or maybe it was Angelina, her ghostly spirit standing hopeful on the other side, waiting for the one who would somehow set her free.

By a drop of her blood being brought to the light.

Staring at her wish, she suddenly felt foolish, not because she was *making* the wish, but because her own personal sadness seemed . . . small. Not unimportant—Clara believed all pain mattered—but hers was a part of the natural order of things, wasn't it?

She released a loud breath. "How silly and selfish you must think we all are," she muttered, crumpling the paper in her fist and shutting her eyes. "Coming here to make our own wishes when you've been waiting decades for your own to be granted. When the life you led held more heartache than we'll ever know."

Clara hesitated for a moment, considering, before she un-crumpled the paper and removed a pen from the purse slung over her shoulder. She tore off the wish she had written, stuffing the small piece of torn paper in her pocket and then wrote a *different* wish. After folding the paper back up, she slipped it through one of the thin cracks.

She started to turn away and then impulsively turned back, peeking through the slit in the stone. Movement made her blink, and she startled slightly, drawing back and inhaling a quick breath.

Cautiously, she moved forward again, peeking through the crack once more. This time she saw nothing. She couldn't even make out a house beyond, as the gaps in the rock were so small and narrow. She could only discern a hint of green. Of course, looking up told her that massive oak trees beyond the wall, would most likely shield the house from view anyhow.

What did I see? She waited . . . for what she didn't know, when she swore she heard the sound of paper crinkling. She stepped closer again, placing her fingertips against the wall. "Hello?" She didn't know why, but she had a vague notion that whatever or whomever was on the other side of the wall stilled, just as she did.

When she received no answer, she turned, unsure of what to do, sliding down the wall until her spine was pressed against it, her head leaned back, listening. She sensed that someone was on the other side, waiting, listening as well.

She closed her eyes and after several minutes, she heard faint rustling again. If she hadn't been pressed right against the wall, she'd have thought it was a bird in some distant tree, flapping its wings for takeoff and lifting through the branches. She pressed her cheek against the stone, her ear right over the ancient, cracked, and porous mortar, and she heard . . . *breathing.* Her eyes widened and her heart quickened. There was no ghost on the other side, but a flesh-and-blood human.

"I hear you breathing."

The breathing suddenly halted, and Clara waited a second, two. "I didn't mean that you should stop."

After another moment, a loud whoosh of breath could be heard. Clara blinked.

"Who are you?" she asked, not knowing if she expected an answer or not.

For a long moment there was no response, and she was about to try again when a masculine voice finally said, "My name's Jonah. What's yours?"

Surprise gripped Clara. There was a man sitting on the other side of the wall, his back pressed to the same place as hers, only a layer of stone separating them. For a second her own name eluded her. "Uh, Clara."

"Clara," he repeated. A whispered caress. She had no idea who he was, but she liked the way her name sounded in his voice, the way his tongue rolled over the *r*.

"Who *are* you?"

He sighed, a weary sound, and there was another long pause. "I'm not sure I know."

Clara frowned, not understanding his meaning. "Do you . . . live here?"

"Yes." The word sounded farther away as if he'd turned his head, and she pressed her ear harder against the stone, picturing a faceless man gazing into the distance. When he spoke again, it was closer, as if he'd turned his head to the wall again.

"I . . . I was told no one lived here."

"Told?"

Clara blushed and then shook her head at herself. The man couldn't even see her. "The locals like to talk about Windisle. I . . . asked around about it."

"And you came to make a wish."

"Yes. I . . . wait, did you read my wish?" Was that the sound of the crinkling paper she'd heard?

He chuckled softly, a rusty sound as if he didn't use it much. "It *was* tossed onto my property."

"I guess you're right." She paused. "So it's you . . . *you* read all the wishes."

"I don't read them all. I just collect them."

"You collect them," she repeated slowly. "So I guess you're the wish collector, then?"

He paused. "The wish collector. I guess I am."

"And what do you do with them?"

"I'm not sure you want to know."

She released a breath on a smile. "You grant them, of course, right?"

"I throw them away."

Clara inhaled quickly. "That's awful."

"What *should* I do? Leave them on the lawn to turn into mush in the rain? To blow all over the property?"

"I don't know. Throwing them away just seems . . . it seems . . . well, sacrilegious. A sin."

"Sacrilegious. That *is* serious. The problem is, Clara, I don't know if that sin trumps all the ones I've already committed."

She wasn't sure what to say to that, so she remained silent.

"What do you think I should do with them? Mount each one in its own special frame and hang them on my wall? *The Gallery of False Hope,* I'd call it."

"You're being sarcastic," she said, hearing the indignity in her own voice. "About people's personal wishes—their hopes and their dreams. Their sorrows."

"And yet *you* didn't make a wish for yourself." Clara heard the rustling of paper as if he was unfolding her wish once more. Reading it.

"That was private."

"It was given to me. It landed right at my feet." There was the hint of amusement in his tone and Clara stiffened, letting out a small, angry huff.

He chuckled again and despite herself, Clara liked the sound of his laughter. It was rusty, yes, but it was also deep and rich.

"Well," she said, standing and brushing her hands off. "I have to go. I can see that making wishes at this particular wall is pointless."

Clara knew he stood too, as she could hear rustling on the other side and his voice came from above her own when he spoke. He was taller than she was. "Wait. I'm sorry. I was just teasing you. Please . . ."

He stopped speaking and she found herself leaning toward the wall. The way he'd uttered the word . . . the blatant loneliness she'd heard in his tone caused her heart to squeeze tightly. For a moment, he'd sounded desperate that she not leave. "What?" she asked softly, her mouth over one of the paper-thin cracks.

"Nothing."

Clara paused, placing her hands against the rock. “I suppose . . . living here, you know a lot about the plantation. The history.”

“Yes.”

“Would you be willing to share some? If I came back?”

“Came back?”

“Sundays are my day off . . .”

"I, uh, that’s usually when I do my wish pillaging as a matter of fact. For some reason, not many people show up on Sundays. Maybe that's the day they make their wishes in church.”

"Wish pillaging." She laughed softly and swore she heard his lips part in a smile, but of course, she couldn't be entirely sure. “So if I were to come up with an idea of some other way to deal with the wishes besides just tossing them out, maybe you’d be open to suggestions? And in return, you could tell me a little more about Windisle?”

“Maybe.”

“Then I’ll see you Sunday.”

When he spoke this time, there was no mistaking the smile in his voice. "Same time?"

Clara slipped her cell phone from her purse and glanced at it. "Six o'clock?"

"Yes." There was something in his voice she wasn't sure how to classify . . . hope? Excitement? Nervousness? Perhaps even bewilderment. But at what? Her heart beat steadily, a warm feeling pressing against her chest. She was delighted that she now had a personal connection to Windisle through the mysterious man on the other side of the wall.

"See you next week."

"See you then."

She pulled out her phone and began calling an Uber, smiling as she walked away from Windisle, up the empty, tree-lined street. She wondered if Jonah stood on the other side of the wall peeking through the cracks, catching small glimpses of her as she moved away.

CHAPTER THREE

June, 1860

Her sister Astrid's eighteenth birthday party was in full swing, the laughter and chatter of guests underlying the music floating dreamily from the windows and pouring off the balconies of Windisle Manor.

"Ouch," Angelina hissed as a thorn pierced the soft pad of her thumb. She put the tiny wound to her mouth for a moment and then, unheeded, continued to climb the rose trellis, which was dripping with fragrant pink and white blooms. *And thorns,* she reminded herself. *Take care with the thorns.*

She peeked over the railing of the balcony, her eyes growing round as she watched the guests dance and mingle in the lavish surroundings. A table laden with desserts had been set out—desserts she knew well as she'd helped bake them all morning and afternoon, and on the other side of the room sat a pyramid of champagne flutes, the bubbly, golden liquid sparkling in the candlelight.

She would never be part of any of this, but oh she wanted to *see.*

Her gaze snagged on the tall form of a man in uniform as he picked up a glass flute, bringing it to his mouth and taking a drink.

From across the room, she saw the lady of the manor, Delphia Chamberlain, grab her daughter—and Angelina's half-sister—Astrid's arm and begin leading her toward the champagne fountain, or perhaps the soldier. When Angelina looked back at him, he was watching the women's approach as well and caught Angelina off guard when he suddenly turned, his eyes locking on hers. She sucked in a startled breath, pulling her head to the side and out of view.

For a moment she was utterly still, only pulling very small inhales of rose-scented air into her lungs, before letting out one large gust of breath. Surely she had imagined their eyes meeting. The house was bright, sparkling with light, and the garden dim.

Her heart calming, she slowly looked over the side of the balcony, her eyes focusing directly on the champagne pyramid. The man was gone. And when she looked to the place Mrs. Chamberlain and Astrid had been, she saw that they had been stopped by a party guest, who was laughing and gesturing while Mrs. Chamberlain looked annoyed and Astrid smiled politely.

Angelina glanced around the party for a few more minutes, drinking in the splendor of the birthday decorations: extravagant bouquets of flowers on every surface, tables piled high with brightly wrapped gifts. Her father had spared no expense for his firstborn daughter. She watched as the women's brightly colored dresses twirled to the music and the men—

"That doesn't seem like the safest place to be."

Angelina drew in a sharp breath, her hands grasping the wood of the trellis, another thorn piercing her palm.

The man moved quickly, coming to stand beneath her as she stared at him, wide-eyed. Angelina swallowed, descending the trellis as the man stood back, allowing her room to lower her feet to the ground, his arms raised to his waist as if prepared to catch her should she slip and fall.

She smoothed her dress, heat infusing her face as her heart raced madly beneath her breast. "I was just . . . ah, reaching for—"

"A star?"

A rose for my mother, she'd been about to say, but his words caused her to pause in surprise. She blinked as his lip quirked minutely. "A star, yes," she said hesitantly. She glanced up, the stars like scattered diamonds on the black velvet of the nighttime sky. "Why, there are so many of them. I hardly thought anyone would miss a mere handful."

"Ah. And do you do this often? Snag stars directly from the sky?"

Angelina tilted her head, her courage gathering. This man was teasing her and something about the way his eyes danced—even as his expression remained serious—caused a warm flush of something tingly to spread under her skin. "Of course. Several now."

The man reached forward suddenly, and Angelina drew in a breath, leaning away. Their eyes met as he plucked something from her hair, bringing his hand back so she could see that it was only a rose petal that had been ensnared in her unruly curls.

"And what do you do with them? The stars?" He tilted his head. "Wear them as jewels perchance?"

Angelina let out a small laugh, stepping away from the handsome soldier. His closeness was causing her to feel quite funny—flushed and dizzy, yet energized simultaneously. And her heart, it was beating as if it might leap from her chest.

"Oh no, I have no use for jewels." She began walking, trailing the back of her hand along the petals of a velvety red rose. The soldier followed, linking his hands behind his back. "No, I squeeze the magic right out of them and bottle it up." She shot him a quick glance, nerves scuttling along her spine.

She was used to talking to white people. She'd been sitting on her daddy's knee and telling him stories since she could remember. And she often played with her half-brother, and one of her half-sisters, but this was the first time she'd spoken for longer than a minute or two to a white person who wasn't part of her family, and she felt apprehensive.

The man's lips tipped into a smile and despite her nervousness, Angelina noticed he had a small dimple in his left cheek. "I see. And what do you use this bottled stardust for exactly?"

"Well, I . . . haven't decided yet." She glanced at him. "What would you propose?"

The soldier appeared to consider it for a moment. "Well, you could drink it up and provide light for an entire city."

Angelina laughed, a small, somewhat uncertain sound. But the soldier was smiling too, so she exhaled, looking at him shyly. Their eyes met again, and they both stopped walking.

"What is your name?" he asked, as though it were the most important question he'd ever posed.

Angelina glanced at the house where someone let out a loud shriek of laughter. "Angelina Loreaux."

The soldier held out his hand. "John Whitfield."

She took his hand in hers tentatively. She'd never been offered anyone's hand before, most especially not a white man's. It was big and warm. Strong. "Nice to meet you, sir."

"Please"—he dipped his head—"call me John."

Their gazes caught and she looked away, letting go of his hand, but the pull was too strong for her not to look back, straight into his blue gray eyes. "John," she whispered, his name ghosting over her lips and lingering in the space between them.

She heard the back door open and her name being called and glanced toward it, although the garden hedges concealed them. "Coming, Mama," she called back. She looked at John. "I have to go."

She lifted her skirts and turned away, but her name said in John's deep voice stopped her. She paused, looking over her shoulder.

"I think you already drank some of that stardust, Angelina Loreaux."

She blinked. The look on his face was so earnest that it caused her breath to halt. His eyes moved to her parted mouth and then immediately returned to her eyes. She saw his throat move as he swallowed. "Goodnight, John Whitfield," she said, backing away, and then she turned and ran, the scent of roses falling behind her, her heart beating to the cadence of her footfalls on the stone garden path.

Above her, the stars glittered, and she felt as if she *had* drunk them up, felt as if they glittered inside of her too. She laughed, the wondrous sound swallowed by the boisterous noise from the party beyond.

CHAPTER FOUR

What the hell was I thinking?

Jonah slowed to a jog, then came to a halt under the shade of the bald cypress. His chest rose and fell rapidly as he bent over, placing his hands on his knees as he worked to steady his heart rate.

He'd pushed himself too hard and felt mildly nauseated, but the doubts in his head continued unabated nonetheless.

Clara. He'd surprised himself by talking to her—despite that she'd heard him breathing. Others had heard him behind the wall before, had even called out a questioning, "Who's there?" But he'd just ignored them, listening in amusement as they giggled and whispered that it must be Angelina they'd detected.

This was different.

But to agree with meeting her again? To sound so damned desperate for her to return? For what fucking purpose?

Am I really that lonely?

God. He straightened, swiping his fingers through his short sweat-drenched hair.

I am. Shit. I am. He was *cracking* from loneliness, and now he was so needy for company he was willing to talk to unknown women through the cracks in a wall. *Pathetic.*

Only . . . it wasn't *just* that he was lonely, though Jonah could admit that much was true, even if he did have Myrtle and Cecil to talk to.

No, it had been her wish.

Help me help you, Angelina.

A mild cramp took up in Jonah's calf, and he began moving to walk it off, heading in the direction of the dilapidated structures that had once been the slave cabins.

He entered the copse of trees, meandering the pathways, reaching a hand out to touch the sun-warmed wood and turning his head so he could look through the window of the cabin he stood next to with his good eye.

The cooler air of this wooded space washed over him, the simple pleasure causing his shoulders to relax. The birds twittered in the trees and for a moment, a deep, inexplicable peace settled in Jonah's chest. Leaning forward, he looked into the empty cabin, dried leaves piled in the corners.

Angelina Loreaux had lived here once. *Help me help you, Angelina,* the girl, Clara, had written.

As if that were actually possible. Still . . . it intrigued him. He'd spoken to her so briefly, and yet *she* intrigued him. Her kind of unselfish compassion was rare. *I should know.*

He'd been collecting between ten and twenty wishes a week for almost eight years now. Not as many wishes showed up on the lawn as in years past. Windisle and its legend were known only among the locals, and especially the old-timers. The ones who knew about it and passed it along were all dead or dying off now, and the legend with them.

The weeping wall was solely a local attraction—if it was even popular enough to be *called* an attraction—due to the fact that the property was private. It wasn't as if it could be listed as a place of interest for tourists, or included on sites meant for visitors to New Orleans.

So the wishes that showed up were from people who'd heard the legend from someone or another and were desperate or curious enough to give it a try.

Jonah read them once in a while, but mostly not anymore, despite what he'd said to Clara.

"Clara," he murmured aloud, rolling her name over his tongue again, liking the way it sounded. Liking the slight shiver that moved across his skin as he repeated it once more.

The truth of the matter was, he'd become *bored* by people's wishes a long time ago. They were always one of three things: a wish for money or some material item, a wish for love, or a wish for the healing of either oneself or a loved one. He didn't judge the wishes; he'd just grown tired of them. And it wasn't as if he could make them come true. He *lived* at Windisle—if anyone knew the legend was only that, it was him. So the wishes, those scattered slips of paper, they'd become nothing more than a cleanup chore.

But he'd never once read one for Angelina, never once read one cast for a stranger at all. It surprised him. And it had been a long damn time since he'd been surprised—him, the monster behind the wall. No, not the monster, *the wish collector*.

One half of his lips tipped. Talking to her, those brief moments, he'd been transformed from the former to the latter. And it'd been a heady feeling. As if by magic, for just a moment in time, he'd not been hideous and deformed, ruined, but something good and . . . mysteriously enchanting. At least that's what the winsome tone in her voice had expressed as she'd uttered the title.

Her wish had made him feel curiously charmed by her, and their brief conversation had only strengthened that feeling. But it also made him *yearn* for things that were long out of his reach, and *that* was not welcome. That was decidedly dangerous. Unconsciously, he ran a hand over his ruined skin, feeling the repugnant grooves and ridges with the pads of his fingers. *Yes, dangerous.* And foolhardy.

So he'd spent the night before moving the encounter from his mind whenever it pricked at his thoughts, and this morning pushing himself so hard on his run that he'd practically passed out from exhaustion.

And still she lingered. This stranger. This wishful visitor with the soft, melodic voice, the unusually compassionate heart, and the deep interest in Windisle Plantation. He'd heard that in her expressive voice as well. He wondered what it would be like paired with the unknown features of her face, and it sent a strange little jolt through his system.

Yes, she'd wanted to know more about the plantation, the history. And there was that too. Her request had made him feel useful, as if he had something to offer when he'd thought himself worthless for so long. It wasn't much but . . . well, it was something and it had seemingly lodged inside of him in a way he was having a difficult time digging out.

Moisture from the nearby Mississippi had formed a morning mist and it hadn't yet burned away. It feathered into the trees, wrapping around his legs as he moved through it and toward the cabin his gaze was always drawn to as he ran past it on his jog. It was situated a bit farther from the others, under the shade of a moss-draped willow tree, its trunk twisted and bent as if it had decided to conform to the shape of the wind rather than try to fight against it.

Jonah rarely went inside of the cabins, but he did today, the ancient floorboards creaking under his weight as he entered. She'd love to see these, he'd bet. He made an exasperated grunt in his throat. *She'd love to see these?* He didn't even know her. Still, who wouldn't love to see these? They were a part of history. For all he knew, they held secrets in the walls . . . under the dusty boards. Although they'd been cleared out years ago, maybe they held relics in some hidden place. He knew the preservation society was chomping at the bit to get their hands on this place. And for the sake of history, he could appreciate that. But these grounds . . . the manor house . . . it was his home, his sanctuary . . . his hiding spot from the daylight. It was all he had. The only thing still important to him in an existence that otherwise held no importance at all.

He walked around the room, making his way back to the doorway quickly. The space was small even for one person, and from what he knew, entire families had occupied these tiny cabins. *Unbelievable.* A part of the Chamberlain family history he certainly wasn't proud of.

And yet, there were stories here. Stories that deserved telling, he supposed, and for that reason, he should set up a will, leaving the plantation to the preservation society. He was the last of the Chamberlains. After him, there would be no more.

The depressing thought spurred him out of the cabin and back on the path toward the manor. It was another humid day, the heavy warmth of summer draping over him, sunshine caressing his skin, uncaring about the ruin. And normally, he would have enjoyed the sensation. But today, that old familiar feeling of keeping himself sequestered from the world pressed down upon him. It'd been *years* since he'd been leery of even allowing the sun to see him, but just then, the feeling returned, the one he thought he'd left behind as he'd grown accustomed to his scars, grown used to the way the light affected his injured eye.

No, suddenly, all he wanted to do was sink into some dark corner of the library and lose himself in a book.

"And just what is it you're frowning about?" Cecil asked.

Jonah looked up, so caught up in his own depressing thoughts that he hadn't realized he was so close to the house.

Cecil and Myrtle were sitting on the porch, drinking lemonade.

"Can't a man frown without it being about anything in particular?"

Myrtle looked at him suspiciously and made a *hrrmph* sound.

"And anyway, I'm always frowning." He gestured to the side of his face that remained in a perpetual glower. "I don't have much of a choice."

Myrtle took an unaffected sip of her lemonade. "Yeah, but there are levels of your unpleasant expressions. And that one just on your face? It rates pretty high."

Jonah turned his head to give her a better view and then, satisfied that she could see it clearly, narrowed his good eye at her. "Don't you two ever work?"

Myrtle took another long sip of lemonade. "It's a full-time job worrying about the likes of you. I'm plumb tuckered out. How about you, Cecil?"

Cecil nodded. "Tired doesn't begin to cover it, Myrtle. Why, I might have to take me a nice long afternoon nap in the hammock out back after this."

It was Jonah's turn to *hrrmph.*

Myrtle patted Cecil's knee. "You refresh yourself with a nap. I'm running to the grocery store for some items." She turned her attention back to Jonah. "You want anything specific for dinner? You wanna come with me maybe, Mr. Sourpuss?" She raised her own brow.

"Whatever you make for dinner is fine by me, Myrtle. And no, I don't want to come with you. Stop asking."

She shook her head, the beads adorning a myriad of tiny braids in her hair making soft clinking sounds with the movement. "Nu-uh. You're gonna have to fire me to get me to stop asking. One of these days, you're gonna say, 'Why yes, Myrtle, you pretty thing. I'll come with you, because I'm done pretending to be a vampire who melts in the sun, and I'm ready to join the world again because I still have something to *offer.*' Your personal patronage at Winn-Dixie is as good a start as any."

Cecil chuckled, evidently apathetic to the particularly high-level glare Jonah turned his way.

Jonah moved past them both and into the house. "Don't hold your breath. I'm a lost cause, Myrtle," he muttered. And he had *nothing* to offer. Unless scaring small children was considered a worthy endeavor.

Myrtle and Cecil must have heard him because Cecil shouted, "If we believed that, we'd a hightailed it outta here a long time ago."

Jonah sighed, but gratitude filled him nonetheless, partially replacing the dismal emotions that had filled his chest as he'd stood in those cabins and then followed him back to the house like spirits who could reach inside of his chest and squeeze. Because the truth was, he loved Myrtle and Cecil and couldn't live without them, and they very well knew it. If *not* for them, Jonah Chamberlain would be utterly and completely alone.

He couldn't hope for things he'd never have. He couldn't. Yes, he had been charmed by the girl. By Clara. But he wouldn't allow himself to be charmed any more. She might show up at the wall next week. She might not. He couldn't care. *Because either way,* he promised himself, *I won't be there.*

****

Why the hell am I here?

Jonah sat at the base of the wall in the shade of a giant, ancient oak, the same spot he'd sat the week before. He brought one knee up, resting his arm on it as he waited. The day was turning to evening, that hush that came with the lowering sun descending upon Windisle. His heart beat anxiously, and he attempted to slow it by breathing deeply. "Idiot," he murmured.

You don't even know her. She might not even show up.

You promised yourself you wouldn't either.

A few minutes later he heard the distant closing of a car door and then the soft footsteps of someone approaching. "You there, Jonah?" she asked, her voice moving from up high to the spot right beside where his cheek rested on the stone.

He tried not to answer. He really did. If he was silent long enough, she'd go away and take these unwanted feelings with her.

"Yeah," he finally said, attempting to sound bored, but not managing it. Instead, his tone was laced with excitement, and he shut his eyes as he chastised himself. But before he got too far, something sharp and tangy smelling came through the crack, hitting his nose and causing his expression to slip into a confused frown. "What's that smell?"

She smelled *bad*. This was . . . No, this was good, a positive discovery. He couldn't possibly hope to get to know someone better who assaulted his nose. Not like he really had room to be picky. After all, he'd assault her *view* if she got a look at him, but still. It was a positive development . . . something to hang on to.

Clara laughed softly and the sound was musical. Sweet. "Liniment. Can you smell it from there? My neighbor, Mrs. Guillot, swears on it for sore muscles. I've been woozy all day from the odor. I think the way it works is it causes you to pass out so you don't move all day, resulting in zero muscle strain."

Jonah smiled, charmed yet again, *despite* the odor. "Why is your neighbor offering you liniment anyway?"

"Oh, I'm a ballet dancer. Sore muscles come with the job."

"You're a ballet dancer?"

"Yes. I'm an apprentice ballerina with the New Orleans Ballet. I just moved here a couple of months ago. I'm renting an apartment in The West Bank of Jefferson Parish from someone my teacher knows."

"Huh." He could honestly say he'd never known a ballerina before. "So no family here?"

"No, it's just me. My family—well, just my father now actually—lives in Ohio." Her words ended more quietly than they'd begun, a sort of defeat lying just beneath the surface. Jonah recognized that tone, knew it well. It was . . . sadness. *Is Clara lonely too?* he wondered, the small pinching in the region of his heart taking him by surprise.

"So, uh, any ideas on the whole wish discarding thing?"

She paused and he heard her moving as if she was adjusting the position she'd been sitting in, straightening perhaps due to the gravity of the subject.

He wondered what she looked like. *A ballerina.* He pictured someone slim with her hair pulled back in a tight bun. He'd already been able to tell by her voice that she was young, and now he was even more sure about that. From what he knew, ballerinas didn't have very long careers. And from the sound of it, hers was just beginning.

"I do actually. I've been thinking about this all week, and I've come up with an idea."

"Okay, shoot. I'm all ears."

"Well," she started and her voice sounded so serious, so filled with resolve that he couldn't help smiling. It was tight and the muscles in his face hesitated awkwardly for a moment, but yeah, he remembered now what a smile felt like. "It's the wish that's important, but the paper it's written on must hold some sort of . . . oh, I don't know . . . power, too."

"Okay."

"Right. So the paper should be discarded in a way that's meaningful."

"Which is the case you made last week."

"Mm-hmm," she said, and he could see her nodding her head. She was a girl with a sweet laugh, a voice that was light and pleasant, a charm that captivated him, and a face he couldn't visualize. She *sounded* so pretty though. *Is that possible?* "So let's consider Angelina. You do know the whole story of Angelina Loreaux, right?"

"Of course. I've grown up hearing about the legend. My housekeepers, Myrtle and Cecil, swear they see her wandering in the garden."

"Oh." Her voice took on a breathy, almost dreamy tone.

Jonah felt like he should dispel the hope he heard in her voice. "Though Myrtle's half-blind and Cecil, well, let's just say Cecil pretty much goes along with whatever Myrtle says."

Clara laughed and then was quiet for a moment. "Okay. In any case, you know that Angelina met and fell in love with John Whitfield in the rose garden, and that's also where she took her own life."

"In front of the fountain."

She paused. "Oh. I didn't know that." She sounded sad suddenly as if she were picturing the scene, Angelina's body lying prone in front of the fountain as the water cascaded and bubbled next to her, her blood soaking into the grass. At least, that's how Jonah had pictured it when he'd been told the story as a boy. And the image had stuck with him as childhood imaginings tended to do.

Clara cleared her throat. "Okay, so the rose garden was significant in Angelina's life as well as her death. What if you soaked the wishes in water and mixed them with the mulch for the flowers? Paper is biodegradable, after all."

Jonah frowned. "That's your idea?"

"Yes. What's wrong with it? It's meaningful. You'd be bringing the wishes to the place she's said to wander."

"It sounds like a lot of work."

She paused and then sighed. "I know. I'm sure you're busy—"

"I'm not busy. I actually . . . well, I'm the opposite of busy. Still, I don't do much in the way of gardening."

She was silent for a moment and just as he was about to call her name, she asked, "Why are you the opposite of busy? What do you mean?"

"Nothing. Plus, the majority of the pieces of paper are white. I don't know that white mulch is a popular look."

She paused and he had the notion that she was dejected. When she spoke, the tone in her voice told him his instincts had been correct. "You're right. From the pictures I've looked at online, it's a stunning property. I'm sure it's important that it's kept in tip-top shape."

A pinprick of shame caused him to shift positions. "Well, honestly, I could probably do better on that front." But the truth was, keeping the property the way it should be would require more help than just Myrtle and Cecil, and he didn't want anyone other than them coming beyond the gate. And so in the time he'd been living there, the place had continued to fall to disrepair.

The further truth was, he liked her idea. Not because he would execute it—he did not piddle around in the garden—but because it spoke to a sweetness that only added to her charm. And she'd obviously spent time considering her answer, which meant she'd thought about him during the week and he couldn't help liking that knowledge.

"Tell me about yourself, Clara."

"There's not a lot to tell. Midwestern girl. I've been dancing since I was four. My"—she cleared her throat and Jonah heard her back slide up the rough stone—"dearest dream came true when I was chosen to join the New Orleans Ballet. We'll be performing Swan Lake in a couple of months and I was lucky enough to get a role. I'm one of the swans. It's a dream come true," she repeated, though her lackluster tone made him wonder if that was true.

"Then why do you sound so sad about it?"

Clara released a surprised sounding breath. "I . . . I'm not sad. It's a . . ." Her words faded away and he again heard the fabric of whatever she was wearing slide against the stone—in a downward motion this time. "My father, he has Alzheimer's. He raised me by himself on a bus driver's salary. He sacrificed so much so I could dance. He never missed a show—never. He was always there, with a single red rose after each performance. All the money for lessons, and then for shoes, costumes . . . When I was fifteen, I landed a big part in the local ballet theater. I was so proud, but it'd been a rough year. There had been a strike where my dad worked and he didn't get paid for a couple of months and . . . I remember waking up early one morning and hearing him just coming home. I got up and looked out the window and saw him taking a pizza delivery sign off the top of his car. My fifty-five-year-old dad had taken an extra job delivering pizzas so he could pay for me to dance in that show. I never mentioned it and neither did he, but I never forgot."

She inhaled a sudden breath and then a small sniffle. Jonah's chest tightened. There was something about hearing of Clara's sorrow that brushed over every ache in his own heart. "Sorry," she uttered.

"For what?" Jonah asked softly.

"For . . . oh, I don't know. Getting emotional. You don't even know me."

That was the thing though. He sort of felt like he did somehow, or at least . . . he'd learned things about her he could have only learned after knowing someone in person for much longer. Was it because a different level of honesty existed when you didn't meet and talk face to face? *Or is it her?* "That's what we're doing though, right?"

"Yes," she said, and he could tell she'd turned her head so her mouth was closer to the crack in the wall on his left.

He lifted a finger, tracing around that small crack. He almost felt foolish, but she had no way of knowing and so what did he care?

"So," he said, after a moment, "your dad, who sacrificed so much for you to dance, won't see the payoff for all that sacrifice."

"Yes," she said. "Yes, that's it. He has moments of clarity, but they're so few and far between now. He didn't even know me when I left, and it's been weeks since I heard his voice on the phone and even then, he couldn't place me, and God, it hurt. I should have told him more often how much I appreciated his sacrifice and that I realized how hard he worked for me. I never really got a chance to say goodbye even though he's not really gone. And"—she paused for another small intake of breath—"it breaks my heart, Jonah. It kills me inside."

Jonah was silent for a beat, taking in her words. "I'm sorry, Clara. It must have been so hard to leave him."

"It was. I wanted him to come live here, but he insisted on staying in Ohio. It was one of the last wishes he spoke to me, and I really think he wanted to give me wings. But, some days I feel like I should quit all this and go back to him, to spend what remaining time he has left enjoying those last few lucid moments, even if there are only a handful left. Instead, I'm here—"

"Doing exactly what he'd want you to be doing, Clara. He'd *want* you here. I don't know your dad, but I'd bet anything he'd tell you that you're exactly where he wants you to be. Honor the sacrifice he made by dancing your heart out—for him. He wouldn't have wanted anything more than that."

Clara let out a soggy-sounding laugh and her voice was closer again. "You're right. Thank you, Jonah. Thank you for saying that. I needed to hear it. You have no idea—"

The sound of a car approaching and then the squeaking of brakes met Jonah's ears right before the rustle of Clara standing. "My ride is here. I have to go."

Her ride? "Okay. Hey, it was nice to talk to you."

"You too." She paused and Jonah found himself holding his breath. "I gave you my idea about the notes—failure that it was." Jonah opened his mouth to tell her she was wrong. He'd liked her idea, but she let out a small laugh, continuing on. "But you didn't fulfill your part of the deal. You were supposed to impart some historical information." There was a teasing tone in her voice and his lips tipped.

"No, I guess I didn't, did I?" She seemed to be waiting. He heard her breath ghosting through the crack in the wall right at his throat. "If you wanted to come back, I could—"

"Great. Next Sunday, then." There was a smile in her voice and when she spoke again, it was from farther away. "Goodbye, Jonah. Have a great evening."

He walked quickly to where he thought the car might be parked on the other side of the large barrier between them and brought his good eye to one of the larger slits in the rock. He couldn't make her out well. He only had the vague image of a slim body in a white top and honey-blonde hair blowing sideways as she jogged toward the vehicle. Away from him.

He didn't want to feel dissatisfied with the short amount of time he'd had with her, but he did. He did.

CHAPTER FIVE

He'd brought her peace—Jonah, the man behind the wall. The wish collector. Clara executed a perfect grand jeté, hitting her spot and coming to a standstill as one of the male dancers performed center stage.

That feeling of peace she'd been thinking about continued to surround her like a warm blanket. Yes, she thought. *Yes!* This is where her father would want her to be, nowhere else. *Dance your heart out,* Jonah had said, and that's what she would do.

How funny, she mused. That had been her original wish—to find *peace* concerning the situation with her father. And she had. In one single moment, Jonah had found a way to grant her greatest desire.

She smiled to herself as she began moving again, the other dancers fluttering across the stage along with her. She'd called him the wish collector, but perhaps he had the ability to grant them too. At least in her case.

"Clara," Madame Fournier said as Clara was exiting the building, her duffle bag slung over her shoulder. "You danced beautifully today." She smiled, thin-lipped, an underwhelming display of expression, but Clara's heart soared nonetheless.

"Thank you so much, Madame Fournier. See you tomorrow." She grinned, letting the door swing shut behind her.

It was already seven p.m. and Clara had the sudden urge to go to the weeping wall, to call out Jonah's name, to tell him about today and how he'd helped her beyond measure with a few heartfelt words. But of course, that was silly. They barely knew each other. He wouldn't want her showing up at his house—even outside—without first being invited. After all, wasn't he sick of all those people coming by randomly all the time as it was? Friends occasionally showed up unexpectedly, but *they* weren't really friends? Were they?

Thoughts of Jonah, of the unusual bond she felt forming between them, kept her company as she traveled home, and when she stepped off the bus, she spotted the man who sold produce and flowers under a temporary awning on the corner, packing up his things.

A flash of red caught her eye and she saw that today, he had red roses. On a whim, Clara crossed the street, smiling as she approached the old man.

He smiled back, his wrinkled skin settling into a hundred folds, his eyes squinting with kindness.

"Sorry, sir, I know you're closing, but do I have time to purchase a bouquet of roses?"

"Course you do. What color would you like?" The man gestured to the red bouquet and one of pale pink.

"The red please. They're my father's favorite."

"Ah. A classic gentleman. I like that."

Clara took out her wallet, tilting her head as she handed the man the money on the sticker. "He is. I just moved here from Ohio, but I saw the roses and thought of him. Sort of seemed like a little touch of home."

The man waved her money away. "Well now, you consider those roses a welcome from me to New Orleans."

"Oh no, I couldn't." Clara thrust the money toward the man, but again he waved it off, chuckling. "Best get home to put those in water before they start wilting." He winked at her, his smile warm and kind.

Reluctantly, Clara lowered her arm. "Well . . ."

"And here"—he handed her a small flowering plant in a terracotta planter—"some lagniappe." He chuckled at the confused look on her face. "It's what us New Orleanians call a little something extra. Now you have something pretty for the inside, and a small something for the outside. Put that on your stoop. My mama always did say that the best way to welcome folk to your home was to show that you cared about decorating their first impression."

Clara held the plant against her body in one hand and the large bouquet of roses in the other, inhaling their sweet fragrance and thinking she better leave before he started giving her more free things and causing her to feel even guiltier. Although . . . the truth was, despite being a person who always, *always* paid her way and dealt with others honestly, the two small gifts—gestures of pure kindness—made her feel warm inside. *Lagniappe.* This man might not know it, but he had a customer for life in Clara.

She grinned at him. "Thank you. Truly. I'm very appreciative. And by the way, I'm Clara." She figured he'd know why she couldn't shake his hand.

He smiled back. "Clara, very nice to meet you. I'm Israel Baptiste."

"Thank you again, Mr. Baptiste." Clara clutched her items close and walked the short distance home. When she got there, she stood in front of the door to her apartment. She didn't have a stoop, per se, but there was a corner near her door just large enough for a plant. She bent, placing the terracotta planter down with a smile.

On Sunday, she'd go back to see Mr. Baptiste and purchase some fresh ingredients to make a vegetable lasagna. She wondered suddenly, if Jonah liked lasagna. She could . . . *no, I won't go that far,* she decided. *Not yet.* She'd take one to Mrs. Guillot. But it was nice to know that when she considered cooking, she had a couple of people now who might want to share a meal with her.

She looked at the plant again, admiring the way the yellow blossoms brightened the once dismal concrete space. A touch of home. *My dad would like that.* She was settling in after all.

****

On Sunday, as planned, Clara walked the few blocks to Mr. Baptiste's stand, greeting him with a warm smile as she approached.

"Well hello, Clara. How are you this fine day?"

"Good, thank you. The roses still look as fresh and beautiful as they did a few days ago."

"Oh good. My wife, Marguerite, tends the flower garden at our house and does a mighty fine job."

"She must love gardening."

"She sure does. That woman could spend the whole day with those plants. Comes back in with dirt smeared all over her, looking just as happy as a lark." His eyes warmed at the mention of his wife and Clara sighed inwardly. To have a man's whole expression change when he spoke your name . . . it was something she could only dream of. "Do you like gardening, Clara?"

"I don't know. I've never done it." She leaned her hip against the edge of the vegetable-laden table, the smell of ripe things and earth meeting her nose. "We had a small yard in Ohio, nothing but grass. My father worked a lot and didn't have time to maintain more than that. And I was always busy with school. And here, well, I barely have room for a houseplant."

Mr. Baptiste chuckled and Clara gave him a smile.

"I'm going to fill a basket with some of these delicious-looking vegetables," she said, grabbing a basket and placing two large tomatoes inside. She glanced at Mr. Baptiste and considered something. He looked old—maybe not quite as old as Dory Dupre, who had to be close to a hundred, but definitely in his eighties or nineties. "Mr. Baptiste, have you always lived in New Orleans?"

"Yup. Born and raised."

Clara nodded as she chose a couple of deep green zucchini. "I've been learning about the Windisle Plantation and the ghost story attached to the weeping wall."

Mr. Baptiste frowned slightly. "Ah. Sad tale, isn't it?"

"It is." Clara put a vibrant yellow squash in her basket and then paused. "I'm completely intrigued by it."

"I don't blame you. There's quite a bit of mystery surrounding that old place. It's a shame it's been abandoned."

Clara opened her mouth to mention Jonah but then closed it, reconsidering. She wasn't sure why she hesitated telling Mr. Baptiste that someone did live there, other than the fact that Jonah obviously preferred it that way since everyone believed it was deserted.

Certainly, he must come and go covertly, in a way that didn't alert anyone to his presence. Did he also keep the electricity off at night? These questions suddenly occurred to Clara, and she made a note to ask Jonah about it. Why the secrecy? In any case, and whatever his reasons might be, she wasn't going to give him away.

And strangely, she felt covetous of him. He was *her* wish collector.

"Yes, a shame." She chose a few more vegetables, thinking for a moment. She knew about the legend, the curse, and the riddle. She had researched Windisle itself and hoped to learn more from Jonah later that afternoon. But it probably wasn't likely that Jonah knew much about John Whitfield, was it? Perhaps Mr. Baptiste could shed some light on who he'd been. "Mr. Baptiste, do you know anything about John Whitfield? The man who betrayed Angelina Loreaux?"

Mr. Baptiste stroked his jaw, running his fingers over his scraggly gray beard. "I don't know much about his family. Let's see. He was engaged to the eldest Chamberlain daughter, Astrid, at some point, wasn't he?"

Clara's hand stilled as she put a pepper into her basket. "He *was*?" Was *that* the way he'd betrayed Angelina? He'd become engaged to her half-sister? And yet he'd never actually married her?

Mr. Baptiste's gaze remained fixed on the sky as if he were attempting to grasp his memories from the clouds. "It's been so long since my grandmother told me the story."

Thank goodness for all the mothers and grandmothers, Clara thought. They seemed to be the ones who had told Angelina's story, who had passed the information down through the generations. Perhaps by bedsides, and firesides, from rocking chairs and porch swings.

Men told stories too, of course. But it was the women who recalled the details of the heart. It was women who passed on the souls of those they remembered.

Mr. Baptiste shook his head as if in defeat at his attempt to recapture memories and Clara's shoulders dropped. But then he raised a finger. "Although! I remember my mama saying that her great, great aunt Lottie had been to John Whitfield's house to care for him when he contracted tuberculosis. Aunt Lottie was a nurse, and back in those days, house calls were very common. The doctor diagnosed him with tuberculosis, and I remember my mama mentioning that John refused to be treated. According to Aunt Lottie anyway. They could have saved him, she said. He had a mild case of it when they examined him. Too prideful, I suppose. Or maybe he had a death wish. They say he suffered flashbacks."

Clara nodded, frowning. "Yes, I heard that." She wondered why a man would refuse medical treatment offered to him. From what she knew of TB, it was an awful, painful way to die. Why would a person ever *choose* that? Or was it as Mr. Baptiste had said, he was simply too prideful and believed he could beat the disease on his own without the aid of medical intervention?

Clara chatted with Mr. Baptiste for a few minutes longer, but customers were beginning to join Clara, taking baskets and filling them with fresh farm produce, so she paid for all her items, and bid Mr. Baptiste a good day.

She would go home and make a couple of pans of lasagna, one for her and one for Mrs. Guillot—though Mrs. Guillot would probably insist on "paying" her with a bottle of her toxic liniment. And then she was going to pay a visit to her wish collector. Clara smiled all the way home. Her small world was growing.

CHAPTER SIX

August, 1860

Angelina ran her hand nervously along the wood bed frame as she moved toward the window. A thin breeze blew off the Mississippi River, the willow tree just outside bending its young, slender trunk. The wisp of air cut through the heat and Angelina sighed as she tipped her head back and let the brief moment of cool reprieve flow over her flushed skin.

She heard the floor squeak behind her, and a combination of elation and terror ricocheted through her blood, causing her heart to leap.

She turned, gripping the window ledge behind her as she took him in, his face flushed, sweat gleaming on his forehead.

He raised his arm and used his shirtsleeve to swipe at the perspiration, a grin lighting his face. "There were enough tomatoes today to feed an army." He set the basket on the stool near the door and Angelina's eyes followed it, taking in the colorful array of garden vegetables, still caked with the soil he'd pulled them from.

Angelina moved her eyes back to his self-satisfied expression, unable to stop herself from laughing softly. "Someone's going to catch you picking vegetables in the Chamberlain garden and then what will you say?"

"You told me no one tends the garden except you."

Angelina turned her head and glanced down and then into his eyes, a smile still playing at her lips. "Well, you just never know who might happen by and see I'm not there. I'm not certain it's worth the risk."

John had been visiting her every other week for almost two months now under the guise of being at the plantation for the sole purpose of taking tea with Mrs. Chamberlain and Astrid. Twenty minutes after John bid farewell to the women and Angelina cleared the tea service, Angelina would tell her mother or the kitchen help she was going to the garden to pick vegetables and instead, she'd meet John in the empty cabin near the sapling willow tree.

To cover the vegetable-picking lie, John himself would fill a basket for Angelina to return with, ensuring they could spend as much time together as possible.

And then they'd meet there, where they talked and talked as long as they were able until Angelina had to race back to the house lest someone come looking for her or become suspicious.

And then later, in her tiny bed in the cabin she shared with her mama, she would go over the words they'd spoken to each other, the stories he'd told her about the army, his family, his life, so vastly different from her own. She'd close her eyes and picture the way his cheeks moved when he smiled, that tiny dimple appearing and causing her belly to flutter. She'd recall the way he'd sometimes trace her fingers—so tentatively—as they spoke, and it was as though she could still feel his touch tingling along her skin.

He touched her as if she were precious, and perhaps breakable. And once he started, some small part of him—his hand, a finger, the side of his thigh—continued to touch her until they parted ways.

John moved closer, and Angelina could smell the tangy scent of his clean male sweat—the sweat he'd expended for *her,* and happily if the look on his face was any indication. It made the blood in her veins do something crazy . . . speed up or slow down, she wasn't sure exactly. She only knew it scared her and thrilled her at the same time.

"It's worth it to me. I hope it's worth it to you too," he said, and she swore there was a note of nervousness in his words as if he was afraid she might tell him it wasn't. The idea caused her muscles to feel loose, as if they'd melted a bit. He enjoyed their time together as much as she did. He wanted more of it, more of *her.*

Still . . . speaking of risks brought the danger of what they were doing to the forefront of her mind, and she looked away on a frown. This dalliance—meeting this way—was foolhardy. There was no real point to it at all. So why couldn't she stop showing up at this cabin week after week, with this sparkly glee in her heart, her eyes so eager just to *see* him that she could hardly *think* straight?

"What is it, Angelina?" He moved closer, taking her hands in his, those warm strong hands that made her feel both safe and unsafe all in the same breath.

She let her eyes linger on their joined fingers for a moment, his pale golden, and hers a deeper bronze.

She released her grip, turning from him and staring out the window at the very edge of the sugarcane fields. The plants were too tall for her to see the workers amongst them. But she knew they were there. Oh, she knew very well. She'd helped her mama tend their wounds when they came in after a long, brutal day. She mixed the salve that would bring relief and soothe their weary muscles and broken skin.

"I haven't told you why this cabin is empty, John."

He didn't reply but she felt the heat of his body behind her, smelled the musk of his skin, knew how close he'd moved by the way the hairs on the nape of her neck felt charged.

"One of the slaves named Elijah and his mama lived here. Elijah was a brawny, big-shouldered man with the mind of a small child."

Angelina pictured the boy/man who had had a perpetual smile on his face and at the thought of him, her stomach twisted. "A man in town said Elijah exposed himself to his wife. Said he dropped his pants right in the middle of the street and caused her such trauma, she fainted dead away." Angelina paused, gathering herself. "Elijah, he was always toying with that rope belt of his. Always . . . tying and untying it. He was shy, nervous, just a child at heart. He didn't mean anyone any harm. They say he smiled even as the noose was slipped around his neck."

Angelina turned and looked into John's eyes. His gaze was filled with the same sadness that she was certain was in hers as well. The sadness that would forever reside in her heart when she thought of Elijah and the injustice he'd suffered. But she saw an angry glint in his gaze as well, and it was that, more than the sadness, that made her trust him.

"Mr. Chamberlain didn't stop it?"

Angelina shook her head. "It was done before he knew what happened. Oh, he raised a fuss at not being made aware of the situation right away, but what good was that? Elijah was already dead."

John moved his hands up her arms and then pulled her to him. Shock lodged in her chest for a moment before she leaned into him. She'd never been held by a man, never been this close to *anyone,* except her mama when she was a little girl. And oh, to be held in someone's arms. It felt so good. Too good. Too . . . *necessary.*

"Angelina," he murmured against her hair, "I won't let anything like that ever happen to you. I'll protect you. The world, it's changing, day by day. So many things are happening. You have no idea." *Of course I don't,* she thought, the words drumming through her mind. How could she? Her small world began and ended at Windisle Plantation.

She tipped her chin, looking into his face, their lips so close she could feel his breath ghosting across her skin. It smelled like the peppermint tea he'd recently drunk with

Astrid, who looked at the man so close to Angelina now with undisguised covetousness. The man Mrs. Chamberlain wanted her daughter to marry because of his family's fortune. A plan she was very obviously working diligently toward.

Oh yes, Angelina was flirting with danger in so many ways. "But not soon enough, John. And how can you protect me? You're one man. You tell me the world is changing, but I see no proof of it. And yet"—she pressed herself closer to him—"I don't seem to be able to stop meeting you, to stop . . . wanting . . ."

What do I want? She didn't even know, and yet the yearning without a name lay heavy within her nonetheless. A constant wanting of this man she shouldn't have.

"John, this . . . this . . . meeting this way is wrong and it makes no sense. It's—" But before she could continue, he lowered his mouth to hers gently, pressing his lips against hers and then pausing.

Their breath mingled, their heartbeats joined, thrumming swiftly in time, and it occurred to Angelina that he was waiting for her to deepen the kiss. Or not. She shouldn't do it, shouldn't encourage this forbidden kiss that was danger, and mystery, and a thousand fireflies spinning recklessly inside of her.

Angelina let out a small, breathless sigh and pressed her mouth closer. John made a strangled sound of his own, pulling her against him as he tilted his head and ran his tongue over the seam of her lips. She opened her mouth to him, allowing him entrance, and lost herself in his taste, in the feel of him, in the sudden certainty that though they must hide it, their relationship was *not* wrong. Not at all. She felt it in a place deep inside that recognized only love and nothing else.

The world might change. It might not. She had no way of knowing. But what Angelina did know was that, either way, for her, there was no turning back.

CHAPTER SEVEN

Jonah walked slowly toward the weeping wall, the birds in the trees singing gleefully overhead, the leaves rustling with their play. Clara was already there. He saw her shifting body in the blocked light of the cracks near the base of the wall. His heart lurched and the feeling caused him to consider backing away slowly. But, ah, what the hell? They were just going to chat for a bit. And he owed her some information, didn't he? For all his faults—and they were vast and many—he'd always been true to his word.

"Hi, Jonah."

He sat down, leaning against the wall and bringing one leg up so he could rest an arm on it. "You have good ears."

"The crunch of the grass gave you away."

"Ah." The summer heat had turned the grass mostly brown. New Orleans could use some rain. "How have you been, Clara?"

"I'm good. I feel like I'm finally settling in." There was happiness in her voice and it made Jonah smile.

"I'm glad."

He heard Clara shift. "Me too. And Jonah, I want to thank *you* as well." Her voice was slightly hesitant as she continued. "Coming here, talking to you, it's made me feel . . . I don't know, like I have a friend and, well, I hope it's okay if I consider you one. A friend."

For a moment Jonah didn't respond, as his heart thumped steadily against his ribs. He'd convinced himself she *wasn't* a friend, and it'd made him feel less anxious about talking to her. But now . . . damn it. "Yeah," he found himself saying, his words followed by a grimace because what the hell was he doing?

He should tell her he was nobody's friend and she was a fool if she wanted to consider him one. She didn't know him. He wouldn't ever really allow her to and so any "friendship" they had would be limited and very temporary. But that in itself was a reassurance that it was okay to title this thing they were doing, wasn't it?

He could rest assured that she'd stop coming once cooler weather set in, or sooner if her social life picked up, which it undoubtedly would as she "settled in" even more, and he'd wrap himself back in his safe cocoon behind his wall and that would be that. "Sure, Clara, you can consider me your friend." *Your temporary friend.*

She let out a whoosh of air as if she'd been holding her breath in anticipation of his response and when she spoke, there was a smile in her voice. "Great."

Her clothing scraped softly against the stone as she resumed her position. "There's an old man who sells home-grown produce near my apartment. I asked him about John Whitfield, and he told me something interesting." She then went on to tell him about the tuberculosis and John Whitfield refusing treatment. "Did you know that?"

"I didn't. But I don't know a lot about the Whitfield family. The stories that I heard as a boy were mostly having to do with this plantation and the people who lived here."

"Ah. Did you know John Whitfield was engaged to Astrid Chamberlain?"

Jonah furrowed his brow. "I have heard that rumor, but when John came home from the war, they definitely didn't marry. Astrid married Herbert Davies."

There was silence from Clara's side of the wall for a moment. "They say John came home with psychological issues. Maybe that's the reason they never married. He became a recluse, from what it sounds like."

Maybe, Jonah thought, that was why he'd always felt a strange affinity for the man—he identified with the need to shut yourself away from the world. John was also the villain of the story, and sadly, Jonah could identify with that as well. "If he was troubled, I can understand why. The Civil War . . . there was nothing pretty about it. The things he must have seen . . ." *Blasts . . . fire . . . heat . . . blood, so, so much blood.* Jonah clenched his eyes shut and shuddered, reaching a hand unconsciously to his mangled cheek.

Clara was quiet as if she'd heard something in his voice he hadn't intended to reveal. After a moment, she spoke, but her voice was tentative. "Yes. I can only imagine." They were both quiet for a moment before she asked, "Jonah, will you tell me a little bit about the condition of Windisle? What's it like in there?"

Jonah sighed, shaking off the fiery visions as best he could. "It's not in the best of shape. It needs an exterior facelift, and the grounds have gone to hell. The rose garden is a mess, though Myrtle does her best to tend it. But the slave cabins are still in good shape—"

"The slave cabins are still standing?"

"All fifteen of them. The furniture's been removed, but they're still there."

"Wow," Clara breathed. "Do you ever go inside them?"

"Once in a while on my morning run."

"Your run?"

"A man's gotta keep his body strong." Although, in actuality, Jonah didn't *have* to do anything, and he suddenly wondered why he'd implemented the rigorous workout schedule he'd kept up every morning. For eight years. Something he could control, maybe?

He couldn't do anything about the part he'd played in the awful tragedy all those years ago, and he couldn't do anything to fix his ruined face—not that he would even if he could, he deserved every scar he wore—but he could keep his body strong. He could keep his heart beating. And that surprised him. It seemed like a small act of hope. He'd thought he'd come to Windisle to die, but . . . he'd worked hard to keep himself healthy and alive. Maybe it was something he'd contemplate later.

"I suppose that's true. I have this liniment if you ever get sore—"

Jonah groaned. "It's bad enough that one of us is covered in that smell. We'd kill the grass on both sides of the wall if I used it too."

Clara let out a laugh that dissolved into sweet giggles. Jonah's heart lurched, and he smiled in reaction to her happiness. "I'll have you know that the grass is just fine over here." Her laughter faded and she was quiet for a moment. "Will you describe it to me? What it looks like on your side?"

So Jonah did, week after week, as Clara returned to the weeping wall, sitting in the grass on the other side of the wall, the summer days dwindling like particles of sand through an hourglass. He told her about the old willows draped in veils of lacy moss, and the sugarcane fields that grew dense and uncultivated, having reclaimed the paths that men and women had once forged. He told her about the garden behind the cabins that somehow kept bearing vegetables though no one tended it now.

While the rose garden had mostly withered and died, growing thorny and sparse, that vegetable garden—though weedy and wild—continued to flourish without care.

It drank from what rain it got and drew nourishment from the rich Louisiana soil and bore fat juicy tomatoes, crisp sweet cucumbers, and hot crunchy peppers of all varieties, among other things.

If her back was younger and stronger, Myrtle said, she would have given it more attention, but why bother, Jonah thought, when it seemed to do just fine on its own?

Jonah described the rooms of the plantation—the way the hardwood floors squeaked and creaked and yet still gleamed with polish in some areas. The house had been redecorated in the thirties, but never since, and though the furnishings, curtains, and the dishes showed signs of age and wear, they still held beauty.

As he spoke, Jonah noticed his accent became thicker, his drawl more pronounced as he heard the voices of those who had first talked about Windisle Plantation and told him the story of Angelina.

Clara listened, seemingly enraptured, to each detail Jonah imparted. And then he asked her about dancing, about the schools she'd attended, about the first time she knew she wanted to dance for a living.

She told him about her teachers, the other girls in the ballet. She told him about arabesques, and soubresauts, relevés, and brisé volés. And he laughed as she rhymed, speaking the terms in a haughty French accent, her own laughter sparkling through him—sweet, effervescent—like champagne bubbles. Like magic she'd tossed over the wall and he'd swallowed from the air.

And yes, their time together *felt* magical to Jonah—a reprieve from his life as a monster. He knew it couldn't last, but he didn't let himself think too much about that while he was with her. When it ended, as it would, he would deal with it.

For now they were just a boy and a girl, sitting on opposite sides of a wall, a layer of thick stone between them, but their hearts connected nonetheless. And for now, he would enjoy the moments they had.

****

"What on God's green earth are you doing there, Jonah Chamberlain?"

The sound of Cecil's voice brought Jonah from his thoughts and he stood straight, wiping a bead of sweat from his brow, and propping the shovel he was holding in the mulch. He leaned on it, attempting to look casual as he watched him approach.

"I'm"—he looked around—"I'm mulching."

Cecil stopped in front of Jonah, his face twisted in confusion as he looked to the mulch at their feet and back to Jonah's face. He scratched the back of his neck. "All right." The words were dragged out as if he were trying to buy himself time to back away slowly before calling the men who brought the buckled jackets.

Jonah couldn't help chuckling softly. "It's just a . . . thing someone I know suggested I do."

Cecil tilted his head, looking back over his shoulder. "Myrtle?"

Myrtle appeared on the path. "What?"

"Jonah here's got a . . . someone."

Oh, Lord. "Cecil, it's not that big a thing."

"A someone?" Myrtle walked closer, a look of blatant hope on her face that was so obvious, Jonah groaned.

"Please stop it, you two."

"Who is she?" Cecil asked. "Someone you met on the email?"

Jonah propped the shovel against the bush he had been adding mulch to and removed his gardening gloves. "I think you mean the Internet. And no, I didn't meet her on some dating site."

Although the idea was amusing in a pitiful way. What would his bio say? Perhaps something along the lines of:

PATHETIC AND HIDEOUS RECLUSE SEEKS . . . WELL, ANYONE FEMALE REALLY, TO MEET IN THE DARK OF NIGHT IN A DILAPIDATED, GHOST-INFESTED PLANTATION HOME.

Jesus.

Cecil and Myrtle exchanged a look. They both knew Jonah didn't leave the house and had to be wondering if he'd finally cracked and started seeing the ghosts everyone claimed lived at Windisle.

Jonah abandoned his task and started walking toward the house. He'd lost his will to garden. Cecil and Myrtle followed, close on his heels. He considered turning toward them and explaining, but the thought brought a sharp, panicky feeling to his chest. What would he say? I met this girl through the wall. I've never seen her, but I think I could easily fall in love with her?

He stopped dead in his tracks. His heart slammed against his chest and alarm bells rang in his head.

Ridiculous. In love? He sounded *pathetic,* even in his own damn head.

His relationship, *if you could call it that,* with Clara was an invention formed from his loneliness and isolation. Nothing more. Yes, she'd called herself his friend but in actuality, she was barely an acquaintance. She was someone he talked to now and then. If he'd lived a normal life, he'd have equated her to the chatty mailperson, or the neighbor you stop on the street to catch up with. *Inconsequential.*

She'd made him consider things he hadn't considered in a long time, that was true, but *she,* Clara, the individual, did not matter.

Talking to anyone other than Myrtle and Cecil would have brought about the same feelings in him. And yet, the thought rang hollow in his head. He knew he was lying to himself. And he knew what he had to do about it.

****

Later that day, Jonah arrived at the weeping wall, sliding down and taking his usual spot under the oak tree. A bright green leaf floated down, landing in Jonah's lap. He picked it up, tilting his head so he could see it with his good eye, spinning the delicate thing between his fingers, noting the subtle yet vibrant striations of gold and yellow that wove through the veins. Something he only noticed because he'd taken the time to examine it closely. How many things had he overlooked in his life because he'd been too busy—too self-important—to take a moment to dig deeper, look closer, understand more fully? The thought was depressing. If only . . . if only . . .

A slight breeze wafted over him, the mineral scents of the Mississippi River finding him through the woods and marsh that separated him from that vast body of water, behind a wall, protected by the dim shade cast by centuries-old trees. Some things you simply couldn't hide from. Some things you could never escape. He'd already discovered that, though. He'd learned the lesson well.

He heard a car door open and close and a moment later, Clara's breathless voice greeted him as she took her seat on the other side of the wall. "How are you?"

"Good. How are you?"

"Sore." She groaned. "We stayed late at practice last night. I stopped using Mrs. Guillot's liniment because of the smell, but I'll tell you what. That stuff works. I might have to make you suffer through it again."

Jonah chuckled. "I'm on the other side of a wall, Clara. You should probably be more concerned with the people you spend face-to-face time with."

There was a moment of awkward silence and Jonah cleared his throat. "Speaking of which, I never asked who drops you off here each week." He assumed she was getting a ride from a friend but she'd never mentioned him or her.

"Oh, I take an Uber."

"What's an Uber?"

"You know, a personal taxi. It's a location-specific app." She paused. "Have you really never heard of an Uber?"

Jonah was embarrassed. Not only had he never heard of an Uber, he couldn't even remember if he'd ever used any apps. "I don't get out much, Clara. I guess the world has sort of . . . passed me by in some ways." How many ways, he couldn't even begin to guess. Just the thought of what was going on "out there," on the other side of the wall, sent a shock of anxiety coursing through him, and he put his palms down on the cold, solid ground, gripping the grass, and feeling it slide between his fingers. The contact made him feel immediately calmer.

"You don't get out much?" Clara repeated, hesitance in her voice. She had asked him questions about himself before, but he'd always neatly sideswiped them, bringing the topic back around to Windisle.

She'd asked him why everyone thought the place was deserted, whether he used lights at night, or kept them off, and he'd answered her truthfully, that though the landscaping lights had ceased working years ago, the lights from the house simply couldn't be seen because of the trees that surrounded the grounds.

But he didn't tell her that he also kept the lights very low, or even off sometimes, because by the end of the day, they hurt his injured eye and brought on headaches.

He closed his eyes then, reminding himself what he had to do. Knowing it was the right thing, knowing he *should* be forthcoming. She should know that he didn't leave this plantation—not ever—and they might be temporary friends, but he wouldn't leave this place under any circumstances. And she should know the reason why.

"How often, Jonah?"

"Never," he said quietly. "I haven't left Windisle in eight years."

He knew her silence was due to surprise, confusion probably. "Never?" she repeated. "What? Why? What do you . . . what do you do?"

"I . . ." God, what *did* he do? Existed. Barely that. "I just . . ." He leaned his head back against the stone, turning his cheek so it was pressed against the cold, hard rock.

"What, Jonah? What is it? Tell me, please."

The clouds above moved over the sun, momentarily shutting out the already-dim light, creating a further sense of intimacy. It felt like the world had shrunk to only the two of them.

He searched for the right words, weariness washing through his soul. There *were* no words that would make this right, and God, but he was tired. He was so *damned* tired of hurting all the time. And this, here, it suddenly felt like a confessional. Or maybe it always had. Maybe it was the draw that kept him coming back to the wall to meet her over and over again. And yet it wasn't fair to her, was it?

He knew he had to stop this charade—for both of them. To tell her the truth. But poised on the brink of confessing his greatest sin, he also had the notion of being trapped and wanting something so desperately, only he didn't know what. To cleanse his soul? To feel alive again? Even for a moment? Were any of those things even possible? "I regret," he breathed, "I just regret. I've made a career of it, here, behind this wall."

"Oh," she said, and there was so much feeling in the word that he turned, kneeling, putting his palms against the wall, wondering if maybe her hands were pressed to his in the same way, her mouth somewhere close by. What color were her eyes? What did her expression look like right then? He wanted to know, and yet not knowing—the anonymity—was what had allowed him to speak from his heart for the first time in so, so long.

"I know what that feels like. What do you regret, Jonah? Will you . . . will you tell me?"

Her startling empathy made his heart clench. He didn't deserve it. She would know that soon enough and she would go. And that's what he wanted, wasn't it?

He leaned his forehead against the cool, smooth stone and closed his eyes, seeing the way the clouds had looked above him that day as he'd lain on the ground, half dead, wishing he were.

He could feel the agony of the blast, the way his face had burned—hot, searing—and then the blessed numbness, the fading noise, the disbelief, and then the grief. Nothing but grief, and it felt as though that part had never gone away. "I killed my brother." And others. So many others. Six innocent people and he knew all their names by heart. He repeated them sometimes as he ran, the syllables of each one drilling into his heart like tiny knives. He deserved that. He did. And so he kept doing it—all of these years. He'd never stop.

He heard her let out a soft gasp. "You . . ."

"I didn't mean to, but I did. I was responsible for his death. For others as well. I'm the monster behind the wall, Clara. That's what I am."

Anguish ratcheted through him, and he let out a whoosh of breath as if the admittance was a tangible thing with a soul of its own and had been residing inside of his chest for years, buried underneath the words. And yet, the admittance of it didn't extinguish his guilt. It only added fuel to the fire. Now she knew too, this girl who had spoken to him gently, who had called him the wish collector and come *back*.

"Oh, Jonah. What happened?"

Why was she asking him *that*? Why was she still here? Why hadn't what he said made her run? Did she really need the details after a confession like that? Did she really still want to be his "friend"? Maybe she was just plain stupid. Or a glutton for punishment. Or one of those do-gooders who thought she could save his soul.

Those people had come by when he'd first moved in to Windisle Plantation. Maybe they'd watched his story on the news and somehow knew he lived there. Or maybe it was a coincidence they'd shown up with pamphlets and booklets about redemption. He'd yelled at them through the gate, telling them he'd call the cops if they didn't fucking go away and never come back.

And *fucking hell,* he suddenly felt so zapped of strength as though he could lie in the grass and sleep. He didn't answer her question, and it lingered between them as much a barrier as the stone wall.

Clara was quiet now and Jonah was glad. He turned back around, pressing his back to the wall as memories assaulted his mind, his heart: Justin, leaning over the top of the bunk bed they'd shared as kids, talking about their dreams for the future, what successes they were going to be, how they would change the world.

He saw his brother the summer before he'd gone to college, doing a backflip off their boat and coming up out of the water laughing, and then his laugh morphed into a frown in Jonah's mind—the frown he'd worn that day he'd left his office. *We'll talk later.*

He snapped back to the moment, leaning his cheek on the wall, sighing and putting his hands flat in the dry grass next to his thighs. The pain of the memories made his stomach contract. He recalled things after that, but it was all such a blur. A horror-filled blur. And he'd been a shell of himself ever since. Just as he deserved. *Why should he get to live when they no longer could?*

"Jonah."

His name brought him back from all the memories swirling together in his grief-drenched mind—wonderful, tragic, unchangeable. *Too much.*

He stood up, feeling sick and distressed. "I have to go."

Jonah heard her stand too, her voice coming from right below his head. "Wait. I'm sorry if I—"

"It's not you, Clara. I'm just . . ." His gut was roiling, and he felt like he was going to vomit. "I'm back here for a reason. My name is Jonah Chamberlain. Look me up. Then don't come back." He knew the final directive was unnecessary. Once she learned his story, she'd *never* come back.

He walked away quickly, not responding to Clara calling his name from the other side of the wall.

CHAPTER EIGHT

The Main Library was open until nine on Tuesdays and Clara took the bus there, asking for directions to the public computer terminals at the information desk once she arrived. Her steps were slow, her mind troubled as she made her way to the place the woman at the front had told her to go. Something about what she was there to do—look Jonah up—felt . . . wrong. Invasive. And yet, he'd told her to. *My name is Jonah Chamberlain. Look me up.* Chamberlain.

She wasn't sure exactly why, but she hadn't imagined he was a member of the Chamberlain family. She'd thought he was part of the staff that kept the place running along with Myrtle and Cecil, or a distant relative maybe.

Perhaps it was the way he'd sounded when he'd spoken briefly about the Chamberlain family, a certain . . . removed tone, laced with disdain. An employer he did not respect, she'd assumed.

She'd asked him questions, of course, but he'd always changed the subject or brought the topic back to Windisle. And she'd let him, figuring he'd open up to her about himself if and when he was ready. She didn't want to push because she sensed so much sadness in him. So much . . . loneliness.

And now she knew she was right. He was a recluse. He *never* came out from behind the weeping wall, not even covertly. *Why?*

She remembered the way he'd spoken about John Whitfield, so much understanding threaded through his voice when he'd mentioned his war trauma. She'd wondered if Jonah had once been a soldier too.

She placed her duffle bag on the floor next to her chair and turned on the computer. She'd like to buy her own laptop, but she was saving up for a car and wanted to put every penny toward that. Also, she assumed the large main library offered more access to a variety of archived news articles.

She'd resisted typing his name into a Google search. If she was going to look him up—and she hadn't decided she would until that day—she wanted all the information at her disposal. *Eight years,* he'd said. He'd been behind the wall for eight years. Meaning, whatever he'd encouraged her to look up must have happened about that time.

Don't come back, he'd demanded. His final words had been ringing through her head for the past two days, the disappointment and confusion continuing to grow. The heartache. Because the truth was, she'd spent each week for the past month and a half looking forward to that brief time on Sunday evening when she sat on the other side of the wall from him, talking and learning and—she'd thought—forming a deep friendship unlike anything she'd ever known.

Growing up, she'd never had a lot of time to cultivate friendships outside of her rigorous practice schedule and constant performances, never had time for parties or shopping, or the things other girls spent time doing together. Even the couple of boyfriends she'd had, had eventually grown bitter at the little time she'd had to offer them. Then again, maybe she hadn't made them more of a priority by choice. Maybe her heart had never been invested in either relationship.

Perhaps all of that was the reason the bond she felt with Jonah meant so much to her.

She loved spending time with him, loved sharing parts of herself she hadn't shared with anyone else. And she loved listening to him as well, loved the way he described his world. The way he added in small tidbits that she knew were only *him,* only his own vision of a certain something, like the way he likened Myrtle to a hedgehog: round and prickly at times, but ultimately the most loyal and lovable person you'd ever meet.

And though he hadn't shared very many personal things with her by choice, she knew those were small pieces of him that he'd unwittingly given, and she grasped them and held them as precious gifts, the same way she held each minor comment Mrs. Guillot made about her deceased husband in the midst of a story.

Those were the tiny treasures all people doled out, but *only* to those they trusted, and Clara recognized them as such.

She'd been intrigued by Windisle when she'd arrived that first day, but Jonah had made her fall in love with it. He'd described it to her in such loving detail, his deep, accented drawl winding through the cracks in the wall, and weaving around her, lush and honeyed, like the blossom-heavy vines that climbed the gates, taking over the swirling iron until it looked to be created entirely of petals and greenery. That's what he'd done to her, as she'd sat there, the colors in the sky bleeding together and melting into darkness. She'd felt *consumed.* Completely engulfed by something strong and sweet.

Jonah.

Her wish collector.

Her grit and velvet-voiced dream weaver.

Her fingers hovered uncertainly over the keys for a moment before she finally exhaled, lowering her hands and typing in his name.

So many hits came up immediately she barely knew where to start. She was shaking, she realized, and something unnamed was moving through her. This was going to change everything, of course. If the miniscule amount he'd given her—*I killed my brother* and *I'm the monster behind the wall*—hadn't, this would. She felt it in her gut.

She clicked on images first and leaned toward the screen as he—Jonah Chamberlain—the voice behind the wall, became a flesh-and-blood man.

She sat back in her chair, blinking at his smiling photo. She hadn't given too much thought to what she expected, but *this,* this was definitely not it.

Her gaze moved from his chiseled jaw to his full smiling lips to his high cheekbones and his light brown eyes topped by dark deep-set brows. *Dear lord.*

He had a face made for fantasy and fairy tales, created for artists, fashioned for stages and film screens and for dark, starlit nights. His hair, which he wore combed back, was wavy and a deep chocolaty brown, a widow's peak dipping from his thick hairline and seeming to point to the perfection of his face.

She swallowed, chills breaking out over her skin. His beauty, formed from tiny pixels, and staring one-dimensional from a computer screen, felt painful to her somehow and why, she did not know.

Clara forced herself to scroll down the screen. The majority of the images were of Jonah in a suit, looking powerful and confident, as he leaned toward a microphone. Others were of him in what looked like a courtroom, and the close-up, the one that had first stopped her breath, was his photo from a law firm pamphlet. Jonah Chamberlain was a lawyer. Or he had been.

Clicking off the images, Clara opened the first article, and began to read, bile moving up her throat as horror gripped her.

An hour and a half later, Clara stood unsteadily from the computer terminal where she'd been glued to her seat. She reached with shaky hands to grab her duffle bag, knocking over the plastic cup of pencils in her jerky movements. They clattered across the surface of the desk and a woman sitting across from her shot her a glare.

Without taking the time to replace the pencils, Clara turned, fast-walking out of the library, drawing in a much-needed lungful of air as she ran across the street, away, away.

But she couldn't escape the information she'd learned, and the photo of her grinning wish collector as he'd drunk champagne and toasted his success right before so many worlds would crumble—including his own—remained in vivid color in her mind's eye.

****

"You felt tense today."

Marco lifted Clara's bag and slung it over his shoulder as she stood. She reached for her bag, but he moved back, grinning his trademark grin and beginning to walk.

She sighed and took a few quick steps to catch up. "I pushed myself too hard yesterday. I just wanted to take it easy today so I didn't pull something."

He gave her a dubious look, raising one dark eyebrow as they pushed through the double doors to the parking lot. "Where are you parked?"

"I'm not. I bus it."

He stopped, turning toward her. "You take the bus to and from the theater every day?"

"For now." She shrugged. "I'm saving up for a car."

He shook his head, muttering something in Italian she didn't understand. *Poor thing,* maybe? *Helpless female? Easy prey?* Any of those were likely. Marco was the biggest ladies' man in the ballet—and Clara was quite certain he didn't limit himself to coworkers. "I'll give you a ride."

"No thanks." Clara held her hand out for her duffle.

Marco opened his mouth and then closed it, and Clara almost chuckled at his perplexed expression. He was obviously unused to being turned down for anything.

From what she had witnessed, the other female dancers—and some of the males—went all googly eyed when he tossed them a glance.

Oh, he was attractive, she'd give him that. But he was also cocky and narcissistic and as a general rule, she didn't date other dancers anyway. Now would be an especially bad time to break that rule; she was distracted enough.

She used his awkward pause to snag the bag from his shoulder and put it over hers as she turned away. "Bye," she sang.

He caught up to her and she glanced at him as she sighed, speeding up her steps, though he kept up with her easily, and she knew exactly how. She was well acquainted with those long, muscled dancer's legs of his. "You don't think very highly of me."

"I admire you very much, Marco. I think you're an extremely talented dancer. But I don't date other dancers." *And I'm distracted and sad and confused and . . . I just want to be alone.*

"I didn't ask you for a date. I just offered you a ride."

That stopped Clara up short, a heated blush rising in her cheeks. He was right. She'd been presumptuous. In actuality, she'd thought too highly of *herself.* Sure, he was a ladies' man, but that didn't mean he was interested in *every* lady. It didn't mean he was interested in *her*. She'd been selfish and rude. She grimaced. "Sorry, Marco, I—"

"Not that I *don't* want to date you." He dragged his gaze down her body and then back up to her eyes. "I was waiting to get you in the car before I put the real moves on."

He gave her a wolfish stare, but she caught the small quirk of his lips. He was teasing her. Maybe only in part but it was enough to disarm her.

She laughed, glancing over his shoulder to where the cars were parked. "No moves, okay? But I'll take the ride. Thank you very much. It's nice of you to offer."

Marco grinned. "Follow me." He removed her bag from her shoulder again, and she let him, rolling her eyes as she did. *Flirt.*

As they were driving away, a group of fellow dancers exited the building, talking and laughing. They caught sight of Clara sitting in Marco's passenger seat as they drove past, their chatter halting as every gaze followed. Clara looked away, focusing on the street ahead as Marco pulled out of the lot. *Let the gossip commence,* she thought. *Awesome.*

"So, Clara, what have you been doing for fun since you moved to New Orleans?"

"Fun? Who has time for fun?"

Marco chuckled, shooting her a grin. "We should all make time for a little fun. All work and no play . . ."

She raised a brow as his words tapered off, a particular whispery lilt to the word *play*. She understood exactly the type of fun Marco was referring to. "I have made a little time to get to know New Orleans." *And a man who keeps himself hidden behind a wall . . . a man who collects wishes, who has a voice that wraps around my bones . . . a man who played a part in such a terrible tragedy.*

"Sightseeing? That's what you consider fun?" Marco sighed. "It's clear how much you need me, Clara." He patted her knee then removed his hand. "If I'd have known it was such an emergency, I'd have come for you sooner."

Clara was surprised at the laugh that bubbled up her throat after the sad direction of her thoughts only moments before. "I'll bet."

Marco gave her a crooked grin, and they drove on for a few minutes in silence, but it was comfortable.

Clara watched the city go by out the window and wondered what Jonah was doing in that moment and then made herself turn her mind away.

Even after two weeks, she still didn't know how she should feel about the man who had become her friend, about the man she'd come to care about despite the stone wall that separated them.

"Do you have a date for the Masquerade Charity Ball yet?"

"No," Clara answered. The Masquerade Charity Ball was an extravaganza that benefitted the ballet, and all dancers were expected to attend, but Clara hadn't been planning on taking a date. And it was in two weeks. Which reminded

Clara that she still needed to find a dress . . . and a mask, though she didn't figure finding a mask in New Orleans would be a problem. The city was known for its love of dressing up, transforming from ordinary to extraordinary.

"Then it's settled. I'll escort you."

Clara laughed. "I thought we agreed no moves."

"I agreed to nothing. And if you think these are my moves, you don't know me very well."

Clara rolled her eyes but couldn't resist a smile. "Anyway, that's not necessary. We'll all see each other there."

He glanced at her. "And you don't date other dancers."

"That's right. So really, Marco, I'm not worth your time."

He smiled as he pulled up to the address he'd plugged into his GPS when they first got in the car. "I think, Clara, that might be exactly why you're worth my time."

He grinned as he got out of the car, and she let herself out as well. He came around, holding her duffle bag he'd taken from the back seat and handing it to her. "I'll pick you up at seven before the ball?" He inclined his head. "One coworker innocently escorting another."

Clara opened her mouth to say no, but hesitated. She had a feeling Marco's whole "one coworker innocently escorting another" shouldn't be entirely trusted, but the truth was, she'd much rather be picked up by a friend, than take an Uber in a ball gown. That scenario sounded very lonely, and she'd had about all the lonely she could handle recently.

Despite her confusion and turmoil, she'd missed Jonah. She *missed* feeling like she wasn't completely alone in this strange city. She missed their talks and their connection. She hadn't simply *imagined* that they had one, or she wouldn't miss it so much.

"All right. Seven. As coworker friends." She gave him a measuring look.

"Perfect." Marco turned and headed toward his car. "I'll see you on Monday, friend." He winked as he got inside and Clara shook her head on a small laugh as she watched him pull away.

Friend.

We're friends, right? she'd asked Jonah, and he'd said yes, though so hesitantly she'd held her breath as she'd waited for his answer.

I just regret. I've made a career of it, here, behind this wall.

Oh, Jonah. She still couldn't mesh the man she'd read about, the man who'd sounded ruthless and self-serving with the sensitive man she'd shared her heart with all those weeks. He'd never once come across as selfish or uncaring, but rather intuitive and introspective.

Don't come back.

And she hadn't. He'd probably *figured* she wouldn't, *counted* on it maybe. He hated himself; she'd heard the painful self-loathing in his voice as he'd told her a small part of what he'd done. What he felt responsible for. What she still couldn't come to terms with.

And now that she hadn't returned, did he think Clara agreed with his self-exile? Or was it self-imprisonment? *Both,* she guessed.

Rain began to fall, fat droplets that splattered the sidewalk and pinged on the metal roof of the porch. Clara stepped backward under the roof's cover and watched as the world blurred into muted watercolors. Despite the downpour, rays of buttery sunshine peeked through the dark, heavy clouds, causing the sheets of water to glitter and glisten.

Clara began to step away from the porch and turn in the direction of her apartment when a sound broke through the whooshing rain. It was Mrs. Guillot's voice that met her ears, the sweet spiciness falling over her like sprinkled sugar with a hint of pepper.

"Amazing Grace how sweet the sound, that saved a wretch like me."

A wretch.

That's how Jonah thought of himself, she was certain. And he was, Clara supposed. Or . . . he had been.

"'Twas grace that taught my heart to fear, and grace my fears relieved."

Grace. Forgiveness. Understanding. She'd always considered herself a forgiving person. But could she even begin to understand the things he'd done? The role he'd played?

Again, Clara began walking toward her apartment door, but decided against it, turning and running through the rain to Mrs. Guillot's. When she got there, Mrs. Guillot stopped singing, smiling widely at Clara and ushering her under the covering of her porch.

"Well now, Clara darlin', I haven't seen you lately. How are you?"

Clara joined Mrs. Guillot on her porch, running a hand over her damp hair and sinking into the other rocker. Mrs. Guillot's smile made her feel warmer inside than a freshly made cup of tea. "I'm okay."

Mrs. Guillot's smile wilted into a frown. "How's your father?"

"About the same. I spoke with him a couple of days ago. Just for a minute, but still . . ."

"Well now, that's wonderful. So why do you seem troubled, darlin'?"

Clara worried her lip. "Mrs. Guillot, do you think everyone deserves grace?"

Mrs. Guillot gave Clara a long look. "I'd say you're asking less about everyone than about a certain someone. Am I right?"

Clara nodded. "Yes . . ."

"And is this someone a friend, sweet girl?"

"I thought so, Mrs. Guillot." Clara paused, amending her answer. "Yes, he was a friend." Was? *Is? Oh, I'm so confused.*

"Someone you trusted?"

"I . . . yes."

Mrs. Guillot leaned forward and patted Clara's knee. "I believe everyone deserves grace, Clara. What you will have to ask yourself is if you should offer that grace from near or from afar. Offering grace does not mean offering your heart. That, my darlin', must be protected at all cost."

Clara nodded slowly, taking Mrs. Guillot's words in and turning them over. Yes, that was exactly what she'd been struggling with these past few weeks. Should she offer grace but stay away from Jonah, or should she offer grace and remain his friend? She still wasn't sure . . . but talking about it for a moment with Mrs. Guillot had settled something inside of her.

She needed to go back to the weeping wall at least one final time. They'd been friends, and maybe they still could be.

She needed to speak to Jonah in person about what she'd read. She owed him that much, if nothing else.

CHAPTER NINE

The tree branches swayed in the slight breeze, creating a gentle hushing sound that might have lulled and calmed under ordinary circumstances. But Jonah was too heavy-hearted to be lulled. Too troubled to be calmed.

He stared at the trees in front of him, his eyes on the sliver of Windisle Manor that could be seen from where he sat.

He heard a vehicle approach and his heart jumped, settling into a quickened beat as a car door slammed and footsteps approached. But then he heard murmuring on the other side of the wall and a slip of paper landed on the grass to his right.

After a moment, the footsteps retreated and Jonah's heart slowed, the disappointment he hated himself for feeling twisted through him like thick, noxious smoke that filled his lungs and made it hurt to breathe.

Why was he out here again anyway? To torture himself? To rub it in?

She'd never be back.

He reached for the wish, opening the folded piece of paper with one hand, and turning his head slightly so he could see the small, precise writing with his good eye. *My little boy needs surgery and I can't pay for it. Please help me find a way.*

Fuck.

He hated when the wishes involved kids. It made him feel more depressed than he already was, and there wasn't anything he could do about it. So he just had to try not to think about the fact that there was some unknown woman out there with a sick kid she couldn't help. God, if Justin were here, he would have—

Another vehicle pulled up, the car door closing with a soft click. Jonah drew air into his lungs and let it out slowly, evenly. He tilted his head and waited for a wish to fall through one of the cracks and instead heard the sound of the car pulling away. He tensed.

"Hi, Jonah," she said, and he heard her slide down the wall as she took her usual seat, the one that had sat empty for the past two Sundays. He knew because he'd come anyway, forcing himself to sit alone and bear the loneliness that was so much worse than it'd been before her. Before Clara.

I won't say a word. I won't, he promised himself. He'd let her think he wasn't there. He'd told her not to come back, so why *would* he let her know of his presence? That he was waiting like a pitiful fool for something he himself had put an end to?

And why in the hell was she there anyway? Had she not listened? Had she not looked him up after all?

"I know you're there. I . . . I was hoping you would be."

Okay, so she could probably hear him breathing, the same way he could hear her. She could probably see the small slips of blocked light where he leaned against the wall. Hell, maybe she could *feel* him the way he felt her. Some type of inexplicable magnetism that pulled at him, which made him want to dissolve through the wall and touch her warmth. *No!*

No. This was why he'd told her to leave. These thoughts that ran untethered through his brain whenever she was near, the way he could smell her soft scent even underneath that god-awful liniment she sometimes had on.

Clara sighed. "Fine. If you won't talk to me, I'll talk to you." She paused and he pressed his ear against the cold stone as if she might be whispering under her breath and if he leaned closer, he could make out the soft, secretive sound.

"I read about what happened, Jonah. I read about Amanda Kershaw. I read about Murray Ridgley and all his victims. I read everything I could."

She paused again, and Jonah's heart tightened painfully with the absolute knowledge that she knew. She knew why he'd called himself a monster. She knew. "I saw your photo, Jonah."

His heart skittered, shame arcing through him. "I don't look like that anymore." He clenched his eyes shut. He hadn't intended on the outburst, but he'd heard the gentle, approving way she'd said the word *photo*, as if she were picturing him right that moment. And that was unthinkable.

She couldn't believe he still looked the way he used to. She couldn't think he was still the man he'd been when women's eyes widened as he entered a room. Oh, they might still widen now, come to think of it, but it wouldn't be for the same reason as before.

When he'd told her he was a monster, he meant in every way. He would *not* have her coming there because she'd liked what she saw online and decided it was worth dismissing his evil deeds.

He ran a hand through his thick hair, frowning. That wasn't the Clara he knew. She wasn't shallow like that, but . . . why the hell *else* was she there?

"No," she murmured thoughtfully. "I don't suppose you look the same. The scarring must be"—*terrible, hideous, ugly*—"considerable," she finished. "The pain you must have endured . . . I can't imagine."

For a moment, Jonah didn't know how to respond. He'd heard hurt in her voice . . . sadness. Compassion. It both unsettled him and brought forth a sudden sweeping emotion he couldn't identify, or perhaps was afraid to. "It's the very least of my ugliness. Didn't you read the stories?" he demanded.

"Yes, but I want to hear about it from you."

"Why?" he rasped. What else did she need to know? Every damning and sordid detail was available online. He'd looked it up once when he'd just been released from the hospital. He'd read the comments below the articles, and they'd made him retch into the bedpan that Myrtle had left next to his bed.

He'd gone back to those comments day after day, forcing himself to read each and every one, every vile word of hate and judgment, knowing he deserved them.

He'd told Myrtle it was the pain medication that was making him sick and though she'd glanced worriedly at the laptop beside him, she hadn't said a word.

"Because everyone deserves to tell their own story in their own voice, and I know I stayed away for a little while and I'm sorry about that, Jonah. I needed time to process, but I hope you trust me enough to share your version with me. I'd like to listen."

Jonah was silent as her words wrapped around him. Did she imagine his version would be different somehow than what she'd already read? Was it?

For the first time since that horrific day, he wondered if it was, even in some small but possibly important way he'd never considered.

No one had ever asked him to tell his version, and he wondered if he could separate it from the story everyone else had told. And yet, none of the *facts* were different, so what did it really matter? Hopelessness descended over him like a damp, heavy cloud. "It won't *change* anything, Clara. It won't undo what happened."

"No, of course not. You can't change the past. You can only change the future. But I'm not asking you to do that either. I'm simply asking you to help me see that terrible day from your perspective, not from those who only looked for the villain to cast all blame upon."

Jonah sighed, the old familiar weariness coming over him. He leaned his head back against the wall. *What the hell?* Clara wanted to hear the story from his own lips. Fine, he'd tell it. For the first time, and the last time, he'd tell it. Because it was *her* asking and no other reason.

"I was a lawyer, you know that." He told her about finishing college early, about the accelerated law school he'd attended, about taking and passing the bar exam. He told her about being hired on at Applegate, Knowles, and Fennimore, and his lofty career aspirations.

"Were you always so driven? Even as a boy?"

He paused, considering that. "Yes. I'd always planned to follow in my father's footsteps. He was a lawyer, as was my brother, Justin." Justin's name ended in a rough whisper and Jonah cleared his throat. "I was the one who emulated my father, and Justin was the one who denounced everything he stood for."

"What did your father stand for?"

"In my mind at the time? Power. Success. To Justin he was greed and narcissism."

"You said *at the time.* What about now? Do you think of your father differently?"

Jonah paused again, thinking about Clara's question for the first time. "I haven't thought about my father very much since . . . I've come to live here."

He was quiet again for a moment and so was she as if she knew he needed to gather his thoughts and was allowing him the time to do that. "But, now . . ."

Jonah closed his eyes, picturing his father as he'd been. Dismissive, and then quick to snap, sarcastic, cutting. The things he'd said when he was displeased with Jonah had wounded him. Yes, he could admit that now. And so Jonah had striven to be *like* him, to make him *proud,* to stop the pain of his disapproval, with no thought to anything else. God, he'd been a coward.

Justin had been the brave one. Justin had had the guts to go *against* his father. "I see that my father had many of the qualities Justin claimed. And because I emulated him, so did I." Shame was a thousand prickly thorns piercing the underside of his skin.

You're choosing a path here, Jonah.

Ah, yes. Justin had been right. And that path had led him there, to Windisle, to life as an outcast and a monster. But Justin . . . the brave one, the good one, had lost his life. Because of Jonah. Because of the path Jonah had chosen, the one Justin had begged him not to travel.

"Justin knew who my father was and did everything to be the polar opposite of him. He fought for justice, he took many pro bono cases, and he gave practically every cent he earned to charity. He made the world a better place." *Unlike me,* hung in the air between them and somehow Jonah *knew* she heard the silent sound of the unspoken words too.

"There are lots of ways to avoid pain," she murmured. "None of them are healthy if they're based on fear. A reaction—a rebellion if you will—rather than something from the heart."

But he didn't want to consider what might or might not have been his brother's faults, what his brother might have been doing solely to avoid pain instead of acting from pure sincerity. He wanted to continue to see Justin as he deserved to be seen: good and righteous. "Maybe," he said without conviction, pushing the idea to the back of his mind.

They were both quiet for a moment before Clara said, "Tell me from the beginning, Jonah."

The beginning. He forced his mind back to a time when he'd only heard Murray Ridgley's name on the news, when *he* was the monster, not Jonah. Not yet.

He sighed shakily. "When I first started at the firm, there had been several girls found in New Orleans the year before, raped and murdered. The police were still on the hunt for the perpetrator, but had little to go on. When a girl was picked up on the side of the road, bloody, beaten, half-alive, they got their first break. Her wrists were still bound and the way she'd been tied up, the particular knot that was used, was the same one used on the murdered girls."

"Amanda Kershaw," Clara whispered. "She was the lone survivor."

"Yes. She was able to help the police pinpoint the location where she'd been taken, where the man later arrested and identified as Murray Ridgley had raped her and almost taken her life before she'd managed to escape."

Jonah's stomach tightened in distress. To have escaped him once, only to be murdered by him later. The pain of that, the bleak, cosmic injustice in which he'd played a part, still haunted his every waking hour. It was terrible and tragic and *wrong*. And he could have *stopped* it.

"Anyway," he said, and even he could hear the despondency in his own tone, "when Murray Ridgley contacted the firm, the partners decided to take on his case. And later, they assigned it to me."

"Did you believe him to be innocent?" The way she said the final word, quickly and with a soft intake of air, led him to believe she was holding her breath.

He paused because something inside of him knew it was very important he be truthful, not necessarily for Clara, but for himself.

He'd described their talks as a sort of confessional and though he'd never expected to confess *this* to her, if he was going to, and if any small crumb of redemption was available to his blackened soul, he must first be truthful.

"I wasn't positive—there was no concrete evidence, only a mountain of circumstantial—but I knew it was a possibility."

Jonah heard the small whoosh of air as it flowed from Clara's lungs. "Did you withhold evidence, Jonah?"

"No. God, no. I wanted to win, Clara, so I was focused on that. But I didn't lie or cheat to do it."

He thought back to the whispered words behind closed doors, the way the partners had ceased talking when he walked into a room, and he wondered again if they had been keeping something from him . . . The thought flitted through his head, but he let it go without attempting to catch it. What did it matter now anyway?

"The thing that ultimately got him acquitted was Amanda Kershaw's testimony."

Jonah clenched his eyes shut, letting his head fall against the stone with a heavy thud. "Yes. She . . . she wasn't strong, Clara, and I knew that. She wasn't like you."

He paused, thinking back to the first time he'd met Amanda at the courthouse, the way she'd shaken when she spoke, the way her eyes had darted around, the way she'd drawn her shoulders in as if to appear smaller, as if to hide from the world. He'd seen the way she pulled at her sleeves to conceal the needle marks on her arms, and he'd used that too.

"I used her weaknesses against her when she got up on the stand." He banged his head against the stone again, a dull thud, and he heard Clara shift. "I demolished her. They practically had to carry her away, she'd gotten so emotionally distraught. She appeared unstable and unreliable—almost insane—just as I'd planned. The partners all congratulated me later. They slapped me on the back and told me how brilliant I'd been."

Jonah laughed, but it was a raw scraping sound, no humor infused in it at all. "Brilliant. I'd *brilliantly* obliterated a girl who'd been the victim of a horrific crime that most people wouldn't have survived."

You're choosing a path here, Jonah.

His heart beat hollowly in his chest, the reminder that he was still here, living, breathing, and the *further* reminder that life held no true justice. Or maybe it did sometimes. He brought his hand to the half of his face that was ruined and ran his fingers over the ridged and melted skin covering the planes of his bones, tipping his head back as he gazed up at the stone structure that kept him separated from the world. Yes, maybe it did.

For maybe this *is worse than death.*

"Then what?" Clara whispered. She knew. She already knew, but she wanted to hear it from him. And he'd come this far. He just needed to go a little bit further.

"The jury acquitted Murray Ridgley." He closed his eyes again, picturing that day. "I felt . . . I don't know. I expected to feel happy . . . proud, but I just felt kind of . . . empty I guess. I attributed it to what I knew Justin's reaction had probably been. I knew, to him, the news would have been very bad. But I didn't take his calls. It was *why* I didn't take his calls."

"You felt ashamed."

"I . . ." Had he? Had he felt ashamed for winning? *Maybe.* Maybe it had been teasing the edges of his conscience, though he hadn't allowed himself to fully consider it.

Winning had been his intention, and win he had. Only, it hadn't *felt* like victory.

He'd thought maybe it would be a delayed reaction. He was tired. After all, he'd been working like a dog since he'd been put on the case. "Yes, though I didn't admit it to myself at the time. And truthfully, I might have just let it go if things hadn't . . . taken the turn they did."

"What about the video?"

"The video was a lie, Clara. I did plenty of disgraceful things, but that wasn't one of them, nor did it truthfully portray the way I was feeling after Murray Ridgley got off, despite that his acquittal was largely because of me."

The video had been part of every news story that aired about the case. It was a clip of Jonah popping the cork off a bottle of champagne as he and the partners laughed and cheered.

"A legal secretary who worked there shot it after a case we'd won many months before, a case that I hadn't even worked on. It was in no way associated with the Murray Ridgley case, but of course, the news didn't care about that, nor did they bother to fact-check."

It had made him appear giddy and excited. They'd mixed it with a video of the carnage that occurred later, showing it again and again, and the story it told was awful and shameful. But it was only partly true.

Clara paused as if soaking that information in. "Tell me, Jonah. Tell me about that day."

That day.

That day.

That day.

The words rang in his head the way the gunshots had, the way the screams still did.

That day. He'd thought he'd never ever talk about that day, but here he was. And it occurred to him that only this girl, in *this* way, could have made him do it. And he wondered if it was a blessing, or a curse.

CHAPTER TEN

Clara waited with bated breath for Jonah to speak. Her heart filled her throat, her arms wrapped around her body as he told his story, as he bared his soul, for she knew that's what he was doing—though she still wasn't sure whether her final grace would be given from near or from afar.

Jonah had called her brave, and she wasn't sure why he had that opinion of her, because recently she hadn't felt courageous at all—just lost and uncertain.

But she *was* a girl who followed her heart, and she would do so in this case as well. After all, it was her *heart* that had led her here in the first place. To Windisle. To the weeping wall. To Jonah.

"I was going to the courthouse for something involving a new case that day. I was . . . distracted, tired I guess . . ." His words dwindled away.

She'd heard the same hesitation in his voice when he'd described his feelings about winning the case. He'd been troubled by the outcome, and confused by his ambivalence, or at least that's what she suspected. But she didn't want to put words—or feelings—on his tongue, and she didn't want to assign emotions to him that he hadn't already assigned to himself. Not just because it wasn't her job, but because she didn't want to let him off any hooks of which he didn't deserve to be let off.

Clara followed her heart, *yes,* but she wasn't willing to knowingly be a fool or an enabler.

"I don't know," he finally continued. "But anyway, I didn't notice the news conference until I'd reached the courthouse steps where it was being held. I saw my brother first. He was on the steps listening. He didn't see me. He was watching Amanda Kershaw who was there with her lawyers and they were answering questions, talking about the grave injustice of Murray Ridgley being acquitted. Amanda looked . . . uh, in shock I guess. She was just . . . staring at the crowd. And then her eyes widened in this way . . ."

He let out a sharp raspy breath. *In shock,* Clara repeated in her mind. Drugged more likely from what she'd read about the woman's past. She'd been a drug addict who prostituted for her habit on occasion, though Jonah hadn't mentioned that just then or when he'd spoken about tearing her apart on the stand, and Clara wondered why.

He had used her weaknesses against her once—from his own mouth—but seemed unwilling to now. Apparently,

Jonah Chamberlain was bound and determined to carry every ounce of blame.

"I followed Amanda's gaze and that's when I saw him. Murray Ridgley standing at the edge of the small crowd, all the way at the back. Time seemed to . . . slow and I watched him reach for something in his jacket and then it was just . . . gunshots and screams and people scattering everywhere, diving for cover."

Clara's throat closed as she pictured that moment in her mind's eye—the sheer terror, the sudden chaos as Murray Ridgley pulled a gun from his coat and began firing first at Amanda Kershaw and then into the crowd.

Jonah paused for so long that Clara tipped her head toward the wall, listening for his movement, wondering if he was going to continue, sensing his pain even through the thick barrier between them.

"I couldn't get to him fast enough. People were fleeing, bumping into me. I . . . fell and got up and that's when I saw the wires going from under his jacket to his pocket. He had a bomb. I ran toward him as fast as I could, but it . . . it wasn't fast enough. I tried to tackle him, but he was already pushing the button in his pocket and then . . . I don't remember much after that."

The silence lingered, thick and heavy like the blood that had surely pooled on the courthouse steps that day. A dreadful blemish that could never be completely removed even when it had been scrubbed away. A stain that would forever remain between the cracks and crevices, in the deep, unseen places that could never ever be reached. *Is that what it feels like inside, Jonah? Deep in your soul?* "Why did you run toward him instead of running away?"

"What?" Jonah rasped.

"He was shooting. You saw a bomb. Everyone else was diving for cover. Running *away*. Why did you run toward him? What made you do that?"

"Why? Because . . . I don't know."

"Jonah—"

"No, Clara." She heard him shift, sit up perhaps, gather himself. "I know where your mind is going, and you think far too highly of me if you're suggesting I was being heroic. It was just a reaction, not a choice. I didn't even think about it."

"Maybe that's what makes it truly heroic."

He laughed, but it was cold and sharp like the uneven stones that poked at her back causing her to shift in discomfort when they dug too deep. "You want to believe that, but it isn't true."

Clara sighed. "I don't know if it's true or not, but can't you give yourself a little bit of grace? You made some bad choices and the result . . . well, it's all so tragic. But you didn't intend for any of that to happen. You didn't know. How could you? Murray Ridgley is the true monster of this story. Not you."

"There can be more than one monster, Clara." But his tone had softened and there was something in it that hadn't been there before, though she couldn't tell exactly what that might be.

Maybe, she thought. Maybe we were *all* some shade of monstrous given the right circumstances. "You're not all bad,

Jonah," she whispered. He'd done bad things, but the results had been unintentional, and he'd *suffered* for them. Still. He *let* himself suffer for them. He *made* himself suffer for them. She knew he did. And he'd relentlessly held on to that suffering for eight long years, and from the sounds of it, planned to forever.

"Is anyone?" he asked, and then laughed, an ironic sound she didn't understand.

"No, perhaps not, but I believe there's redemption for those who *truly* want it. Who work to achieve it."

"Oh, Clara, you're naïve. There's no redemption for me. Do you know what happened when I left the hospital? There was a crowd outside, and they yelled and spit on me as Myrtle wheeled me out of the door."

She had momentarily bristled at being called naïve, but that was quickly replaced with sorrow. Her heart ached and she closed her eyes, hanging her head at the vision his memory evoked in her mind. "I'm sorry. I'm sorry you experienced that at a time you must have been in terrible pain. I'm sorry people were cruel to you when you were injured and grief-stricken and in need of love, not judgment."

"Why? I deserved it. And I accepted it. I was the face of the trial, and I was the face of the carnage later. And what a recognizable face it is."

"Is that why you stay behind this wall? Because people will see your scars and recognize you? Because you're worried they'll be cruel again?"

He was silent for a long moment as though he wasn't quite sure how to answer the question. "It's just better this way."

"I don't believe that." Clara wasn't sure at which point during his telling of the story she'd decided to offer him grace from up close rather than from far away, but she realized very suddenly that whenever it had happened, she had.

The conviction wrapped around her and made her spine straighten as though an invisible cord had somehow been roped around her and connected to him. It pulled tight and she rose onto her knees and turned toward the wall so that her mouth was pressed against one of the whisper-thin gaps. "I believe you deserve grace, Jonah Chamberlain."

The rough stone was abrasive against the soft skin of her lips but despite that, she pressed even closer, hoping somehow she could breathe that grace through the tiny opening and over to the other side where her broken wish collector sat, despairing and in pain. Alone. "I believe—"

She felt moisture on her cheek and drew back, tipping her head to look up at the rain. But the sky above her was bright blue and cloudless, not a raindrop in sight.

Clara looked at the wall again as more water droplets ran slowly down the stone face. She sucked in a startled breath. *It's weeping!* "Jonah," Clara exclaimed, pressing her palms against the damp rock. "The wall is weeping."

A sweeping joy raced through her, a hopefulness filled with awe that caused her to laugh out loud. "Do you see it? Is it weeping on your side as well?"

"Yes." The place where her lips had just been pressed was suddenly shadowed and she saw the rosy tint of his mouth through the stony gap. Unbidden, she brought her finger to the spot and though the wall was too thick and the gap too thin for her to touch him, she felt the exhale of his warm breath and tingly goosebumps prickled every inch of her skin.

"Jonah . . . " she whispered, the feeling dreamy and strange. She didn't understand it and yet she wanted more of it. She dropped her hand, replacing her finger with her lips and breathing his name again, their breath mingling.

For a moment they only breathed together and she closed her eyes, picturing them as they must appear from above, their bodies in the same position, pressing toward each other, the barrier of the wall separating them. It was the most intimate moment Clara had ever experienced.

The wall's tears ran over her cheeks and into the corners of her open mouth. She darted her tongue out to taste them and laughed. "It's salty, Jonah." Just like real tears. *Angelina's tears.*

Sadness mingled with the joy coursing through Clara's heart, the wonder of the sight of the wall weeping dampened by the memory that the legend said the wall would only *stop* weeping when Angelina was set free.

Perhaps Clara couldn't set Angelina free. Perhaps the wall wept for reasons other than magic or legend that Clara couldn't explain. But Jonah Chamberlain was very real, and maybe she could help set him free from his self-appointed isolation. Perhaps she could help do good here at Windisle Plantation after all.

"Meet me, Jonah," she whispered through stone, over his lips.

"What?" he croaked. "Why?"

She drew back slightly so she could speak more easily, immediately missing the intimacy of their mouths being so close. *A kiss, only not.* "Because you can trust me. Because I'm your friend. I know you have scars. I know it's . . . hard for you. I understand. I do. But if you take the first step, if you come out from behind this wall, just for a short time, I'll be there to do it with you."

Hope soared in Clara's chest. She hadn't felt this type of overwhelming joy in years, not since before her dad got sick. *Time is so precious.* She had learned that it should never be wasted. Sometimes there wouldn't be a second chance.

"Meet me. Come out from behind the wall and meet me," she repeated.

He drew away too, and Clara could practically feel the tension and the indecision pouring off of him. "I can't."

"You can. Jonah, you can." She thought about asking to go inside, but somehow Clara felt that it was more important that he come out. Maybe after that, he'd invite her inside of his personal sanctuary, maybe eventually she'd be allowed to see Windisle rather than only hear the description. But this was for him, and she believed if Jonah stepped outside, just once, he'd see that he didn't have to live the life of a trapped monster. And maybe he could begin to forgive himself.

Angelina would never live again. But Clara's wish collector could. And she would help him do it. "You can," she whispered with all the conviction in her heart.

Clara stood and watched the shadows move through the cracks in the wall as Jonah stood too. They were pressed against opposite sides of the wall again, only this time, the entirety of their bodies.

A warm tingle moved over Clara's skin and she swallowed. "I get out of rehearsal at nine this Thursday night. There's a park only about a mile from here with a fountain and a few benches. Do you know it?"

"Yes," he said haltingly.

"Meet me there. I'll wait by the fountain. There's never anyone else there when I go by it on the way here. It'll be late, and it'll only be me."

"Clara, I—"

"Please. I'll be waiting for you. All you have to do is join me."

He was silent for several long moments before he let out a loud whoosh of air. "Okay."

Clara grinned, such intense happiness rushing through her that it turned into a joyful laugh. "Yes? Okay," she said, backing away before he changed his mind. She'd order her Uber from down the block. "See you then. See you then, wish collector," she called.

CHAPTER ELEVEN

November, 1860

The cool autumn breeze flowed over Angelina's bare skin, causing her to shiver slightly, though her lips remained tipped upward in happiness. She felt John's mouth on her shoulder, his lips warm and soft as he kissed her there, nipping softly as she laughed.

The old bed springs squeaked as she turned into the cradle of his arms, trailing one finger over his smooth jaw and then nuzzling her lips where her finger had been. Under the blankets she felt him stir again and smiled against his skin. "I have to get back," she whispered.

He groaned, pulling her closer. "Just a few more minutes."

She hesitated, wanting nothing more than to spend the rest of the day hidden away in that empty cabin with him, but knowing every minute she was away was a moment they were risking being caught. "I want to, John, but—"

"I know," he said, giving her a quick kiss on the lips and sitting up. She followed suit, turning and reaching for her dress where it lay discarded on the floor. One of the buttons was hanging loose. She'd need to repair it later.

My, but John had been in a hurry to get it off of me. She smiled again at the very recent memory of their lovemaking.

Behind her, John's hand moved slowly down her back and when she glanced over her shoulder, the look on his face was reverent as though the feel of her mesmerized him. "Someday we're going to have all the time in the world together," he murmured. "Someday we're not going to have to worry about who catches us, or who knows we're together." His voice was hushed, introspective as though he almost didn't realize he was speaking aloud.

"That will be nice," she answered, standing as his hand fell away. *Nice? What an understatement. Glorious, more like.*

She knew they were playing a game of what if, but it felt too good not to participate. What if . . . oh, *what if* he could be hers to fall asleep with and wake up to? To walk hand in hand down the street . . . to eat meals with and marry and—She cut off the thought as she pulled on her dress, turning back to him where he still sat on the bed, his bare golden skin shining in the dusky light filtering through the burlap curtains.

She was willing to play what if, but if her mind spun too far, the game became painful. Angelina knew very well how important limits were, though looking at John's naked chest now reminded her she'd surpassed several already. A chill went down her spine, and this time it had nothing to do with the cool air flowing through the cabin.

"Come here," he said, seeming to read her sudden melancholy. He pulled her to him and held her, stroking her back for a moment before letting her go and pulling on his own clothes.

He stood before her, taking her upper arms in his hands. "We are going to find a way. I don't care if we have to travel to some other continent and live in a cave in the desert."

She laughed and his eyes twinkled, but in truth, that might be their only true option. Still . . . a cave, with John, all to herself, day and night . . .

"Or a den under a massive oak tree." She'd seen that once, watched a whole family of rabbits hop right down a hole in the ground. She'd been jealous of them, truth be told. How peaceful it must be down there. How utterly safe. "We'll string a hammock from the roots to sleep in, and eat acorns for dinner."

John laughed, but she perceived the note of sadness in his smile. He twisted a finger into one of her curls, pulling on it slightly and then watching as it sprang back. For a moment, his eyes filled with wonder as if her hair were some form of miracle he'd never known existed. "There's a place for us, Angelina. Somewhere in this wide, wide world. Do you trust me?"

"Yes," she whispered with all the conviction in her pure and gentle heart. "*Yes.*"

They kissed for long minutes, for centuries, for eons, and it wasn't enough, but Angelina knew their time was ticking.

She felt it in her blood as if she carried some sort of internal clock that was counting down the hours and moving toward some unknown ending. *Please let it be a good one,* she thought. *Please, please.*

She left John in the cabin, his hair mussed and his lips red from her kisses, and hurried back toward the house, the basket of vegetables slung over her arm.

She entered the kitchen breathlessly, placing the basket on the counter. "Hello, Mama." Angelina smiled but her mother didn't smile back, returning her gaze to the potato in her hand, the knife moving swiftly over the skin, which dropped into the basket at her feet in long strips.

"You need to be careful, Lina."

Angelina's blood chilled, but she did her best to appear unaffected, removing the vegetables from the basket and placing them on the counter. "I'm always careful, Mama."

Her mother stood, her deep-brown, knowing eyes moving over Angelina's face then down her body, landing on the loose button and lingering before meeting Angelina's gaze again. Angelina felt heat infuse her skin and unconsciously she reached for the button, fiddling with it for a moment before letting go, her hand dropping heavily to her side.

Her mama looked at the vegetables sitting on the counter and reached for one, picking up a yellow squash and turning it over before setting it down again. "Seems you forgotten recently when a vegetable be ripe for the pickin' and when it not. Funny since you been pickin' since you be a chil'."

"I've been tired, Mama. I haven't been sleeping well."

Her mama eyed her, and Angelina swore she saw fear in her mama's eyes, mixed in with the disapproval. "We all tired, Lina." She turned away. "Know who to trust." She turned back to her, her eyes glittering as if with tears. Angelina stilled. She'd never seen her mother cry, not once in all of her life. "And who not to trust."

Her mother picked up the knife again and continued with her work as Angelina unpacked the rest of the basket, filled with the half-ripe vegetables John had chosen, obviously in his haste to get to her.

She couldn't help the small smile that teased at her lips. She looked at her beautiful mother, took in the ebony smoothness of her skin, the high, proud bones of her face, the wide-set eyes that seemed to see everything, and understand it on a level others did not. "Did you love him, Mama?"

Her mother didn't glance her way as she answered, and she didn't pretend not to know who Angelina asked about. "Love? There ain't no place for love here."

But her mama was wrong. Angelina loved. And Elijah's mama had loved him. She'd wailed like a wild woman when she'd seen him strung up in that tree, and it'd torn Angelina's heart in half. And though she didn't express it often, Angelina knew her own mama loved her too, despite whether there was a "place" for that love or not. No, Angelina didn't think love worked that way. "Love makes a place for itself even if there isn't one, Mama," she said quietly. "Love carves into the hardest of places."

Mama Loreaux halted in her peeling again, the sharpness of her gaze piercing Angelina, as stripping as that knife she held expertly in her calloused hands. "That kina talk gone get you hurt or worse."

She set the knife down on the counter with a harsh clack, turning her narrow shoulders toward her daughter. "No, I did not love your father, and he did not love me. We made you on the floor o' the cellar while his wife was havin' herself a fine tea party in the parlor. He got the idea to lift my skirts while I was puttin' the canned beets away, and I let him do it 'cause things easier that way."

Her eyes narrowed, but then she let out a long sigh, her gaze softening very slightly. "He ain't a cruel man, and he ain't all bad neither, but he gone choose his real family over you any time, any day. You can talk fancy like them, and you can *love* all you want, but they ain't never gone love you back the same way, and they ain't never gone think a you as one a them. You got that?"

Angelina stared at her mother's regal face, picturing the scene in the cellar she'd just described, picturing the damp, musty floor where she'd come to be. She flushed, looking away, not knowing how to feel about what she'd just learned, hurt welling up inside of her.

What had she imagined? That her father secretly loved her mother? That to him, Angelina and her mama were special somehow though he couldn't show it lest his wife be angered? That because he'd rocked her on his knee and called her his little hummingbird, he loved her as much as his other children? Yes, she supposed she had. It had made her feel . . . worthy in a world where she was no such thing.

Heaviness descended upon her. But then she thought of John. She thought of how *different* things were between her and John than the way her mother had described what happened with her father. Their coupling was not a quick interlude on a dirty cellar floor. Their time together was spent in soft touches and shared laughter, with sacred promises and woven dreams. And the comparison gave her a resurgence of hope. *Do you trust me?* he'd asked. *Yes,* she'd answered, and she'd meant it. She'd meant it with her whole heart. They *would* find a way. Despite that there was no "place" for love between them, despite that the whole world was against them, or so it seemed. They would find a way. They *would.* Because where there was love, there was always, *always* hope.

Angelina turned away from her mother, but she felt the heat of her worried gaze on her back nonetheless, prickling her skin as if she'd stepped too close to a flame and was about to be burned.

CHAPTER TWELVE

Do it.

Jonah stared at the latch of his gate, unmoving.

Or . . . not.

He glanced back. Myrtle's car wasn't far from where he stood, but he wasn't going to ask her if he could use it. For one, he didn't want to involve her in this at all, and for two, his driver's license had expired many years before. But the real truth of the matter was, he still hadn't decided if he would go through with meeting Clara. He still didn't fucking know exactly why he'd agreed in the first place.

Or maybe I do. Yes, he admitted to himself with a sigh of acceptance. *I do. I know.*

It was because he'd been infused with her hopefulness—her *joy*—and filled with the wonder of the grace she'd given him even after hearing his story, knowing each and every grisly detail. She'd offered him her compassion—her understanding—and the awe of that made him dizzy.

Meet me, she'd said, her voice so full of hope and joyful astonishment when the wall had started "weeping." Her wonder had been infectious. For a few minutes, Jonah had felt part of it. Part of Clara's vibrant spirit. For that's all he really knew of her. He didn't know what she looked like, except that her hair was the color of spun gold—he'd seen that much through the small crack in the wall—and she must have a dancer's slim, athletic body. Otherwise, he only knew she was compassionate and sensitive and deeply loyal. Come to think of it, that might be the most Jonah had ever known about any girl, even the ones he'd known more intimately in a physical sense.

His thoughts caused his mind to move to the moment Clara had kissed him. And yes, he knew it wasn't *really* a kiss, and he knew they were only friends, but it had been one of the sweetest moments of his life. It had made him feel like a flesh-and-blood *man* again when he'd been nothing but an invisible monster for so long.

He put one hand on the latch and released a harsh exhale, pulling his collar up high and the beanie he was wearing down low so most of his face was hidden.

The sliver of moon above went behind a cloud, causing the night shadows to grow deeper. Clara was waiting for him. He could *do* this.

In one swift movement, he unlatched the gate, moved to the other side, and let it swing shut behind him.

His heart raced, his hands becoming clammy as he worked to catch his breath. He hadn't been outside Windisle for eight long, miserable years.

He stood in the shadow of the gate for a moment, gathering his courage before he stepped away, stuffing his hands in the pockets of his black, lightweight jacket and moving down the empty street.

He stepped between dim patches, his head bowed as if against the wind, though there was no breeze that night. His heart continued to pound heavily the farther from Windisle he moved, and several times he almost turned and darted back to the plantation, as a child races up the stairs at night, sure there is a demon at his heels. But Jonah was the only monster on this street tonight, and he suddenly understood that it was much better to be *pursued* by ghouls than to be the ghoul yourself. If only he'd known.

He arrived at the edge of the park fifteen minutes later and leaned against a tree, a stunned laugh rising in his throat, born half of surprise and half of terror. He'd done it. He'd left Windisle and made the full trip to the park where Clara waited for him. Yes, it was only a handful of blocks from home, but to Jonah, it felt as if he'd traveled a million miles. Fear still sat heavy on his chest, but underneath that there was the bubbling of triumph. God, he hadn't felt that feeling for so damn *long. I didn't think I'd ever feel it again.*

Jonah stilled completely, focusing on the whisper of water, a tinkling sound that let Jonah know the fountain was very nearby. *Clara.* Was she there already? He'd been so much closer to her than this and yet, in that moment it felt as if they'd never been closer. He was going to lay eyes on her for the first time.

He was going to put a face to the sweet voice through the wall, the woman who had given so much of herself to *him,* a stranger who didn't come close to deserving it.

But she was going to see his face too. Would it horrify her? Would she grimace and turn away? Oh God, he was terrified of her reaction. He was so fucking scared.

He pictured the faces of those who had looked upon him right after the explosion, their expressions of disgust. He shivered as he remembered the way it had *hurt,* how it had punctured something soft and vulnerable way down deep inside of him. And he didn't think he could take the same thing from her. *Not her.*

Stealing a breath, he moved through the trees, following the sound of that flowing water, the promise of Clara drawing him forward.

The fountain came into view, the bubbling water catching the glow of the streetlight that shone upon it.

He stood among a grouping of trees, stepping around one ancient trunk and then pressing himself against it. She was there, sitting on the edge of the gray stone, her hands on her knees as she waited.

The light picked up pieces of gold in her hair and flashed them in the air surrounding her. She turned slightly, her eyes scanning the entrance to the park, then moving briefly to the dark area of forest where Jonah hid, his body motionless against the solid strength of the massive oak.

His heart stalled for a moment and then took up a quickened beat as he caught sight of her face. He groaned, so softly it mixed with the night sounds, disappearing before it could reach outside his darkened hiding spot.

She's beautiful.

Jesus, she's beautiful.

Clara, the girl he'd only previously known as the soft voice on the other side of his fortress, the woman who both soothed him and caused him to question everything, was *beautiful* both inside and out. *Oh, fuck, fuck, fuck.*

His heart sank lower in his chest, pressing against his lungs until he couldn't breathe. Why did he suddenly feel so devastated? Had he hoped she was unattractive so she might want to give someone like him a chance? To kiss him again, only the next time with nothing between them? And was he really so insensitive—so superficial—that he thought unattractive women had to settle for disfigured men like him anyway? Or that people loved each other based only on looks? Then again, why shouldn't he? Hadn't he chosen women solely on their physical characteristics once upon a time? Hadn't he been proud to enter a party or a restaurant with some beautiful woman on his arm that he'd replace with a new one once things grew stale as they inevitably always did? He'd never loved any of them. Not one.

God, but his mind was everywhere. And *Jesus.* Love? What was he even doing *thinking* about love? Him, the scarred man standing behind a tree in the park, too intimidated and ashamed to emerge from the bushes and approach the girl waiting for him.

Jonah sighed, the energy draining from him as he leaned more heavily against the tree. He felt confused, sad, lonely, and he just wanted to slink back to Windisle and hide again.

As if she'd heard his tiny exhale of breath, Clara turned her head, her eyes probing the darkness around him. He froze, her gaze moving over him without seeing.

A car pulled up near the park entrance and Clara stood, watching, her stance tense until it pulled away. She sat back down on the edge of the fountain, turning toward the splashing water dejectedly and running her fingers through it.

Her movements were elegant, heart-achingly feminine, and everything masculine inside of Jonah responded to her. She'd dance beautifully, and Jonah felt a tiny tremor of grief move through him to know he'd never see it.

He watched her as she waited, memorizing her movements, seeing the way she glanced at the stars now and again. *What are you thinking when you do that, Clara?* he wondered, the need to know an ache of despair within his chest. *What are you looking for?* He'd never know, of course, not after this.

An hour went by and still she waited, Jonah's heart growing heavier by the moment. She waited for him, and he needed her to *leave* so he could return home as well. But he wouldn't abandon her alone in this dark, deserted park even if she thought that's exactly what he'd done. He'd wait for her ride to appear and then he'd go. But when Clara finally stood a few minutes later, looking around one final time before walking toward the park entrance, there was no car waiting for her.

What the hell?

It was a relatively safe area but still . . . she shouldn't be walking through strange neighborhoods by herself.

Jonah followed, keeping to the shadows, raising his collar higher and lowering his head in case someone passed. But the streets were mostly empty as he trailed Clara, far enough behind, he hoped, that she wouldn't hear his hollow footsteps.

Despite his raw emotions and the guilt he felt over standing Clara up, he experienced that surge of triumph he'd felt earlier. He was outside his self-ordained prison, walking down a residential street like any other normal person. He'd done it!

He closed his eyes, breathing in the freedom, breathing out the fear.

If he took precautions, covered himself so no one looked twice, he could walk around just like this. He'd remain hidden—he *deserved* a life of shadows—and had no desire to be seen. But he didn't *have* to torture himself any further than he already did with days of nothing but boredom and sameness. Did he?

The area became less residential the farther Clara walked and when she finally entered a mostly empty, well-lit diner, Jonah took a sigh of relief, standing in a darkened doorway as she sat at a table next to the window across the street, her hands wrapped around a steaming mug of coffee.

He could see her more clearly in the bright lights of the diner, see the pretty heart shape of her face and the beautifully wide set of her eyes, the sweeping elegance of her cheekbones, and the full lip that she chewed on as she stared forlornly out the window.

And he ached. He ached with longing so intense it left him breathless. *She* was his Clara. That beautiful girl in the window, who looked so deep in thought.

He leaned his head so he could see her better with his good eye, knowing he'd let her down, but also knowing it was better this way. He took that moment to merge *this* Clara with the girl he'd come to know until he could not only *hear* her in his memories, but picture her as well, sitting on the other side of the wall, her shiny hair pulled into a ponytail as it was now, her long slim legs pulled beneath her.

He startled when Clara suddenly stood, digging in her purse for money that she then placed on the table before rushing out of the diner.

He hadn't seen her call for a ride, but he figured she must have and that's where she was heading. But when she looked both ways and then jogged back across the street, he ducked into the doorway, looking out when he heard her footsteps hurrying away, back toward the park, back toward Windisle. What was she *doing?*

He followed her again, only this time in reverse, as she hurried down the darkened streets, moving fluidly through the night. She was going to Windisle. He had stood her up—or so she thought—and now she was going to confront him.

Or, wrong choice of words. She was going to give him a piece of her mind through the stone that would forever be between them.

Some part of him thrilled at her audacity.

This girl didn't give up. She might have made a damn fine lawyer if she hadn't been given a body made for dancing. And he could see that she definitely had been given a body made for dancing. She was slim and strong, her lean legs encased in a pair of fitted jeans, her every movement elegant and graceful. *God, to see her dance.* To carry that vision in his mind forever. Maybe it would sustain him all the rest of his lonely, sheltered days behind that damn wall he both hated and was forever grateful for.

But he couldn't make it to the gate at the back of the property—the one she didn't know about—without her seeing him. So he'd remain hidden until she went away.

CHAPTER THIRTEEN

Clara's fingertips brushed the rough stone as she leaned her forehead against it, listening for him.

The slice of moon in the sky didn't provide very much light, but enough that she could see he wasn't in his usual spot. Not that she'd expected him to be, but still, she called his name, just in case.

She waited a moment but there was no answer. Was he sitting somewhere else close by? Against one of the massive trees on the other side of the wall, perhaps? She could *feel* him, she swore she could, only . . . well, that was silly. It was just this place, *his* place, and she was here now, and that was the reason for the warm prickly feeling on the underside of her skin that she associated with him.

She'd felt it in the park as she'd waited too though, and he hadn't shown, so obviously the feeling was something unrelated to his presence—her own singular focus on him perhaps.

Still, just in case he could hear her, she needed to apologize, or maybe she just needed to voice her feelings out loud, here, against the wall where she'd felt so certain Angelina was sending them a sign.

"I'm sorry, Jonah." She sighed. "I got carried away when the wall wept. I . . . I was pushy and selfish. I practically forced you to say you'd meet me and you probably weren't ready." Clara's shoulders sagged. "You obviously weren't ready. Do *not* feel bad about that. It was my fault."

She was silent for a moment as she gathered her thoughts in this place where honesty seemed to come more easily. "I'm your friend, and I should have taken more care with your fears. I should have . . . asked you what you were ready for instead of making plans."

A soft rustling sound whispered from the thick greenery behind her and she turned her head, peering into it. A squirrel probably, or maybe just an errant breeze that hadn't touched her where she stood.

She turned back to the wall. "I care about you, Jonah. I feel this . . . pull toward you that I've never felt before and you're back there, and I'm out here and—" She broke off on a frustrated exhale. "But I will be your friend in whatever way you need me to be. I want you to know that. I just . . . want you to know that, and that's all."

She removed the slip of paper she'd written on as she'd sat in the diner deciding what to do and slipped it through a crack. She hoped Jonah would read it rather than just discarding it along with any other wishes he collected. *My wish collector,* she thought with a sad sigh.

Clara turned from the wall, pressing her back against it, the vegetation rustling again just as a cloud covered the small sliver of moon, causing the already thick shadows to merge and grow and come alive.

A shiver went down her spine, her skin prickling. Although she hadn't seen anyone else on the street as she'd walked, adrenaline had kept her nerves at bay. But now . . . she felt *watched* and because it was from outside the wall, alarm rang within her.

She pulled out her phone and called for an Uber. A driver arrived ten minutes later but that feeling of being observed didn't go away until Windisle faded from sight out of the rear window.

****

The feeling of being watched persisted. Clara was being paranoid of course. She knew it for sure now because she was across town from Windisle, at rehearsal, and still the feeling was there.

It was late and she was tired, but Madame Fournier insisted they all stay until they did one perfect run-through.

Her muscles ached and her toes were bloody and blistered in her pointe shoes, but she knew the other dancers were experiencing the same pain, so she plastered a smile on her face and moved through the steps unflinchingly.

Marco lifted Clara in the air, his hand lingering on her backside a heartbeat longer than necessary and Clara shot him a narrow-eyed look before she twirled effortlessly, spinning away. She saw his wink at the moment before her head turned, her gaze finding her spot.

Movement in the back of the theater caught her eye and she stumbled slightly, catching herself and glancing at Madame Fournier who, *thank the heavens,* was looking in a different direction.

A man—she could only make out his tall outline—stepped around the corner. Just a custodian, or someone there to pick up one of the dancers, she guessed, but her stumble reminded her she needed to *focus* if they were all going to get out of there at a decent hour.

After what felt like forever and a day, Madame Fournier clapped her hands twice, telling them rehearsal was over and that she'd see them the next day. *Thank you, God of Blistered Feet,* she thought with a small wince.

Clara grabbed her bag, pulled sweats on over her tights, and changed her shoes quickly.

The other dancers groaned and stretched and commiserated about sore muscles and backaches as Clara ducked out of the theater. The door closed heavily behind her and she made her way to the corner bus stop, pulling out her phone as she walked. No missed calls. Her heart sank, though she hadn't truly expected that he'd call.

As she'd slipped her number through a crack in the wall after racing back from the diner, she'd wondered why she hadn't given him her phone number before. But then she realized that she had wanted to visit him at Windisle.

Giving him her number might have made her visits seem unnecessary when she enjoyed everything about sitting on the other side of the weeping wall and listening to him as he spoke right next to her ear, his melodic tone dancing over the wall and settling around her like a comforting caress.

But in any case, he hadn't called.

Maybe he didn't have a phone, or had no desire to turn it back on if he'd shut it off when he'd gone to live at Windisle. Maybe he just didn't want to talk to her anymore at all.

Sadness pierced her, indecision close on its heels. Should she return so she could make an apology, this time one he actually heard? What if he hadn't opened the slip of paper she'd meant for him? What if—

Clara groaned, massaging her temples as if doing so could stop her from obsessing about Jonah. She'd been doing just that—for one reason or another—since she'd met him, and she needed a break.

She should pick up a bottle of wine and drown her sorrows alone in her apartment, but she'd never been much of a drinker. There was another rehearsal bright and early the next morning, and if she hurried, she had just enough time to make it to the costume shop she'd looked up online earlier that day.

The night was humid and damp, the rain sprinkling the dirty windows as Clara rode the bus to the French Quarter.

The masquerade ball was part of her job and she needed to make sure she had something appropriate to wear rather than waiting until the final hour and finding herself with very limited options. Although she supposed two days in advance *was* the final hour and she said a silent prayer that the right costume would be waiting for her.

The sidewalks were filled with laughing, chattering people leaving restaurants and entering and exiting tourist shops, some wearing bright-colored boas and carrying colorful drinks in their hands.

It seemed that in New Orleans there was always a party going on somewhere no matter the time or the day of the week. Clara could get happily lost down here, people-watching and wandering from shop to shop.

A man laughed boisterously, bumping into Clara, the large plastic cup he was holding in his hand tipping precariously. He managed to right it but not before several drops splattered. The man raised his brows in apology, but continued grinning, as he ducked by.

"Crap," she muttered, stepping into a doorway and brushing at the bright red droplets staining the front of the pink leotard she was still wearing under her light zip-up sweatshirt.

She sighed, pulling her sweatshirt closed and looking up at the door in front of her. *Madame Catoire's Palm and Spiritual Readings: Past, Present, Future.*

Clara hesitated, curiosity getting the best of her as she leaned toward the smoky glass, gazing into the tiny shop.

She could see tables inside holding small trinkets and candles and other items and after a short hesitation, Clara pulled the door open to the sound of a tinkling bell and stepped inside.

It smelled smoky and cloyingly sweet, and what sounded like wind chimes and piano music filtered softly from somewhere beyond.

A slight breeze brushed Clara's skin, though there were no windows open anywhere she could see, and the door was now closed.

Nerves cascaded through her, but she was too curious to turn around, her gaze snagging on one interesting object after another. She walked slowly around the shop, leaning in and looking at the assortment of crystals and geodes that glittered atop one table, and stopping to study the names on the tiny amber bottles on another. They were each labeled in handwritten print: Money, success, love. *My, but there are so many ways to make wishes in this world,* she thought.

"And what is it *you* wish for, dear girl?"

Clara spun around to see an older woman in a purple dress standing in a doorway half covered by a curtain at the back of the shop. *What do you wish for,* she'd asked. It was as if the woman had read her thoughts.

The woman moved closer, and Clara saw that though she was older, she was still stunning with large turquoise eyes and hair that was a mixture of white and a blonde so pale, Clara could only discern the difference between the two shades now that the woman was standing in front of her.

"It is love you wish for, no?"

"I . . . I suppose so." *Doesn't everyone?*

The woman tilted her head, studying her for a moment. "It is hard for you to wish for things for yourself? Very rare."

The woman had phrased it as a question, but she turned away from Clara as if requiring no answer. "Come, I am closed, but I will read for you. No charge."

"Oh, I'm so sorry. I didn't realize—"

The woman waved her hand dismissively and held the curtain open for Clara. Clara hesitated, but the urge to hear what the woman would read for her was strong, her inquisitiveness overwhelming the unsettled feeling she'd had since she'd entered the shop.

Clara glanced back once, and as she did a shadow moved away from the doorway, leaning back as if he had peered into the shop for a moment.

She turned back to the woman, and the woman was watching the door where the shadow had been a moment before, too, a frown marring her beautiful face. But as quickly as Clara had seen it, it was gone and the woman gestured to her once more and then disappeared behind the heavy red curtain. Clara followed.

The back of the shop was dim and mostly empty, twinkle lights strung across the ceiling, a round table positioned in the middle of the floor, the woman already seated on one side. Clara took the empty chair opposite her.

"I am Madame Catoire. And your name is?"

"Clara."

She smiled a thin smile and pulled a deck of cards from the middle of the table. "Shuffle these, please."

Madame Catoire handed them to Clara and she did so, handing them back to the older woman who then shuffled them herself, peering intently at Clara all the while.

Madame Catoire laid the cards out one by one, each containing symbols and numbers that meant nothing to Clara. The fortune teller looked them over for a moment before sitting back in her chair.

"There is sadness in you. You have experienced a loss only . . ." The woman's brows creased as if she was trying to find the right words. "It is not *quite* a loss." She looked at Clara. "Someone you love is very ill."

Clara nodded. "Yes," she breathed. "My father."

Madame Catoire nodded. "What the doctors have told you is correct."

Clara nodded again slowly, sadly. Yes, she knew.

Madame Catoire studied the cards once more. "You seek answers to a mystery."

Clara's heart jumped but she took a slow breath, going for a casual response. Fortune tellers were like salespeople after all, weren't they? Letting them see your excitement gave them an edge. "I am actually."

The fortune teller didn't look up at her though, as if she neither wanted nor needed her validation. She leaned forward, her eyes seeming to shimmer in the golden light cast from the strings of twinkling lights above. "Keep seeking. Do not stop. It is very important."

"Okay—"

"Very important," she whispered again before looking back at the cards, her full red lips tight and tilted downward.

Clara shivered, adjusting herself in her chair. Could Madame Catoire *actually* be talking about the riddle and how to set Angelina free? "Madame Catoire, can you tell me where to find more answers? Where to look?"

"No. The cards do not answer questions nor communicate in specifics. They speak in shadows, and I know only what peeks through the mist."

Well, that sounds . . . vague. Disappointment overcame Clara and she wondered if this was all some trick. If Madame Catoire couldn't speak in specifics or answer questions, couldn't generalities apply to almost everyone? Then again . . . the two things she'd given Clara so far hadn't been things that would be applicable to just anyone. But they'd been very applicable to her. And she'd even insisted that Clara not pay her, so there wasn't really a reason for her to trick Clara anyhow.

Madame Catoire looked Clara in the eye as her finger moved over another card, slowly, almost caressingly. "Be wary of the man with two faces. He'll hurt you if you let him."

Be wary . . . the man with two faces? Could she mean . . . Jonah? He was scarred, she knew that, but what did the fortune teller mean about two faces? His old face and his new face? *He'll hurt you if you let him?* Jonah?

She shook her head, denying her own unspoken thought. She couldn't believe Jonah would harm her. She trusted him. At least . . . well, at least as far as her safety went. Then again, maybe she was being naïve. She felt like she knew him, but could you really know a person from behind a wall? *Yes,* her heart insisted. Yes. But doubt continued to linger . . . he *hadn't* come to meet her. Nor did he wait by the wall.

Madame Catoire said the cards didn't answer questions so Clara didn't ask her to clarify. "Is there anything else, Madame Catoire? Anything about . . . love?"

Madame Catoire sat back in her chair, looking exhausted somehow, which was surprising given they'd only been sitting at a table for ten minutes or so. "Your true love dances between moonbeams."

What in the world? Dances? She was a dancer, obviously, but other than that, Clara had no earthly idea what the words meant and opened her mouth to say so when Madame Catoire stood suddenly. "The reading is done."

She gathered her cards with a flourish, and left through another door in the back of the small room. Clara heard her ascending stairs and stood, confused by the abrupt departure. Wasn't she going to walk her to the door and lock up? She'd said she was closed . . .

Clara took a twenty and a five from her purse and placed the bills on the table so Madame Catoire would see the money when she came downstairs. There was no sign that indicated how much readings were, but she didn't feel right allowing the fortune teller to work for free, and hoped the money she'd placed on the table was in the arena of what she generally charged.

The bell tinkled above the front door again as Clara opened it, closing it tightly behind her as she stepped out into the muggy night air. The street was emptier than it'd been before she entered the shop.

Clara pulled her phone out and glanced at the time, surprised to find that an hour had gone by. *How did that happen?* she wondered with a confused frown.

She turned right, hurrying down the street. She had ten minutes to rush to the costume shop. Ten minutes to find something to wear to the masquerade ball. And then another night alone. She knew she'd continue pondering the fortune teller's words: *Keep seeking. Do not stop. It is very important.*

CHAPTER FOURTEEN

January, 1861

"Mr. Whitfield, you look dashing this evening."

John smiled, though it felt forced. If Mrs. Chamberlain noticed, she didn't react. "Thank you, Mrs. Chamberlain. You look lovely as always."

He turned to Astrid who was right next to her mother. "As do you, Astrid."

Astrid blushed to her hairline and John felt a small, sinking feeling in his chest. He hated that he was using the girl as a means to spend time at Windisle—*to spend time with Angelina*—but at the moment, there was simply no other way.

"Is that Mrs. Holdsworth? I do believe it is. Why don't you young people have a glass of punch, and I'll be right back."

She patted Astrid on the arm, giving her a quick look full of meaning, and John looked away, pretending not to have caught the not so subtle glance.

He cleared his throat, nodding at Mrs. Chamberlain as she breezed by him. "Punch?" John asked Astrid, raising an eyebrow.

She blushed, but a small apologetic grimace accompanied it. "Subtlety is not my mother's forte. But, yes, thank you, I'd love some punch."

John chuckled. He had no romantic notions toward her, but Astrid was a nice girl. And she was pretty. She resembled Angelina a little bit with their father's same almond-shaped eyes and high forehead. She would catch the eye of some other man someday soon, and that man would be lucky if she looked back at him, despite her dragon of a mother.

He led Astrid to the punch table, pouring her a cup and then making one for himself. "Happy New Year, Astrid," he said, clinking his glass to hers.

"Happy New Year, John," she said softly, taking a sip of her punch.

A man in a top hat and a black mask laughed, walking past with a woman in a red boa and a dainty hat that looked like it was supposed to be a cardinal's plume. "I didn't realize people were dressing up in costume."

"Oh, it wasn't on the invitation. My parents had a New Year's Eve costume party many years ago, and some people still dress up as part of tradition."

"Ah, I see." John took another drink of the watery punch, wishing someone had spiked it or that he'd brought his own so it would be easier to endure the social triviality of this night.

All he wanted to do was push through this crush of people, and burst outside into the night air. He wanted to go to *her*. He wanted her so badly he ached with it.

Suddenly, as if his thoughts had conjured someone who looked like her . . . or rather, someone who *moved* like her, his eyes snagged on a woman in a high-necked, pale pink dress wearing a full-faced cat mask that also covered the top of her head. John attempted to shrug it off, to move his gaze away, but no, she *definitely* moved like his Angelina. He should know, he'd spent long hours reliving every moment with her, picturing over and over every stretch of her lean body, every gesture, every small twitch of her muscles. But Angelina would never have been invited to this party or any other. She was somewhere very close by, yes, but God, she was a world away.

"So, John," Astrid said, and John pulled his eyes from the woman across the room, to look at Astrid who was biting her lip nervously. "I've ah, enjoyed having tea with you very much. I hope, well, I . . ."

John's eyes moved back to the masked woman, Astrid's voice fading. The woman reached out with her gloved hand and took a bite-sized piece of cake from a passing tray, holding a hand over her lower face, as she discreetly delivered the morsel under her mask. Her spine bent back very slightly as she lowered her hand, chewed and swallowed.

That small spine bend . . . it was the same way Angelina experienced pleasure, arching back into it, feeling it with her entire body— *Holy hell.* The sound of the party exploded in John's head.

"John? Are you all right? Did you hear what I said?"

"I beg your pardon?" he muttered. John looked at Astrid who was staring at him, her expression a mixture of hurt and concern.

"I asked you if—"

"Forgive my rudeness, Astrid, I need to speak to someone."

"Oh, certainly, I—"

John moved around her, trying to walk as calmly as possible to the woman standing by the window, the woman—no, not *the woman*. Angelina. *His* Angelina, and she was playing with fire.

His gut clenched and he bit back a curse, plastering what he hoped was a casual smile on his face as he walked past her. "Follow me," he said softly so only she could hear. Then he moved past, exiting the room and walking down the hall where he glanced back once to make sure she was indeed following him and that no one else witnessed them.

He entered the library at the end of the hall, leaving the door open a crack. When she slipped in a moment later, he pulled her into his arms, closing the door and locking it with a quick turn of his wrist. "What in the hell do you think you're doing?"

"How did you recognize me?"

He removed her mask and flung it aside, tightening the arm that still held her and released a harsh exhale. "I'd know you anywhere, don't you know that?"

She stared up at him, her lips tipping sweetly. She placed her hand over his heart that was thundering in his chest, part fear at the risk she'd taken, part joy in having her in his arms when it was the very thing he'd been wishing for so fervently.

"I wanted to be near you, John. I wanted to dance with you and drink champagne. I wanted to taste one of those cakes my mama spent all day baking. And I saw the masks and I—"

John crushed his mouth to hers and her words became a breathless moan. Their sounds of pleasure mingled as their tongues twisted together, their kisses frantic and full of longing, full of the knowledge that there would be no dancing, no champagne, not for them. *But there is this. Ah, there is this,* John's fevered mind told him. Even if it wasn't nearly enough.

"I don't want to hide," she said, her mouth breaking from his, "not in a cave or a burrow. I want to live in the light, John."

Oh, fuck. Fuck, *fuck. This is madness,* John thought. It was driving him mad, making him insane with the need to *do* something, to find a solution for them. But despite being unable to sleep for thinking about her, staying up late into the night just staring at the ceiling, he could envision nothing that didn't risk her life. *Her life,* that was more precious to him than his own.

"Angelina," he whispered, the word full of love and the helplessness he felt in his heart. He needed some time. What would they do?

He kissed her one final time, trailing a finger over her smooth cheek. "We'll *both* drink that starlight you bottled up. We'll shine for the whole wide world."

Angelina let out a small laugh that didn't hold much humor. "Only that isn't real and you know it."

John looked into her eyes, this woman who had rearranged his soul somehow. "Isn't it?" All he knew was that he felt brighter, hotter when she was with him. He felt like he could do *anything* if it meant caring for her.

Angelina let go of him, bending to pick up the mask that had landed on the floor as she walked to the nearby desk.

She picked up a book and glanced at it, her shoulders bunching before she placed it down. When she turned, her expression was still troubled but she quickly replaced it with a smile. She opened her mouth to speak when a key jiggled in the lock and before either of them could react, Astrid burst into the room. Her eyes were wide and she looked from John to Angelina and then back to John, an arrested expression on her face as John's stomach dipped. *Oh God, no.*

John moved to stand in front of Angelina, an instinctive protective maneuver, when the sharp sound of heels clacked on the hardwood of the hallway seconds before Mrs. Chamberlain joined her daughter.

She looked from one stricken face to another. "What, pray tell, is going on here?"

John's mind spun. They would hurt her somehow—perhaps not physically, but they'd find some way to hurt her. He wouldn't let it happen.

Astrid stepped forward, a brittle smile turning her mouth up. "Mama, I asked Angelina to fetch one of my masks from my room and deliver it. I wanted to surprise everyone."

She walked to where Angelina was standing and held out her hand for the cat mask.

John could see that Angelina was trembling and it caused his muscles to tighten painfully with the need to go to her, but he knew it was better that he didn't. "Isn't that right, Angelina?"

John stared, ready to move should it be necessary, wondering what Astrid was doing. Was she *covering* for them?

"Yes, ma'am," Angelina said, her voice whisper soft as she thrust the mask into Astrid's outstretched hand.

Astrid took it, smiling that same thin-lipped smile as she turned back toward her mother. Mrs. Chamberlain narrowed her eyes at Astrid. "Was that really necessary, Astrid? Only the older people still carry on that tradition." She looked at John. "What were you doing in here, John?"

"I, uh, wrong door. I was looking for the washroom."

"Oh goodness, you've been in this house enough times to know." She waved her hand. "Well, I suppose not long enough to become well acquainted with *all* the rooms." She paused. "I do hope that will change."

"Yes, well"—he turned to Angelina—"I'm sorry I scared you, miss."

Mrs. Chamberlain glanced at Angelina as if she'd forgotten there was an actual person there.

"John, maybe you recognize Angelina. She's the kitchen help and has served tea at our luncheons," Astrid supplied.

John looked at Angelina, trying to convey with his eyes how damn sorry he was for this situation. A part of him wanted to shake her for taking the risk in the first place that had brought them to the brink of disaster. Thank the Lord for Astrid. He'd figure out an explanation for her later. But she must suspect the truth if she willingly lied for them, and *why* she'd chosen to do so was a mystery.

He nodded at Angelina. "Yes, hello." He looked away from her, to Astrid. "I never received that dance you promised me."

Mrs. Chamberlain clapped her hands together, satisfaction clear in her expression. "That must be remedied then. Astrid, John has just asked you to dance."

Tension coiled inside of him, along with the knowledge that it was hurting Angelina to have him ignore her the way he was, but he knew caution was necessary. And they were used to this, used to the small brushing of fingers as she handed him his teacup, used to the glances and the pretending, the polite smiles and the outright lies.

I don't want to hide. I want to live in the light, John. He pushed the memory of her words away. The time for that had not arrived.

"I'd love to dance, John," Astrid murmured, taking the arm he presented to her as the three of them turned toward the door. He didn't dare glance back at Angelina.

As John and Astrid made their way to the dance floor, a slow song replaced the more cheerful music of a moment before—due to Mrs. Chamberlain's directive, no doubt.

John took Astrid into his arms, turning her slowly along with the other dancers. "Thank you," he said softly.

She tensed for a moment but then nodded, and he was grateful she wasn't going to pretend she didn't know what he was thanking her for. "Astrid—"

"You don't have to explain. I already knew. Or, I suspected anyway. The way you watch her, John . . . it was clear to me many weeks ago."

He blew out a breath. "Do you think your mother knows?"

"I know she doesn't. If she did, Angelina . . . well, you're taking a very big risk," she ended softly as he spun her around once more. "Are you certain it's worth it?"

John spied Angelina from the corner of his eye, ducking out the door and heading back downstairs. For a halted heartbeat, their eyes met before she disappeared. His body remained in the room, but he swore his soul followed her. "Very," he said softly, resolutely.

"Then you'll need to be more careful. If I've noticed, it's only a matter of time before my mother notices as well. She's self-centered, but she has a nose for things that might potentially disrupt her plans."

"Like her plans for you and me," he said, a spear of guilt probing at him.

Astrid paused. "Yes, like you and me."

"I'm sorry, Astrid. If—"

Astrid laughed softly. "Smile, John. You look like I'm holding a revolver underneath my petticoats and forcing you to dance with me. And if you were going to say that if things were different you'd be happy to have me, please don't. I can only take so much."

"I *was* going to say that, and I'd have meant it. You're going to make some man very happy one day, Astrid."

"It just won't be you."

"No . . . it won't be me." He pulled away from Astrid slightly, looking her in the eye. "Will you help us, Astrid?"

Astrid paused, glancing away for a moment and then back at John. This could be disastrous. He knew he sounded both discourteous and utterly desperate, *but it was worth that risk for Angelina.* She deserved to shine in the light. *They deserved a chance surely.* His only hope was that Astrid would see past her own hurt in the name of love.

Astrid took a deep breath. "Yes, John, I'll help you."

CHAPTER FIFTEEN

"If I haven't told you yet, you look stunning," Marco said as he took her hand and she stepped from his car.

Clara laughed softly. "You have said it a time or two. Thank you again."

Marco grinned, handsome in a black tux and a simple black mask that only covered his eyes and nose, offering her his arm as they headed for the luxury hotel where the charity masquerade ball was being held.

Clara *felt* stunning in her gown of black satin, the skirt full, and tiny capped sleeves that fell off her shoulders, the fitted bodice overlaid with hundreds of aqua and green sequins.

The pickings at the costume shop had been slim, but she'd found an azure mask with gold thread filigree, featuring a cascade of blue and green feathers on one side. It was delicate and beautiful and unique, and it'd appealed to her immediately. It reminded her of a hummingbird.

She'd planned on wearing a simple but pretty long black gown that she'd worn to a friend's wedding the year before, but as she'd been passing a vintage clothing shop, she'd spied the gown with the sequins that perfectly matched her mask and ended up fitting like it'd been made for her. It'd felt meant to be.

Clara was used to dressing up in costumes—she did it for a living—but this dress felt more special than anything she'd worn before. Shimmery. Satiny. *Romantic.*

It didn't feel as though she was dressing up for a part, but rather wearing a gown that was simply *her.*

"Wow," Marco said, stopping and looking around the room appreciatively. Clara agreed with the simply stated sentiment. *Wow, indeed.*

The entire room was decorated in black and white and gold, extravagant overhead chandeliers bouncing light around the room and causing the golden accents to sparkle.

There were full vases of decadent white lilies and trailing greenery on all the tables, each set on a mirror that reflected even more shimmery light around the room.

Clara inhaled deeply, closing her eyes with delight as she took in the sweet, heady fragrance of fresh flowers.

"Dance with me," he said, leaning toward her on a whisper.

Clara allowed him to lead her to the dance floor where masked couples swayed to the music of the live band set up in the corner.

Marco took her in his arms and Clara looked around at the couples moving past her, admiring their masks, their beautiful formal attire.

The party was decorated in black and white and gold, but the women's dresses were like bright, opulent jewels standing out even more so because of the lack of color in the surroundings.

"Are you so used to my hands on your body that you zone out when I'm holding you?"

Clara shook her head. "I wasn't zoning out. I was admiring all the costumes."

"And here I am admiring you," he whispered against her hair.

Clara forced herself to focus on Marco. He looked so debonair in his tux. She'd thought of him as a ladies' man, but he was only looking at her, and maybe . . . maybe she could think of this as a real date. Maybe her rule about not dating coworkers was too limiting. After all, where *else* would she meet someone? At the wall of some abandoned plantation?

She scoffed inwardly. Maybe it would be good for her to focus her attention on someone other than a troubled man who couldn't forgive himself and had chosen instead to lock himself behind a wall forever and ever and ever.

It wasn't that Clara was impatient or unkind, but if he never wanted to be found . . . *should she continue to try to find him?* She wanted to live *now.*

She brought her hands up around Marco's neck and pulled him closer. He looked briefly surprised but then tightened his arms around her back. She gazed at him, attempting to see him as more than just Marco, a fellow dancer. She looked at him as a man, who, yes, seemed to enjoy a variety of women, but who maybe was just waiting for the right one to come along.

And maybe she was waiting for the right person too.

Marco leaned in, his eyes moving to her lips. He was going to kiss her, and she was going to let him.

"Excuse me," a female voice interrupted. Annoyance flashed in Marco's eyes before he pulled away, glancing over his shoulder as whoever she was, cleared her throat. "We're up in ten minutes." It was Roxanne, a fellow apprentice, and she gave Clara a curious, though not unkind, stare before turning and walking away.

Marco shook his head. "Sorry."

"Don't be. I almost forgot you're performing. You should go get ready. You only have ten minutes."

Marco released a frustrated breath, giving a terse nod. "Yeah."

He pulled back, taking her hand and walking her to the edge of the dance floor. "The performance is only thirty minutes or so. Wait here?" He gestured to a table at the edge of the dance floor that would be the stage where a handful of dancers performed for the guests.

Clara hadn't volunteered—there had been plenty already—and now she was glad. It was nice to be part of the audience for once, and her feet could always use the break anyway.

Sitting at the table, she smiled at Marco before he sauntered toward the stage. "Good luck," she called, knowing very well Marco didn't need any. He was one of the most skilled dancers she'd ever met.

She ordered a glass of wine when a server came by and sat sipping it leisurely until the ballet dancers were introduced and the lights dimmed.

Clara loved this moment, loved it from either side of the stage, loved those breath-stealing seconds when her heart was hanging by a string as she waited for something wonderful to happen. *There's nothing else like it,* she thought as happy anticipation prickled her skin.

The lights came up and Clara's breath released on a slow exhale. Marco stood in the middle of the stage with Roxanne, posed and completely still.

A saxophone began playing, the smoky sound filling the quiet room as the couple began to move in sync.

Something overhead caught Clara's attention and she glanced up. It was a moon, suspended above the dance floor/stage, a thousand tiny lights sparkling in the ceiling to mimic the stars.

Roxanne spun away and Clara returned her attention to Marco as he moved alone under the glow of the created night sky.

Your true love dances between moonbeams.

Clara's heart jumped. Had the fortune teller been referring to Marco? She watched him for a moment, trying again to see him with newer eyes than the ones that had first judged him. The eyes that had seen the women waiting for him after rehearsal—different ones each week. The eyes that had watched as he flirted with co-workers as they looked at him with hope in their eyes, only to be crushed days later when his attention moved elsewhere.

He moved beautifully, skillfully, his expression filled with such intense concentration. He wasn't an emotional dancer—he didn't pull at her heartstrings like some of the other dancers she loved to watch. But he was good. Amazing, in fact. But she didn't think the music, the *story* of the dance, filled his soul.

She was probably the opposite. She felt the story *too* much, and forgot to execute the movements with perfect precision. The greats had both, Clara thought. And that was the rarest of all.

Her small evening bag buzzed softly, the screen lighting up in her purse and creating a soft glow. Clara snatched it, her mind immediately going to her dad. She stood from the table as the music soared and slipped away into the darkened room, waiting until she was far enough away not to interrupt the show before taking her phone from her purse and reading the text from an unknown number.

You look beautiful tonight.

Clara stared at the words, a shiver moving through her. *Who in the world?*

She brought her head up, glancing around the darkened room, her eyes moving to Marco still dancing under the starry moonlit ceiling and then away.

A shadow moved near one of the exits, stepping through the doorway. She swore the man glanced back and directly at her before he disappeared around the corner.

Clara moved in that direction, her heart skipping a beat as she texted back.

Who is this?

I've been called the wish collector.

Clara sucked in a sharp breath, halting for a second in surprise and then moving forward again, stepping around a couple who was standing at the back of the room.

The couple spared her a quick glance and then went back to watching the dance performance. Clara hurried toward the door through which the man had disappeared. *You're here, Jonah? How?* And how had he picked her out from the crowd? Half her face covered by a mask nonetheless.

The door exited into a courtyard with a fountain bubbling in the middle. Large potted trees were placed around the perimeter of the space, their fronds casting moving shadows on the cobblestone. He had disappeared.

She ventured slowly forward, her heart galloping, her skin prickling. The air was mild, but her skin was flushed with nervousness, doubt, and a tinge of fear.

A shadow moved to her left and she let out a surprised squeak, turning in that direction.

It was a man, tall and broad, his shadow mingling with all of the others and then becoming sharper as he stepped forward.

Clara was uncertain, scared, poised to run, only . . . this was *Jonah. There's nothing to be afraid of,* she told herself, the internal words buoying her confidence.

The wonder of him standing directly in front of her outweighed her doubt, and she stepped forward in order to see him better.

Something inside of her whispered softly, a warning that told her everything was about to change. *Everything.* She took another step, her vision adjusting further to the dark.

Her eyes widened as his face became clearer, her mouth falling open in shock, her pulse jumping at the skeletal lines of his face. Her breath rushed out. But no, it was just a mask, half of it fully covering his face and painted to look like a skeleton, and the other half only covering one eye and a portion of his nose.

Though her gaze didn't stray from his face, she also noticed he was wearing a black tuxedo, the white bow tie standing out in stark contrast, just as the milky bones of his mask glowed against the darkness covering most of his skin.

The air stilled, the scent of night-blooming jasmine reaching her nose, the tinkling sound of splashing water breaking through her excitement and fear and confusion, and a hundred other emotions she didn't have the wherewithal to separate.

"This isn't the fountain where you were supposed to meet me," she uttered breathlessly taking several more steps toward him.

He appeared frozen, the set of the half of his mouth she could see a grim line.

He paused and then it twitched up slightly as he apparently registered her words. "No, I know." *It was him*—her wish collector. She'd recognize that deep tenor with the lilting accent anywhere, the voice made for storytelling, for weaving spells, for convincing and cajoling. For seducing and luring and for making dreamy-eyed girls do things they hadn't intended on. Was that what he'd been doing to her right from the beginning? *And if so,* she wondered, *why do I love it so much?*

Clara stepped right up to him and felt the heat of his body. There was a sudden shift in the air, something chemical Clara couldn't explain but still *felt*. Like the way she could tell when a thunderstorm was approaching. The colliding of atoms, the buzz of ozone, only in this case it existed exclusively in the small space between them.

He's here, her heart whispered. She was standing right in front of him, no wall between them.

Awe filled her, a sense of unreality as if this were merely a dream and she might wake up at any moment.

She extended her hand and touched his arm, her fingers skimming the stiff material of his jacket. There was nothing separating them, nothing at all. Well, except their masks.

She reached for hers, swallowing nervously as she pushed it up so it rested on the top of her head. She brought her eyes to his shyly, her face fully exposed to him as she tilted it toward the light. From what she could see, his expression didn't change.

"Hi, Jonah," she whispered. *This is me,* she thought. She had no idea what he expected, if he expected anything at all, but nerves assaulted her all the same and made her blood tremble within her veins.

"Hi, Clara." His tone was gravelly, unsure, and when she reached for his mask tentatively, he leaned back into the shadows again. Her hand fell away. "You're beautiful."

There was a note of something almost reverent in his tone and her heart swelled as relief washed through her.

It surprised her that she was so pleased by his compliment when she'd never been a girl who cared overly much about her appearance, instead choosing to focus on her talents, her skills, the things she was in control of.

But she was still a girl, and to hear that this man, whose opinion she'd come to care about, thought she was beautiful brought her joy. It made her very aware of the reason he was so fearful of revealing his scars to her.

"I went to meet you that night," he said, turning his head in a way that made her think he favored one eye. "I watched you. I . . . just wasn't ready."

He'd been there that night? Oh. She exhaled a breath, stepping ever closer, seeking his warmth. He wasn't ready to show her his face yet—his scars—and she wouldn't push him, but there had already been so much separation between them, and the pull she felt toward him was difficult to resist.

"It's okay. You're here now." Her brows drew inward as the reality of that settled over her. "How are you here now? How did you know about this?"

He let out a soft, embarrassed-sounding chuckle. "I wanted to see you dance. I went to your rehearsal." He shook his head slightly. "I'm sorry, I know that sounds sort of—"

"It sounds sweet. I wish you had told me. I wish I had known you were there. I would have danced just for you."

Their gazes locked for a single heartbeat, and even though his was mostly hidden, something still flowed between them that Clara wasn't sure what to name.

Jonah broke eye contact, leaning against the wall behind him. In the moonlight, Clara could see the beat of his pulse in the exposed portion of his throat. It sent a strange thrill through her. She wanted to touch it, to feel the life throbbing through him, but she sensed it would cause him to retreat further. He already seemed poised to leave at the slightest provocation, and she was desperate for him to stay.

"There was a flyer for the masquerade ball in the lobby." His lip—the beautifully shaped half of his mouth she could see—quirked slightly again. "It seemed too perfect to resist." His mouth straightened out. "I won't stay long."

"Why?" She took his hands and he glanced down at their joined fingers. "You're safe here with me." She smiled at him. "I'm so proud of you. It must have been hard to leave Windisle. But you're here. You did it."

"Yes. I did it." He cocked his head very slightly. "I don't know how often I'll do it from now on, but thank you for helping me remember there's a world outside Windisle. And if it's dark enough—"

"Oh, Jonah"—she squeezed his hands—"you don't have to wait for the darkness to come outside. You can live in the light." But a small needle of guilt poked at her chest. She felt like she was pushing him again and didn't want him to resent her for that. She wanted to inspire him, to make him feel safe, not to pressure him. "But at your own pace. This"—she squeezed his hands again—"is the most wonderful surprise of my life."

He laughed softly, but there was something to the set of his mouth that told her he was pleased by what she'd said. And she hoped he knew she wasn't exaggerating in the least.

Jonah glanced toward the door where the music from the performance came to a lingering end and then back to their linked fingers.

He held on to her as he turned his palms up, looking at the tops of her hands. He ran a thumb over one of her knuckles and let out a shuddery breath as a tremor went through her too, and the muscles in her stomach clenched as their eyes locked once more.

She couldn't see the entirety of his face, but lord, no one had ever looked at her with the same intensity. She'd called him her friend, but *this* didn't feel friendly to Clara. Just the touch of his hands, his presence felt . . . erotic, and she swallowed, feeling out of her element, overwhelmed by feelings she hadn't experienced before, her blood pulsing so furiously in her veins she felt lightheaded.

She'd had two serious boyfriends and had been physical with them. But it hadn't been like *this*—nothing close—and all she was doing was holding Jonah's hands, a man whose face she'd only seen online, a man who was terribly scarred under that mask of his. Although, he really only had one side completely covered. The skin that was exposed on the other side was smooth and uninjured and she could see the same beauty in that small portion of him that she'd seen in his online photograph.

Be wary of the man with two faces. He'll hurt you if you let him.

Spiders skittered down her spine at the memory of the fortune teller's words. She shook them off and they scattered, disappearing into the fragrant night air.

"Do you believe in prophecy, Jonah?" Her words were halting, as she'd uttered them without thinking. Truly she felt half in a daze and half so singularly focused it was making her head ache.

Jonah's thumb did another stroke of her knuckle and she swore more heat emanated from him. It was a pleasant night, not overly hot. But Clara felt positively flushed.

"Prophecy?"

"Yes. Do you believe our futures are already determined?"

Jonah shook his head. "No, I believe we choose our own paths. I chose mine and it—"

"Brought you to me," Clara finished, though she knew that's not where he'd been going. He'd been about to say it'd brought him to Windisle or that it'd made him a murderer or something like that. She wouldn't let him.

Jonah's lips tipped. "Yes." He sounded thoughtful. "Yes, I guess it did."

He raised their hands, loosening his fingers and pulling back slightly and then pushing them forward again. Clara let out a sigh laced with pleasure, and Jonah's fingers tightened on hers. "Why do you ask about prophecy?" His voice sounded strained, deeper.

"I . . . I." She shook her head, having lost the thread of conversation as his fingers did a slow glide through hers. No, this definitely did not feel friendly. "Never mind."

A new song began, the music inside of the ballroom flowing softly through the open door of the courtyard. "Dance with me?"

He hesitated, his fingers halting in their movement as a breath escaped him. "Clara—"

"Just one dance?" she whispered. What if he decided not to venture out again? What if this masquerade ball, where he could safely hide his face, was the only chance she got to dance with him?

"All right," he murmured, stepping toward her and slowly, so slowly, taking her in his arms, his solid heat enveloping her. She melted into him. "It's been a long time since I've danced."

His breath ghosted her cheek as she wrapped her arms around him, beginning to sway slightly to the music barely making its way to where they stood.

She danced every day. She was used to men pressed against her, to their hands on her body. She was *so* used to it, that sometimes she became desensitized to how her body *could* react to physical touch in her personal relationships. A hazard of the job, she'd told herself. And yet *this,* this slight grazing of Jonah's body against her own, made her feel as if she were buzzing with electricity.

"I was wondering . . ." Jonah began, his words trailing away.

"Yes?" she whispered, the word breathy, shivers breaking out over her skin at the sound of his voice so close to her ear.

"That night you were waiting at the fountain, you kept gazing up at the stars." He paused, bringing his mouth even closer and causing her body to pulse. "What were you thinking?"

For a moment she was caught off guard by the question, her entire being so present in that moment, it was difficult to cast her mind back to a different time. "I . . . I was wondering how many lifetimes we might get to be with the ones we love. I was wondering—*hoping*—that there's something after this. Another life, another chance." She turned her head minutely, bringing her mouth closer to the side of his neck and a small tremor went through him. "Love can't just disappear when this life is through, can it, Jonah? Even if our bodies turn to dust, the love we feel must go somewhere."

He was silent but he gripped her more tightly as she, too, pressed closer, seeking *more,* hearing his breath halt and feeling his muscles tense and harden. They swayed together that way for several moments before he pulled away, stepping back, breathing more harshly as if their short dance had exerted him. "I should go."

She opened her mouth to ask him not to, to tell him she would leave *with* him if he insisted on going, when the door to the courtyard swung fully open, clattering against the wall of the building. Sharp footsteps sounded and she heard her name.

Clara frowned, turning toward the voice and stepping out from beneath the small overhang where she and Jonah were enveloped in shadows.

Marco turned toward her as she came into his view. "There you are. I've been looking for you."

Crap. Marco. She knew it was rude to do so, but she would be leaving with Jonah. How could she not? *Well, this is about to be awkward,* she thought, cringing internally.

"What are you doing out here?"

"I was talking to someone. Marco, this is—" She turned back toward Jonah but he was gone.

Marco came to stand in front of her, peering into the darkness where Jonah had been only moments before.

Clara looked over her shoulder at the door that exited the other side of the courtyard, her heart sinking. He'd left. He was already gone.

CHAPTER SIXTEEN

Jonah pressed his back against the wall of the building next to the hotel, attempting to catch his breath.

He'd ducked out of the courtyard and walked quickly down the stairs and out of the hotel, but it wasn't as if he'd exerted himself overmuch, and it wasn't as if he was out of shape. No, his inability to breathe properly was because of Clara. *Clara.*

Fuck, his body was still hard, still pulsing with the memory of her body pressed to his, her scent enveloping him, the way she'd gazed at him with those beautiful brown eyes. *Brown. Her eyes are golden brown. Like rich, sweet caramel.* And they had seemed to *see* him despite his covered face. He closed his eyes, willing his heart rate to slow, willing his body to relax.

When he felt more in control, he pushed off the wall, shoving his hands into the pockets of his jacket and lowering his head a little.

He was still wearing the mask he'd donned for the masquerade ball, and it gave him more freedom to walk the streets uninhibited by the need to hide his scars.

He received a few strange looks from passersby, but this was New Orleans and seeing people decked out in strange outfits and costumes wasn't outside the norm, and so after a curious look or two, each person went on their way without a word.

Still, Jonah didn't like the attention, never liked being looked at. He wished to God he could be anonymous once again. But that would never be the case. He ducked his head further, bringing his collar up around his neck.

Stares reminded him of who he was now, of who he'd never be again. Stares made his heart heavy and his hackles rise. Stares made him realize why he'd never walk through the world with someone like Clara in any capacity.

There was a group of people waiting at the stoplight on the corner, and Jonah lingered in a doorway, not wanting to walk through them, preferring to wait until they'd crossed the street.

He leaned into the darkness, moving the larger expanse of his body before his feet followed, stepping gingerly, attempting to reveal as little movement as possible.

It was a sort of dance, he thought ruefully, this shifting between the shadows, knowing just where to step and how to spin away from the light, even that of the moon.

Once upon a time, he had been a man used to the spotlight and now he was a man who danced between moonbeams.

It would sound romantic, Jonah thought with a humorless huff of breath, *if it weren't so damned pathetic.*

The group of laughing young people moved on and Jonah did as well, his mind returning to his short time with Clara.

God, she was beautiful and kind. Her curious mind contemplated love and life and mysteries beyond herself. She was good and selfless and she smelled like heaven . . . and he wanted her to be *his*. It filled him with a sharp yearning—piercing and painful.

He thought back to the night in the theater when he'd gone to see her dance, when he'd convinced himself he'd do that one thing, make that one trip, and then he'd return behind his wall and live off of the memory forever.

He'd stood in the plentiful shadows at the back of the theater, melding with the darkness as her body had spun and leapt and moved in ways that made his heart expand and break all in the same breath.

She'd been mesmerizing, not just her body, but the expression on her face as the music had swelled, reaching its crescendo and then dwindling, the notes of a solitary piano drifting away.

Her expression had held the very soul of the music and told him the story of the dance she executed. He didn't know its name, but he knew it was a tale filled with heartbreak and grief, and finally, with redemption. She had told it with her body and her face, with the tears that shimmered in her eyes under the bright lights of the stage. *He had felt it all and he'd fallen in love.* Right there, just like that, her chest rising and falling as she stared blindly into the darkness where he stood, wanting her so desperately it made him dizzy.

He'd fallen in love, and she hadn't even known he was there. Hadn't known that his heart had beat to the same tempo of the music she'd moved so gracefully to. Swelling and receding . . . in rapture. In pain.

He'd ducked outside, too overwhelmed to continue watching her, and that's when he'd seen the flyer for the masquerade ball.

He heard a couple arguing as he passed by an alleyway and slowed his steps, his mind returning to the present. The woman's voice was shrill with fear, the man's voice threatening.

Jonah ducked into the shadow of the overhang. Why was he listening to this? Why had he stopped? This wasn't any of his business, and he needed to get to his ride—the motorcycle he'd bought and learned to ride a year or so before Murray Ridgley's trial, intending on driving it to work, a toy he'd found impractical once he'd used it a time or two.

He'd started it up a few times over the years, tinkered with it for lack of anything else to do, half-heartedly contemplated going out for a short trip around his neighborhood under the anonymity of the dark helmet, but ultimately fear and shame had always stopped him. He'd decided he wouldn't leave Windisle at all. Not ever, not even for a trip around the block. He hadn't had the will, nor the motivation. Not until Clara.

"I'll get you the money," the woman said, her voice shaky.

"That's what you said last week, you two-bit whore. I don't run a goddamned charity. Either pay what you owe me, or you can work it off right here. Your choice."

"Please, Donny. I don't trick. And my little girl's at home alone. I need to get back to her."

"Then you better get down on your knees and make it good and quick."

Jonah watched as the man advanced on the woman, grabbing her by her hair and forcing her onto her knees as she yelped in pain.

Oh Jesus. Jonah inhaled a slow breath through his nose and let it out. He should turn and leave—the woman had obviously gotten mixed up with the wrong person and was going to learn a harsh lesson, but maybe she needed it.

This has nothing to do with me. His muscles tensed to turn.

You're choosing a path here, Jonah. He froze, sure he'd heard his brother's voice right next to his ear, but knowing it'd only been his imagination.

Justin wasn't there, but the memory of another time he'd felt the way he felt now—torn, indecisive, riddled with . . . was it guilt? Yes, that's exactly what it was. *Guilt* at turning a blind eye, at participating, even by inaction, in something he'd innately known was wrong.

Jonah stepped out of the shadows. "Let her go."

The man grunted, turning toward Jonah but not releasing the woman's hair. In front of him, her eyes were wide and filled with fear and she grimaced as the man's hand apparently tightened, pulling at her scalp. "Get lost, man. This ain't none a your concern."

Jonah stepped closer, into a patch of low light given off by the glow of the street at the end of the alley and the man's eyes widened. The woman's mouth parted in surprise, the fear still present in her eyes.

Jonah, in his skeletal mask, obviously looked even more frightening than the filthy meathead attempting to assault her.

"What the fuck are you?" the man asked, his gaze skittering over Jonah's tuxedo and back up to his skeletal face.

"I'm the guy who's making this my concern," Jonah said, his voice a low growl that barely rose above the air conditioning units humming noisily on the outside of the building next to where they stood.

The man let go of the woman's hair, and she crumpled to the side before catching herself and skittering backward like a frightened crab.

The man laughed, a sound as oily as the hair that hung lankly around his blubbery face. Jonah sighed. Great, now he was going to have to touch this dirty bastard.

"It's not Halloween yet, little boy. Go home and tell your mommy she dressed you in your costume too soon."

"Maybe what's under here is even scarier, you fat fuck."

The man squared his shoulders. "Do you know who you're messing with?"

Jonah stepped forward, taking the bait. Something violent inside of him suddenly thrilled at this situation—not the fact that a woman had been about to be someone's victim, but that he might have a good reason to shed this guy's blood, to see him laid out flat in front of him. His palms itched with need.

Do I know who I'm messing with? Jonah laughed. "A greasy bully who preys on women half his size in a garbage-strewn alley." Jonah realized his fists were clenched at his sides, his feet spread, ready for whatever battle this guy brought.

The man narrowed his eyes and shifted uneasily, obviously shocked by the lack of fear in Jonah's voice, and the fact that he was advancing instead of turning away. And though the man had mocked the skeleton mask, that—and the fact that Jonah's expression couldn't be seen—probably made him creepier, a greater unknown.

The man pulled something shiny from his pocket and Jonah pulled back. It was a knife and the man pushed it toward Jonah. "Go on, get out of here, freak show."

Freak show.

Jonah glanced quickly at the woman still on her knees and cowering on the ground, taking one step backward, pretending to reconsider the fight. The man lowered the weapon minutely, and Jonah turned away slightly and then swung around, advancing speedily and kicking at the man's arm with all the might in his legs, the legs that had run miles and miles around Windisle every day for the last eight fucking years.

The man yelped, the knife clattering to the ground. Jonah kicked the weapon away and swung at the man with his fist in one coordinated move.

Cracking bone sounded and blood sprayed as the man let out a high-pitched scream, clamping a hand over his nose. "You broke my fuckin' nose, you motherfucker."

Then he began swinging wildly at Jonah, connecting one shot before Jonah ducked and sidestepped, his own fist connecting with the man's squishy gut. The man doubled over, gasping for air.

Jonah swung his leg again, connecting with the side of the man's head. He went down hard, splashing into a puddle of unknown origin, the dank liquid raining over Jonah's shoes. *Well, fuck.*

Jonah took a few steps, picking up the knife he'd kicked away and returning to the man, still groaning on the ground.

Jonah brought the knife to the man's neck, digging the tip of the blade into his skin and the man let out a wheeze, following the glinting blade with his fear-filled eyes as Jonah ran it over his sweaty skin. "Come near her again and I'll make sure a blade just like this one slices right into your flabby gut. You got me?"

The man bobbed his head, stopping when it caused the blade to dig into his skin again. "Get up."

The man hesitated for one beat as if he wasn't quite sure if Jonah was playing with him or not and then he sat up, scooted backward and pulled himself to his feet, panting as if he'd just run twenty miles.

Blood continued to drip from his nose and the spot where Jonah had pierced his throat, settling into the rolls around his neck.

"Go," Jonah rasped, stepping aside. The man ran, splashing through the murky puddles as he went.

"Thank you, mister." Jonah turned around, returning his attention to the woman still kneeling on the ground. She rose slowly, obviously attempting to gather herself as she smoothed her clothing and ran her hands under her black-rimmed eyes.

Jonah nodded. "Go home to your little girl. Whatever you were doing to get yourself into debt with a bottom feeder like him, don't do it again. Your daughter needs you to make good decisions. To make a stand for her. She's counting on *you* to choose the right path."

You're choosing a path here . . .

The beaten-down woman in front of him still had a chance to make the right choice, to turn and head in the right direction. He sincerely hoped she would.

The woman nodded, swiping at a tear. "I will. Thank you. You have no idea . . ." She gulped. "Thank you." She ran past Jonah, turning out of the alley in the opposite direction the man had limped a few minutes before.

You have no idea . . . Only, Jonah did have some idea. He knew what it was to feel beaten down, damaged beyond all fixing, hopeless, helpless . . .

Freak show.

Only he hadn't felt helpless just then. He'd assisted someone more helpless than himself. Jesus, wouldn't Justin be proud of him? He laughed softly to himself. "That one was for you, bro."

The words brought him sorrow, but they also brought undeniable warmth to his chest that he hadn't experienced for a long, long time. For a moment there, he'd felt *useful,* not the purposeless person he'd lived as all of these years.

As he walked, he put his hand in his pocket, feeling the solid smoothness of the phone he'd had Myrtle turn on for him the day before. He pulled it from his pocket now, glancing at the screen. There was one text message.

Clara: Where did you go?

He typed in a quick reply. **Sorry, Clara. I had to leave. Thank you for the dance.**

Fuck. Thank you felt far too inadequate. Or maybe it was what he was thanking her *for* that felt wrong. *Thank you for making me feel alive again, even if for a moment. Thank you for making me feel like I might be worth something.* Shit, talk about the best way to scare her off. No, true or not, he wouldn't say anything like that.

He closed his eyes, picturing her as she'd been earlier, her shimmery ball gown draped over her beautiful body, making her look like something out of a fairy tale. Her hair had been curled, hanging down her back in shiny waves, the vivid blue and green mask that hid half her face making her lips—the only feature that could be well seen—appear especially pink and lush. God, he'd wanted to kiss her, to taste her—

Stop. Don't even think about that.

He'd sworn there had been something full and weighty between them in that garden, something that felt a whole lot like mutual attraction, but if she was attracted to him, it was only because she hadn't been able to see what he'd become.

And he'd watched her before letting her know he was there. He'd watched as she danced with the other ballet dancer he'd seen on stage at the theater and wondered if there was something between them.

For a second there, he'd thought the guy was going to kiss Clara and some feeling, spiky and hot, had made him grit his teeth. *Jealousy,* he'd thought. *This is what jealousy feels like.* But he had no right to that. None at all.

Clara: When can I see you again?

Jonah frowned, putting the phone back in his pocket, not sure how to answer her question.

The ride home went by in a blur as Jonah relived every moment he'd spent with Clara. He was still partially in a daze when he removed his helmet, the mask slipping off as well and landing on the ground.

"We've been worried about you."

Jonah practically jumped. "Jesus, Cecil. You almost gave me a heart attack."

"Well, now we're even. What in God's name are you doing out riding around town on that thing?" He gestured to the sleek black motorcycle.

"You've both been trying to convince me to leave Windisle for years, and now that I do, you're complaining?" Jonah placed his helmet on the seat of the bike and turned more fully toward Cecil.

"Not complaining exactly. This just seems like a sudden leap, and we're wondering why all the secrecy. Where have you been going? What's motivating this? What have you been doing?" Cecil frowned as Jonah moved more fully into the light. "What happened to you?" he asked, his gaze squinting as he seemed to peer more closely at Jonah's face. What? Was the man going senile?

"A bomb blew up in my face."

"Oh, for God's sake, not that. You're bleeding."

Jonah brought his fingers to his lip where the man had gotten in his one shot. When he brought his fingers away, there was a smear of blood on them. "I . . ." He shook his head, dropping his hand. "I saw a woman being assaulted. I stepped in. It was nothing."

Cecil regarded him for several long beats. "Nothing," he repeated.

Jonah turned, heading for the door. "Right. Nothing."

"Like you going out after dark on secret missions around the city?"

Jonah stopped, laughing as he turned to Cecil. "Secret missions? Jesus, Cecil. I . . ." He tossed his hands up and let them drop. Cecil was a nosy bastard. "I went to see a girl."

That seemed to bring Cecil up short. "A girl? The one you met at the wall?"

Jonah sighed. "Yes. Her name is Clara. She's a . . . friend. There was a masquerade ball, and I went to see her. That's all."

"That's all."

"Are you a parrot now?" Jonah let out a breath, running his hand over his short hair, feeling the scarred spots on the left side of his scalp where the hair had never grown back. "I'm just . . . getting *out,* Cecil. I was anonymous tonight at that ball, and I'm anonymous under that helmet, so I can ride my bike and be someone else for a while, okay?"

"Clara," Cecil repeated, clearly picking that out as the important piece of information Jonah had just given.

"Yes, Clara."

"Who is she?"

Jonah turned again and headed inside of the house, toward his room. Cecil trailed. "Just a girl."

"Just a girl."

Jonah let out a frustrated breath, turning once more. The old man came up short. "Yes, just a girl. A girl named Clara."

Cecil leaned in, looking at him closely. "You're pining."

"Pining?"

Cecil crossed his arms. "Mm-hmm. Definitely pining. The way you say her name. It's like you're saying a prayer."

Oh lord. The old man was losing his marbles. Or maybe he was extremely perceptive. Jonah preferred to believe the former. Although . . . *Christ, yes,* he did want Clara. Yes, he pined for her.

He let out a defeated breath. It didn't matter, and he wouldn't tell Cecil or Myrtle how far he'd fallen. That was for him to know, and no one else. "It's not a big deal."

"If you say so," Cecil said, raising one disbelieving brow.

Jonah paused before heading down the hall toward his bedroom. "There's nothing to worry about. It's all . . .

temporary." The nature of his life would never include another person on any permanent basis, especially a vibrant woman like Clara.

He enjoyed the freedom of cruising the streets on the motorcycle, but he wasn't sure if the risk was worthwhile. At some point he might get pulled over. He wouldn't have a license . . . he'd have to reveal his face to the officer.

A small shudder went down his spine. Hell, he had risked a run-in with the law earlier that night when he'd confronted the goon in the alley.

No, this was all just a temporary diversion from his lackluster life. But it'd be over soon. He'd end it himself. Nothing was worth exposing himself to the world.

He turned toward the old man, who he suddenly realized had far more white in his hair than black, far more wrinkles creasing his brown skin.

Myrtle and Cecil were getting older by the day. They wouldn't be there forever and the sudden knowledge brought forth a burst of fear. He sighed. "I'll let you know if I go out again, Cecil. Tell Myrtle not to worry."

He didn't wait for the old man to answer, though he swore he heard Cecil mutter, "Yup, definitely pining," under his breath, a hint of worry in his tone.

Jonah walked quickly to his room and shut the door behind him. His phone dinged again, and he pulled it from his pocket.

Clara: Jonah, are you there?

Jonah: Yeah, sorry. I'm home now. Are you still at the ball?

Clara: No. I called a ride and left right after you.

A feeling of relief drifted through Jonah. If she'd arrived with the dancer, he hadn't driven her home.

Clara: Jonah, do you want to talk on the phone for a few minutes? It's okay if you don't.

Jonah hesitated. She always gave him an out, and he didn't think he deserved such kindness all the time. Before he could respond, another text came through.

Clara: I just sort of miss your voice.

God, this girl. He wanted to hear Clara's voice too. To close his eyes and talk to her the way they'd spoken so often as she sat on the other side of his wall. He flopped down on his bed, putting one arm behind his head as he dialed her number.

"Hey," she said, her voice sleepy. His heart rate accelerated at the sweet sound of her right against his ear.

"Hey," he answered, picturing her as she might be, lying on her bed in whatever she wore to sleep in . . . a tank top maybe, something sheer and soft. His body tightened at the image his mind conjured, and he willed his blood to cool.

"This feels familiar but different. If I close my eyes it's like you're still just on the other side of the wall, but a different wall, one that's just a paper-thin sliver of rock," Clara said. Jonah smiled at the image but when she spoke again, her voice was serious, "Will there always be something between us, Jonah?"

"Yes," he said, and even he could hear the regret in his tone. There would always be something between them. If not a wall, then a phone, a mask, the shadows he hid amongst.

She paused and he sensed that she was trying to figure out how to answer, whether to accept or convince. "I hope someday you'll change your mind."

"I won't, Clara."

"But you said you'd never come out from behind the wall either and you did that." There was a note of satisfaction in her voice.

Jonah smiled. "You got me there. You're a very convincing person. You should have been a lawyer."

Clara laughed. "Oh God, no, I'd be awful. My jaw locks up when I speak publicly. It's a scary sight."

Jonah chuckled, but her words caused a frisson of shame to roll down his spine. She had no idea what scary was. If she saw the frozen, scarred side of his face, she'd re-evaluate the usage of that word.

"Jonah . . . I hope you don't mind me asking but . . . how is it that you don't have to work? I mean, I know that's personal and I don't mean to—"

"It's fine. It's not that personal." Especially considering everything he'd already shared with her. "The truth is, I'm rich."

He rolled over, looking out the window at the dark lace of the trees outside. "The Chamberlain family has always been well-off, but my father made a lot of money, and then he invested it well and when he died, he left it all to me and Justin. When Justin died, I got his share."

"Oh," she whispered, seeming to understand that Jonah took no satisfaction in his wealth. It had come at far too great a price.

"I'd give it all back if I could," he said softly. "Every cent."

"I know," Clara said, and he truly felt like she did.

"But, in all fairness, I'm grateful for it too because it's allowed me to live the life of solace that I want." *Solace.* That felt like the wrong choice of words—Jonah had felt little solace—but he didn't correct himself and neither did she.

"Why Windisle? Why choose a place you yourself have described as run-down and in need of repair?"

"At first, it was the only place I could think to go to get away from all the reporters, the cameras, just . . . *people* in general. The Chamberlain family abandoned Windisle a long time ago. Everyone knew it was empty. Cecil and Myrtle were the caretakers before I arrived, but at that time, they didn't live on the property. After that . . . I don't know. I guess it became easy to hide here."

Clara was quiet for a moment, and he pictured her face, pictured those wide, sensitive eyes blinking at her ceiling, pictured her pulling her full bottom lip between her teeth the way he'd seen her do when she was focusing on something her teacher was saying the night he'd watched her dance. "What about your mother? Is she still alive?"

"Yes."

"Yes?" She sounded surprised.

"My mother lives in the south of France with her new husband."

"Oh, I . . . well, she must obviously know what happened to you."

"She does." There was a small painful clenching in his chest, and it surprised him to know he could still feel the ache of his mother's abandonment after all of these years. Her *emotional* detachment.

"They were already living out of the country at that time. She came back briefly, but then she left again." He'd been too zonked out on pain medication to remember much of her short visit. "It was all too much for her . . . Justin's death, everything that happened to me."

"Too much for *her*?" Clara sounded incredulous.

"My mother is selfish, Clara. She always has been. I didn't expect more from her." That was the truth, and a lie, and they were both wound so tightly together, Jonah had no clue how to separate them. He hadn't thought about all this in so long.

Up until now, he hadn't had a phone, but his mother sent postcards from different places she was obviously vacationing in, and he always read her singular scrawled line—*Wish you were here!* Or, *Love you bunches!*—and he never knew whether he should laugh or cry. He sort of felt like doing both, but what he generally did instead was rip the card into a hundred tiny pieces and watch as they rained down in the trash. He never wrote back.

"Oh," Clara breathed. Jonah heard her sadness even in the single syllable, uttered half under her breath.

"What about your mother, Clara? You've never mentioned her."

"My mother died when I was eight. I don't have many memories, but the ones I do have are good ones."

"You're lucky for that."

"Yes, I . . ." She trailed off and Jonah waited for her to collect her thoughts. "I'm sorry you've been so alone."

His heart squeezed. He deserved it. He deserved his solitary life. And it's what he *wanted*, what he'd carved out for himself, despite a few motorcycle rides, despite an appearance at a masked ball. So why did Clara's words—said so sincerely—make him ache? Make him pine? Christ, that old bastard Cecil was right on the damn money.

"You're not alone anymore."

He smiled at Clara's sweetness, though it felt sad upon his lips. "You sound tired," he said, picking up on the slight slurring of her voice and using it as an excuse to change the subject.

"I am." She yawned and then laughed softly. Jonah closed his eyes and took every small sound she made inside of him as if he could hold on to tiny pieces of her forever. "And I have to get up early. Can I call you again?"

"Of course."

He heard the smile in her voice when she said, "Goodnight, Jonah."

"Goodnight, Clara."

Jonah rolled onto his back, dropping the phone on the bed next to him. He was exhausted, but it was a long time before he fell asleep that night.

When he did, he dreamed of Clara, lifting her ball gown as she ran, glancing behind her with both sorrow and fear in her eyes. The vision mixed with murky images of dark alleys and tall rows of sugarcane, of a woman kneeling in a dark puddle that reflected the silvery sheen of a knife that then morphed into a razor blade.

There was a strange pounding in the background that made his heart race with fear. *Hurry! Hurry!* And then he saw Justin at the end of the alley beckoning to him, a smile on his face right before he disappeared into the mist beyond.

CHAPTER SEVENTEEN

Everything felt brighter to Jonah the next day, as if there'd been a veil of gossamer fog hanging over the world he hadn't known about, and it'd suddenly lifted.

He knew why. It was because he'd fallen asleep to Clara's voice in his mind, and despite the way his dreams had twisted and turned, she'd been a part of them.

He went for his early morning run and then strolled aimlessly around the property, stretching his arms and breathing in the sweet fresh air as his heart rate slowed and the sweat dried on his skin.

As he was turning to go back to the house, he swore he heard soft weeping. He paused, listening. Yes, underneath the loud morning bird chatter someone was crying.

He moved tentatively toward the wall, taking care not to step on anything that might make a sound and give him away.

He leaned forward, turning his good eye toward one of the larger cracks. He couldn't make out much through the thin space, but he could see it was a woman. She was standing back from the wall enough so that he could tell she was young with dark hair. For a moment she continued to stand there weeping quietly.

He leaned away, feeling awkward about intruding on this moment, one the woman obviously believed was private. But he halted in his movement when she began to speak.

"I know I've already come here once and made a wish, but I didn't think it would hurt to try again. I'm sure you get so many, and . . . if mine stood out . . ."

She hiccupped and then let out a strangled sound, half chuckle, half sob. "God, I'm desperate, aren't I?" She paused for a moment. "It's just, I was thinking that maybe my last wish wasn't specific enough. You might be a spirit, Angelina, but it doesn't mean you're a mind reader, or, well, maybe you are but . . ."

The woman let out a shuddery breath and Jonah waited, unwilling to move and let her know he was there while she was pouring her heart out in what she thought was a confessional. *I know what that feels like,* he thought, closing his eyes as he ran his fingers over the coarse rock, picturing Clara on the other side, listening as he'd bared his own heart.

He felt like an ass listening to her, but the birds had quieted, her sobs had halted, and he was afraid to back away and make a noise. He was stuck.

"Anyway," she continued, and he noted that her voice sounded more dull as if she had lost hope in her own wish, as if she'd already talked herself out of any possibility of it coming true before she'd even made it. "My son's name is Matthew Fullerton, and he's at Children's Hospital. He's very sick and he needs surgery . . . if there's any hope for him. I can't afford it, and I need help. Just"—she let out another small choking sound—"fifty-thousand-dollars-worth of help."

Her words faded away and Jonah's heart clenched as he closed his eyes. *Fuck.* Was this the woman whose wish he had read about her sick son? It must be.

"That's all." She sounded drained, her voice a mere whisper now. "I need help to save my boy."

Jonah heard the sound of her footsteps moving away and pressed his eye to the crack again, watching as a blue car drove away, leaving only silence in its wake.

Jonah sat down on the grass, his heart heavy just like it'd been the first time he'd heard that woman's wish for her dying child, feeling helpless all over again.

But you're not helpless, are you?

The question wandered through his mind and for a second it felt as if someone else had asked it. Where had that come from? Did he think maybe he was some sort of masked hero now that he'd assisted one helpless woman who was being assaulted in an alley?

He ran his hand over his head, his hair now completely dry from the soft breeze blowing through Windisle. *Oh Jonah, you fucking fool.*

Although . . . this time, the person in need of help was requesting something that would require far less effort on his part: all she needed was money. *My son needs surgery and I can't afford it.*

He blew out a breath. Was he seriously considering *granting* one of the wishes that had been made at the weeping wall? God, wouldn't Justin *love* that?

He stood up, the idea taking hold in his mind, the ease with which he could do it forming.

He might not even have to leave his property. Although . . . no, he did not want this attached to him. He'd have to make the delivery in person. He'd have to make sure Matthew Fullerton's mother received the money she needed. Fifty thousand dollars. It was nothing to him, but it would be everything to her.

And for the first time in many, many years, someone else's woes outshone his own.

Maybe he could still be useful to the world after all. And he didn't have to wait to stumble upon a drug deal gone wrong in a dark alley. Maybe *he* could be Angelina.

He smiled, feeling the skin stretch over the damaged side of his face, reminding him of his limitations. Still, there was a lightness to his heart, and the day grew even brighter.

****

Translucent marigold rays streamed from behind the silver-plated clouds, bringing light and warmth to the day that had begun in shades of sallow gray. Jeannie wished it could penetrate the pewter sorrow that surrounded her heart.

She glanced up at the hospital room window where Matthew lay sleeping, her precious boy who wouldn't be long for this world. She had no idea how she would survive without him.

She sat heavily on the wooden bench, warmed by the sunshine, and stared blankly out at the path where patients exercised, some holding the arm of a nurse, others being pushed in a wheelchair. Everyone was taking advantage of the break in gloomy weather to take a stroll outdoors.

A man approached the bench and she saw him in her peripheral vision, though she didn't turn in his direction. She caught the image of bandages on his face and a black, athletic jacket with a collar that was turned upward, shielding his neck and chin.

He walked crouched over as though he were old, but something about the size and breadth of his body didn't fit his movements. If she had to describe his body type, and even though she hadn't looked at him full on, she'd go with . . . *strapping*. Odd, though she moved the strange feeling aside as he sat down on the edge of the bench, hunching over, his elbows on his knees, as he watched the other patients amble by on broken limbs, and sickly bodies.

She was curious but she wasn't afraid. She was out in the open, a dozen other people strolling directly in front of her, and frankly, she didn't have any more fear to offer the world.

Her greatest terror was losing her baby boy, and the imminence of that hung heavily over her like a boulder attached by a thread. And when the crushing came, it would flatten her.

"Your son is sick?"

Jeannie turned toward the man then, surprised at his words. He was looking out at the path in front of them and she could only see his profile, heavily bandaged in white gauze.

He wore a baseball cap so she couldn't tell anything about whether his injury extended to his head, or only involved his face. And she couldn't see his hair that might have given a clue about his age, though his voice was young and deep and smooth.

"I'm sorry. Do I know you?"

The man paused. "I've heard you talk about your son. Matthew, right? He's very sick?"

Jeannie frowned. This man must be a patient here. He must have overheard Matthew's diagnosis, maybe seen them walking in the halls. She knew a lot about the other patients too, simply because she spent so much time at the hospital.

She'd never seen this man, though perhaps he'd recently had his surgery and when he'd been in the same room as her before, he'd looked very different.

Jeannie sighed. Everyone here had a story, obviously his held trauma too. "Cancer. He's very sick."

There was another pause, and then the man said, "I'm sorry. I thought I heard you say he needs surgery."

Jeannie glanced at him. He was definitely a patient here then. Lord knew she'd been talking and crying and practically begging the doctors to help her find a way to get Matthew into the study that was performing a surgery on kids with his disease.

They'd already been having huge successes, even in advanced cases, and Matthew was a great candidate, but insurance didn't cover the experimental treatment, and she didn't have anywhere near the money to afford it.

The doctors were sympathetic to her case, and they cared deeply about Matthew, she knew they did, but other than listen to her cry, there wasn't much else they could do.

Jeannie didn't have any family who could help her, Matthew's father had taken off the moment he found out about his existence, and she was all her son had in the world.

And I'm failing him.

She told the man all this, a tear slipping down her cheek. She wasn't sure why she opened up to the stranger who had obviously been wounded so badly, other than that she didn't seem to be able to help herself—the words just tumbled out of her as though they'd been dammed up and finally allowed to flow freely.

And there was also the fact that his voice held an empathy that only those who had felt pain themselves seemed to carry. She'd never recognized it before, but she'd know it now, she'd hear it in others for the rest of her days. Anguish did that, she supposed, honed your senses to hear and see and *feel* the unspoken sorrow in others.

"I'm sorry," she said, shaking her head. "You probably weren't looking for all that."

He let out a breath and she sensed there was a smile with it, if he could manage one with whatever was happening with his face under all the gauze. "I'm sure you weren't looking for all that either. Sometimes life just . . . bowls you over."

She smiled and it surprised her. It felt unpracticed, as though she hadn't smiled in a very long time. But it felt good too, as if she should try to do it more often.

She wanted to be strong for Matthew. She wanted him to see that she'd be okay when he was gone. Whether she believed it or not, she knew it would bring him peace. Her tiny caretaker, the boy who'd taken on the role of man of the house as if he was born to protect.

God, he would have grown up to be an amazing man. A leader. A force of *good* in the world. She felt it deep inside, not just as a proud mother, but as a woman who had made too many bad choices when it came to men and finally learned how to spot a good one because he had been placed right into her arms.

"I'm already thinking about him in past tense." Another tear slipped down her cheek. "I need to stop that," she whispered. "The truth is, he's what set me on the right path. Before him, I was heading for, well, nothing good, let's put it that way."

Jeannie made a small, embarrassed sound, but the man remained silent. It was a comfortable silence, and she lingered in it for a moment, picturing her life before Matthew, and thanking God for him and the change in direction her unplanned pregnancy had caused her to make.

"You wished for the ability to get this surgery for him."

She frowned. He must mean in general. There was no way he could know of her desperate attempt to take advantage of a local legend she'd heard about once as a kid.

"Yes, yes, I wish for it every day. He won't be a candidate at all if he gets any worse."

"I'd like to grant your wish." He reached into his pocket and pulled out an envelope and handed it to her.

She took it, staring down at it in confusion. "What is this?"

"Stay on that path you're on," the man said, standing. "Make sure your son stays on the right path too. Help him grow into a good man."

Jeannie could see then that she'd been right about the size of him. He was tall and broad and yes, strapping. And yet, he'd first appeared to walk as though he was old and sick.

He turned to her for a brief moment and her eyes widened. He turned away quickly, but before he had, sunlight had flashed on his bandage wrapped face and it'd appeared that underneath the gauze, he was wearing a skeleton mask, the fakeness of it obvious in the stark black and white contrast.

Jeannie was momentarily shaken, taken off guard. She glanced at the envelope she was now clutching tightly in her grasp, tearing it open. Inside was a cashier's check made out to her in the amount of fifty thousand dollars.

She stood, looking around frantically for the stranger who'd just granted her greatest wish, the stranger who may have very well given her son a death reprieve.

Patients strolled and hobbled all around her, but the man was nowhere. He'd disappeared.

Jeannie let out a joyful sob, and ran toward the hospital, toward her boy.

****

"You sound happy, Jonah."

Jonah smiled, sitting in the chair in the corner of his bedroom and toeing his shoes off. *Am I?*

He sat back, pushing his hair off of his forehead. He thought back to what he'd done earlier that day, the look on the woman's face as he'd begun speaking to her.

She'd been wary of him at first, with his bandaged face, even if he was in a hospital courtyard. And she'd looked briefly terrified when he'd looked at her full on and she'd realized he was a skeleton under the bandages.

But it'd been the first time he'd been outside Windisle in the bright light of day, and the dual cover had felt *necessary*. Creepy stuff, he knew. But damn if it hadn't been worth it to see the blatant hope that had filled her eyes when she'd realized what she was holding in her hand.

So . . . maybe not happy exactly. But not miserable either, and damn but it was a nice reprieve. "Happy-ish," he answered, putting a teasing note in his voice.

He heard the smile in hers as she said, "It makes me happy to hear you happy . . . ish."

Jonah laughed, quickly pulling his shirt over his head and tossing it in the direction of the clothes hamper.

"Jonah, do you remember the other night when I asked if you believed in prophecy?"

"Yeah."

"Well . . . I asked because I went to this fortune teller and she said some stuff that made me wonder."

"A fortune teller, Clara?"

"I know. I never really believed in all that stuff before either. But it was . . . I don't know, eerie, I guess. Anyway, she told me I was seeking the answers to a mystery and told me it was very important that I keep looking."

"You mean, the mystery of the curse put on John and Angelina?" It *was* the reason Clara had shown up at Windisle in the first place, he remembered that now. *Help me help you, Angelina.*

"Yes."

He blew out a breath. "Who *isn't* searching for the answer to a mystery though, Clara? Even if the 'mystery' is just an unknown . . . you know, will I find success in my career? Will I find love? Will the Mets win the World Series?"

The explanation of how the unknown fortune teller had struck on Clara's searching for answers to a mystery felt a little weak, even to him, but fortune tellers were con artists, plain and simple. Whatever method she'd used to land on something that happened to apply to Clara, it had been an accident. Trickery.

"I guess." She drew out the words, clearly unconvinced. "In any case, whether her statements came from the great beyond or not," she said with an ironic lilt to her tone, "I don't want to dismiss anything, and she renewed my desire to find out more about Angelina and that curse."

"Okay." Jonah unbuttoned his jeans and let them fall to the floor where he kicked them off. He sat on his bed, clad only in his boxers, leaning back on the pillows against the headboard.

He loved the decisiveness in her voice, loved that quality about her in general because he knew it was the reason she'd kept coming back for him. Clara had decided there was something worth knowing in Jonah, and because she'd decided it, she hadn't given up even when he'd told her to. She was . . . God, she was amazing. The thought filled up his chest until he felt he might overflow with his admiration for her.

Clara was beautiful and elegant, and he couldn't help noticing those things, but damn if he didn't also like the hell out of her. "And how are you going to do that?"

"Well, I've been thinking about the avenues I still have to explore. There aren't many, but . . . I was hoping you might be able to help me. What can you tell me about Astrid Chamberlain?"

"Astrid Chamberlain? Not a lot, to be honest. Justin was a big family history buff. He would have been able to tell you anything you wanted to know."

He was quiet for a moment as he remembered Justin prattling on about Windisle and the things he'd discovered. Justin had wanted to sell the property to the preservation society, and Jonah hadn't been against it at the time, but he'd been busy . . . he kept putting Justin off whenever he mentioned it . . . told him they'd deal with the sale of Windisle once Jonah had more time. Of course, looking back, Jonah could admit that would have been never.

"He had some folders of information, family trees and whatnot, that I think I put in the attic. I could get them out for you."

"Would you?" She breathed the question and Jonah smiled, thinking that her reaction had exceeded the actual worth of some dusty paperwork in the attic of Windisle.

"Of course."

She was quiet for a beat. "The thing is, Jonah, I have this feeling that the answers are all *somewhere.* I just . . . they're *waiting* to be put together and I don't know, but I sense this . . . ticking. Does that sound crazy?"

It did, sort of, but the real funny thing was, at her words, he felt it too. This drumming right under his ribcage that made him feel like rushing to the attic that second and getting that paperwork for her. Or maybe it was just his intense desire to please this woman in any way he was capable. And the truth was, his capabilities were very limited.

"No, it doesn't sound crazy. It's an interesting story, Clara. And the people who can provide answers, or pass on stories are either dead or very old."

"Yes," she said, but he sensed something in her voice that told him his explanation about the rush to find answers didn't feel quite right to her.

"What about the old priestess who spoke the riddle to breaking the curse at the party in the '30s. Do you know her name?"

The name appeared in Jonah's head as if it'd been scrawled across his brain. "Actually I do, strangely enough. It's one of the things in Justin's files—an original invitation to that party. It was one of the things he showed me, and it had the priestess's name on it. She was the entertainment."

He'd glanced at the invitation, other things on his mind at the time, but he remembered the priestess's name because it had been unusual and he'd repeated the alliteration in his head. "Sibille Simoneaux."

Clara said her name softly once and then again, as though to commit it to memory. "Do you think her family might be alive?"

"I have no idea, but even so, you can't just go knocking on strangers' doors alone. There are dangerous people and lots of unsavory parts of New Orleans."

"Come with me."

Jonah expelled a breath. "You know I can't."

Clara was quiet for a moment. "Maybe I could go there."

"Here?"

"Inside Windisle. I could help you look through those papers."

"I don't think so." He shut his eyes, hating that he was rejecting her in any capacity. He'd stood her up once and this felt like he was doing it again but . . . no, he couldn't allow her to go beyond the weeping wall, to see the place where he showed his scarred and ruined face. Not only did he not want her to see it, but this place was safe for him. Here, he didn't hide. Not from the trees or the ghosts or Myrtle or Cecil. And not from a beautiful girl who would grimace when she laid her eyes upon him the way all the others had. Even his own mother hadn't been able to bear the sight of him. His heart beat dully. No, he couldn't invite her in.

"Okay," she said softly, understanding lacing her tone and causing him to feel even guiltier. "But will you call me tomorrow if you have a chance to look through those papers? Anything you find, Jonah, will you share it with me?"

I'd share everything with you if I could. Even my blackened soul . . . "Yes. I'll call you tomorrow."

"Okay." There was a smile in her voice. "Sleep tight."

"You, too. Goodnight, Clara."

CHAPTER EIGHTEEN

April, 1861

Angelina removed the hood obscuring her face and shut the door behind her, turning to John with a smile that immediately fell. "What is it? The look on your face, John. Is something wrong?"

He walked to her, his boot steps loud on the old wooden floor of the boathouse on his family's vast estate.

They'd been meeting there since Astrid had begun covering for Angelina by sending her on fabricated errands in town. Instead, Angelina would go to the small structure on the edge of the Mississippi, and she and John would spend a few hours together in a location where they didn't have to worry about being caught. It still housed equipment and tools, but no one came to the Whitfield estate boathouse since John's father had passed away earlier that year.

As he approached her, John's expression was so solemn it caused Angelina's heart to contract and nerves to flutter in her belly.

He took her face in his large hands and for a moment he simply gazed at her. She looked back at him, searching his eyes and finding the love always present in his gaze.

She released a pent-up breath. Whatever it was would be fine. As long as he still loved her, she could endure anything else.

"I'm going to war, Angelina."

A lump formed immediately in her throat, and she turned away, his hands dropping from her face as she leaned against the wall.

"When?" she choked.

"I leave day after tomorrow."

Her heart squeezed painfully and she brought a hand to it. "Day after tomorrow? Why, John?"

He turned away, pacing as he ran a hand through his hair. "The Confederacy needs me." He said it quickly, his tone making the hairs on the back of Angelina's neck rise. His tone was different, one she'd never heard before. She had the vague notion he was lying to her, or leaving something out, and she didn't know why she felt that, but she did.

He turned back to her. "This war, Angelina, it could change everything. It could *free* you." The sentence was uttered on a burst of breath and then his mouth settled into a thin line as a muscle jumped in his jaw.

Angelina stared at him for a moment. This war that John had spoken of for months had all seemed so unreal, so *distant* and disconnected from her world. But she suddenly realized that that would not be the case for long.

"But, John, you'll be fighting for the South." Fighting against the side that would see her free, that would see her mama free, and all those men and women and children who came back from the fields sweaty and dirty and without hope day after day after day.

John let out a grunt of frustration. "I know. It's the way it has to be."

He closed his eyes and took a deep breath as he grasped her upper arms in his hands, holding on to her as though she might disappear at any moment if not for his strong grip. "It seems wrong. Damn it, Angelina, it *feels* wrong. But I . . . I have to. I'm sorry."

Hurt trickled through her. She couldn't help it. She knew it wasn't his fault, knew he was only doing his job as a soldier, following orders delivered by other men with other ideas. That's how war worked, wasn't it?

But the knowledge that he would be fighting against her freedom was an arrow to her soul. Despite having no choice, the knowledge that his weapon would be aimed at the hearts of men who would *free* her if they could, crushed her on a level that defied logic or reason.

"I know," she breathed. Because she did, even if she couldn't feel it.

"Listen to me, Angelina. Keep your head down. Don't take any risks. Just do as you're supposed to do until this war is over."

She wanted to laugh, or cry, or both. What did he know about keeping her head down? She'd been *raised* to keep her head down—*born* to do so maybe, although that thought was too hopeless to consider—and everything else along with it. It was *all* she knew. All she'd done her whole life . . . until him.

And now *he* was the one telling her not to take any risks. That would be easy, wouldn't it, now that he was leaving? The thought should have brought her relief—there would be no more hiding and lying and sneaking around.

And maybe the idea of him telling her to keep her head down should have made her angry. But her feelings were all over the place, and the only one she could identify was anguish.

She didn't want him to leave. She didn't want a war—especially one the South might win. She *just* wanted to love him and feel loved in return. Why was that too much to ask? Why must the color of one's skin determine destiny? Determine wars. Separation. How did the color of one's skin create such distinction when no one *asked* to be born what he or she was? Surely God on High hadn't intended that. Had He?

"Kiss me, John."

His gaze moved over her face for a bated breath, hot, fierce as if he was memorizing her features one by one. Then his mouth was on hers, demanding, urgent, and she had the sense that time was ticking . . . ticking, because of course it was.

He brought her to the floor, his hands moving under her dress, and something rough dug at her back. It didn't matter.

As long as he was with her, she'd sleep on dirt or rocks or the thorns of a hundred prickly rose bushes.

He entered her body in one smooth thrust. "I *love* you. I will come back to you, do you hear me?" he breathed, his words punctuated by his pounding hips.

"Promise me," she gasped, her nails sinking into the damp skin of his back.

"I promise you, Angelina."

She took his promise inside of her and locked it safely away. It was all she had in the world that was hers and hers alone. Nothing else belonged to her—not her future, not her happiness—not even herself.

CHAPTER NINETEEN

Steam rose from a nearby manhole cover as Clara stepped off the curb, glancing both ways before crossing the narrow, deserted street.

This was obviously not the safest of neighborhoods, but Clara was determined to get to the address she'd looked up online, the address of a shop belonging to Fabienne Simoneaux, who advertised herself as a voodoo priestess providing healing and spiritual comfort. It was the small line at the bottom of the ad that had given Clara the most hope: "Descended from a long line of voodoo priestesses."

Clara had called the number listed on the ad—repeatedly—only to get a message telling her the voicemail connected to that number was full.

So she was headed to the address where she hoped to have better luck. She didn't know if Fabienne Simoneaux was a distant relative of Sibille, but apparently, there was only one way to find out.

Clara glanced over her shoulder, swearing she'd heard footsteps, but the street behind her was deserted, not a soul in sight.

Despite that the sky was still light, no shadows to fear, a strange bristling at the nape of her neck caused her to shiver, and she unfolded the printout of the ad, double-checking the shop number. It should be right ahead, on the next block. She hurried toward it.

Jonah had warned her not to do this, and realistically, she knew she should be cautious. Bad things happened to women alone in questionable neighborhoods all the time. But that damn ticking feeling was growing louder, more insistent, and she could not sit idly by if there might be information somewhere waiting for her. It simply wasn't in her nature to hesitate.

She gripped the address in one hand and kept her other hand in her pocket, her fingers curled around the container of pepper spray.

Clara walked past several boarded-up businesses, a Laundromat, a framing shop, and what had once been a deli. Was this one of the neighborhoods still recovering from Hurricane Katrina?

Mr. Baptiste had told her some sections of New Orleans were still struggling to get back on their feet, though the disaster had occurred over a decade before. *How awful.*

Were any of the shops still open for business? A sinking feeling descended over Clara, right before she spied the one she was looking for, the sign chipped but *there.* She was even more relieved to see light coming from under the door, even though the windows had been painted over with black paint.

Clara tried the door but it was locked, and so she knocked, putting both hands in her jacket pockets as she waited. She heard footsteps from within and then the door was pulled open to reveal a woman with long, black curly hair and one of the most beautiful faces Clara had ever seen in her life. She was wearing low-slung jeans and a crop top that exposed almost all of her smooth, mocha belly. "Yeah?"

"Hi. Are you Fabienne?"

The woman eyed her. "Who's asking?"

Clara held out her hand and Fabienne took it suspiciously. "Hi, I'm Clara, and I was hoping you were open for business and I could ask you a couple of questions?"

"Questions about what?"

Clara heard voices in the street and glanced behind her. "May I come in?"

Fabienne glanced over Clara's shoulder, pressing her lips together before looking back at Clara. She sighed. "Spiritual readings are a hundred and fifty."

"Oh, I don't want a read—"

"Spiritual readings are a hundred and fifty."

"Right," Clara said, drawing out the word as understanding dawned. This woman was only going to answer questions if she paid her.

"I don't have that much cash on me."

"I take credit."

Clara stared at her for a second, the woman's dark gaze steadfast, without a hint of apology. "All right, but before I pay for a spiritual reading, I need to know if you're a relative of Sibille Simoneaux."

Fabienne looked over her shoulder and pointed to a picture high up on the wall in a grouping of other photographs.

Clara walked toward it, squinting her eyes as she peered at the picture of an old, old woman, her eyes milky white, as she seemed to stare straight into the camera. "That's her?" she murmured, a small chill moving down her spine.

Those eyes . . . Clara swore they followed her as she walked slowly back to where Fabienne stood, though obviously even in life, they'd followed nothing.

"That's Sibille," Fabienne said.

Clara pulled her credit card from the inside pocket of her jacket, handing it over to Fabienne.

Fabienne took the card and swiped it on the card reader already plugged into her phone and then handed it to Clara to sign. Clara scrawled quickly, trying not to think about the fact that she had just given up a hundred and fifty dollars toward her car down payment. *This had better be worth it,* Clara thought, though she was already skeptical.

"What do you want to know?" Fabienne asked, sitting down on a black velvet sofa that had seen better days and crossing her long legs.

"Do I get a spiritual reading along with my questions?" Clara asked, taking a seat on the wooden chair across from her.

"That's extra."

That made absolutely no sense and Clara stopped just short of rolling her eyes. Not that she wanted a spiritual reading from the woman, who she had a feeling might have scammed her out of a hundred and fifty bucks.

"I'm interested in the story of John Whitfield, a southern soldier, and Angelina Loreaux, a slave. They're the two spirits said to be trapped at Winisle Plantation."

"Okay." Clara was relieved. Fabienne knew of them and was willing to give information.

"Your"—what would Sibille be to Fabienne? A sixth great-grandmother maybe?—"relative spoke a riddle at a party that she said would break the curse put upon John Whitfield. The curse that somehow tangled Angelina as well and keeps them both trapped at Windisle Plantation. Do you know the riddle?"

"Refresh my memory." Fabienne's eyes darted up the stairs as a baby began to cry, but when the crying stopped a moment later, Fabienne's gaze returned to Clara. Either the baby had cried out in sleep or someone had responded to it.

Clara bit at her lip, moving her mind back to their conversation. "Sibille said the *only* thing that could break the curse that Angelina's mother, Mama Loreaux, put on John Whitfield, is a drop of Angelina's blood being brought to the light."

Fabienne stared at Clara, unmoved. "You believe in that?"

"Believe in . . . curses? Or that they can be broken?" She wasn't sure about anything involving ghost stories, or curses, or riddles said to break them. It was all so . . . beyond her. But she didn't know which other leads to follow that might provide the answers to the many questions swirling in her head.

Maybe the legend of Angelina and John being trapped wasn't even true. Perhaps their spirits didn't wander the rose garden, blind to the presence of the other, eternally trapped, despite the stories and the reported sightings, despite the definite weeping she'd experienced at the wall that day with Jonah.

But there was a reason John betrayed Angelina, a reason he never married Astrid Chamberlain, a reason—

"No. Curses are very real." Fabienne leaned forward. "And every curse has a weak spot—something that, if done in the right way, will break it and set the person free."

Fabienne pointed her finger at the gallery of portraits hanging on the wall. "That's what that old blind priestess must have meant. Good luck solving the riddle."

Clara frowned. Good *luck?* "That old blind priestess? I thought she was related to you."

Fabienne shook her head. "I never said that."

"But your last names—"

"There are thousands of Simoneauxes in New Orleans."

Good grief. Clara sighed. She couldn't even be mad. Clara had made all the assumptions while this woman had neatly convinced her to hand over a decent sum of money that she could have used better elsewhere. *Great.* She almost demanded Fabienne give her a refund, but was interrupted by the baby who began crying upstairs again, this time in earnest. Clara looked at Fabienne. "Do you have any knowledge at all of John Whitfield and Angelina Loreaux?"

Fabienne studied her nails for a second, though Clara sensed that her casual display was an act. Her muscles looked tensed to go to the crying baby. "Just what you told me. Sounds like quite the story."

Clara's shoulders dropped and she began to stand. "It is. You should look it up." She turned to leave.

Fabienne stood too. "I can tell you one thing, though." Clara turned back toward her. "Curses do not trap those they're not intended for."

"What . . . what do you mean?" Clara asked as the baby's wail increased in strength and volume and Fabienne began inching toward a set of stairs that obviously led to living quarters.

"If there was a curse put on John, Angelina isn't locked in it. If Angelina lingers, she lingers for him. For the soldier man."

The baby let out another sharp wail and Clara nodded at Fabienne, thanking her before letting herself out the door of the shop.

For a moment she stood in the doorway overhang, Fabienne's words ringing in her head. *If Angelina lingers, she lingers for him.* But *why?* Why would a woman linger for a man who, until the moment of her tragic death, she believed had betrayed her? Or . . . so the story went.

The bare bulb hanging in the doorway suddenly extinguished and Clara realized that in the time she'd been in the shop, sunset had come and gone.

The streets were now dark, though sounds—both distant and nearby—told her that this place was not as deserted as it seemed.

A dog barked, another answering, something that sounded like the lid of a garbage can clattered on the ground, someone laughed and glass broke just down the street, spurring Clara to begin walking toward the bus stop a couple of streets over.

She had planned on hiring an Uber to get to the shop, but there had been a wait for a driver when she'd gone to schedule one. A quick check of the bus schedule had told her she could get there more quickly that way.

She'd assumed it was an area full of plenty of well-lit businesses, but if that had been the case once upon a time, it definitely wasn't now.

However, the chill that moved down her spine convinced her that rather than walking a few blocks in the unfamiliar, questionably safe neighborhood, she'd call for a ride.

She stopped walking, stepping into a shadowy doorway and taking her phone from her pocket.

"You here for me?"

Clara let out a startled yelp, whirling around to see a homeless man slumped in the corner. He laughed, holding up a bottle in a paper bag. "Join me, sweetheart."

Clara stepped quickly from the doorway, mumbling some form of apology that didn't even really register in her terrified brain. The man laughed as Clara hurried down the street.

Behind her, she heard footsteps, the sound of a shoe splashing in a puddle and she sped up even more.

"Hey, you," someone else said, the voice deeper than that of the homeless man and close behind her. Another man called something to her she couldn't hear, and when she looked behind her, she saw two men walking with a pair of muscled pit bulls. Her heart rate spiked, adrenaline racing through her.

Clara crossed the street, holding the pepper spray in a death grip in her pocket, her fear escalating when the men crossed the street, too, the dogs growling. *Oh God.* What had she gotten herself into?

She should have remained in Fabienne's doorway and called an Uber from there and waited. *Stupid, stupid.*

The men were conversing with each other behind her as if this situation was the most casual thing in the world to them, which scared her even more.

Something shattered in an open courtyard next to where she walked, followed by the sound of someone swearing viciously and the dogs behind her began growling.

"You best get home, girl. You don't belong here," the person in the courtyard tossed out at her. Clara ran.

The well-lit bus stop in front of an open gas station was just two blocks away. If she could make it there, she would be fine.

"You don't want to go that way," one of the men called. She didn't answer, didn't look back.

She ran one block, her heart thundering in her ears, the sound of pounding feet following her and ratcheting up her terror. *Oh God.*

Tears streamed down her face and her breath came out in sharp gasps as she turned the corner onto the street where the bus stop was—and that well-lit gas station where a clerk would call the police for her—only to find that she'd made a wrong turn somewhere.

It was another dark, deserted street and Clara let out a sob as she sprinted down it anyway, trying desperately to outrun the men following her. *Get a hold of yourself. You're strong. You have the stamina to outrun anyone.* A burst of adrenaline spiked through her. *Yes!* Her muscles were strong and toned. She would outrun the bastards behind her.

She heard the dogs' pants as they followed, heard their nails hitting the pavement along with the sounds of the men's boots, and Clara sprinted into the dark street, devoid of any street lamps.

A fence met her at the end of the street and Clara let out a fearful, frustrated grunt, banging her hands on the chains. *Oh God, oh no.*

She glanced behind her to see that the two men were at the end of the street, walking slowly, the dogs straining at the leashes.

"Hey, stop, we just want to talk to you." *As if.*

Clara swallowed down the lump of fear in her throat, turning back to the fence and climbing. She swung one leg over gracefully, and for a moment, her heart lifted, hope dancing through her veins. She was going to make it and the dogs would not be able to climb this high.

Clara swung her other leg over, her foot trying to find a spot to land in the holes of the fence when a shadow moved behind the men, growing in a small shaft of moonlight until it loomed up behind them, impossibly huge.

She gasped and her foot slipped just as the men turned toward the approaching shadow.

"What the fuck are you?" one of the men asked and Clara heard the uncertainty—the fear—lacing his question.

She grabbed for the fence, but she'd leaned too far back and her finger merely brushed a metal link.

Clara screamed, turning her head to see the pavement rushing toward her and all went black.

CHAPTER TWENTY

Clara smelled him—*Jonah. My wish collector.* His scent was against her nose, that clean, masculine smell she'd breathed in in the masquerade ball's courtyard and had yearned to breathe in every day since.

She was sleeping and in her dream, he was carrying her, his strong arms wrapped around her body.

Her head cleared slightly, a small moan coming up her throat as some distant fear poked at her memory.

"Shh," he said. It was his voice. She wasn't mistaken. She might not be as familiar with his scent—it would have been possible to get that part wrong. But his voice? *No,* she'd know his voice anywhere. It flowed through her veins and invaded her cells. It had become part of her.

"Can you hold on to me?"

"I am holding on to you," she said, her speech garbled, feeling the lean strength of him as her arms tightened very slightly around his shoulders.

"I mean tightly." He sat down on something, holding her on his lap.

She burrowed into him, the fog clearing slightly as she opened an eye and then clenched it shut again, the bare slip of light causing her head to throb.

"Never mind," he said very softly as if to himself. She just wanted to sleep. She was safe—safe with Jonah—and she just needed to shut her eyes for a little while. "Too dangerous."

What? What's too dangerous?

She drifted, swearing she heard him speaking to someone. But his arms were around her and it felt so good, and she was so warm. There was no danger at all.

She slept and when she woke, she heard the slamming of a car door, and then another. Someone spoke to Jonah, his voice raspy and filled with concern, and then she was in Jonah's arms again, being laid on something soft. "Don't leave me," she whispered.

Clara turned, her eyes opening slightly, vision blurry. His face swam in front of her, her heart jumping slightly as he drew closer. The light was so dim and he was so shadowy.

His face moved closer, her breath hitching, skeletal bones sharpening as the gap between them closed.

Clara's breath released on a loud whoosh of air, her fingers tracing the rubber cheekbone on his mask. "Don't leave me," she said again. He could wear a mask if he wanted to, he could put a paper bag over his head if he chose . . . she only wanted him *there,* with her.

He seemed to still very slightly, and she saw his eyes moving under his mask.

"You were following me," she murmured, reality flowing in and bringing with it the memory of the men, the dogs, the fence. It had been *him,* the shadow behind them that had made her lose her footing and fall.

"Good thing." His voice was gritty, and she saw a muscle in his exposed jaw tick. "You might have a concussion."

He brought his hand to her hair, moving it off her forehead. She noted a stinging sensation and her head throbbed again. "How do you feel?"

"Sore. And I have a headache. Where am I?"

"Windisle."

Excitement thrummed through her, but right then she was still in pain, her head was foggy, and she was more interested in the man in front of her. *Physically.* She understood his need to hide, but he still felt distant too behind that mask of his.

Jonah moved back into the shadows and Clara sank into the soft pillow behind her head. It smelled even more strongly of him. She was in *his bed*?

A tremble went through her right before he reappeared, handing her a glass of water and two tablets. Clara placed the tablets in her mouth and swallowed them with a sip of water.

She closed her eyes as Jonah moved away and when he came back, he applied something cool and wet to her forehead. It stung very slightly, though Clara didn't grimace.

When he brought the white cloth away, she saw a trace of dried blood. It should concern her, but she was in his bed. He was by her side. Touching her. *I'm safe. Even if I'm slightly hurt.*

"I'm not used to playing the damsel in distress."

The corner of his mouth tipped upward. "No, I imagine you're used to running the show." He paused as he dabbed at her cut again and then smeared some type of ointment on it. "And I thought dancers knew how to leap."

Clara laughed then winced when her head throbbed. "Not quite that high. There were men after me—men with *dogs.*"

Jonah peeled the backing off a large Band-Aid and laid it on her wound with a little more pressure than Clara thought was necessary. "The Brass Angels."

"The . . . what?"

"They're a gang, but the good sort. They protect the streets of New Orleans, especially neighborhoods like the one you were in. There had been a robbery in the area. They wanted to ask you some questions, that's all."

"Oh." Right, *oh. Good grief.* Now she really felt like a fool.

"Still," Jonah said, his voice grating over her skin though not in an unpleasant way, "it was plain stupid to be wandering those streets alone."

"I wasn't wandering. I'd gone to see a voodoo priestess I thought might be related to Sibille Simoneaux."

His hand stilled and he sighed. "I never should have given you that name. You couldn't sit still once you had it, could you?" He was scolding her, but she loved the underlying warmth in his voice.

Clara sat up slightly, flinching when a slice of pain lanced through her skull. "No. I told you, Jonah, I feel this . . . I don't know, *urgency*."

Despite her declaration of urgency, she suddenly felt zapped of strength and sank back into the softness of Jonah's bed, her limbs and her eyes heavy.

"You can get back to ghost hunting tomorrow," he said. "For now, you need to sleep. I'm going to wake you up a few times in case you do have a concussion. Myrtle will see you out in the morning."

As if she'd heard her name, an old woman with deep brown skin and beaded cornrows that danced around her full face, came into the room. Clara knew immediately she was Myrtle and smiled at her, attempting to sit up.

"No, no," Myrtle said, gesturing for her to lie down. She looked at Jonah, pushing her thick-lensed glasses up on her nose and scowling. "Good gracious, you could put someone in an early grave wearing that thing."

She looked back at Clara, squinting slightly despite the glasses. "I heard he almost did. You're lucky you just got a bump on your head."

She moved closer, studying her with those dark, magnified eyes and laid her cool palm against Clara's forehead and then put her knuckles on Clara's cheek as if testing for fever. Seeming satisfied, her expression evened out, and she sat on the side of the bed.

Jonah stood, walking to Clara's side of the bed where he picked up the empty glass. "I'm going to go fill this so you have water during the night if you get thirsty."

Clara nodded and watched him as he walked to the door. Her eyes lingered on his tall physique, apparently not too concussed to appreciate his muscular backside and strong, broad shoulders.

When she looked back at Myrtle, Myrtle was watching her with a small smile on her lips, and Clara blushed, looking down.

"Jonah wanted me to come in and introduce myself and let you know I'm in the bedroom right next door if you need me."

Clara frowned. "Oh, okay. Thank you."

"I suppose he imagines you might be frightened if you think you're alone here with him."

Clara shook her head. "I'm not scared of him, Myrtle. Not even a little bit."

Myrtle smiled, and it was warm and soft, her deep-set eyes shimmering under her lenses with what Clara thought were tears. "No, I can see you're not."

Myrtle reached out and took Clara's hand, squeezing it softly. "I'll let you rest now. You come on down to the kitchen in the morning, and I'll make you something good and hearty to eat before you go."

Clara nodded, biting at her lip. Jonah had said Myrtle would show her out in the morning, meaning he likely wouldn't be around. Why? Because he'd only allow her to see him—even in a mask—in the dark of night?

Myrtle stood and began to turn. "Myrtle?"

She turned back toward Clara, tilting her head.

Clara sat up just a bit, leaning on her elbow. "Myrtle, what does he look like under that mask?" She asked it on a whisper, feeling as if she were betraying Jonah by even posing the question, but too curious to let the opportunity pass.

Sadness passed over Myrtle's expression for a fleeting moment, her eyes filling with the unconditional love Clara could already see she had for him. "He looks like a man who's been terribly hurt by the world and believes there is nothing left to love about him anymore."

Clara's heart constricted so tightly it was almost a physical pain.

Myrtle gave her one heart-rending smile and quietly left. Clara heard her say something right outside the door and a response in Jonah's smooth, rich voice, then he was entering the room.

He put the full glass of water on the nightstand. "Here you go. If you need anything else tonight, Myrtle—"

"Please don't go, Jonah. Lie with me."

Jonah hesitated, bringing a hand to his mask as if unconsciously, opening his mouth to speak and then closing it.

"Keep that on if you want. I'd just like you to stay. Please."

"Clara—"

"Please."

He let out a gust of breath, hesitating again, then nodding slowly. He reached across her, shutting off the lamp that had emitted a very low light, darkness draping over them.

He lay next to her, and for a moment she held her breath, the nearness of him causing the blood flowing through her veins to hum.

She turned slowly toward him, resting her head on his shoulder and closing her eyes. She felt his muscles tense for a brief moment, but then he relaxed, bringing his arm up and turning slightly so she was warm and protected in the cradle of his arms, her head resting under his chin.

Clara closed her eyes, loving the way he made her feel both safe and agitated in some twisty way that was pleasant and exciting. And she liked that she couldn't see that mask that hid him from her.

The mask was unsettling because it stared at her, expressionless and unmoving. And that wasn't the man whose arms held her. He wasn't expressionless. Unmoving. He was sensitive and deeply caring whether he believed it of himself or not.

I do. I believe, she whispered inside of herself.

She reached her hand up and ran it down the portion of exposed jaw and he stilled under her touch.

"Jonah," she whispered. "In the dark, I picture you the way I saw you in the pictures on the Internet because it's the only thing I have to go by."

He remained silent, though she sensed his sudden tension.

"But that feels wrong. Because I know you're not that man anymore, and I want you to know that I don't need you to be. I want to *see* you. I want to *know* you."

She drew back and in the pewter light of the darkened room, lit only by the moonlight slipping through the edges of the gauzy curtains, she looked into his masked eyes.

Jonah made a small strangled sound in the back of his throat and broke eye contact, pulling her to him.

"You can picture me the way I was, Clara. I'm glad you know I'm not, but, trust me, it's better this way."

Clara was silent. She couldn't believe that. She cared about him so much, cared about him as a person, as a man. She wasn't so superficial that she couldn't accept his scars. And wouldn't it *free* him to show them to her? He couldn't enjoy wearing a mask. But . . . she couldn't force him to reveal himself. She kept *doing* that . . . pushing him when he wasn't ready and then regretting it later. She burrowed into him. "I'm pushy, aren't I?"

He chuckled softly. "Yeah, you are." But he didn't sound mad about it, and his hand was doing something wonderful and calming on her lower back, making her feel warm and sleepy.

And when his arms were around her like this and he was touching her, there was nothing more important in the world—not curses, or riddles, or stories about people long gone from this earth. Not scars or masks or walls or things that kept him from her. There was only his tenderness and his heart and his voice. Only *him.* And only her.

When she woke, the sunlight was streaming into the room.

Clara sat up, blinking as she looked around. There was still a dull ache in her head, but she felt better and remembered blearily Jonah waking her up several times during the night, speaking to her for a moment in that hypnotic voice of his and then letting her fall back into sleep. Clara sat up, swinging her legs over the side of the high bed and looking around the room.

There was a beautifully carved fireplace on the opposite wall and the mahogany furniture was obviously vintage. It was old and sparse except for the few pieces of furniture, but it still held charm and elegance due to the molding on the walls and the wide-planked wooden floor that squeaked as she put her weight on it.

Something on the bedside table caught her eye and she picked up a folder with her name written on the front in blocky print.

She opened it, her eyes widening with delight when she saw what it was. It was the folder Jonah's brother, Justin, had put together of Chamberlain family information. Jonah had hunted it down and left it for her. She squeezed it to her chest. *Please,* she thought, hope and excitement swirling through her, *please let there be something important inside. And let me recognize it when I see it.*

CHAPTER TWENTY-ONE

Jonah stood off to the side of the house as Myrtle showed Clara out, his heart clenching as he watched her leave.

The women chatted animatedly, Myrtle's arms moving as she punctuated her words the way she did. Clara laughed and the sound carried to Jonah, making his gut clench with want, where he stood watching them from the dimness of the surrounding trees.

He wanted to see her out, he did, but he couldn't wear the mask during the day. It would make what was already creepy, just weird and clownish. At least in the dark of night, the creepiness sort of took on an edge of *fiendish,* and fiendish he could live with. Clownish he could not.

Beasts were alluring in the dead of night, weren't they? There was a reason they hid in the light of day. And anyway, the damn mask was uncomfortable after a while—rubbery and sweaty—and he longed to rip it off and toss it aside, to feel the cool air on the damaged skin of his face.

Myrtle said something and Clara looked beyond her for a moment to the plantation house.

Jonah turned his good eye toward her, straining to see the expression on her pretty face. *Awe,* he thought. Yes, the look on her face was full of wonderment as if she were gazing upon some place of worship. And damn if he didn't feel jealous of the inanimate structure.

Clara returned her gaze to Myrtle and smiled warmly as she waved, slipping through the gate on the side of the property as Myrtle latched it behind her. The sound was lonely, reminding Jonah of the empty day that stretched before him.

A moment later, Jonah heard a car moving away, taking Clara home. He watched as Myrtle ambled back to the house, talking to herself as she walked.

And despite his mundane thoughts about hiding in the trees, his heart rejoiced. Clara knew of his scars and cared for him anyway. And God, it had felt so good to be held. To feel her softness against him, to listen to the sounds of her breathing as she'd slept. And yet it unsettled him too.

He had thought that to watch her dance once would sustain him all the rest of his long, lonely days—but in fact, it had done the opposite. It had made him long for *more.* So yes, Cecil was right. He pined. God damn, but he pined. It was a constant pang throbbing in his veins.

And now, to have the memory of her arms around him, his name on her lips as she drifted into dreams, it just increased his longing for life, for her, for things he could never have.

He put his hands in the pockets of his sweatshirt, feeling the small, smooth card within. He brought it out, staring at the information printed on it. Who knew gang members had business cards? Just a name and an address and the memory of the offer the man named Ruben with the obvious prison tattoos on his face had made: "You ever need a night gig, masked man, you call me. We could use you." And then he'd laughed, but it hadn't been unkind. In fact, it'd been laced with respect, and it had made Jonah feel damn good, despite that a moaning Clara lay limply in his arms, and he'd needed to get her someplace safe.

Speaking of which . . . he'd have to have Myrtle or Cecil come with him to collect his motorcycle later. Once he'd determined Clara was still too out of it to ride behind him safely, he'd called them to pick them up, leaving the bike chained up where he'd secured it after following Clara's bus.

Jonah sighed, stepping out of the trees and tipping his face to the bruised sky. It was going to rain.

He walked to the wall, laying his palm on the solid stone. Right there was where it'd all started to change. And he still couldn't decide if the change that had begun in him was a good thing or would bring nothing but deeper misery in the end.

Several feet away he heard the sound of footsteps on the other side of the wall and then a male sigh just before a piece of paper was slipped between one of the cracks, landing on the dewy grass.

The man's footsteps moved away, the sound of a car starting up and then driving in the opposite direction meeting Jonah's ears a minute later.

The ink was already bleeding because of the dew it'd landed in as Jonah unfolded it carefully, reading the wish.

"I wish I had a reason not to jump from the CCC tonight. Anything. Just anything." *Christ. The CCC.*

The Crescent City Connection, the bridge that spanned the Mississippi River, connecting downtown New Orleans to the West Bank. He'd driven it often when he'd lived a normal life.

Jonah leaned against the wall, swearing it trembled beneath his weight. The ancient thing was getting so old, it would probably crumble at the barest of touches one of these days.

He fingered the message, putting it in his pocket and then bringing it out along with Ruben's card.

Some guy was planning to jump off a bridge tonight and was looking for a reason—any reason—not to. Jonah thought about that, thought about the fact that if anyone knew how destitute a person could feel, how hopeless and clueless about their own place in the world, it was him.

He'd considered—maybe not strongly, but still—ending his own life a time or two, but Myrtle and Cecil's relentless love and care of him had stopped him from considering it too closely. He'd had that. He'd had *them,* and gratitude suddenly spiked within his chest so fiercely that it caused a physical pang. A tightening.

Maybe Justin had been right when he'd often said that there was always something to be grateful for. He'd written off half the things Justin said—he was practically religious in his optimism and it had, frankly, annoyed Jonah. But . . . well. Maybe that one held some truth.

Would he have actually survived this long without Myrtle and Cecil? Had their unwavering belief in him been an unnamed consolation within his grief and anger and pain? *And this man has nothing.*

Yet.

In any case, how negligent would Jonah be if he didn't do something to try and stop a man from ending his own life? He stood there for another moment, considering, and then pushed off the wall.

He had plans tonight after all.

****

Eddy stared at the churning water below. Fear rumbled through him, but not loud enough to quiet the roaring emptiness that gaped open like a festering wound inside of his soul. The emptiness that felt vast and unending, a black hole of pain.

He'd have thought emptiness would dull his senses, but no, it seemed to make everything sharper, more piercing somehow. He couldn't live with it any longer. He just wanted it to *end.* And that water below was going to do just that.

Drown out the noise, the hurt, the memories, and yes, the breath from his lungs . . . because he couldn't see another way.

He *wanted* to. He wished he had *something*, some form of hope that things could get better. He'd even gone to that stupid wall, which was, well, stupid. But nothing was going to change, and he couldn't face another day of this never ending agony.

"Pretty far drop."

He sucked in a startled breath of exhaust and river-water-scented air, gripping the metal bar in his hand more tightly as he turned his head.

"S-step back," Eddy demanded in a voice that sounded less than commanding.

He'd chosen a spot that was out of sight of the cars driving by on the bridge. How had this guy spotted him?

The older black man wearing a leather vest and a dark bandana around what appeared to be a completely bald head didn't flinch and didn't move back. In fact, he stepped forward, his eyes locked on Eddy's. "You're a Marine."

"Was," Eddy said. He wasn't sure why he'd put on his uniform before going out there. It'd seemed to make sense at the time. He should have died on that stretch of desert highway half a world away like all six of his buddies did, but instead, he'd been saved for some unfathomable reason that brought him nothing but regret. So he'd die in his uniform after all, even if his death would be by his own hand.

"Yeah," the man sighed, as if he'd understood far more than was contained in that singular word. "It's never really past tense though, is it?"

He leaned against the giant metal support, putting his hands in his pockets as if this were a situation he came across every day of the week and therefore wasn't fazed in the least.

Eddy tilted his head, taking the guy in. He was probably in his sixties, but still muscular. He obviously stayed in shape, and his attire made him look like some kind of biker.

Eddy couldn't read the patches sewn onto the front of his vest from where he stood, but he assumed they spoke of whatever organizations he belonged to. *Belonged to.* The words rung in his head and he wasn't sure why. They made him wince. They made him yearn. "You were a Marine too?"

"Yup. Came back from Vietnam in sixty-nine. Stood right where you are now more than once."

"You tried to jump off a bridge?"

The man chuckled though there was something painful in it. "Nah. Drugs and alcohol were my ledges."

"Oh." Eddy turned toward the water again, looking into that swirling vastness once more. It looked choppier than it had before. Colder, darker.

"Thing is," the guy said from behind him. Eddy looked back at him again. "Thing is, we could use a guy like you. A retired soldier who's already trained."

Eddy frowned. "Use me for *what?*"

"The Brass Angels."

"You're a Brass Angel?" Eddy had heard of them. They were a volunteer crime-fighting force in New Orleans who patrolled high-crime neighborhoods.

"I'm the head of the New Orleans chapter as a matter of fact." The man moved closer. "Name's Augustus Bryant."

"Eddy Woods." Augustus took another step closer, reaching his hand out to shake.

Eddy reached out tentatively, taking it. Augustus gripped his hand and though his hand was being held tightly, something inside of Eddy loosened. Eddy pulled in a huge breath.

"Come on down, Eddy. Maybe we can talk about how you can fit with us."

Eddy paused for the fraction of a moment, recalling the wish he'd made earlier that day. The wish he'd called stupid a few minutes ago. *I wish I had a reason not to jump from the CCC tonight. Anything.*

Anything, he'd asked for. Well this was something wasn't it? Hell, it *felt* like something. It felt like the first *something* in a long, long time, maybe since that day he'd seen his buddies blown to smithereens in front of his face. That day when he'd stood up with nary a scratch on him as the blood of the men he'd been laughing with moments before rained down from the sky to drench the sand in shades of scarlet death.

Eddy gripped Augustus's hand and stepped down from the ledge. Augustus didn't let go.

"I know, man. I do. Feels like it's too painful to live in a world where God allows things to happen like what you've seen. Nothing makes sense. No purpose."

"Yes," Eddy said, something else unknotting inside of him, making him feel weak.

"Yeah," Augustus said. "Yeah." He looked straight into his eyes. "There's light in the darkness, man. I promise you.

And you're going to be a part of it. There's *no one* better than you to be a part of it."

Eddy swiped at the tears that had filled his eyes, suddenly so overwhelmed with gratitude for the trickle of hope moving swiftly through him that he could only nod.

"Come on out, guys," Augustus called, and Eddy's head whipped to the side where two men emerged. As they stepped from the shadows, Eddy's heart jolted. One of them was wearing a skeleton mask that covered half his face.

"What the fuck?" Eddy muttered.

Augustus chuckled. "That's what I thought too." He gestured to the man without the mask, the man who didn't look much less sinister with the tattoos marking up his face. "That's Ruben." Then he pointed to the guy wearing the skeleton facade. "And that's Jonah."

Jonah walked forward and shook Eddy's hand. "I'm glad to meet you, Eddy." There was something in his eyes, some deep solemnity. Eddy didn't know the exact reason why, but he bet any guy who went around wearing a mask had some kind of story to tell.

"Jonah."

Augustus smiled, putting one hand on Jonah's shoulder, and one on Eddy's. He looked at them, something that looked like pride shining from his knowing eyes. "We've got ourselves a kickass team."

Eddy laughed. Nothing about him felt kickass, but something about the motley crew surrounding him offered quiet calm. *And he could live with that.* He could *live* with that.

****

"How are you, Jonah?"

"I'm good." He smiled as he swiped the rain that had fallen earlier that evening off the garden bench and sat, leaning back and wiping his wet palm on his sweatshirt.

"You *sound* good. I can hear it in your voice."

He leaned his head back, closing his eyes to the stars, bringing the memory of her lips to the forefront of his mind.

That achy pulsing took up in his veins, and he supposed he should hate it—hate that it signified what he couldn't have—but he couldn't manage to do it in that moment. He felt too good, too filled with something that felt dangerously like hope.

Jonah heard something that sounded like a drawer opening and closing. "Are you just getting home?"

Clara sighed. "Yeah. Late practice. When I get off the phone with you, I'm going to take a hot shower and then fall face first into bed."

He couldn't let himself think too much about that hot shower and less about Clara in bed, but the *face first* thing made him think of her fall. "How's your head?"

"Better. I had a bit of a headache earlier today, but a couple more Tylenol took care of it."

She paused for a moment. "Jonah, I didn't ask why you were following me last night. I don't mind," she rushed on, "in fact, I'm grateful you were, but . . . well, why? Why do you follow me?"

Jonah opened his eyes, his gaze moving between the stars that made up the big dipper.

It was so clear tonight, so vibrant, and bright. Those stars, they'd watched it all unfold, every story since the beginning of time. He wondered how many times their hearts had been broken by what they saw.

"Because I want to be near you," he said without considering his words. *I crave you. I want to protect you.*

There was a small pause and Jonah's heart jumped. He sat up, blinking. "I'll stop," he said, letting out an uncomfortable chuckle. "I wasn't always this creepy. It's just—"

"Stop," she said softly. "I want to be near you too. You don't have to follow me anonymously. I want to be near *you.*"

Jonah's heart jumped again, this time with happiness, though that thread of disappointment, of the knowledge that he could never have more than what they had right that moment, pulled at his joy, making it feel tight and breakable.

"Anyway," she said, changing the subject, perhaps sensing that his thoughts were meandering toward bleakness, "I called because I looked through Justin's folder during lunch today."

Justin's folder. He loved that his brother was a real person to her, loved hearing her acknowledge him. "Yeah? What'd you find?"

"Something interesting, actually. Do you know a lot about Reconstruction?"

"The basics, I guess. That after the Union won the Civil War and millions of slaves were freed, there were lots of societal challenges."

"Yes. And did you know that the man Astrid Chamberlain married, Herbert Davies, was a champion for the rights of former slaves during that time?"

Jonah frowned. "I didn't know that, but I never knew a lot about Herbert Davies."

"Apparently, he was a prominent activist. I still need to read through all the information your brother printed, but what's really interesting is that some of what I read implies that his wife, Astrid, worked alongside him in his efforts. There are letters included in the file where they trade ideas about his work."

"Huh," he said. "I mean, it's good to hear that one of my ancestors was on the side of right. But what do you take from all that?"

"I don't know yet." Her voice was thoughtful. "I guess it speaks to Astrid's later beliefs on the subject of slavery. And it makes me question what her role may have been in her half-sister's tragedy. Nothing that I've heard, until this, indicated Astrid might have been sympathetic to Angelina's circumstances, or that she might have disagreed with her family's owning of slaves."

"Huh," he said. Although in all honesty, Jonah couldn't see how the information shed any more light on what may have happened so long ago in the very place where he was sitting.

He glanced at the broken fountain, empty except for the small amount of accumulated rain and the leaves that had fallen into it and turned to muck. *Right there.* Right there was where Angelina had felt so barren of hope that she'd taken a razor blade to her own wrists. A tiny shiver went down his spine.

"It's just another piece of the puzzle, you know? I feel like . . . I feel like we're getting close to something."

He loved the hopeful tone in her voice, the underlying excitement, and he wouldn't dash that, but even if there were a mystery to solve, how in the world would they confirm any of it?

Too many decades had passed, too much evidence had turned to dust, and too many stories and truths had died along with those who'd carried them.

"Thank you for helping me."

"I'm happy to." And he was, despite his lack of belief that any of this would come to anything. But he'd damn near do anything for the girl on the other end of his phone.

"I didn't tell you about what the priestess I went to said."

Oh right. *The priestess.* He'd seen her enter that shop and waited in a doorway until she came out. "What'd she say?"

Clara sighed. "She might have been a bit of a . . . well anyway, she gave me some good general information. You know how the legend says that Angelina is trapped at Windisle because she somehow became tangled in the curse put upon John?"

"Yeah."

"The priestess, Fabienne, said that it isn't how it works. Other people cannot become tangled in curses that aren't put directly on them."

"Okay . . ."

"So," Clara said, speaking faster, that energy that made her eyes sparkle, filling her voice, "Fabienne guessed that if Angelina lingers at Windisle, it's by choice. It's because of John that she stays."

"I don't get it."

Clara let out a breath. "The legend is wrong. There's something about it that's not accurate."

"What?"

"That's what we have to figure out. Why would Angelina choose to stay trapped for eternity, waiting endlessly for a man who betrayed her? It has to be important, Jonah. Angelina lived her life in chains—almost literally. She wouldn't choose to spend her afterlife in such a way if it wasn't vital to her soul. Is she waiting for some sort of revenge? Or does she continue to love John despite his betrayal? There's a reason she won't leave him, Jonah, and we have to figure it out.

"And for that matter, why does John linger at Windisle? Is it because Windisle is the place where the curse was placed upon him?" She paused. "Or," the word rushed out on an excited breath, "is Windisle somehow involved in breaking it?"

For a moment Jonah had gotten lost in the earnest passion in her voice, and he had to take several seconds to go back over her actual words to respond. "Clara, I don't know that I believe in ghosts, but unless you can speak to them, I don't see a way to solve any of this."

Clara sighed and Jonah regretted his words. He hated to say something to dampen her exuberance, but he also wasn't going to pretend to believe things that had no basis in real life.

There was not only no point to that, but it was dangerous to him on a personal level. Jonah was not a man who could afford to get lost in fantasy. There was no telling where his mind would go if he gave it free rein to dream. Even if the topic involved those long dead and gone.

"There's a way," she murmured. "I realize all the ghost stuff is supposition, but . . . I still think there's something to be found if we know what we're looking for."

The foliage rustled around him and he sat up, a shaft of pearly moonlight highlighting a thorny rosebush empty of all blossoms. Next to it, a walking fern, which was mostly disguised in shadows, shook. Jonah's skin prickled, as if Angelina herself had heard him speak his doubt and was about to prove how wrong he was.

The fern shook more vigorously and a small bunny jumped suddenly through the leaves, startling him. Jonah rolled his eyes, sinking back into the bench as the rabbit stared at him, wiggling its pink nose.

"Let me know if you find anything else in that file, okay?"

Clara yawned. "I will. I better go. Hey, Jonah?"

"Yeah?"

"Thank you."

"For what?"

"For being you."

CHAPTER TWENTY-TWO

June, 1861

"Angelina, follow me to the parlor please," Mrs. Chamberlain said, her voice clipped, as she stood at the doorway to the kitchen before turning and immediately walking away.

Angelina wiped her hands slowly on her apron, fear pooling in her belly. She'd done nothing but lie low for the past three months, as John had said. She barely had the strength to do more than that anyway—the heartache of missing him made her feel weak as if an invisible layer of fog constantly surrounded her.

Angelina shot her mother a quick look where she stood slicing an onion at the counter, the knife moving smoothly and steadily in her adept hands. Her mother frowned back, her eyes questioning. Angelina forced a smile to her lips, shrugging nonchalantly as she turned from the kitchen to follow Mrs. Chamberlain.

The windows were open in the parlor, a rare summer breeze causing the gauzy curtains to float into the air, and bringing with it the scent of garden roses. *Garden roses.*

The memory of the first time she'd laid eyes on John came back to her then, infusing her with strength.

Mrs. Chamberlain stood at the fireplace, her back to Angelina. "Yes, Mrs. Chamberlain?" she asked softly as her gaze landed on Astrid who sat on the other side of the room, her pallor ghostly, her eyes downcast.

"Something nagged at me after that party when you brought Astrid the mask. I couldn't figure out what it was until a few days ago. And then I did. You were wearing your Sunday best, Angelina." Mrs. Chamberlain turned toward her slowly, holding a book in her hands. "Why was that when you were only delivering something to Astrid?"

Angelina clasped her hands together, her mind spinning quickly. "I"—she swallowed heavily—"I didn't want to embarrass you, Mrs. Chamberlain. It was a party."

Mrs. Chamberlain's eyebrows rose slowly. "It didn't make sense," she said as if Angelina hadn't spoken at all.

Her hands rose and she waved the book she was holding around, turning her nose up at it as if it emitted a bad odor. "I never understood the need to keep a diary," she said. "Especially when one has so many dirty secrets."

Angelina glanced at Astrid as Mrs. Chamberlain turned away again and Astrid's eyes met hers, the bereft look on her half-sister's face sinking all of Angelina's hope, and making her realize that Mrs. Chamberlain hadn't really needed an answer to her question. She already knew.

"I'm sorry." The words were whispered and they dropped heavily from her mouth, weighed down by surprise and terrible fear.

Mrs. Chamberlain turned back toward Angelina again. "Dirty, filthy secrets," she said, her gaze raking down Angelina's body in disgust.

"Mrs. Chamberlain," she said, her voice cracking, her mind searching for some way to explain what Astrid had already revealed in her diary. But maybe she hadn't revealed everything. Maybe there was still a chance. "I'm sorry, I don't understand."

Mrs. Chamberlain laughed, a nasty sound full of mocking. "No? Well, let me ask you this. Do you *understand* what happens to old used-up slaves like your mama when their owners no longer have a need of them and toss them away like the garbage they are? Do you *understand* what happens to negro whores who seduce white men from wealthy families with their evil voodoo? Is that what you did, Angelina? Put a spell on John Whitfield? Made him falsely believe you were something worth having?"

Horror washed over Angelina, so suddenly and with such strength that she reached for the wall, holding on to it so as not to fall.

"Mama," Astrid said pleadingly.

"Shut up, you little ingrate! You filthy liar! How dare you speak a word to me?" Mrs. Chamberlain's face strained with anger as she screeched the words, her skin almost purple with rage.

Astrid sank back in her chair, her face full of misery, her hands grasped so tightly in her lap that her knuckles were bright white.

"Now," Mrs. Chamberlain continued, "here is what is going to happen. When John returns, you will cease your whoring and animal seduction and allow the proper relationship between John and Astrid to develop. Is that clear?"

The blood buzzed in Angelina's head and her knees grew weaker. Angelina couldn't speak, her lips slack and useless, unable to form words. Again, Mrs. Chamberlain didn't seem to require an answer and turned away, toward Astrid. "Is that clear, Astrid?" she practically hissed.

"Yes, Mother," Astrid agreed.

Angelina's eyes moved sluggishly toward Astrid. Astrid was gazing at her lap again, her expression blank. She'd helped them, yes, when she believed their secret would remain undetected. But Astrid was no match for her mother. She never had been.

"Now then," Mrs. Chamberlain said, reaching for a match on the mantel and striking it quickly. She held the diary over the fireplace grate and brought the match to it. The pages ignited quickly, the flame billowing so that Mrs. Chamberlain was forced to let go of it. It fell into the fireplace where it continued to burn to ashes.

A sob rose up Angelina's throat, her hands shaking as she willed herself to remain calm. This was a warning. A bone-chilling warning of what was to come.

The war John was fighting had found Windisle Plantation. The storm approached. And Angelina was its eye. *Defenseless.*

CHAPTER TWENTY-THREE

"I called you last night," Marco said. "You never called me back."

Clara grimaced and turned toward him. She sincerely felt bad for basically ignoring his attempts to get hold of her the last week. "Sorry, Marco. By the time I got your message it was late." The truth was, she'd been talking to Jonah and had seen his call come through. It'd been an easy choice to let it go to voicemail.

"And I knew I'd be seeing you today. You were amazing out there, by the way. You're going to knock them dead at the performance."

"Thanks," he stepped closer, leaning his head forward and peering at the place where she still had a bruise on her forehead. She'd dabbed stage makeup on it before heading to work, but she'd apparently sweated it off. "What happened?"

Clara brought her fingers to the sore spot on her forehead. "I walked into a door."

Marco raised a brow, looking dubious. "You? One of the most graceful, sure-footed people I know, walked into a door?"

Clara laughed, uncomfortable with her obvious lie—she'd *never* been good at coming up with believable falsehoods but wasn't willing to get into how her bruise had actually occurred.

"Even the most graceful trip or stumble every once in a while." *Sometimes graceful people fall over fences onto their faces as a matter of fact,* she thought with an internal cringe.

"I guess. Anyway, I—"

"Hey Marco," Roxanne said, coming up behind him, a flirtatious smile on her face. He turned toward her. "I was wondering if you have some time tonight to go over the scene in the—"

Clara took the opportunity to duck away and head toward the door. She didn't want Marco to offer her a ride. She didn't want to engage in idle chitchat with anyone. She wanted to get on the bus and lose herself in her own thoughts, the roar of the bus's engine allowing her to drift from the world around her back in time to Angelina's. And maybe, if she let her mind wander, some of those elusive puzzle pieces would begin to fit together.

She also wanted to spend more time looking through Justin's folder, the folder now kept safely in her duffle bag.

Thankfully, the bus was coming around the corner as Clara walked to the stop at the end of the block. She jogged to make it just as the doors opened and she swiped her phone, smiling in greeting to the driver.

Each time she boarded a bus, it reminded her of her father, how hard he'd worked day in and day out for her. How he'd come home with a smile on his face even though he must have been exhausted. The thought always caused a pang of love to tighten her chest. It'd been so long since they'd sat and talked about their days, about the funny things that happened at work, to the frustrating prima donnas she'd dealt with dancing. How she missed him. Down deep to her soul.

Clara took a seat on the mostly empty bus, leaning her head back and enjoying the white noise of the engine, and for the first time all day she sat still and gave her muscles a rest.

Physically, she enjoyed the stillness, but the ten minutes didn't serve to connect any drifting puzzle pieces in her mind. Clara sighed in frustration, sitting up and lifting the Chamberlain family file from her bag.

She rifled through it, reading over a few of the documents she'd already looked at, and then opened a manila envelope near the back that contained several old letters to Herbert Davies that appeared to be business correspondence, but that she already knew were letters from his wife, Astrid.

She hadn't had time to read through all of them the day before, because the script was so formal and full of flourishes that reading was slow-going.

She'd read enough to know that Astrid was working with Herbert in his construction efforts, but no more. But she took the time then to read through a few more, stopping at several lines that Astrid had written in all capitals and underlined in two heavy strikes of ink. "We must never choose safety over right. Safety is the blanket under which cowards sleep. Safety smothers hope and extinguishes all fight."

Clara read the lines once, then again. They had obviously meant something deeply to Astrid. Clara noted again the way the writing grew bold and slightly shaky as if her hand had trembled as she'd clutched the pen and scrawled the words.

Clara returned the letters to their envelopes slowly, feeling troubled. But why? What was she missing?

Her brow drew inward as more puzzle pieces appeared, still without any matches. The picture was *there*, she felt it. She just needed to arrange the pieces properly so it became clear. She'd call Jonah when she got home and ask him what he thought.

Safety is the blanket under which cowards sleep. Who had been the coward? And what safe option had someone chosen over right?

She straightened the large stack of papers in the folder, the family tree at the top catching her eye.

Clara ran her finger down the list of names she'd already looked at, her finger stopping at Jonah's as she circled it lightly, her finger halting when she noted the date. "Oh my God," she whispered, stuffing the folder quickly into her bag as her stop came into view. And of course, he hadn't said a thing.

Clara looked at her phone, noting the time. She had just enough to make it to the shop about ten blocks from her house where she'd seen something that would be perfect for the occasion of which she'd just learned.

****

Clara took a deep breath before rapping loudly on the gate where Myrtle had let her out a few days before.

If she hadn't been shown the gate, she would have never known there was an entrance other than the one covered in thorns at the front of the property.

What she now knew had at one point been an unpaved driveway, was so overgrown by reedy grass that it looked like a field, and apparently, even the sedan that Clara had seen parked inside and knew must be used at least occasionally, could not keep it flattened permanently.

If an outside observer looked around that side of the wall, they would see that the river all but butted against it, only separated by that weedy strip of what looked like marsh.

It looked unstable, and perhaps dangerous, and she certainly wouldn't have ventured beyond the tall grass had she not known that there was an entry gate beyond it.

"Who's there?" Myrtle demanded.

"It's Clara, Myrtle," she said and there was a pause before Clara heard Myrtle unlatching the gate and then pulling it open.

"Clara dear, is everything okay?" She stood at the entrance, blocking the opening, squinting mightily without her thick glasses, and Clara's heart squeezed.

This old woman who could barely see was acting as Jonah's protection, a barrier of love from the outside world. And somehow Clara knew she would fight viciously to defend him.

"Yes, Myrtle, everything's fine." She held up the gift, offering it to Myrtle. "It's a birthday present for Jonah. Will you give it to him for me? I called his phone but he didn't answer, and then I called his name at the weeping wall, but he didn't answer there either, and I'd . . . I'd really like him to have this."

Myrtle took the small blue gift bag, her expression half troubled and half contemplative. "This is very thoughtful."

Clara smiled, beginning to turn away when Myrtle reached out a hand, stopping her.

Clara turned back to Myrtle questioningly and Myrtle opened the gate wider, stepping aside. "He's out back. There's no light out there. I suppose . . . well, I suppose if you call out, if you let him know you're there, he wouldn't mind if you delivered it yourself."

"Oh," Clara breathed, uncertainty enveloping her. "I wouldn't want to upset him, Myrtle."

"No," Myrtle murmured, her unfocused gaze sliding away from Clara as she chewed at the inside of her cheek. "But . . . yes."

Clara frowned, not knowing exactly what to make of her conflicting comments.

Myrtle moved her eyes to Clara again, and she put a hand on her arm. "You must give him warning that you're there. Don't surprise him." Myrtle handed the gift bag back to Clara.

"I promise, I won't."

Myrtle ushered her inside of the gate and told her which path to take, giving Clara one more tip of her chin as Clara turned away, following Myrtle's directions.

As she rounded the house and began heading toward the trees, the light waned, only darkness before her.

She set the gift bag on a garden bench, wanting both her hands available before she stepped into the dark.

"Jonah?" she called softly, a chill moving down her spine, born of doubt and excited anticipation. She was close to him. He was here, somewhere, just beyond her reach, but not for long.

She tossed his name into the lightless void in front of her again, letting her voice lead the way, making no attempt to quiet her footsteps.

Was this how Angelina felt but minus the hope—the promise—that the man she was searching for would hear her call? What an awful, desolate feeling, to know that the man who made your heart swell and your blood tremble was there, so close, and yet completely and utterly out of reach.

What torture to wonder if he might be looking for you too.

"Jonah?"

Clara stepped forward, the canopy of trees and moss covering the moon and shading the surroundings in tones of darkest gray. She held her hand up and watched it disappear as she moved it away from her face.

"Jonah?" she called again, her heart thumping rapidly. "It's Clara."

She heard footsteps to her right and whirled in that direction, staring sightlessly into the inky blackness.

"Maybe you like monsters? Is that it, Clara?"

Jonah. His voice was deep, raspy, the voice she'd know anywhere, though she couldn't quite discern his tone.

Despite his unknown mood at her showing up uninvited, relief flowed through her along with the thrill of his presence.

"You're not a monster, Jonah. But if you insist on calling yourself one, then yes, I must like monsters."

"Silly Clara," he said, but now his tone had changed, and though his words mocked her, his silken voice held warmth. "You're in my lair now, you do realize that, right?"

"Y-yes," she said as the direction of his voice changed and she turned blindly toward it, unable to see anything, not even his movement.

He chuckled then and it drifted to her, falling over her like magic, causing goosebumps to erupt on her skin.

"You're playing with me." It was a statement, but also a question. She should be annoyed, perhaps, but she couldn't help her excitement.

Clara did not consider Jonah a monster, but apparently, she still enjoyed being his prey. *Am I really considered prey if I want to be caught?* she wondered, as a tremble of delight moved through her.

"What are you doing here?"

"Myrtle said you were out here. She thought it would be okay if . . ." Clara bit her lip, shifting where she stood, feeling strangely naked standing together as they were in the dark.

"If what?" He was closer now, but she hadn't heard him move, and it felt as if tiny bubbles popped under her ribs.

"If I warned you I was coming."

"Nothing could have warned me you were coming," he said, half under his breath, his voice right next to her ear.

She startled, turning toward the place he must be, letting out a small laugh.

"Stop," she said, her voice more breathy than she'd meant, the pleasure in that one word belying it entirely. "I can't tell where you are."

She heard the small crunch of something then and the warmth of his hand taking hers.

"Follow me."

She grasped his hand, holding on to it as though it were a lifeline, stumbling slightly as he began to move ahead of her. "I can't see where I'm going."

"You don't need to," he said, his voice carrying back to her. "I know this land like the back of my hand. I won't let you fall."

She grasped him more tightly, reveling in the solid strength of him.

He sped up, pulling her slightly and she laughed with joy as she moved her legs more quickly to keep up with his long, sure strides. They wove through trees maybe, or perhaps around rocks, she had no idea, but he obviously did and she trusted him. If she hadn't known it before, she knew it now. She trusted him with her safety and was willing to let him lead her where he may, even in the pitch-dark of night through unfamiliar territory.

He wouldn't let her fall. Though in all honesty, it was far too late for that. She'd fallen. Somewhere along the way, she'd already fallen.

When he stopped suddenly, she ran into him, laughing in surprise as he turned, both of them colliding softly right before he stepped back, out of her field of vision. "We're in the woods?" she asked.

"Yes. Don't you know it's dangerous to follow monsters into the woods?" But she knew he was teasing her.

"I must like danger too." She smiled but then grew serious. "Because I think I'd follow you anywhere, Jonah." Her tone held all the gravity contained in her heart, the truth of her confession. Yes, she would. She'd follow him anywhere.

Jonah was quiet for a moment before he uttered, "Clara." There was a warning in his voice, but she didn't care. She wouldn't heed it, and he must know that by now.

She heard the rustling of what sounded like tall grass nearby—the overgrown sugarcane fields maybe—and the hoot of an owl, the soft whistling of the wind.

"Happy birthday, Jonah."

There was a pause before he said, "Thank you. How did you know it was my birthday?"

"The family tree in Justin's folder."

"Ah."

"I brought you something. A gift. It's why I came. To deliver it in person."

"A gift?"

"Yes. Just a . . . it's nothing really, but . . ."

When he didn't interrupt her awkward stuttering, she rushed on, nervous that he was displeased. "I tried to call you first—"

"I was out here."

"What were you doing?"

"Just walking."

It was then she heard the squeak of hinges, tilting her head in surprise as she realized exactly where they were standing. *Oh.*

"We're standing among the slave cabins," he said, confirming her thought. He pulled on her hand and she followed. "There's a small step up," he said, guiding her so she didn't trip. "Go on in. Turn on the flashlight on your phone so you can look around. I'll stay out here."

"You don't have to stay outside. I won't turn the flashlight on you, I promise. I wouldn't do that." Her voice was a whisper, filled with the solemnity of her promise.

He paused for the span of two quickened heartbeats and then she heard him step up behind her. *Trusting her,* she thought, and the knowledge brought a warm flush of pleasure to her skin. The door swung shut squeakily behind him, and she heard him step to the side, not moving any farther into the room. She smelled old wood and the sweet, rotting scent of wet leaves.

Clara turned away from Jonah, swiping at her phone, the sudden bright light causing her to squint against the glare. She turned on the flashlight and set it to its lowest setting, sweeping it once around the room.

It was empty of furniture, just four bare walls that surely held secrets they'd never tell and wouldn't want to if they could.

Clara walked to the window, running a fingertip down the cracked and dirty glass. Even if there had been light beyond, the visibility would be poor.

Clara walked around the room, pointing the low light into the corners and at the ceiling, careful not to turn it in Jonah's direction, careful to allow him the darkness where he felt safe.

After a couple of minutes exploring the room, Clara shut her phone off, returning it to her pocket.

She turned back toward Jonah, stepping carefully as she moved blindly to where she knew he stood. She heard his breath as she drew closer, the steady exhale that told her where he was.

"Reach for me?" she asked and he did, grasping her outstretched hand so she could find him.

She stepped closer, right up to him, and their breath mingled, the slow exhales she'd heard moments before growing less steady.

Something sparked in the air, something Clara was surprised didn't illuminate the darkness, something that felt bright and shimmery and she swore was raining upon her skin like the fallout of a broken star.

"I thought there'd be sadness here," she said. "I thought . . . I don't know, that I'd feel heavy hearted or—"

"I know. There's something about this one. I feel the same way when I'm here. It's funny that you do too."

Clara wasn't sure what to make of that, but it felt as though she was sharing something with Jonah, something indefinably special.

She took his other hand in hers and stepped even closer, their bodies meeting. This is how they'd stood in that hotel courtyard, and she'd longed for it again. *Now?* It was even better, *fuller . . . more.* "Do you think places hold memories?"

She heard his arm move and then felt the tentative brushing of his hand on her cheek and sucked in a breath, leaning in to him.

A small groan rose from his throat, so quiet that she wasn't sure she'd have heard it if she'd had possession of all her senses. The ones she was using were so attuned, so highly sensitized, so acutely aware.

"No."

For a moment she was confused about what question he was answering. For a moment she'd been lost in his touch, and for a moment she'd forgotten she'd asked about places holding memories at all.

"No," he repeated. "Only people hold memories."

She smiled, pressing her face more firmly against his palm. He turned his hand over, moving his knuckles down her cheek and she sighed.

People . . . souls, Clara thought. Then maybe Angelina was really there, and the old cabin was a place that held happiness for her. She liked the thought, but it brought sadness too.

Clara turned her head, brushing her lips against his knuckle and he groaned, louder this time, her name following an exhale of breath.

"These walls, though," Jonah said, "they're sacred. They belong to others."

He took her hand, and she inhaled a quick breath of air as he pulled her from the cabin, back out into the night. He was walking ahead of her and she laughed as she hurried to keep up, running into the solid breadth of his back when he stopped, turning so they were facing each other again. He turned them around slowly as though dancing, and she felt something hard against her back. "Just a tall fencepost," Jonah murmured.

Clara lifted her chin, breathing in the air. She smelled something sharp and sweet and fresh. "The garden that grows on its own," she said, a note of wonder in her tone. "I can smell it."

"Yes. It's the tomatoes." She could feel his breath on her face and moved in even closer as he again brought his knuckle to her cheek the way he'd done a minute before. "They're so big and sweet you can eat them like an apple."

Clara smiled against his knuckles, darting her tongue out to taste him.

He froze, her tongue dancing lightly over his fingertips, tasting the clean saltiness of his skin. His breathing was coming out more jagged now, as if he'd just begun to run, and she realized her heart was pounding quickly too, moving the blood through her to the rhythm of Jonah's.

Jonah brought his hands up and used them to frame her face as if he could somehow see her, though there was no light in the darkened corner where they stood.

Clara tipped her head back instinctively, her lips parting as she waited. A hot, liquid thrill went through her, cascading down her limbs and pooling at the apex of her thighs.

Foggily, she remembered thinking that there was nothing like the anticipation right before a stage curtain opened. Nothing at all. But oh, how wrong she'd been. Waiting for Jonah's kiss was like that moment, only infinitely better. *Oh yes. Something wonderful is about to happen,* her heart sang.

His lips landed on hers, soft yet firm, and it felt like a thousand fireworks exploded in her belly. His hand moved to the nape of her neck where he gathered her hair between his fingers, pulling gently as he pressed her mouth more firmly to his.

She moaned, and it seemed to ignite him. He swept his tongue into her mouth, and she met his with her own, learning the taste of him, the feel of his body pressed to hers, the way he swelled and hardened against her hip.

Their kiss went deeper, something seeming to possess them both—neediness, desperation, only without a painful edge. Clara loved it, whatever *it* was.

Both of Jonah's hands were in Clara's hair now, and she reached her arms up, gripping the muscles of his biceps as he explored her with his mouth.

She wanted to reach up higher and touch his face, to learn the *feel* of him if he wouldn't let her see him with her eyes. But she knew that would put a stop to what he was doing, and she would do nothing to discourage his kiss, the magic that was sparking around them, the joy coursing through her heart.

Jonah's hips moved back slightly and then toward Clara again, an unconscious gesture of arousal—of his body's *need* to thrust—and it made Clara throb with her own desire.

"Jonah," she gasped between kisses, her hand moving between them, over the hard planes of his chest. He moaned as if her touch pained him, drawing away slightly, but then pressing himself toward her again as if he couldn't help himself.

Clara nipped at his lip, running her tongue over his bottom one, feeling the ridges there and the way it dipped slightly into an unnatural sort of frown, that part of him he thought made him unlovable, the proof of all his sins. She wanted the chance to prove him wrong. Someday.

Someday.

He made a small movement with his head, taking charge of the kiss once more and leading her away from his scars, his message clear: *not this day.*

God, but the man knew how to kiss and apparently an eight-year dry spell—if she was assuming correctly—had done nothing to dampen that particular skill.

She felt like she was floating in a vast midnight sky, his lips her only anchor to reality, the only path out of the darkness. It was a kiss born of a thousand starlit dreams. A kiss she never wanted to end.

After a minute longer, he broke away, his breath coming out in soft pants as he leaned his forehead against hers.

She went up on her tiptoes, seeking his mouth again and he laughed, a sound that was some humor but mostly frustration and ended in a pained groan.

"Was that my present?" he asked, and she heard the smile in his voice. She didn't dare reach for him to trace the curve of his lips with her finger. *Someday,* she told herself again, repeating it in her mind. Someday he'd trust her with everything he had. Someday he'd allow her to see all of him.

Clara laughed, wrapping her arms around his waist and holding him the way she'd held him in his bed a few nights before.

She turned her nose into his chest, inhaling his scent, the one she was coming to know as well as she already knew his voice.

"We should get back," Jonah said, kissing the top of her head and breathing in the scent of her hair. He rubbed his cheek on it, the side of his face that had less scarring if it had any at all. She'd only really seen his chin, half of his mouth, and a portion of his cheek.

"Do we have to? I like being here, in another world with you. It's like it's just us in all the universe."

He chuckled. "That would get lonely for you, wouldn't it?"

Clara smiled, thinking of the people she'd miss—her father, of course, but she already lived with that. But she'd miss Mrs. Guillot and Madame Fournier, and the myriad of people she looked forward to seeing day after day, surprisingly even a few of the other dancers who had been treating her more warmly of late. "Maybe a little, after a while."

She rested her cheek on the soft cotton of his shirt. He'd phrased the question in a way that excluded himself, and it made her realize that he'd already been lonely for so very long, perhaps he didn't even consider that he could ever get any lonelier than he already was. It made her heart hurt for him. All because he believed he *should* be an outcast.

He looks like a man who's been terribly hurt by the world and believes there is nothing left to love about him anymore.

Oh, Jonah. She held on to him more tightly, wanting to assure him she wouldn't let him go, but very aware that he might be the one to push her away.

She hoped with everything in her that that wouldn't happen, that she could convince him there was a life for them outside this deep, fathomless darkness.

She would meet him here as long as he let her, but her most fervent desire was that at some point, he would take her hand and let her lead him out of the emptiness of this universe built for two, into the light of the world.

He had so much to offer. Not just to her, but to others as well. She believed it with her whole heart, even if he didn't yet.

And he made her so blissfully happy. She wanted to share that happiness with everyone.

"Come on," he whispered. "I'm going to walk you back so you can get home. Go to the house and call for a car. Myrtle prefers not to drive at night, but I'm sure Cecil would be more than happy to drive you."

Clara started to protest. She wanted to stay there longer. She wasn't ready to say goodbye. But it was late, she had early practice, and she should do the responsible thing and get the rest she needed.

"I'm going to dream about you," she said as she leaned up and kissed the underside of his jaw, the side he'd already exposed to her. She felt his chin move and the light ghosting of an exhale from his nose and knew he was smiling.

"I've been dreaming about you for a while now," he said softly, very seriously, as though it were a dangerous confession.

"What do you dream?"

"Things I shouldn't."

"No," she breathed. "Whatever you dream, I promise you I want to make them all come true."

He breathed her name. "If only you could."

"I can, if you let me."

He smiled again but it felt sad to Clara, even in the darkness, even without her sight. He kissed the top of her head once more and then took her hand in his.

He guided her through the forest area once more, around obstacles, and through trees that rose up in front of her so suddenly that she gasped a few times. But he gripped her hand more tightly, pulling her close to his side as he walked the path he obviously knew by heart.

Eight years, she thought. Eight years of walking this property, day after day, night after night. Again and again. His world condensed to the acreage of Windisle and nothing more.

The stars came into view first, their twinkling glow dancing through the darkness above and creating singular pricks of silvery light.

Clara could make out the movement of Jonah in front of her now, though barely. He turned very suddenly, and she let out a startled laugh as he pulled her into his arms, kissing her firmly but quickly and releasing her just as fast with a small push.

Clara took a step forward, spotting the light of the house through the break in the trees in front of her.

"Goodnight, Clara."

She reached for him, and she saw the bare glimpse of his fingers, reaching for her too before he melted into the unlit woods. *My monster. My wish collector. My* love.

"I left something for you on the bench behind the house," she called. "Goodnight, Jonah. Happy birthday." And then she turned, heading for the light of Windisle. Away. Always away from Jonah.

When all she wanted was to draw nearer.

CHAPTER TWENTY-FOUR

Jonah smiled as he set the music box down, watching as the tiny ballerina spun to the tune of *All I Ask of You*.

He ran a finger over the blonde dancer, spinning endlessly and to his heart's desire. If only he could ask the same of Clara. This was her sweet way, he supposed, of asking him to think of her even when they were apart. God, if only she knew. He did nothing *but* think of her. *Ache* for her. Want her with a desperate need that made his stomach cramp and his muscles clench. Heartache, he'd learned, was a very real thing. He suffered from it.

And yet there was a sweetness beneath the suffering. Torment that he kept seeking out, over and over as if Clara were not only the symptom, but also the cure.

Christ, I'm a goner for her, he thought with a pained sigh.

Jonah wondered if she'd chosen the music with purpose. He recognized it because he'd seen The Phantom of the Opera several times, once on a business trip to New York where he'd scored Broadway tickets. He'd taken a date, and yet when he tried to picture her now, he couldn't even see the vague outline of her face.

The love song the music box played was from a story told about a masked phantom, unwilling to show his damaged face, and the woman who loved him anyway.

God, Clara.

Yes, she tormented him, but she'd also begun to loosen the immovable noose around his neck. He wasn't sure if it was wise to even consider *that*. But since the very first day he'd spoken to her from behind the weeping wall, her life-giving essence had . . . infused him. Before her, taking full breaths again had been almost unimaginable.

Jonah ran a hand over his rough and ridged face, his finger tracing a particularly nasty upraised scar that ran from his damaged eye, down the curve of his cheekbone, outlining the shape of that bone.

Maybe she *could* learn to accept him. Myrtle and Cecil had. Yeah so, Myrtle was half blind without her glasses and Cecil had been a pig farmer for the first part of his life, so he was used to looking in the eye of less than attractive creatures. But neither one batted an eyelash at the sight of him anymore.

Did he even dare entertain the thought?

His finger moved over his bottom lip, the melted side she'd felt with her tongue. It hadn't seemed to disgust her then. She'd even tried to do it again, but he'd distracted her from it. But of course, feeling something with the tip of your tongue and seeing the full scope of the injury front and center in the glaring daylight would be a completely different experience.

Jonah remembered the journalist who had followed Myrtle and him the day he was released from the hospital. Jonah's bandage had come loose because of the mad dash to the car away from the yelling, spitting crowd and as part of his face was revealed—the red, raw meatiness of his wound exposed—the journalist had looked shocked at first, his expression morphing into horror as he'd stumbled back. *Disgusted.* And Jonah had been glad for the reaction at the time because the sight of his disfigured face had gotten rid of the guy. Or at least that's what he'd told himself.

The music ended and the ensuing silence felt sad.

Lonely.

Normal.

He didn't *want* it to end. But it would have to, wouldn't it? He felt himself changing, emerging, only there wouldn't be a caterpillar to butterfly transformation for him—he'd forevermore look like the back end of an insect. That was not going to change.

He thought back to the week before when he'd roamed the darkness with Clara, when he'd tasted her, felt her pressed against him. God, he longed to taste her again. Not just her lips, but her throat, her shoulders, the warm sweet place between her thighs.

He'd only spoken to her on the phone since that magical evening. She'd been busy with rehearsals, and he'd been out almost every night, patrolling with the angels for an hour here or there.

It had given him that purposeful feeling that he now coveted. Plus, he'd felt somewhat responsible for Eddy. The kid was obviously still struggling. But the guy kept showing up, just like Jonah, and he thought that was a positive sign.

He saw him walking with Augustus, talking, laughing a few times. He knew that feeling, what it felt like to connect to another person after having felt disconnected for so long, to finally have an understanding ear. And watching them, he'd felt relief that he'd made the right call that day he'd received Eddy's wish—his silent cry for help—and reached out to Augustus rather than the police.

He'd heard Augustus say something to Eddy the week before about seeking forgiveness from those he'd wronged being part of his healing process, and later, it'd started Jonah thinking. He needed to apologize. He had no misconception that his apology would be accepted. Hell, he didn't believe it should be. But he needed to make one. He *needed* to. Not to everyone who hated him because of what happened—he didn't owe those people anything, but he did owe an apology to at least one. He had no idea if there was any hope beyond the life he was living now, but if there was, God, if there was even a kernel of possibility, he needed to do this one thing in order to move forward.

And even if there wasn't, he owed it anyway. In fact, it was long overdue.

Jonah waited until the moon appeared in the star-studded sky, just a slip of pearly yellow against the velvety indigo of night.

When he pulled up to the dilapidated bungalow in the Lower Ninth Ward, his heart was beating harshly in his leather-covered chest.

The roar of the motorcycle's engine echoed in the silence of the night for a moment before the crickets took up their song again.

Jonah looked down the block. It seemed as though most of the houses on this street were still unoccupied. Ghosts may or may not linger at Windisle, but there was no question that the ghost of Katrina still haunted this devastated area.

Jonah kept his helmet on as he ascended the three rickety steps that led to Lucille Kershaw's door. Before he could talk himself out of it, he raised his hand and knocked at the screen, the door rattling on its hinges, clearly at risk of coming loose entirely and falling off.

"Who's there?" he heard called from directly on the other side of the door.

"Uh, I'm looking for Lucille Kershaw, ma'am," Jonah said unsteadily.

"You found her. Now who the hell are you?"

Jonah paused. He didn't have another choice than to tell this woman his name, but then she'd tell him to fuck off and he wouldn't have the chance to deliver the apology he'd rehearsed.

"Jonah Chamberlain, ma'am," he said on one exhaled breath, speaking quickly. "Before you tell me to go—"

The lock disengaged and the door opened a crack. "Jonah Chamberlain? The *lawyer?*"

Jonah was so surprised that for a moment he didn't compute the question. "Ah, yes, I was. I was a lawyer. I worked on the case ah—"

"Yeah, I know who you are," she said, opening the door a tad more. She stared out at him, her expression blank.

He was very aware that he must look threatening in the black motorcycle helmet, the visor closed, and he reached for it, but couldn't quite force himself to lift it off. "What do you want?"

"I'd like to talk to you if you can spare a few minutes. I won't take up much of your time."

She opened the door wider and stepped back, surprising Jonah. "Yeah, I recognize your voice, Jonah Chamberlain. Well, come on in then."

She turned and Jonah followed her into a small family room where Jeopardy was playing on a box television set.

The room was furnished in mismatching, well-worn pieces, but it was clean, with blankets folded neatly on the back of the ugly brown sofa, and the torn armchair.

Lucille Kershaw took a seat in the recliner, picking up a remote and muting the television while Jonah sat on the edge of the sofa. Lucille looked at him again, and he took in a deep breath, lifting the helmet over his head and placing it on the couch next to him.

He raised his gaze to her slowly, bracing for her reaction. He could feel his pulse racing and laid his sweaty palms on his denim-clad thighs as he made full eye contact. Her expression didn't change. She continued to stare at him without so much as a muscle twitch.

Jonah watched her back for a moment, understanding dawning.

She's blind.

For fuck's sake. He almost laughed out loud. His biggest moment of courage and it fell on blind eyes. Literally.

"Well?" she asked. "If you have something to say, then say it."

"Mrs. Kershaw, I came to . . . I came to"—his voice broke and he gathered himself, sitting up further and clearing his throat—"to apologize to you. I know what I did can't be forgiven. I know that. I just had to tell you how sorry I am. And I know I waited far too long to say it. I know that too. I just . . . you have no idea how sorry I am." Jonah's voice faded away, trapped in the sorrow, the deep, deep regret that he carried inside and now rose up and filled his throat.

Lucille Kershaw, the woman whose daughter he'd eviscerated on the stand that day, the woman whose child had died because of *him,* stared, her forehead creasing into a frown. "I never blamed you, young man."

"What?" The word was a whisper, mostly made of that blockage of exhaled regret. It was raspy and rough, and it scratched Jonah's throat as though it had been wrapped in sharpened barbs.

Lucille Kershaw shook her head, her gaze fixed on Jonah, her sightless eyes boring into him somehow, some way. "I never blamed you," she repeated.

She sighed, reclining back in the chair, her hands folded in her lap. "If it's the way you questioned her on the stand that you're referring to? Making her cry?"

Jonah bobbed his head, his throat filling again so that he didn't think he could speak. But he finally forced out a cracked, "Yes. I was wrong."

"You weren't wrong. Hell, the Lord knows I railed at that girl enough times myself. Said far, far worse than you did. Called her a junkie and a loser. Told her she was a waste of space. I tried that tough love. Oh, she'd cry and break down, sometimes she'd make promises. Never changed nothin' in the end though."

A deep sadness had come into Mrs. Kershaw's expression as she spoke, and Jonah felt his heart constrict. And yet her lack of blame still caused a buzz of shock to reverberate through his chest. Awe. He didn't believe he deserved it.

"You're her mother, though, Mrs. Kershaw," Jonah said, putting his thoughts to voice. "What I did was not done out of love."

"Maybe that's why it would have worked"—she paused, sighing loudly, her shoulders rising and falling—"if that damn psycho hadn't shot her in the heart." She shook her head again. "Nah, I know that some do, but me? No, I never blamed you. You didn't kill her." Her blind gaze found his face again somehow. "And in any case, from what I hear, you paid your price."

Jonah reached unconsciously for the side of his face that had sustained the burns, the scarring, his hand lowering before he could run his fingertips along the damage, a gesture of insecurity, of remembrance.

"Yes," he said, acknowledging her statement. He may or may not have deserved what he got—and that he was even questioning it made him feel confused, overwhelmed—but he had most *certainly* paid a price. A debt he'd be making good on for the rest of his life whether he wanted to or not.

Mrs. Kershaw nodded solemnly. "I'm sorry about that, young man." And the thing that pierced Jonah in the gut, the thing that made him bow his head as a tear escaped his eye and ran down the ruined side of his face, was that he could see that she was. This woman, who he'd felt he had wronged so cruelly, had offered him grace *and* sympathy for *his* pain.

He didn't know how to feel, what to think. It seemed as if a giant balloon was expanding slowly in his chest.

"Another man, a lawyer like you, came here once too, you know. Offering his condolences. I could tell from his voice it was all a pack of lies though. Oh, he was smooth, said all the right things. But I raised a liar. I know how to spot one."

"What?" Jonah asked with a breath that released a smidgen of building pressure. "Who was it?"

Mrs. Kershaw shrugged. "I don't remember his name. I wasn't in the best place. A contractor I'd finally hired to fix the water damage in the house had taken off with the money. Everything was displaced . . . a blind woman can't live in chaos."

She sighed and Jonah looked around again, noting the precise placement of the furniture, the clear walking path around each and every object.

There was still a faint line on the wall where the floodwaters had risen, and a very slight mildew scent hung in the air. The carpet was obviously new and the furniture—it had to be secondhand—was undamaged.

This woman had done what she could, but over a decade later and she still hadn't completely rebuilt—just like the neighborhood where she resided.

"Anyway, he was real old, I could tell by his voice—old but smooth, that one. Almost"—she paused as if searching for the right word—"*oily* sounding. He asked for Amanda's phone under some ridiculous pretense. I told him I didn't know a thing about her phone or where it was, but I lied."

Jonah had been stunned by Mrs. Kershaw's forgiveness, and now surprised by this unexpected and perplexing information.

"Applegate?" he asked. "Was his last name Applegate?" The two original partners he'd worked for, Applegate and Knowles, were *both* old, but out of the two, Palmer Applegate had the voice of a snake-oil salesman. Pair that with his big, overly white dentures and his bony face and he was downright disturbing.

Not that Jonah had any room to talk. Not now anyway.

Mrs. Kershaw nodded and snapped her fingers. "That's it. I remember it now. Applegate. I remember the name didn't seem to fit him."

No, Jonah agreed. Apples were sweet and fresh. Palmer Applegate was older than dirt and smelled of mothballs and denture paste.

"Why would he want Amanda's phone after the trial was already over?" Jonah asked. *After she'd died?*

Mrs. Kershaw shrugged. "Don't know. It's not as though I can look through the thing. I don't even think Amanda knew it was here. She left it when she was by asking for money. She was as high as a kite." She sighed. "I didn't have any way to get in touch and let her know I had it, so I put it aside and figured she'd be back at some point."

Mrs. Kershaw looked blankly off to the side, probably staring into a past that was forming in her mind. "Later, after that Applegate came by, I figured I'd be better off not knowing the things Amanda might have had on her phone anyway. Not much good ever came from the paths Amanda chose to walk. Maybe I couldn't keep her safe in this life, but I can let her rest in the next one."

Jonah nodded. "I understand, Mrs. Kershaw. I won't say anything about that phone."

Questions about why Palmer Applegate had been interested in it swirled in his mind, but he did his best to squash them. *Why after the trial? What had been so important?* He'd never know. He was there to offer amends. Only that.

"I want you to have it."

Jonah pulled his head back in surprise. "What?"

"Because I don't have anyone else I trust to look through it. And maybe part of letting Amanda rest involves whatever truth might be on that phone. I know you'll do the right thing with whatever you find."

"I . . . I don't know what to say," Jonah stumbled. And it was the truth. He was overwhelmed. Relieved. Confused. Deeply grateful. Bowled over.

But a tremor of fear sparked through him too. Not only did he feel unworthy to be given the responsibility of looking through Amanda Kershaw's phone for her mother, but he was afraid of delving back into that case at all. The case that had been his downfall, and had caused the death of so many innocents. And yet, Mrs. Kershaw had unselfishly offered him her forgiveness, her understanding, and now, her trust. How could he possibly say no?

Mrs. Kershaw stood, making her way slowly but surely around the coffee table and down a hallway off of the living room. He heard a door open and what sounded like a piece of furniture moving, some shuffling, and then a minute later she was back, handing him an old flip phone.

Jonah stared at the relic and wasn't surprised that when he flipped it open, it was expectedly dead. "Do you have the charger?"

"No. You'll have to get one of those yourself."

Jonah nodded, wondering if they even made chargers for flip phones anymore. "I will, Mrs. Kershaw." Jonah put the phone in his jacket pocket and stood.

"I'll let you know what I find." He paused, gathering himself. "I can't thank you enough, for taking the time to talk to me. For . . . for your kindness. I would do anything if I could bring her back. If I could go back in time . . ."

Mrs. Kershaw smiled, though it held sadness. "Maybe a better plan is to move forward." She held out her hand and

Jonah took it, grasping it in both of his, squeezing it tightly as he let out a soggy chuckle.

"Yeah," he said. "Yeah."

Her smile grew. "Good. I'm going to have you let yourself out. I've already missed half of Jeopardy."

Jonah gave her another chuckle and picked up his helmet from where he'd left it on the couch. Mrs. Kershaw sat back in her recliner and unmuted the TV so that Alex Trebek's voice filled the room, posing a question about ancient Rome.

Jonah took one last look around the dilapidated room. This woman had been wiped out in so many ways and yet she'd *rebuilt,* kept a heart open enough to offer forgiveness to a guilty man, and was still putting one foot in front of the other day after day. Admiration overwhelmed him so completely that he almost stumbled as he turned and headed for the door.

"Marcus Brutus," he heard her say to the TV right before he pressed the flimsy inner lock, stepped out of the house, and closed the door behind him.

For a moment he stood on the stoop, his helmet hanging at his side. He turned his face to the sky, closing his eyes and letting a handful of different stars look upon his brokenness for the first time in eight years.

After a moment, he brought his head down, pulling his helmet on and walking to his motorcycle. As he drove toward Windisle, his lips were shaped in a smile.

****

Lucille Kershaw pulled back the curtains, exposing the room to the morning sun. Not that she could see it. But she hadn't always been blind. It was only habit that kept her pulling open the drapes day after day, she supposed. Or maybe, doing the things she'd always done to greet the sunrise, gave her a smidgen of hope that each new dawn offered promise if you did your part, whether you could see it or not. Sort of like faith.

Just as the coffee machine let out three long beeps, letting her know it had finished brewing, she heard a knock at her front door. *Well, if this doesn't beat all.* She hadn't had a visitor in three years, and now she was going to have two in the span of twenty-four hours?

"Who is it?"

"My name is Neal McMurray, ma'am. I'm a contractor here to look your place over."

"You must have the wrong house. I didn't call a contractor." She might have if she could afford one, *or* if she trusted any of them after what that shyster had done to her so many years before. She still remembered that man's deception with a stabbing pain that made her cringe. After the devastation of Katrina, after all her community had lost, it had felt like the worst kind of betrayal.

"No, ma'am. Jonah Chamberlain sent me. He said you'd know his name."

Lucille paused for a brief second before cracking the door open. The cool air met her nose. She smelled rain. It would be pouring in the next hour or so. Storms still brought a tremor of fear even after all this time. How could they not? "Why'd he send you? I can't afford a contractor."

She had a few friends in the neighborhood who'd helped her over the years when she could pay them a little bit. They'd painted, laid new carpet, patched the places that had the worst of the water damage. She knew it still needed a lot of work, but it was livable, and she'd get more done as she was able.

"He's paying for the work, ma'am. He already gave me a deposit, and told me to let you know the rest would be taken care of. I'm here today to make a list of what needs to be done, with your approval of course. My team can get started on the repairs day after tomorrow."

Lucille was stunned. She'd told Jonah Chamberlain she didn't blame him for what had happened to Amanda, or for any of it, and that was the God's honest truth. He didn't need to feel indebted to her. But she'd heard the intense pain in his voice, and she'd heard the sincerity too. The thing she'd prayed so hard to hear in her own daughter's voice and never received.

She had a notion that accepting this gift would go a ways toward helping the young man move past whatever he still blamed himself for. And lord, but she also couldn't deny the spark of excitement that pinged through her now. "He's going to pay for all of it? The whole bill?"

"Yes, ma'am. Every cent. He said the damage might be extensive."

"Well . . . it might be." Truthfully, she had no idea. She'd only been able to afford cosmetic fixes, but she could smell the mildew that festered somewhere. She could smell it better than anyone.

"Then it'd be best if I got started right away."

Lucille opened the door all the way, a tinge of sunshine finding her face, a ray that must have cut through the scent of gloom she'd caught in the early morning air. "Did he tell you about my disability?"

"Yes, ma'am. I won't disturb a thing. I'll let you know where I am at all times, and I'll explain what I find when I'm done."

"That's good. Otherwise I'd have to hang a bell around your neck like a cat." He chuckled and she paused before adding, "I hired a contractor once when I could afford one. Gave him every cent I had to my name to make this place livable again. He stole it."

There was a pause before Neal McMurray said solemnly, "I'm so sorry about that, Mrs. Kershaw. I can't understand it. How a person can kick another who's down is beyond me." The sincerity in his voice was clear, the same sincerity that had been clear in Jonah Chamberlain's voice the night before, but without the hue of pain.

Lucille nodded curtly, turning her head so he didn't spot the tears suddenly burning her eyes. "Well then, I'll let you lead the way."

CHAPTER TWENTY-FIVE

August, 1861

Homer winced as Angelina's mama rubbed the ointment into his abraded palms, his expression relaxing into relief almost immediately.

"Better?" Mama Loreaux asked as she worked the herb-filled ointment into Homer's raw, bloodied skin.

"Yes, ma'am," Homer said as she slipped some cotton gloves over his hands, the gloves Angelina had sewn herself.

"Sleep with those on tonight and by the morning, you gone be healed right up."

"You a gem, Mama," Homer said, offering her that gentle, gap-toothed grin of his that never failed to elicit a smile from Angelina. He looked shyly at her, his smile dipping slightly. He bowed his head. "Miss Angelina," he said. "You sleep well."

"You too, Homer. Come see us tomorrow if you need another treatment."

"I surely will." With another tip of his head, he left their cabin, the screen door closing softly behind him. Angelina went to stand in front of it, watching him walk into the darkness and wishing for a breeze, even a slight one. But the night was still and breathless and Angelina stared out, the desolation she'd put aside while Homer was there, now filling her once more.

Night after night they came to her mama, seeking relief for lacerations and bloodied hands, for muscle aches and pain of every type. Those were the easy visits, though. Those were the ones that could be soothed with ointment or herbs, with Mama's special oils, or strong-smelling tinctures.

It was the pain that couldn't be mended that pierced Angelina's soul—the loss, the heartache, the deep, deep sorrow.

Somewhere far beyond, under the same moon that was filtering weakly through the trees above her, John was fighting a war. He was fighting against the side that would see an end to the injustices that she witnessed every day of her life, an end to the misery and suffering, an end to the threats of women like Delphia Chamberlain who ruled and ruined lives.

She loved him, she didn't want to fault him for things he couldn't control, but the lonelier she became, the more fearful and hopeless, the more her resentment grew.

Her mama glanced at her, putting the satchels of herbs back into the leather case she kept them in. "You think too much, you gone give yourself a headache."

Angelina laughed, though it didn't hold much humor. "I wish I could stop, Mama. If you have an ointment for that, please apply it immediately."

Her mama gave her a sharp look, thinning her lips. "You *make* yourself stop, girl. All that thinkin' an dreamin' ain't gone come to no good."

Her mama was right, of course. It had *already* come to no good. She'd fallen in love with a man who'd made her life dangerous and uncertain. Delphia Chamberlain's threats sat heavy upon her shoulders, threats that not only included herself, but her beloved mama as well.

She had kept her head down since that awful day in the parlor. She walked through her days weak with hopelessness, foggy with fear. She had no earthly idea how anything could be made right.

Angelina eyed her mother's case. "Mama, how do you curse someone?"

Her mother had shown her how to blend herbs to create medicines, how to make tinctures and oils that soothed and cleansed, and how to apply ointments that cooled and healed, but she'd never shown her the other rituals she performed when Angelina was gone from the cabin, the rituals she knew had been passed down from her grandmother and great grandmother before her mother had been shipped to Louisiana across a vast sea.

"I smell the smoke sometimes when I come back to the cabin. I know you still practice the old religion."

Her mother didn't look at her as her hands continued with the work of returning the items to her case. "You don't need to know any a that. They call me a witch, say it devilry what I do. I never wanted that for you. I can't help what I already know, but I sho enough can keep you from knowin' it. Safer that way."

Safer.

But nothing in their lives was *safe.* Was *safe* supposed to feel this way? Did her mama feel safe? Did any of the slaves on their plantation feel safe, no matter how good they acted, no matter how hard they worked, no matter how many rules they followed? Angelina didn't think so.

"And anyhow," her mother continued, "curses are only fueled with a whole soul a fire behind 'em. They do not work just because you wishin' they would."

"I do have a soul of fire behind my wish," Angelina insisted. She wished Delphia Chamberlain would die a thousand miserable deaths. She would deserve every one of them.

"And for every ounce a hate that fuels a curse, there gotta be a equal amount a love."

Angelina watched her mother, weariness overcoming her. It all sounded confusing and complicated, and unlikely to work.

Maybe she hated Delphia Chamberlain as equally as she loved John, though she didn't have an idea on how to measure that. But it couldn't just be about love and hate.

Surely there were words involved, the whispery chants she heard her mother saying as she passed by the window of their cabin sometimes, the wispy vapors of whatever she had burned, drifting over the sill.

But her mother had never shared it with her, and she doubted she could convince her to begin now. And in any case, she wasn't even sure she believed in any of that.

If her mother knew how to curse people, why hadn't she cursed her father before he made her pregnant with a baby she never asked for on the dirt of the cellar floor? Why hadn't she cursed the men who put her in shackles and shoved her in the vomit-scented hull of a slave ship? Why hadn't she cursed the group who had strung Elijah up and left his body to rot in the sun?

For every ounce a hate that fuels a curse, there gotta be a equal amount a love.

Whatever that meant.

Angelina sat down heavily on the bed.

"It that man who started this," her mother stated, her expression hard, her eyes filled with worry as she looked upon her forlorn daughter. "If he really love you, he would not put your life in danger."

But how could he love her *without* putting her life in danger? Would the war really emancipate slaves? It seemed so far-fetched and inconceivable. Absurd. *Could the world ever really change that much?*

Doubt prickled her skin. She wanted to insist that John *did* love her, that his promises were real and true. But she saw him in her mind's eye, the way his gaze had shifted away when they'd spoken about him fighting for the side that would never set her free. There had been something he'd refused to say to her and the memory only increased her doubt that their love would ever win in the end.

"Yeah," her mama murmured, the glint of something fierce in her eyes. "He nothin' but danger. *Nothin'* but danger."

CHAPTER TWENTY-SIX

Clara pulled her light jacket around her, inhaling the fresh, pure scent of an evening washed clean by a day of rain.

The familiar sound of Mrs. Guillot's voice drifted to her on the breeze, and she smiled with pleasure as the sweet sound rolled through her.

Long my imprisoned spirit lay,
Fast bound in sin and nature's night;
Thine eye diffused a quick'ning ray—
I woke, the dungeon flamed with light.

Clara let herself in the gate, stepping past the tabby cat that sat cleaning himself on the stone path.

Mrs. Guillot stopped singing, her face bursting into a warm smile as she spotted Clara. "Well, Clara, darlin' girl, how are you? It's been far too long since I've seen you."

"I'm good. I've looked for you, but you haven't been on your porch recently when I've walked by. How are you?"

"I'm wonderful. I've been keepin' some company with Harry," she said, and Clara swore the pink in her cheeks deepened just a smidge. "And of course, now that the weather's cooled down a bit, I spend more time indoors in the evening."

"Yes," Clara agreed. "The cooler weather is such a relief."

"Isn't it? I was just going to make myself a cup of coffee. Will you join me? I picked up some of that fall creamer. I've got pumpkin spice, peppermint, and, let's see"—she put her finger on her chin as she rose from her chair—"oh! crème brûlée."

Clara grinned. "How did you know I was a sucker for fall coffee creamer?"

Mrs. Guillot laughed as she opened her front door, holding it for Clara to enter behind her. "Who isn't, dear?"

"No one I want to know."

Mrs. Guillot laughed as Clara closed the front door behind them and entered the cozy room. The furnishings were older, but obviously well kept, with warm afghans on the backs of the chairs and plush throw pillows at each end of the two facing sofas. In the corner, a television was on, the sound turned down so low it could barely be heard.

"You take a seat and I'll put the coffee on. I see you've been to visit Mr. Baptiste."

Clara nodded, placing the bag containing zucchini and yellow squash on Mrs. Guillot's coffee table. "Yes. He's closing up for the season in a couple of weeks. I've been visiting him as much as I can. He's such a nice man, and I'll miss him when he's not there anymore."

"That he is. I'll miss seeing him too. Make yourself at home, and I'll be back in a few minutes. What kind of creamer would you like?"

"Pumpkin spice, please," Clara said as she sat on the sofa, looking around the room at the different knickknacks Mrs. Guillot had displayed.

She glanced at all the photographs atop the side tables, and on the console that held the television, all the people Mrs. Guillot had loved and lost.

She heard Mrs. Guillot humming the tune she'd been singing when Clara walked through her gate. "That's a lovely song, Mrs. Guillot," Clara called to her.

"Yes, it is, dear," Mrs. Guillot said, her voice carrying clearly from the kitchen right next to the living room. "It's called *And Can It Be*. My mama, rest her sweet soul, didn't know how to read, but oh, did she know how to sing. Just like an angel. She taught me every hymn she knew."

"You sing them beautifully."

"Thank you, dear. Oh, I forgot to mention that I bought a ticket for your opening night. I've been checking and when they went on pre-order, I snatched mine right up."

"You did?" Clara asked, the delight clear in her voice.

What a sweet, sweet woman Mrs. Guillot was. And how wonderful to know that even though her father wouldn't be at her opening night—the very first one he wouldn't be able to attend and oh, how that knowledge *hurt*—Clara would have at least one person in the audience just for her. "Thank you, Mrs. Guillot. That means so much to me."

"I can't wait."

The whir of a coffee grinder met Clara's ears and she settled back into the sofa as Mrs. Guillot resumed humming, watching disinterestedly as a news program started playing.

After a minute, Clara sat up, blinking at a clip on the television. She grabbed the remote on the coffee table and turned up the volume, her fingers fumbling slightly in her haste to hear what was being said.

"I just love this story, Genevieve," the male newscaster said to the female newscaster. "It seems this masked man is going around New Orleans doing good deeds for people in need. There have been a handful of stories from folks saying he's part of the Brass Angels, which as you know is a group of volunteer crime-fighters formed after Hurricane Katrina."

"A masked man?" Clara whispered, shocked. That's what she thought she'd seen in the clip that had been part of the news story's opening. The mask was eerily similar if not exactly the same to the one she'd seen Jonah in on two occasions now. Her heart sped up.

"Yes, Brennan," the newscaster named Genevieve answered. "It's so interesting. But the most fascinating part is he's apparently not only helping people as part of the Brass Angels, but he's actually donating money in some cases. A lot of money."

Clara watched as a teary-eyed young woman sat next to an obviously sick little boy in a hospital bed as she told about a man who had approached her in the hospital courtyard, somehow known about the treatment her son needed, and handed over a cashier's check for fifty grand, a check that contained no personal information except the bank where it'd been issued.

"I just want to thank him," the woman said, a tear rolling down her cheek. "My son is scheduled tomorrow for the surgery I hope will save his life, and"—she sniffled, reaching for her son's hand and squeezing it as the little boy looked at his mother with love in his eyes, a small smile on his lips—"and I just really would like to thank the man who made it possible."

"News Eight has obtained the camera footage from the parking garage of the hospital, and if you look closely, you can see this masked man walking around a corner. Unfortunately, the camera on the other side was out of order at the time, but we've frozen the frame where this mystery man looks at the screen. If you are able to identify him, please let us know so this grateful mother and a host of others can thank him for his kindness and generosity."

The screen moved to a grainy picture of a man looking up at a camera above him, his head tilted slightly as though he were peering out of one eye that was stronger than the other.

Clara's heart gave a strong jolt and she put her hand over her mouth.

"A masked man who helps the hopeless," Mrs. Guillot said from behind her before coming around and placing two coffee cups on the table, the delicious scent of coffee and pumpkin spice drifting to Clara and breaking her from her shocked trance. "Well, if that doesn't beat all. Am I the only one in the room who finds that quite . . . alluring?"

Clara couldn't help the startled laugh that bubbled up her throat as she turned to Mrs. Guillot. *Alluring.* No, no Mrs. Guillot was definitely not the only one. "Mrs. Guillot, I . . . I know him."

Mrs. Guillot tilted her head, her eyes filling with surprise. "You do? Who is he?"

Clara shook her head. "I can't tell. I mean, I didn't know either, not until just now. He obviously doesn't want anyone to know."

Mrs. Guillot rested her hand on Clara's. "Is he by any chance the man you weren't sure if you were going to offer grace to from up close or from far away?"

"*Yes.*"

Mrs. Guillot nodded. "And what did you choose, dear?"

"Up close. Very up close."

Mrs. Guillot's lips tipped, and she gave Clara a knowing look. "I see." She glanced at the television that had moved on to a different public interest story. "It seems it was a good call. Any man who acts the way that man is acting is very, very serious about redemption."

She patted Clara's hand again. "Now drink your coffee, dear. And then you go to that young man and offer him a little more grace. And this time, consider getting even closer."

Clara's eyes widened right before she laughed, throwing her arms around Mrs. Guillot and hugging her hard.

CHAPTER TWENTY-SEVEN

"Hello? Jonah, are you there?"

He heard Clara's voice and froze. She was at the side gate, her steady rapping shattering the quiet of Windisle. His heart jumped, excitement flaring inside of him, along with a spark of panic.

What are you doing here, Clara? He paused for the portion of a moment, letting a deep, long breath flow through him. Did he dare answer? Myrtle and Cecil were out on a rare date night to dinner in the French Quarter to be followed by a show, and he was alone.

He reached up and touched his face, running his fingers over the scars, his fear increasing. No . . . no. He wasn't ready. Not yet.

Maybe he wouldn't answer at all, although the thought itself made his panic increase. The idea of Clara leaving more terrible than the thought of her staying. His stomach churned. *Fuck.*

She called his name again, her voice ringing through the property, through *him.* What if there was something wrong? What if she needed him?

He let out a frustrated growl, shutting off the few lamps he had turned on inside of the house and then heading downstairs where he flipped the switch to shut off the sconce that lit the back door.

The blackness closed in, wrapping its fingers of safety around Jonah, calming his heart rate. The knocking ceased. Clara had obviously seen the light go out and knew he was coming for her.

"He arrives in darkness," she whispered when he unlatched the gate, reaching for her and pulling her quickly to his side before kicking the gate closed.

The side door to the house opened into a short hallway that led directly into the kitchen. Jonah closed the door and pressed Clara against the wall in two quick movements.

"What are you doing here?" he asked, close to her face.

She pulled in a breath, and he had the sense she was inhaling his scent, which made a shiver of arousal quake inside of him. "It's *you,*" she said.

"Yes, it's me. Who did you think it was?"

"No, I mean, it was you on the news."

Unease prickled Jonah's skin. "The news?" Those two words were enough to send fear ricocheting through him. *The news* only conjured negative reactions for Jonah. Once upon a time, *the news* had flayed him alive. "I wasn't on the news."

"You *were,*" she said, and there was something in her voice . . . wonder? "You're going around New Orleans helping people who need it." Her voice held a note of incredulousness, and still, that same wonder he'd heard.

"No." Jonah took a step back, turning his face slightly in the darkness that wasn't quite complete because of a shaft of moonlight shining in the kitchen window beyond. He could only see her outline, no details, so he hoped it was the same for her.

"No," he said again, but even he could hear the way the word came out, sounding more like a question than a statement. "What did they say?"

"The way you turn your face like that," she murmured as if she were speaking only to herself. "I recognized that the minute they showed the video."

"Clara, what the hell are you talking about?" Jonah demanded, his unease increasing.

"Sorry." He thought he saw her shake her head slightly, her movement mixing with the darkness that surrounded her as she leaned against the wall.

Without thought, he stepped toward her, seeking. *Always seeking this woman.*

"There was a news story about how this masked guy is helping people anonymously in New Orleans. They had a woman on who has a sick little boy who was just accepted into a study. He's having surgery tomorrow."

Jonah let that piece of information slip past his unease, his heart filling with momentary happiness to know that Matthew would receive the chance he deserved.

"She said this man paid for it, approached her in the middle of the day, wrapped in bandages, and just handed her a check." Clara was speaking quickly now, her voice soft and breathy. "And other people reported him patrolling with these volunteer crime-fighters, the . . . the Silver Angels you told me about the other night. The guys I thought were chasing me."

"The Brass Angels," Jonah muttered. *Jesus.* How in the hell had the news gotten hold of that? And now he was some public interest story? Well *shit*. He had never intended on any of this. It was not welcome news.

"It's you," she repeated. "There was footage of you from the hospital's garage camera. It was the outline of that mask I saw you in and then . . . you tilted your head." She raised her hand and reached blindly for him, running her finger over his jaw. "And I knew. I knew it was you."

"Clara—"

"Don't lie to me, Jonah. Tell me the truth."

Jonah sighed. What did it matter? He trusted her. She wouldn't expose him. What did it matter if she knew the truth? After this, he wouldn't be able to anonymously patrol the streets anyway. They'd probably be looking for him. Looking to make a story out of him again. He wouldn't allow it, so his short but illustrious time of crime-fighting with the Brass Angels was over. "Yeah. Yeah, it was me."

Clara was silent for a beat, and he thought maybe she was gaping at him. He shifted uncomfortably. "Why?" she breathed, that wonder in her voice again. "Why are you doing it?"

"Why?"

"Yes. I mean, it's wonderful, but . . . why did you decide to start helping people? To be a hero to others?"

"Oh Christ, Clara." He let out a soft bark of laughter. "You keep trying to turn me into a hero, and I'm not."

"To me you are. And you can't do anything about it, Jonah Chamberlain. You can't change it even if you want to. To me you are and that's all."

That's *all?* He sighed, feigning frustration, but in reality, a flush of pleasure shot through him, making him feel *alive.* Not because he considered himself a hero to anyone, but because he *wanted* to be one to her. He did. God, but he did. And she'd told him he was. And it wasn't only in her words. Right that minute he could sense it emanating in the space around them, the feeling that he had done well in her eyes and that she was proud of him in a way a woman finds pride in the man she wants to call her own. And it lit him from within. It lit his soul. He lived in the darkness, but Clara, she was his light.

He whispered her name, and she moved forward, bringing her face to his and finding his lips in the dark. "Hi," she whispered right before she pressed her mouth to his.

He smiled against her lips and then took charge of the kiss, eliciting a small moan from her that felt like a zing of electricity straight to his groin. *Hi.*

They continued kissing, and Jonah lost himself in sensation, the accelerated heartbeat, the warm flush that ran through his veins, the excitement that filled every cell of his body. "I missed your mouth," he said between kisses.

He felt her smile. "The things it says or the things it does?"

"Both."

He drank down her laughter, kissing her again, not able to get enough. He ran his hand under the collar of her jacket, along the dip where her neck became her shoulder, his finger hooking on the leotard she wore beneath.

"You came straight from practice," he said, his lips moving down the side of her throat. She tilted her head back, giving him better access to the places his lips wandered.

"Yes. I was heading home and stopped at my neighbor's. That's where I saw the news."

"Hmm," he hummed, and he felt her shiver. His gut clenched with want. He loved the way she reacted to his touch. Loved every damn thing about her. Loved *her.* "And so you headed straight here."

"Of course."

"Of course." He smiled. Of course she would. Clara was thoughtful. She considered a situation if she was unsure about it, but once she'd made up her mind to confront something or someone, she did it right then, without hesitation.

"I loved the music box, by the way," he said between mouth brushes.

"Was I self-centered to give you a gift in the hopes that it would make you think of me every day?"

He chuckled and again, she shivered. "No. But it wasn't necessary. I already think of you every day, Clara. Every morning. Every night. Every second."

"Jonah," she whispered, wrapping her arms around the back of his neck, bringing his mouth back to hers. "Dance with me again the way you did at the masquerade ball."

"That? That was hardly dancing. *You* dance. That was just swaying," he teased.

"So you want me to teach you some ballet moves and make you a *real* dancer?"

Jonah chuckled. "God, no. I would be tragic at ballet. You wouldn't know this, but I had some moves back in the day. Do you know how many galas and charity balls and fancy parties I went to as an esteemed member of a prestigious law firm here in New Orleans? I was the toast of the town."

Clara breathed out a laugh, kissing the indent at the base of his throat and making him groan. "Show me."

He tensed and she shook her head, her nose rubbing against the base of his throat. "With your body. Let me *feel* it," she amended.

His shoulders dropped and he laughed, pulling on her hand, leading her quickly through the kitchen and into another darkened hallway.

"Stay here," he whispered, their fingertips brushing as he left her, walking to the library beyond and turning on the old turntable, feeling with his hands as he placed the needle on the edge of the record already in place. It was the record he'd put on after receiving the gift from Clara, wanting to listen not only to the tune, but to the words of the song she'd chosen for him.

The strains of *All I Ask of You* filled the room, and Jonah turned it up to its highest volume, making his way back to Clara where she waited for him in the blackened hallway.

She gasped softly when he suddenly took her in his arms, having not been able to hear him approach over the music filling the air around them.

"You knew the song," she said, a smile in her voice as he spun her once, and her smile turned into a laugh, bubbling sweetly from her.

"Did you choose it on purpose?" Jonah pulled her flush against him, leading her down the hallway and lifting her slightly when he came to the place where there was a step up into the front foyer.

Moonlight filtered softly through the window high up on the wall and Clara laid her head on his shoulder as she followed his lead. "Yes," she said, her voice wistful, dreamy.

He spun her around once, twice, as she laughed again, moving her through the unlit rooms, the steps he'd known so well once before coming back to him as though it hadn't been too many long, lonely years since he'd held a woman this way.

And this wasn't just any woman, just any partner he might dance with once and forget about after the song ended. This was *Clara,* and she was in his arms, and he never wanted to dance with anyone else again. Only her.

Jonah smiled each time a surprised burst of laughter erupted sweetly from her, spinning more quickly, picking her up as he took the small steps up and down into different rooms of the house he knew like the back of his own hand. The rooms he'd walked through in the dark night after night.

He was leading and she was following, and in the darkness like this, with her pressed so close to him, trusting him not to let her fall, he could almost believe he'd gone back in time . . . he was just himself, just Jonah, unscarred, a man with the freedom he'd taken so much for granted once upon a time.

But no, he wasn't. He *was* scarred—damaged—and it hurt too much to pretend otherwise. This was his new world, but the real miracle was that Clara had come into it of her own free will, and she was holding him just as tightly in her arms as he was holding her.

He spun her past the windows emitting the barest glint of moonlight, a soft pearlescent glow barely peeking through the heavy drapes, but enough to see by if he stopped rather than spinning them back into the shadows.

She laughed, pulling him closer. "You dance between moonbeams, don't you, Jonah Chamberlain?" Her laughter had faded, her voice sounding huskier than it had. Her words sounded familiar somehow, as if he might have heard them somewhere before, or thought them himself, but he couldn't quite remember.

"*We* dance between moonbeams," he said, spinning her again.

"We," she repeated. "Yes."

The music dwindled and then faded away, static from the needle replacing the notes. Jonah stopped, both of them breathing heavily in each other's arms. He could feel his own heartbeat—hers too—the blood pulsing between them, the gravity that suddenly filled the air.

"Kiss me again, Jonah," she said. "Only this time, don't stop."

His heart skipped a beat and then took up the same rapid staccato. "What?"

She took his shirt in her fists and pulled him closer, impossibly closer. "Don't stop kissing me. Take me to your bedroom."

"My bedroom?" His blood was pumping furiously through his veins, he could feel every sweet curve of her softness against him, and his heart was beating so harshly, he couldn't think straight.

"That place where you sleep?" she said, a smile in her voice. She let go of his shirt with one hand and placed it over his pounding heart. "The place where *I'm* going to sleep." He heard her lick her lips, and it sent a hot pulse of blood to the already-throbbing place between his legs. "Under you. And on top of you and—"

She let out a surprised gasp as he swooped her into his arms and headed for his bedroom. He made a brief pause in the library where he switched off the record player now playing a song from Phantom of the Opera that he didn't know the name of.

Silence enveloped them as he walked the rest of the way to his bedroom, kicking the door closed and putting Clara down, her body sliding against his before her feet hit the floor.

He kissed her as she grabbed his shirt once more, leaning into him so his back hit the door. He was losing the ability to think at all, losing the ability to reason, but before he allowed himself to fall into the oblivion of pleasure, he had to be sure she would not regret this. "Are you sure? You haven't seen me. I'm—"

"I don't care," she said between kisses. "Don't you know that by now?"

He groaned. He was painfully hard—desperate—and her hands were everywhere, moving down the plane of his chest, her fingers tracing the muscles of his abs through his T-shirt. *Slow. Slow down. Speed up. Don't stop. More.* God, he wanted everything, and all at once.

He didn't know this version of himself, this Jonah so frantic with lust that he was coming apart at the seams. He'd always been the one in control, the one who set the pace and made the terms when it came to the women he'd been physical with.

But Clara . . . oh God, Clara . . . She was making sweet little panting sounds, making him delirious, causing him to pulse hotly in his jeans with each small utterance. *Christ.* He was going to explode. It'd been so long. This wasn't going to go well. If she pressed her hips into his one more time, he was going to come in his damn pants.

"Clara." His voice was filled with desperation. He tried his best to add a hint of levity, as though he found the situation vaguely amusing, when in fact, he did not. Maybe they could laugh about it. *No big deal. You touched me once, and I lost it.*

"I'm not going to last—" His words left off on a moan as she unbuttoned the top button of his jeans, the sound of his zipper barely breaking through the lust fog he was in. "W-what are you doing?"

"*Helping*." Her hand wrapped around his hardened flesh and he groaned, his back pressing into the door behind him.

"Oh God," he panted, as her hand gripped him more tightly, stroking up once and then down. *Jesus. Jesus.* It felt so good. He should stop her . . . *maybe*. But he couldn't begin to figure out why.

Clara leaned in and kissed his neck, nipping it softly as her hand continued to work its magic. He grew harder, and his gut clenched with pleasure before he came, breathing out her name raggedly as his head fell against the door.

"Better?" she asked on a whisper, releasing him as he fought to catch his breath.

"God, yes." That small trickle of embarrassment returned, and yet the bliss still coursing through him dulled it. He'd be embarrassed about it later. Or not. Because for now the happiness lighting his insides was too great to allow him to fully believe that was possible.

"Good," she said, kissing him again. "I need to take a quick shower. Is that okay? I came straight here from rehearsal and—"

"Let me," he murmured, taking her by the arm and leading her before she could protest.

She clung to him as he guided her around the bed and through the door to the master bathroom, letting her go for a moment as he turned on the faucet, the sound of water splashing into the tub filling the room.

Moist steam, invisible in the darkness, rose in the air, and as Jonah tested the temperature of the water, he could hear Clara's movement, the very soft sound of her clothes as they hit the floor and fire ignited in his veins once more.

He helped her step in and she let out a moan of pleasure as she sat down in the rising water, laying her head back against the porcelain rim of the claw-foot tub.

Jonah sat on a stool behind the tub, gathering her hair and running his fingers through the silken strands.

"This is heaven," she said, the final word ending in a sigh.

She had no idea. But how could she? She hadn't been to hell, not like him.

He washed her hair as the water rose higher, the fragrance of his shampoo scenting the room and mixing with the steam.

"Sorry I don't have anything more . . . floral," he said on a smile, his fingers massaging her scalp. "I didn't exactly expect female company."

Clara laughed, the sound half-drunk as though she was so relaxed she could barely muster the sound. "I love it," she said. "It's like you're all around me. Behind me. In the air. Filling me."

That was all it took. Jesus, he was aroused again, hard, ready. His body trembled as he brought water to her hair with a cupped hand, rinsing the soap.

"Someday," she said softly, a note of trepidation in her voice, "I'd love to do this by candlelight."

Jonah paused, waiting for the fear. But it didn't come. He pictured the steamy room, bathed in candlelight, pictured her turning her head, her gaze ghosting over his damaged face. And instead of terror, hope blossomed inside of him, the idea that maybe, just maybe, Clara *could* look upon him as he was, not with horror, but with . . . love.

He would consider it later, but not now, not when he was so caught up in her, he could barely think straight. "Maybe someday," he said. "But not tonight."

"Okay," she whispered, but she didn't sound disappointed. No, she sounded pleased. And he realized it was the first time he'd given her reason to believe that he would find the resolve, the strength, to reveal himself to her. In fact, he'd surprised himself.

Maybe.

Maybe.

The one little word was so *full.*

Clara handed him the bar of soap that she must have felt in the clip-on dish on the side of the tub and for a moment Jonah simply held it in his hand, his mind blank. If there had been enough light to see by, he would have sat staring blankly at the smooth bar in his hand, uncomprehending.

She seemed to be waiting, and when it dawned on Jonah that she was asking him to wash her body, to run his hands all over her wet, naked skin, he almost groaned aloud.

How had he arrived here? How had it happened? *Is this even real?* He couldn't figure it out. But he wasn't going to waste these moments in heaven—dream or reality—however long they might last.

He ran the soap over her curves, learning her in the warm, wet darkness, his hands seeing what his eyes could not. She had asked for this in candlelight and he had said, *someday.* Maybe. But he yearned for it too. He yearned to *see* her, to know her expression as he touched her, to learn all the shades and details of her body.

But for now he could worship her with his touch.

He rubbed the soap between his hands and then ran them over her shoulders, down and back, massaging her muscles gently.

He used his fingers to trace her collarbone and felt her arch her neck as he moved slowly over those delicate bones. His hands ghosted down her ribcage and then up, over the soft mounds of her breasts. He felt her nipples peak as he ran his hands over them, a soft moan floating from her mouth as his fingers circled that hardened flesh. His name rose in the air, so soft, it was like another tendril of steam. He wanted to lean over her, to take those peaks in his mouth, to taste her, but he forced himself to continue on, taking another ragged breath.

He soaped his hands again and then brought them back to her body, his hands lingering on the dip of her waist, moving slowly downward, over her firm, slim hips.

"Jonah," she breathed, arching her back so the water rose and then lowered. She used her own hand to guide his to the place between her legs, and he let out a shuddery breath as he willed his own body to remain in control.

Fear trembled through him as his fingers explored that secret, vulnerable place. She had no real idea whose hand stroked her there. If the lights suddenly came on, would her eyes widen in horror as she realized who she'd let take such liberties with her sweet, pliant body?

She pressed herself into his touch, gasping his name, distracting him from his thoughts as though she'd known the direction they were taking. And before he could return to them, she lifted herself from the water, bringing him with her so he was standing beside the tub, her arms around him, her wet body saturating his shirt.

"I want you," she said. "*You.*" So she did know then. He had a tell, apparently. One he couldn't identify, but one she'd read as easily as if he'd uttered the words that spoke of his doubts. He was that transparent to her, even in the darkness. It terrified him. *It thrilled him.*

Their mouths met as he lifted her from the water, grabbing a towel and rubbing it over her with the arm not wrapped around her body.

She gripped his shoulders and they stumbled toward the bed, his hands running over the curve of her backside, lifting and pressing so they both moaned into each other's mouths. She laughed, a raw sound as her legs hit the back of his bed and she fell, landing on his mattress with a soft thump.

He kicked off his shoes, barely cognizant of removing his clothes, so eager to get back to the warmth of her arms.

And then his naked flesh met hers and they both stilled, something vibrating between them before he brought his mouth to her breast. He had learned her with his hands, and now he meant to learn her with his mouth.

He tasted and sucked and nipped as he moved down her body, drawing more of those raw, garbled sounds from her throat, sounds that might have been meant as words, as *encouragement,* but lost their way from her mind to her lips.

Her hands came to his head, her fingertips grazing one of the scarred patches of scalp. He tensed, turning so she couldn't explore him there. She didn't protest, but instead brought her hand to the back of his head, pushing gently so his mouth would return to her body.

He held himself away from her so that the rigid, blood-filled part of him wouldn't brush against her and make him as desperate as he'd been before. Amazing that it was possible. How many times would he have to have her before the desperate edge went away and he regained that control he'd always had? Or was part of it about *her,* about the fact that he'd never felt this way about any woman?

He stroked the inside of her thigh, kissing that silken flesh, and she opened to him, inviting. His tongue found the spot that made her press toward him and cry out, and he lapped her there, listening to the soft pants that told him what she liked. His finger found her opening and he pressed inside as more sounds of garbled pleasure spilled from her lips. God, she was wet. She was—

"Jonah!"

He realized blearily that she was repeating his name, and now she was pulling on his shoulders, asking him to move things along, to hurry.

A small laugh, born of wonder, came from his mouth right before he crawled up her body, kissing her as he simultaneously entered her.

Oh God, oh holy hell you feel good.

"Yes. Oh," she sighed, breaking from his mouth and pressing her head back into the pillow. "I want to come this first time with you inside me," she whispered, her legs wrapping around his hips.

This first time. Oh God. He really *had* died and gone to heaven.

He thrust once, distant fireworks brightening the darkness of his mind. He made a raw, garbled sound of his own as he thrust again, her fingernails digging into the muscles of his back.

She repeated his name, her voice saturated with pleasure as he moved inside of her, grasping the back of her thigh so he could raise it slightly. So he could go deeper, claim more of her, feel every part of this beautiful woman beneath him that he possibly could.

He wanted her so much. So much. It pounded through his disfigured body and into his twisted soul. He *loved* her, and that love rang inside of him like the bells of a church on the holiest of holy days.

The song echoed through his soul, a resounding chime of joy that filled the empty hollows of his lonely heart.

I love you. I love you. I love you.

She tightened around him, squeezing his hips with her wrapped legs, her body arching as she cried out.

He came a moment after her, the orgasm hitting him as though one of those distant fireworks had exploded right under him, shooting its glittering light through every cell in his body, her name the final sparkle falling from his inner sky.

"Well," she sighed, and the sound was part awe, part tease. He smiled, his nose in the crook of her neck.

He took a moment to breathe her in, before slipping free of her and rolling away. She rolled toward him, wrapping her arms around his waist and laying her head on his scarred shoulder.

She kissed his chest, nuzzling her nose over his skin until he drew her closer.

"Well," she repeated, and he could feel her grin.

"My thoughts exactly," he said, winding a strand of damp hair around his finger and bringing it to his nose, inhaling the scent of her mixed with his shampoo.

They lay there for several minutes, the bliss of their lovemaking still floating through Jonah, the quiet darkness wrapping around them and making him feel as if they were in a cocoon built for two. God, he wanted this. Wanted her. Forever.

"How long have you been patrolling with the Brass Angels?" Clara asked, her breath warm against his skin.

"Not long. Since a couple of days after your fall." *That* moment, watching her fall, had been horrendous. Time had stood still, desperately needing to get to her, but also needing to know if Ruben and Augustus were threats or allies. Waiting for her to open her eyes had been torture . . .

"Tell me more about what you do."

They spoke into the night, Jonah telling her about the people they'd helped, the wishes he'd granted, and how he'd gathered the courage to visit Amanda Kershaw's mother.

He didn't mention the phone because he didn't see any reason to. He didn't know if there would be anything of any consequence on it and so at the moment, it felt unimportant. He'd found a charger that matched the old phone on eBay and ordered it, but it wouldn't arrive for another few days. He'd check it out then and see what was what.

But for now, there was only Clara, only whispered words and touches that began lazily and took on more focus, more purpose, until their words faded, turning from syllables to sighs.

He hadn't expected to ever experience such pleasure again . . . to be sexually sated . . . held. Monsters didn't deserve pleasure, after all.

But something was shifting inside of him.

"I never blamed you. You didn't kill her." Those words.

"It's like you're all around me. Behind me. In the air. Filling me." Clara's want. Clara's caresses. Her touches. Her willing kisses. And unless he was very wrong, the giving of her heart.

He rose before the sunrise, stealing from the warmth of the bed and pulling on his clothes in the hush of the darkness before dawn.

Clara said something in her sleep, his name he thought, and it washed over him as though the sun had suddenly risen in a rush of bright illumination.

She moved very slightly, her form a mere outline in the blackened room, and he desperately wanted to crawl back into bed with her. To hold her as she woke.

Another hour and the room would be cast in milky shades of light. If she turned, she'd see him and—

No.

He'd lost control of his body, his *heart,* but in this, he couldn't.

He made his way to the door, standing outside of it, visions of the night before bringing him joy and hope. Maybe he wouldn't always be slipping out of Clara's arms before the sunrise lit the world and exposed his damaged face. Maybe . . . *maybe.*

CHAPTER TWENTY-EIGHT

Clara inhaled the sweetly subtle scent of the white rose, its velvety petals tickling her nose. Her lips curved into a dreamy smile as she reached for her phone, placing the singular stem back into the vase filled with eleven other white roses, and fresh eucalyptus that spilled over the sides.

The flowers had been delivered during rehearsal, making all of the other ballerinas whisper and shoot her grins.

Clara: The roses are beautiful, thank you. Did you know white roses stand for purity? Do you still think of me as pure after last night? ;)

Jonah: The woman at the flower shop told me they stand for honor and reverence. But yes, I still think of you as pure . . . ish. ;)

Clara laughed, her heart flipping over in her chest at his claim of honoring her. He'd made her *feel* revered the night before. He'd made her feel precious.

Clara: Then I need to do better next time.

Jonah: Better than last night doesn't exist.

Clara grinned, catching a reflection of herself in the dressing room mirror and biting her lip, realizing she looked like a love-struck teenager. She released her lip, allowing her grin to widen. *Who cares? I* am *love-struck,* she thought with a flush of giddiness. And she was alone, so what did it matter if she wore a goofy grin?

Although speaking of being alone, she should get going. There were probably still a few dancers left in the building, but Clara wasn't certain. She'd remained on stage after everyone had been dismissed, wanting to use the space to practice a move that she still had to think about each time she did it, rather than it feeling like second nature, the way that allowed her to lose herself in the emotion of the story.

Clara: Just leaving practice now. I'll call you when I get home.

Jonah: Talk to you then.

Clara unlaced one toe shoe quickly, removing it and taking a moment to massage her arch with a small sigh. God, it always felt so good to take them off. Her hand moved on her foot, working the overused muscles, and it brought to mind Jonah's hands on her body the night before, the way they'd stroked and—

Clara groaned, moving the memories aside with effort. It would do her no good to get all hot and bothered while in a public dressing room, even if the other girls had already changed and left.

No, she wouldn't *linger* on the details of her night with Jonah just now, but, God, it had been magical. The most magical night of her life. And his body was a marvel. Solid and muscular and perfectly masculine. She'd felt all of it, every dip and curve, each divot and . . . swell.

She'd even felt the scars, that mottled, upraised skin of his back and shoulder that he hadn't even noticed she was running her hand over. It'd only made her want him more, every imperfect part of him.

And her wish collector definitely knew what he was doing. He very obviously knew his way around a woman's body.

Clara felt a momentary twinge of jealousy for all those women he'd been with in the past. Those women who'd had him in the light, perhaps as sunshine streamed in a window, daylight breaking and casting him in shades of gold.

She moved her mind away from thoughts of envy. He was hers now, and she was his. A few bars of *All I Ask of You* hummed from her lips as she recalled him twirling her through a darkened Windisle Manor.

She'd felt as if they were dancing together in some celestial body as he'd guided her from room to room, hopping between stairs, using them for steppingstones as he'd spun her through a midnight sky.

Your true love dances between moonbeams. Ah yes, he did, didn't he? Her wish collector . . . her shadow dancer. Her beloved.

She still hadn't looked at his face, the way it was now, so damaged, or so he thought, that he had disappeared with the morning light, leaving her only memories and the scent of him lingering on her skin.

But whatever he looked like now, she loved him and there weren't enough scars, not enough battle wounds in the world to convince her otherwise. She loved him deeply and with her whole heart.

Clara pulled on her clothes, hanging her costume up on the hook at her station, and grabbing her duffle bag as she left the room.

She was surprised to find that the lights had been turned off. Was she really the very last one in the building? She'd stayed on stage before, practicing a move or two, and there had always been at least a few other dancers who had lingered for one reason or another . . . or janitorial staff or *someone.*

She made her way down the darkened hall, a small smile teasing at her lips. The darkness suddenly had a whole new appeal to her.

The darkness was where he lived.

"You've been avoiding me."

Clara spun around, letting out a gasp of surprise, but then bringing her hand to her chest as she saw that it was Marco. "God, you scared me."

He didn't smile as he approached her, and a small jolt of unease ran down Clara's spine. "This whole hard-to-get thing is getting old."

He moved closer, stopping several feet from her.

Clara shifted, watching him, this strange standoff making her suddenly uncomfortable, his words causing the hair on the back of her neck to stand up. She couldn't read his expression in this dimly lit hallway. But his voice contained annoyance . . . and something else she couldn't identify, something that didn't sound like the Marco she knew. And now she was alone with him.

Be wary of the man with two faces. He'll hurt you if you let him.

Was he *angry?* Why was he confronting her like this? Alone in a building where it was only the two of them? She backed away. He advanced.

"Don't run from me, Clara. You're always running from me."

"Marco, listen—" She put her hand against the wall, feeling for the switch she thought for sure was there. She found it with a gust of relief, flipping it as light flooded the hallway. Marco flinched away, putting his hands in his pockets as he looked back at her. Clara stared. He looked . . . sad.

"I know you're hesitant to give me a chance because you think I'm some sort of player." He gave her a self-mocking smile. "And the truth is, I have been. But I . . . I'd really like to earn your trust."

Clara's shoulders lowered. "God, Marco, a darkened hallway isn't the best place to do that."

He looked briefly confused. "What? You *know* me. I didn't think I'd scare you." He leaned one hip against the wall. "Every time I try to talk to you, you run off before I can get three words out."

Clara studied him, seeing the vulnerability in his expression. He'd tried for teasing, and it had come off as false because it was. He was truly hurt by the way she'd treated him.

Clara took a deep breath, relaxing, a small buzz of guilt vibrating within her. He was right. She'd known he'd wanted to talk to her and she'd all but ducked behind furniture to avoid him when she'd seen him coming. Not cool. Marco might be a lot of things, but he'd never been unkind to her. She owed him the truth.

"Sorry, Marco. You're right. See, the thing is . . ." Clara glanced away. God, how did she explain this? "A friendship has unexpectedly turned into more and, well, I'm—"

"No longer single?"

Clara frowned. Jonah had made no promises to her on that front. Her heart was hanging on a maybe that he'd ever even reveal his face to her. "It's complicated. But I'm no longer interested in dating anyone else."

Marco stuck his hands deeper into his pockets, nodding, the expression on his face full of disappointment. "He's a lucky guy. Does he know it?"

Clara doubted Jonah would describe himself as lucky, but she hoped beyond hope that he felt the same joy she felt in their relationship, however that might be defined.

Rather than getting into things she hadn't even worked through in her mind, she nodded. "Thank you, Marco."

He sighed, pushing off the wall. "All right, well now that you broke my heart, the least you can do is let me drive you home." He walked to her, offering her his arm.

Clara smiled. Marco might be disappointed that she wouldn't date him, but she highly doubted his heart was anywhere near broken. "You sure?"

"Very. Come on."

Clara and Marco chatted about the upcoming performance as he drove her home, their rapport suddenly effortless. He was a nice guy, and she felt guilty for judging him more harshly than she should have. He might be a player, but he had a sensitive side too, and someday he'd find that woman who made him want to commit to only her if that's what he ultimately wanted.

In any case, his romantic life wasn't her business. She didn't feel even an eighth of the magnetism toward him that she'd felt for Jonah even through a layer of rock.

But the situation with Marco also made her consider the ways in which she might have written off the other dancers in the ballet as she'd done with him.

She had been quick to judge others because she'd often felt judged in the past. And yes, girls could be gossipy, but perhaps it was *she* who'd been remiss in making more of an effort at friendship, *she* who'd always left quickly, who avoided the social activities she'd overheard being planned.

Maybe she could apply some of the fault to herself. Perhaps she could benefit from a little self-reflection when it came to the friendships she might have enjoyed if only she'd put herself out there a little bit more. And she vowed to do better in that regard.

When Marco dropped her at her apartment, she thanked him again and then waved, watching as he drove away.

How could she have thought—even momentarily—that the fortune teller was referencing Marco? If there was even any credibility to Madame Catoire's words, the *only* man who held the power to truly and irrevocably hurt her was Jonah. A small tremble moved down her spine. *Oh no,* she thought dejectedly, *please let me be wrong about that.*

Her cell phone began ringing and Clara pulled it from her pocket, the number on the screen making her heart skip a nervous beat. "Hello?"

"Clara, dear, it's Jan Lovett."

"Hi, Mrs. Lovett. Is everything okay?" Clara had spoken to her father briefly a few days before but he hadn't known her name. That was always so hard, to have the joy of his voice in her ear, but the heartache of explaining who she was again and again.

"Yes, dear, it's great. Your father is here and he'd like to speak to you."

Clara had let herself into her apartment as she spoke and now she stopped on the other side of the doorway, her heart soaring. "Really?"

Mrs. Lovett laughed. "Really."

She heard some soft scuffling and then her father's voice in the background. "I told you I could make a call on my own. I'm not helpless."

"Oh, stop being a pain. Your daughter's waiting on the line."

"Clara?"

Tears welled in her eyes. "Hi, Dad."

"Hey there, Tiny Dancer. How's my girl?"

So much emotion flooded Clara's chest and so suddenly, that she let out a tiny hiccup. "I'm good, Dad. It's so wonderful to hear your voice." She made her best effort to pull herself together. The last thing she wanted to do was make her Dad sad on this rare occasion that his mind was lucid. *But, to hear him say her name.* To have him *know* her was a gift beyond measure. "I have so much to tell you."

Her dad chuckled. "Start with the important part. You know I like to get right to the good stuff first."

Clara let out a soggy-sounding laugh. "Okay then." Clara pulled in a lungful of air and let it out slowly. "I'm in love."

There was a very short pause and then her dad asked, "Is he a good man?"

"Yes," she said without hesitation. "He's a very good man, Dad. Like you. He's kind and he's valiant and he cares about others." Clara paused for a moment, wanting to sum up the situation with Jonah for her dad in a way that cut straight to the chase without going through every detail of their story.

Clara was very conscious of time when it came to conversations with her dad. He had told the truth when he said he'd always liked to get right to the heart of a matter, but now, it was a necessity. Their time was limited and she was mindful of every second.

"But he doesn't believe in himself as strongly as I do, Dad, and I worry that, in the end, he won't let me love him the way he deserves to be loved." *In the light. Out in the open. In front of the world. Free from guilt.*

"Hmm," he said. "That is a challenge. If he doesn't have faith in himself, he's going to find it difficult to have faith in you. He'll hurt you if you let him."

"I . . . I know, Dad. That's what I'm worried about."

"So don't let him."

Clara let out a tearful laugh. Her sweet dad had so much faith in her, he thought she could do anything, convince anyone, rule the world. "I love you, Dad."

"I love you too. You're extraordinary, Tiny Dancer. And that young man of yours must be extraordinary in many ways too if he's won your heart."

"He is. He really is. I wish so much you could meet him."

"Me, too. I miss you, sweetheart." There was a short pause. "Do you want to go to the zoo tomorrow? I know you love the giraffes, Tiny Dancer."

Clara's heart sank, pain ricocheting through her. "Yes, Dad," she said on a whispery breath. "I'd like that."

She heard some shuffling sounds and then it was Mrs. Lovett's voice on the phone. "Sorry, dear. I was hoping he'd be with you longer than that."

A tear ran down Clara's cheek and she swiped at it as she smiled. Happiness mingled with sadness and it was almost too much to bear. "It's okay, Mrs. Lovett. I'm so grateful for those few minutes. Thank you for calling me."

"Of course, dear. You be well."

She hung up the phone and sat on her couch for a few minutes longer, a smile on her lips as several more tears ran down her cheeks.

"I'll miss you," she said to herself, her voice echoing back to her in the small, underground space. How many more moments like tonight would she get? How long until he didn't remember her at all?

After a minute she got up and went outside. She needed to feel the breeze on her face, to look at the sky and remind herself there was beauty and joy and magic and mystery in this great wide world, and she wouldn't ever stop remembering that even when she was hurting. Especially then.

It was a beautiful night, clear and quiet, a million shards of diamond stars scattered across the sky.

Clara looked down the block toward Mrs. Guillot's but her porch light was off and there was no light coming from the front room of her house either.

She remembered back to the moment several days before when she'd seen Jonah on the news as she sat in Mrs. Guillot's and a smile played at her lips. *Jonah.*

Clara leaned back against the brick next to her door.

He must be extraordinary in many ways if he's won your heart, Tiny Dancer.

Oh yes.

As she stared in the direction of Mrs. Guillot's porch, the place where she'd first heard about Windisle Plantation, about Angelina Loreaux, her tired, emotionally taxed mind began drifting. It felt good to allow her thoughts to float away, to swirl around, weightless.

Her experiences, the intriguing stories and bits of information she'd received over the past few months mixed together and she let it, not stopping to examine any of it, simply letting the words and memories tumble aimlessly inside of her brain . . . Angelina and John, she and Jonah, the mystery, the curse, the riddle . . .

Amazing Grace, how sweet the sound.

I just regret. I've made a career of it, here, behind this wall.

If Angelina lingers, she lingers for him. For the soldier man.

Vague knowledge drifted just out of her reach, as nebulous as early morning fog. She let it go, not attempting to grasp it . . .

The note. John's betrayal . . .

Amazing Grace, how sweet the sound.

My mama, she didn't know how to read, but oh, did she know how to sing.

Clara's eyes widened as she stood up straight, blinking into the quiet street in front of her. *She didn't know how to read.* Mrs. Guillot's mama hadn't known how to read . . .

Clara pulled out her phone, dialing Jonah's number.

"Clara."

"Jonah, hi."

"Hey, what's wrong? You sound upset."

Clara shook her head. "No, no. I mean, I talked to my father, but it was wonderful. It made me sad, too, but, no, the reason I'm calling is, how common do you think it was for slaves to know how to read?"

"Read? I . . . I guess . . . rare. Why?"

Clara paced, something taking shape in her mind, information repeating, forming. "John's family delivered the note he wrote to Angelina, right?"

"From what I know."

"Would his family have approved of him and Angelina? A wealthy Southern family?"

"I . . ." He paused for a long moment, obviously thinking. "No."

"Right? And how likely do you think it was that Angelina knew how to read?"

He was silent again. "Probably not very likely."

"But what if . . . Oh my God, Jonah. What if they lied about what his letter said? She wouldn't know, would she?"

Excitement made Clara's heart beat faster. She felt it in her gut. She was *right* about this.

"You could be right. But how would it ever be proven?"

"The note. We need the note."

"The note's long gone, Clara. No one's ever found it. If his family did lie about what it said, they probably took it with them."

Clara's excitement dipped and her shoulders sagged. "But they might have left it, thinking it wouldn't matter since she couldn't read it, and no one she was close to could read it either . . ."

"They might have, but if they did, Angelina herself probably disposed of it. Believe me, if that thing existed, it would have been in my brother's file."

Crap. Clara let out a disappointed sigh. "You're probably right." Still, the idea that she'd connected several of the puzzle pieces persisted. Maybe it couldn't ever be proven, but Clara *believed* she was right, and the possibility was both exciting and so horribly tragic. They'd *lied* to Angelina, stealing every last piece of her hope. Had they planned on blackmailing John into marrying Astrid when he arrived home from the war with a threat to Angelina's safety? Her life? Oh how easy that would have been. A sharp pang tore through Clara's heart.

"I'll tell you what, I'll dig through the attic a little bit tomorrow, okay? See what I can find."

"You'd do that for me?"

"I'd do just about anything for you." His voice was suddenly gritty, his tone so serious it made Clara's breath catch.

Just about. She made note of the caveat, but happiness infused her anyway. She'd received a maybe from him the night before when she'd asked about candlelight. *Maybe . . .* Such a beautiful word when previously it had always been no and never.

"Maybe you could come over tomorrow night. I don't have to get up early the next morning."

Although a little lost sleep was worth it to Clara, she did have early practice the next day and the performance season was drawing so close. She needed to be at her best at rehearsal. "I'd . . . I'd leave the lights off."

Jonah hesitated for only a moment. "No, Clara, I don't think so. Not yet."

The stab of disappointment that hit Clara was very small and fleeting. Truthfully, she just wanted to see him. Or, well, *feel* him. She just wanted to be with him, and if that meant she only went to him for a while, that was okay. "I understand, Jonah."

She heard the smile in his voice as he asked her about her day and they began to speak of both mundane and important things. The things couples spoke of. The small details of their lives that were only shared with each other.

She told Jonah about her conversation with her father, and he sounded both happy and sad for her. Clara stared at the darkness of the sky, closing her eyes as her wish collector's velvety voice filled her ear and her heart. Although somewhere in the back of her mind, that ticking grew louder, stronger, more insistent.

CHAPTER TWENTY-NINE

"Did you order something?" Myrtle asked. "This was in your PO box."

Jonah turned toward her where he stood at the sink, rinsing his dishes from lunch. Myrtle placed a small package on the counter as Jonah dried his hands. He peered at the label. The item had come from somewhere in Kansas. Ah, the charger he'd ordered from eBay. "Yeah. Thanks."

Myrtle eyed him suspiciously. "What?"

"I saw Clara leaving the other morning."

Jonah grinned. He couldn't help it. It just spilled over his face like sunshine at the mention of her name *and* because she'd left his bed that morning.

He tried unsuccessfully to wipe it away, clearing his throat and squinting at the ceiling as he tried to distract himself from thoughts of her. "She was, er, visiting. It got late. She was tired."

"Mm-hmm. I didn't just fall off a turnip truck, Jonah Chamberlain." Worry creased the lines of her face, and she leaned in close, adjusting her thick glasses. "I heard you leave your room hours before she did."

"Yeah, so?"

Myrtle reached a hand out tentatively, and Jonah instinctively pulled back, turning the damaged side of his face away from her touch. Shrinking.

Myrtle halted but then brought her fingers slowly closer, the way one might when reaching out to offer solace to an injured animal.

Jonah watched her, unmoving now as she grazed her fingers over his scarred cheek. He released a pent-up breath, closing his eyes at the feel of another person touching that ruined part of him for the first time since he'd left the hospital.

"You have to allow her to love all of you."

He flinched, turning away, her fingers falling into the empty space he'd created. "What if she can't?"

"What if she *can?*"

"I . . . I don't know, Myrtle. What if she can, but what if I'm still not able to give her the life she deserves?" Jonah turned away, looking out the window at the brightness of the day.

"I have faith in you, my boy. But you already know that. You need to find faith in yourself."

He turned toward her, the happiness that had flooded through him moments before crumbling to doubt. "Maybe it's not *about* me, Myrtle. This town, hell, the world at large, isn't going to be accepting of me just because I decide to walk out into it."

"It's *always* about you, Jonah. It's always *been* about you. The world will react the way the world will react. That's not your business. You have faith in your own worth and the world won't matter."

"I don't think I know how to do that," he murmured.

"You do, sweet boy. And if you need a hand to hold, you got old Myrtle. I might walk you right into a tree before I walk you into the world, but I'll be there by your side."

Jonah laughed, love for her filling his heart. "Thanks, Myrtle."

Myrtle nodded on a smile as she picked up the grocery bags she'd brought in along with the mail and began unpacking them.

Jonah took the package, unwrapping the charger and stopping in his room where he plugged Amanda Kershaw's phone in before putting on his running clothes.

As he ran through the trees, doing his familiar loop among the cabins, peace infused him, a sort of unfamiliar . . . *bliss* tripping through his system.

He started to recite the names of the victims who'd died that day on the courthouse steps, the lives he'd felt responsible for, for so long, but they kept drifting away from him.

He attempted to catch them at first, to start at the beginning, the first name on the list he'd thought was tattooed on his brain, but he kept losing focus, losing track, a certain .

. . peace attempting to claim the space, pushing its way inside as the names floated away.

It almost felt as if those names were living, breathing entities and they *wanted* to be set free, wanted to disappear into the clouds above, like maybe his holding on had kept them trapped like him.

He'd run this path for so many years with the same syllables chanting through his mind, but now . . . now there was suddenly room for . . . *more.* There was suddenly so much space, and he wasn't sure what to do with it.

What he did know was that he was in love. Desperately, irrevocably in love. *Clara, Clara, Clara.* Her name echoed through him, and he raised his face to the sun and found the muted rays that had filtered through the breaks in the trees.

Clara. Beautiful, thoughtful Clara. God, Justin would have liked the hell out of her. She was so giving, so determined to right a wrong that actually bore no reference to her own life.

It had all started with her. Everything good that had happened to him in the last few months was because she had shown up at the weeping wall that day.

Yes, he'd fallen in love with her, but even more than that, he'd sought and received forgiveness, done some good for a few people in need, found friends in the members of the Angels.

He was disappointed he wouldn't be able to patrol with them anymore now that the media was looking to make a story out of him. Unless he . . . Jonah brought his hand to the bare skin of his face, running his palm over his scars . . . unless he found the courage to take the mask off. *Maybe.*

Again, that tiny yet immense word.

Jonah came to a stop, pushing his sweat-drenched hair back and walking in a slow circle in front of the main door to the manor. He considered the porch, seeing in his mind's eye a rocking chair and a man sitting upon it, rocking a little girl on his knee. *Angelina.* Had Robert Chamberlain taught her to read? Or had he allowed her to remain illiterate? Only seen her as a slave girl who happened to share his DNA?

He'd promised Clara he'd dig through the attic to see what he could find. He highly doubted he'd locate a letter dating back to 1861, but he'd check anyway. For her.

Back in his room, there was a green light at the top of the flip phone. *Huh.* It still held some charge. He opened it, pacing in front of his window as the screen lit up. No passcode. That made things easier. Did these old phones even have passcodes back then? He couldn't remember.

She had a few text strings and he opened them one at a time. One from her mom. He pictured her blind mother using some speech-to-text feature as she tried to reach her wayward daughter. He'd been thankful when he'd received an update from Neal McMurray, the contractor he'd sent and knew her place was being restored right that very moment, including new furniture and appliances an interior designer Neal had recommended was arranging. Mrs. Kershaw deserved some ease in her life, some comfort.

There was another string from a contact simply listed as "K" and he opened it, scrolling through. There were several "Meet me" and "It's Thursday. What time will you be here?" and when he got to the top of the string, there was an address.

Was that some kind of drug exchange? Or possibly, prostitution services being arranged?

He knew Amanda Kershaw had participated in plenty of unsavory activities for a fix. He'd spoken of them in lurid detail in front of a courtroom of witnesses. He'd seen her shame, her regret. He'd paraded every vile misstep to create reasonable doubt.

I know that some do, but me? No, I never blamed you. You didn't kill her.

And in any case, from what I hear, you paid your price.

Mrs. Kershaw's words rushed back to him, flowing over his soul like a balm. *Grace.* Jonah took a deep breath and opened another thread, drawing away from the phone in shock when he saw his brother's number. There was no name attached to it, but he knew that number well. It was the one he'd avoided in those last days, sliding *decline,* as his phone rang over and over. Justin. *What the fuck?*

The string was short. Justin asked to meet with her several times and that she at least call him back. She never responded via text message. Whether she'd ever called his brother, and for what reason, Jonah had no idea for her call history only went back to the week before she'd died.

Nerves vibrated through him, the feeling that something was wrong, that he'd been left in the dark and finding out why was going to *hurt.*

"Get a grip," he said aloud, forcing himself to enter that unattached state he'd adopted so many times when dealing with a disturbing case. "Relax and focus on all the information available to you first."

Having looked through the text messages, he opened her photo stream, his eyes widening.

For a moment he simply blinked as his mind caught up with what his eyes were looking at. *Sex*. And lots of it.

He sat on his bed, dragging his finger down the tiny screen, looking at what was obviously Amanda Kershaw herself, with man after man in various sexual positions. It looked as if most of the photos had been snapped discreetly while the men were either in the throes of passion—for lack of a better word—or in a position where they couldn't see the phone she'd obviously been holding.

What the hell *was* this?

Jonah stopped scrolling when he saw a face he recognized. *Holy shit*. Was that . . . he squinted, drawing the phone closer. It looked like . . . he couldn't be sure, the photo was blurred and from a strange angle, but he swore it looked like Judge Rowland, the man who'd presided over the Murray Ridgley case. Jonah dragged his fingers through his hair, holding his scalp for a moment as his mind raced.

When he opened one of the individual shots, he saw that Amanda had titled it with his first initial and last name. Each photo was like that, even the ones of the men he didn't recognize.

She had kept proof of each sexual interaction with these men, each picture titled with a name and a date. What *was* this? Had Amanda Kershaw been planning to blackmail them?

Completely confused, his gut churning with anxiety, Jonah scrolled through the last of the pictures, stopping immediately when he recognized another face. Shock hit Jonah. The acidic smell of his own sweat filled his nostrils. *Holy shit.*

It was Murray Ridgley, the man who had been accused of raping Amanda and attempting to murder her. But these pictures told another story. These pictures said in no uncertain terms that she'd been with him willingly . . . at least at some point. She had lied on the witness stand. *Why?*

Jonah opened the texts again, going back to the address at the beginning of the string with the unknown, K. He didn't recognize the street name, nor know why the word Vortex was spelled out below it, but he brought his own phone out and typed the location into his GPS.

It looked to be in an industrial area of New Orleans and was only about twenty minutes from Jonah. It had been almost nine years since that text was sent, and chances were, going to that address would lead to nothing, especially if it was some empty warehouse where she'd met a drug dealer. But it was Thursday, so he knew where he was heading.

****

The rumble of his motorcycle idled away to silence, Jonah taking a moment to look around before he slowly lifted his leg over the bike, removing his helmet and donning the mask.

The night was cold and still, a metallic smell hanging in the air. The massive building in front of him, once some sort of shipping warehouse, was dark and deserted, or so he thought until he saw a light move slowly past one of the windows as though it'd come from a hallway beyond, illumination of some sort slipping under the doorway for a brief moment.

He moved toward the building, looking around. There were no other cars in the parking lot, but if he strained his ears, he swore he could hear music coming from somewhere close by, the steady pulse of bass threading through him and matching his quickened heartbeat.

When he reached the entrance, he knocked on the heavy metal door, three loud raps that echoed in the emptiness. He didn't really expect anyone to answer, so when the door was pulled open moments later, Jonah startled, stepping away as a large man with long black hair pulled into a low ponytail filled the doorway. He peered out at Jonah, nodding once as he took in his mask. "Password?"

Fuck. But then he remembered the random word that had been spelled out under the address. "Last I was here, it was vortex."

The man raised a brow. "Man, that was years ago. No one even wore masks back then." He nodded to Jonah's covered face. "Who invited you?"

"Rowland."

The man narrowed his eyes slightly but then nodded, opening the door wider so Jonah could enter. "Have fun."

Something in the bouncer's tone caused Jonah to pause, but then he nodded, moving into the dark interior of the building.

"And hey," the guy called, looking out at the parking lot, "if that's your bike, park it in the back next time."

Jonah didn't bother to answer, walking down the hallway lit only by weak lights along the baseboards.

The bass grew louder, music pumping steadily as lights pulsed from a room beyond. Jonah had the sense that he was entering a dream, or a nightmare perhaps, something dark and unknown that already felt disconnected from reality.

"The good stuff's that way tonight," a man said, startling Jonah as he walked past. He was wearing a mask, something black and white and distorted that Jonah didn't get a good enough look at to identify before the man was moving away from him.

Jonah walked in the direction the man had pointed, pushing the door open to the room with the pulsing lights.

There were four different groups, naked or half-dressed women in the center of each, men performing various sexual acts on them, some, one at a time, and others, in tandem.

Jonah was briefly stunned, his eyes moving everywhere, taking in this scene. A masked orgy? Some type of exclusive sex club?

As his eyes grew accustomed to the dim lighting, he noticed that the girls looked very young, maybe not underage but very close to it. And they all looked mostly zonked out, not necessarily finding enjoyment in what was happening to them, but then, not protesting either.

Jonah felt sickened, confused. This place, the dim lighting, the bright red walls, it was the background of the photos on Amanda Kershaw's phone. She had been one of these girls. She'd photographed it, obviously before the men began wearing masks as they did now. He could see how easy it would have been to slip a phone out of a robe pocket like the silky black one the redhead in the corner was wearing. To snap a shot, to record what happened.

"Join us," a hand slinked around Jonah's waist, dipping toward his groin and then pulling away as a blonde girl walked past him, her eyes foggy and half closed, three masked men in tow.

Jonah waited for them to pass by and then turned, exiting the room and heading in the opposite direction from where he'd entered.

He passed by room after room, sounds of music and sex coming from beyond, the sounds of both pleasure and what he thought to be pain. He heard noises he couldn't identify, the slashing of a whip maybe, chain running over a concrete floor.

He moved faster through the dark labyrinth, finally spotting a double metal door and pushing through it, out into a back parking lot, his breath bursting from his lungs right before he sucked in another.

What the fuck was that? And what did Murray Ridgley have to do with it? Judge Rowland? His own brother maybe? His mind was spinning in a million different directions, and he wanted answers, answers he knew had to be on Amanda's phone if he could figure out how the evidence fit together.

He walked around the side of the building, heading for his motorcycle as he pulled out the flip phone. He scrolled to the text identified only as K and dialed the number as he strode toward his ride.

A woman answered on the second ring. "Knowles residence, May I help you?"

Holy fuck.

Knowles.

He knew the name well, because once upon a time, that man had hired him, had welcomed him to his firm.

CHAPTER THIRTY

November, 1861

Angelina entered the parlor where she'd been summoned, a dishtowel still in her hands. The sweet, yeasty scent of baking bread followed her from the kitchen. "Yes, Mrs. Chamberlain?"

Mrs. Chamberlain rose from where she'd been sitting, a man standing along with her. He turned and Angelina blinked. He looked like John, only he was thinner, the bridge of his nose narrower, his eyes more deep-set . . . Still, the resemblance made her heart flip in her chest, and her grip tighten on the towel in her hands.

"Angelina, this is Mr. Lawrence Whitfield. He's come bearing correspondence for you."

"C-correspondence?" Angelina whispered, a tremor of hope *and fear* shimmering through her. Was it from John? And if so, why would he expose their relationship by writing to her directly? That wasn't safe.

Mr. Whitfield gave her a thin smile, taking the few steps to where she stood as he removed a letter from his pocket. "My brother, John, asked that I give this to you. It came in a bundle of mail for our family."

Angelina reached for the letter but Lawrence pulled it back. "John explained that you're unable to read. He asked that I read it to you."

Her eyes met his, her heart beating wildly. She didn't know how to read this man's expression, this stranger, and she felt so weak with anxiety, that for a moment all she could do was stare. "Al-all right. Thank you, sir."

Mr. Whitfield unfolded the letter and Angelina felt a gasp of joy rise in her throat when she saw the handwriting. She swallowed it down with effort, watching as Mr. Whitfield donned a pair of spectacles.

That handwriting . . . the tiny precise letters mixed in with the large, sweeping ones. She'd seen it at the boathouse where they met. John had brought along correspondence to work on as he'd waited for her—hours sometimes, depending on when she'd been able to get away—and she'd glanced at the papers on top of the old crates he'd used as a desk.

At the sight of that script, longing swept through her, along with the deep relief that he was alive. Unharmed. Oh how she'd yearned for him. How she'd prayed for his safety. Wished fervently for the news that he was coming home. To her.

"Angelina," Mr. Whitfield read, "I write this letter regretfully and with the knowledge that my words will wound you. But I must be true to my heart. My time away from you has made things abundantly clear. Our trysts were pleasant, but lack a future. When I return home, I will marry Astrid. Surely you can see that anything else is impossible. You must accept your place in the world, Angelina. Only in this way will you live a satisfying life. Sincerely, John."

Mr. Whitfield cleared his throat, folding the letter slowly. Angelina's heart had sunk during the reading and now it lay heavy in the pit of her stomach, misery gripping her.

She raised her eyes slowly to Mrs. Chamberlain's and Mrs. Chamberlain looked back at her, her lips curved into a small smile. This pleased her. Of course it did.

Mrs. Chamberlain brushed her hands as if all that nasty business between John and Angelina was now over and she could move forward with her life.

But Angelina's life had ended. Just a few brief lines had destroyed her heart.

Our trysts were pleasant.

Pleasant.

How could this be true? Had the war somehow convinced him that she was not worth fighting for? He'd told her he loved her.

Know who to trust. And who not to trust.

Mr. Whitfield handed the letter to Mrs. Chamberlain and she took it, tossing it into the fireplace, but drawing back quickly when a spark flew at the sleeve of her gown and it caught flame. Mrs. Chamberlain let out a scream and beat at her sleeve as Mr. Whitfield moved to help her.

Angelina's eyes went to the letter where it had fallen next to the grate and she moved swiftly, taking advantage of the commotion and scooping it up. She slipped it beneath the towel she was still holding as Mrs. Chamberlain turned around, the fire on her sleeve having been extinguished. Angelina looked at her blankly.

"Well, go on then," Mrs. Chamberlain said, glancing at the roaring fire. "You've been dismissed."

Angelina turned without another word. She walked to the door on legs of jelly, Lawrence Whitfield's whispered words to Mrs. Chamberlain following her down the hall: "You see, Mrs. Chamberlain, my brother's foolhardiness is resolved. I look forward to toasting to John and Astrid at their wedding."

The pressure in her head grew, the tears she'd held back in the parlor now streaming down her face. She gripped the letter tightly, a small, small spark of hope still burning in her belly. She swiped at the wetness on her cheeks and tried to keep that small light aglow in her mind's eye.

I love you. I will come back to you, do you hear me?

Nothin' but danger. Nothin' but danger.

"Lina?" her mama called as she walked past the kitchen, catching a glimpse of her daughter's expression, her own draining of color. "Lina?" she repeated, though weakly the second time. Angelina ignored her, walking on, climbing the second-floor stairs and knocking on Astrid's door, entering without waiting for a response.

Astrid was sitting on her window seat reading a book and looked surprised when Angelina entered. "Angelina? What is it?"

Angelina thrust the letter in front of her, the paper shaking in her grip. "Will you read this, Astrid? John's brother read it to me and states that John's affection for me has ceased."

Astrid stared at her for a moment, several expressions flitting over her face. Expressions that Angelina was too distraught to read.

Astrid stood, walking to Angelina and taking the letter from her. She unfolded it slowly, glancing at Angelina as she did so, a frown marring her forehead.

Her eyes moved down the lines as she read and Angelina held her breath, a lump swelling in her throat. *Please, please. Tell me they lied,* she thought desperately. *I trust you, John.*

"I'm sorry, Angelina," Astrid said softly. "It says what Lawrence told you it says." Astrid handed the letter back to Angelina, stepping closer, wrapping her arms around her half-sister.

Angelina sagged into her, the tiny light inside of her extinguishing, hope draining. She felt empty, devoid, a moan climbing her throat, but not seeming to have any sound.

"It's better for you this way," Astrid said, pulling away and gripping her upper arms, her gaze intense. "*Safer.* My mama . . . you have no idea what she's capable of, Angelina, the way hate has carved itself so deeply into her. If she sees you . . . hoping for things, *planning* for things, she'll hurt you, or your mama, maybe both of you. It's *better* this way," she repeated and Angelina had the distant notion she was trying to convince herself as much as Angelina, but she was too sick with grief to consider it any more.

Nothing mattered, nothing at all, especially her. *Especially her.* She was merely something to discard. Something to hurt and throw away. Her mama was right, there was no place for love in Angelina's life. And there never would be.

And Angelina, she couldn't live a life without love.

She nodded, turning slowly and exiting Astrid's room. Astrid didn't try to stop her. She hesitated outside of her father's room for just a moment before going inside.

She felt nothing. She *wanted* to feel nothing.

When she stepped back into the hallway, her father loomed before her. "What are you doing?"

She looked at him, her eyes beseeching, hoping against hope to find that tenderness that used to be in his gaze when he'd bounced her on his knee as a child. "Nothing, Mr. Chamberlain."

His eyes narrowed as he glanced toward his closed door and then back at her. "Well then, get on back to the kitchen, girl."

Girl.

She'd tried so hard to emulate him, like the other Chamberlains who lived and ruled this house. She'd sat upon her father's knee, listening as he'd read her stories. She'd learned to speak like them, even to adopt the same mannerisms so they might come to love her.

But her mama had been right. Her efforts were in vain. It didn't matter what she *tried* to be . . . and it never would. He'd found her charming once upon a time, perhaps a novelty, but now she was a woman and . . . to him, she didn't even have a name.

Girl.

She ducked around the man who'd given her life against her mama's will on a dirty cellar floor and walked slowly down the stairs.

Outside, the breeze was cold upon her skin. She looked beyond to the sugarcane fields, heads bobbing in the distance and her heart sank lower. Lower.

If the world were different, maybe she wouldn't feel this clawing devastation inside, this vast and unending hopelessness. If the world were different, she'd start walking, and she'd *keep* walking. Beyond the high stone wall that contained Windisle, beyond New Orleans maybe. She'd go somewhere where she'd be free to make her own choices and live her own life. But that wouldn't happen.

My time away from you has made things abundantly clear . . . When I return home, I will marry Astrid. Surely you can see that anything else is impossible. You must accept your place in the world, Angelina.

Her place in the world—this godforsaken world that would never change—was as ash.

CHAPTER THIRTY-ONE

The upstairs bedroom was spacious and luxurious, Jonah's feet sinking into the thick carpet as he approached the bed where the man lay dying. Chandler Knowles.

Jonah removed the helmet he wore, the one he'd kept on when the housekeeper had answered the front door. When he'd called, he'd let her know he was coming and was surprised to find himself ushered inside immediately, the woman murmuring that Mr. Knowles was expecting him.

Mr. Knowles's glossy eyes moved over Jonah's damaged face, and despite being sickly and bedridden, he managed to cringe harshly. Jonah told himself the reaction did not matter. He no longer cared whether this man respected him or not. Didn't care if he looked at him in horror.

"I wondered how bad it was," Mr. Knowles said, his voice crackly and raw. He cleared his throat, motioning to the water pitcher on the bedside table where various pill bottles also sat.

Jonah poured a glass of water and handed it to him, and Mr. Knowles raised his head slightly to slurp in a few sips of the liquid.

"Now you know," Jonah said, replacing the glass on the nightstand. Of course the bastard could have known a lot sooner had he ever visited him, even in the hospital after it first happened. But there'd been radio silence from his firm. Not a word. Not even a fruit basket. What would the card have said anyway? "Hey, sorry your face blew up. Enjoy this lovely banana."

"I found Amanda Kershaw's phone," Jonah said. "I went through it."

There was a chair near the bed and Jonah pulled it up, sitting down as Knowles digested that information.

"You want to know the truth, I imagine." The old man let out a wet-sounding cough. "And as for me, I suppose it's natural for a man to want to clear his conscience when he knows he's about to meet his maker."

"I don't particularly care what your reasons are, but yeah, I deserve the truth."

Mr. Knowles grunted, a small sound that seemed to carry agreement. "Tell me what you know so I can save what little breath I have left."

"I went to the warehouse. The club, whatever it is."

"Ah. Yes, well. I thought they should have shut it down after all that mess." He sighed. "They didn't listen to me obviously. Suppose there's some extra turn-on in the risk of getting caught."

"What is it exactly? Who were the girls? The men?"

"The girls are drug addicts and runaways who are only too happy to score a hit or two." He paused. "Did you know that people will do *anything* for drugs? *Anything.* Women will give up their own *children* for a hit. Anything. They steal a person's soul."

As if the man lying in front of Jonah knew anything about having a soul. The low-level nausea Jonah felt increased.

"The members are gentlemen who work stressful jobs and long hours and want to let off some steam by participating in activities that their wives would be less than thrilled to know about. Applegate started it many years ago. He hand-chose the members, and it simply provided a very enjoyable extracurricular night now and again."

Jonah watched the man, digesting the information, feeling sickened. "So basically a group of old pervs preys on the weakness and vulnerability of young girls who've taken the wrong path."

Chandler Knowles laughed and for a moment, he seemed younger before his face collapsed in another grimace and he coughed, patting his chest. "So judgmental. Hence the need for privacy. *Exclusivity.*"

"Murray Ridgley was a member?"

Mr. Knowles made a distasteful sound. "I never liked that kid. Beady-eyed rat. I told them they should deny his application, but his father was a big to-do in the banking system. Some of the members had loans through him . . ." He waved his hand as if it was enough for Jonah to get the gist. Which, of course, it was. *Jesus.*

They'd known him. He'd been one of them, part of their sick little club. They'd accepted him because his father was valuable.

"They didn't listen to me, though," Mr. Knowles went on, his words broken up in a way that told Jonah, talking so much was taxing him. *Just get through this, old man,* Jonah thought. *And somehow I will too.*

He already felt sick, disturbed, overwhelmed. But he forced himself slightly outside his own mind so he could absorb the information, without absorbing the ramifications, and how it all related to him. Not yet. That was for later. He'd been a lawyer. He could compartmentalize with the best of them.

Mr. Knowles glowered. "And then it all went wrong. It was a rule that no one fraternize with any of those girls outside the club. But the little rat didn't listen. He took them home. He got too rough, choked not just one girl but two." He waved his gnarled hand. "Just runaways, junkies, but still, we had to cover it up."

Just runaways, junkies. Jonah's skin prickled. A tide was rising inside of him, and he tried desperately to hold it back.

"Murray was counseled, tossed out. But he waited for one of the girls to leave, offered her a ride. He didn't have to be a club member to reap the benefits, see?" *One of the girls. Amanda Kershaw.* "But she sobered up, got away from him before he could do her any real harm, and that's when the shit really hit the fan."

Jonah remained speechless. He felt unable to form words. Mr. Knowles let out another loose cough and then settled back on the pillows. "One of the club members was a former prosecutor. We sent him in to talk to her. She threatened to expose us all, said she had proof, but we were able to talk her down, promise her things. Whores all like *things,* don't they? She complied. Agreed to appear unstable on the stand."

Jonah's insides felt hollowed out. *A setup*. It'd all been a setup. "And then the firm stepped in to represent Murray Ridgley. You had to or he'd expose you too."

Something that looked like ire came into Mr. Knowles's eyes. "If they had listened to me, and denied that little rat's application in the first place, none of this would have happened. None of it was my fault. I only stepped in to help after the fact."

And yet, isn't this a confession where you're supposed to take responsibility for your sins? Jonah wondered. *Isn't this an attempt to wipe your soul as clean as possible, you sick bastard?*

Mr. Knowles sighed, looking off behind Jonah as though staring into the past. "We told him we'd get him off if he cooperated. Told him we had an ace in the hole, a fiery young buck who was sharp as a tack in the courtroom and would make it all look legitimate."

Me. Jonah's chest constricted painfully. He'd been used. Lied to. He'd been a pawn and he'd played straight into their hands. God, he'd thought he was so *smart,* when all he'd been was an idiotic patsy. *Blinded* by self-importance and ego. He wanted to laugh, to cry, to scream, but he did none of those things. He'd done a fine job making Amanda Kershaw appear unstable, of convincing the jury, but she'd played right along. All of these years he'd carried that guilt, and she'd known exactly what she was doing.

"What happened afterward?" His voice sounded dull, dead.

Something that looked like guilt came into Knowles's eyes. But quite frankly, he didn't care. Knowles's gaze flitted to Jonah's ruined face and then away.

"He always was a loose cannon. We should have remembered that. See, our mistake was that we operated as though we were dealing with someone sane. Ridgley was not sane."

So Murray Ridgley had held some kind of grudge toward Amanda Kershaw, the woman who'd gotten away from him, and he'd shown up that day to exact revenge. And Jonah had walked right into it.

"Where did my brother come into all of this?"

For a moment Mr. Knowles looked confused, but then his lips thinned. "Your brother worked in the neighborhoods where we found some of the girls for our club. He heard rumors, started asking some questions. Amanda told us he had called her and we told her not to talk to him." Mr. Knowles shrugged. "Nothing came of it."

Of course nothing came of it. Amanda had been shot, his brother had been shot, and Murray Ridgley had blown himself to bits. What a stroke of luck that must have been for all those high-status club members. And they still partied on as if lives hadn't been destroyed that day. As if the innocent simply hadn't existed.

It was merely collateral damage that Jonah's face had been scarred beyond recognition, his life ruined. Jonah stood on unstable legs. "Is there anything else?"

"I'll call you a liar if you say I told you any of this. If I'm not dead by then."

Mr. Knowles peered at him from beneath bushy white brows. He suddenly seemed small, shrunken, lying there in his deathbed. But Jonah felt small and shrunken too, hollowed out.

He thought of the evidence he had, the blurry photos that could be of anyone, from the phone of a woman who had no credibility. Thanks in part to him. God, it might be funny if it wasn't so fucking sad.

"For what it's worth, I'm sorry for what happened to you."

Jonah regarded the dying man. "It's worth nothing." He turned and he left, striding past the housekeeper who raced to show him out the door. He opened it himself as she stuttered a goodbye, her eyes widening on his scarred face before he donned his helmet and walked out into the night.

****

"Myrtle," Jonah's voice boomed through the quiet halls of Windisle. "Myrtle!"

"For Pete's sake. I'm right here. What's all the fuss?" Myrtle asked, rushing into the kitchen where Jonah stood yelling for her. Half her hair was in braids, but the other half stood out in a massive puffball on the side of her head. She'd obviously been interrupted mid-braiding session.

"Where did you put the stuff the police gave you after the investigation? My stuff and Justin's? He had a briefcase that day. A brown one."

Myrtle looked startled for a moment, her eyes bugging out even more than usual beneath her thick lenses, and then worry transformed her features.

"I . . . I put all that stuff in a box. It's in the upstairs closet. Wait—"

Jonah tore out of the kitchen, taking the stairs two at a time and throwing the closet door open. He tossed out the coats obstructing his view and pulled out several boxes containing Christmas decorations or some such nonsense, before finding the one he was looking for.

Justin's briefcase sat at the top and Jonah lifted it carefully, grief washing through him. He ran a hand over the soft, worn leather. There were large splotches of something rusty on it. *Blood.* His brother's blood. Jonah swallowed back his anguish and opened the clasp.

There was a stack of papers inside, something pertaining to a case Justin had been working on, nothing of interest to Jonah. Underneath the papers was a yellow legal pad with doodles and small notes on it. He'd scrawled on this thing in court, Jonah remembered. He'd watched him a time or two, wondering what he was writing. Notes to himself it seemed. Random thoughts and small drawings.

Jonah's eyes moved to a spot near the bottom of the page. In small, concise writing, his brother had written: *Amanda Kershaw. No evidence.* Next to that was a list of names, some he recognized from the courthouse, including Judge Rowland's. Men his brother suspected were part of the club?

In smaller writing under that was the name of the law firm Jonah had worked at with several question marks next to it.

And then underlined twice the words that pierced Jonah's already broken heart: *Don't trust Jonah.*

He dropped the pad, leaving it where it was along with the rest of the mess he'd made in the hall. He walked woodenly toward his room.

"What is it?" Myrtle asked, her voice full of motherly concern. But he didn't answer. Couldn't. His brother had come to him that day because he'd known something more sinister was happening behind the scenes—or that it was likely—but instead of trusting him, he'd attempted to appeal to some sense of moral righteousness, and then he'd let it go. He had just let it go, and allowed Jonah to go on his merry, ignorant way. He hadn't even given Jonah the chance to *do* something that might have altered the outcome.

I just have a feeling . . . you're choosing a path here, Jonah.

A *feeling*. Jonah laughed, though the sound was empty. No, he had had far more than that. Far more. He'd been gathering evidence. And then he'd withheld it. *Don't trust Jonah.*

Jonah closed the door in Myrtle's face, her prattling voice muffled as the wood separated them. Jonah stood alone in the empty room for a moment, his chest buzzing with grief, with the enormity of what he'd discovered. *Why, why, why?*

He fell to his knees, holding his head in his hands as he cried.

CHAPTER THIRTY-TWO

"Where *are* you, Jonah?" Clara murmured to herself, replacing her phone in her pocket after calling him yet again, and once more receiving no answer. What the heck was going on?

At first, the fact that he wasn't returning her calls had made her feel insecure—was he *ghosting* her? But now, after two days of utter silence from him, she was beginning to worry.

What if something had happened when he'd been patrolling with the Brass Angels? What if he was hurt? Would Myrtle know how to get hold of her? She told herself that was silly, but it was difficult to convince herself he was just *busy,* when she knew he was nothing of the sort.

The opening night performance was in three weeks, so they'd been rehearsing constantly, but now it was her day off, and she was dying to see Jonah.

She'd spent the earlier hours of the day cleaning, doing much-needed laundry, and making a visit to Mr. Baptiste, where she bought a basket full of squash and even a small pumpkin to sit beside the plant outside her door. But now, the sun had set and she paced her apartment, too antsy to sit still.

Deciding she had to get out or go stir crazy, Clara called an Uber and decided to pass some time while she waited for Jonah to respond to her umpteenth message by attempting to get the answer to a question that had been burning in her mind since just after she'd spoken to Jonah about Angelina being unable to read.

Twenty minutes later, she was dropped off in front of the shop she'd gone to what now felt like a million years before, the shop belonging to Fabienne.

Clara suspected she didn't have much talent for fortune telling, but she did seem to be an expert of sorts on charms and curses and the rules pertaining to such things. It was worth a shot, and it would move her worried mind from Jonah for at least a few minutes.

If he still hadn't called her after this, she'd head to Windisle and seek him out like she'd done before. She had hoped they were past that.

When Clara entered the shop, Fabienne was sitting on the couch she'd sat on the last time Clara had come by, but this time, the baby she'd heard from the background was sleeping in her arms. Fabienne's eyebrows arched. "I don't give refunds."

Clara shut the door, turning toward her. "What?" She shook her head. "I don't want a refund. Actually," she brought her credit card from her purse and held it out to Fabienne. "I'd like another . . . reading."

"A reading?"

"Yes. Like last time."

"Hmm."

Fabienne looked away when a man came from the back, shirtless, dreadlocks hanging down his back. His sleepy eyes moved toward Clara and then back to Fabienne. "He asleep?" He nodded toward the baby.

"Yeah." Fabienne stood, walking the short distance to the man and handing the swaddled baby to him. His full lips tipped as he looked down at the baby and then turned, disappearing into the back room. Clara heard him climbing the stairs beyond.

Fabienne turned back to her. "Two for one."

"What?"

Fabienne nodded to the chair across from the couch. "I had a two-for-one special going the day you came in. This reading is on the house."

Clara took the offered chair as Fabienne sat across from her. "That's nice of you, thank you. I have a question about, um, the afterlife."

Fabienne leaned back, regarding Clara. "Okay."

Clara tilted her head, considering the best way to ask the question. "Say someone died believing something that was false. When they passed over, would the truth somehow become clear?"

"You do know I've never been dead, right?"

Clara laughed. "I figured. It seemed like you knew a lot on the subject, and maybe you'd be willing to make an educated guess."

Fabienne toyed with the edge of the couch, running her fingers along the nailheads as if making sure they were all accounted for. "My mama used to say that when a person passed over, all veils were lifted."

"So . . . they might be able to see the full picture in the afterlife, when they were unable to in this one."

Fabienne shrugged. "That's what my mama and my grandmama believed." She leaned forward. "See, the afterlife is about forgiveness, and you cannot forgive a person if you cannot see the truth cast in every light."

In every light. Something whispered at the edges of Clara's mind but drifted away, too thin to grasp.

Clara nodded slowly, thinking of what Fabienne had said the last time she was in this shop. *If Angelina lingers, she lingers for him. For the soldier man.*

Clara hadn't been able to figure out why Angelina would linger for a man who'd broken her heart, a man who'd hurt her so terribly she'd taken her own life.

But suppose what Fabienne had told her was true? In the afterlife, the veil had been lifted. The truth made clear. Angelina understood that John didn't lie to her, that she was tricked.

Then a curse was placed upon him so he couldn't be with her in the afterlife and so they wandered aimlessly, blind to the presence of the other.

And yet, perhaps they were able to *feel* each other as she'd felt Jonah through that thick layer of stone, forever separated, John by a curse, and Angelina because she refused to leave her beloved to wander alone.

It was all so . . . fantastical. Such conjecture, something that could never be proven. And yet, a great sadness overwhelmed Clara. Even if it couldn't be proven, the idea alone filled her with aching grief. What if she was right? What a heartbreaking tragedy made even worse.

Clara glanced at Fabienne. "Thank you so much. I can't tell you how appreciative I am."

Fabienne nodded. "If you come back in a month or so, this will be a coffee shop. The neighborhood's getting better thanks to the Brass Angels. Crime is down. People feel safer. Businesses are opening again." She shrugged. "I never was much for fortune telling, truth be told. But damn if I can't brew a fine cup of coffee, and I can bake like nobody's business. It feels like the right path for me."

Clara grinned. "I *will* be back. Thank you again." She started to turn, then remembered something and turned back to Fabienne. "The theater where I'm performing is looking to hire a coffee shop to provide coffee and baked goods for the upcoming shows." Clara shrugged. "You could hand out business cards. Could be a good way to start advertising while making some money at the same time. If you're interested."

Fabienne didn't say anything for a moment, but something had lit in her eyes. "That'd be great. Who should I call?"

Clara dug in her purse quickly, pulling out an old receipt and a pen, scrawling Madame Fournier's cell number on it, along with her own name. "Tell her I gave you her name. She'll point you in the right direction."

"I will." She paused. "Thank you very much."

Clara smiled on a nod, letting herself out of the shop. She checked her phone and sighed when she saw there had been no missed calls. The Uber driver she'd paid to wait outside was across the street and she jogged over to the car, hopping inside with a breathless thanks and giving him Jonah's address.

Enough is enough, Jonah Chamberlain, she decided.

Clara knocked at the wooden side gate for a good ten minutes once she'd arrived, and, still receiving no answer, she stood back, her brow furrowing as she considered the barrier. It was high, but she was strong. If she held on with her arms, she could pull her body up and over. She had something to prove in the way of fences, anyway, she thought, grimacing at the reminder of the last time she'd attempted to climb one.

A few minutes later she was standing on the other side, brushing her hands off. She allowed herself a moment of victory before she headed toward the house, knocking on the front door, but again, receiving no answer. *Crap.*

For a moment, Clara stood uncertainly in the low light of the porch, before heading around the side of the house and peering into the darkness beyond.

Maybe you like monsters. Is that it, Clara?

She stepped out of the light, into the shadows, calling his name as she ventured forward.

She could smell pine, hear the leaves crunching beneath her feet as though each one was an explosion of sound, and she knew she was amongst the trees. But she was quickly disoriented, fear settling in her chest. He wasn't here, and she wasn't going to know how to get back.

She fumbled in her pocket, pulling her cell phone out and turning on the flashlight to its lowest setting.

Her heartbeat slowed, calm descending along with the security of the light. She walked farther into the trees, keeping the light pointed down but able to make out the path between the cabins now, the path Jonah himself must have kept clean of debris as he ran the course day after day as he'd told her.

"Put the light away."

Clara gasped, lowered the flashlight, and then turned it off.

Darkness settled around her. She heard his footsteps coming toward her and her pulse quickened. "I've been worried about you," she said as his hand brushed hers. "No one answered at your gate."

"Myrtle is helping her niece with something across town, and Cecil sleeps like the dead. How'd you get in?" That *voice.* God, it was like an aphrodisiac. He pulled her along and she followed.

"I . . . I . . ."

"You scaled my fence?"

"Yes."

"Of course you did." He didn't sound displeased, just sort of . . . weary, and Clara felt confused and uneasy about his mood. The last time they'd spoken, his voice, the things he'd said, had been full of warmth. Full of *love.*

"Jonah? What's wrong?"

She heard a door opening and then he was telling her to step up and she did, stumbling slightly, but recognizing the old wood smell of the cabin they'd been in before, the way the dim shaft of light flowed through the small, grimy window.

Clara felt for the wall and leaned against it, needing to orient herself with something solid. She heard Jonah pacing in front of her, heard his exhale of breath.

"It was all a setup."

"What? What was a setup?"

"The case. My role. Everything. And worst of all, my brother knew. At least . . . some of it. He knew and didn't tell me."

Clara heard the despair in his voice. She wanted to reach for him but was afraid he'd draw away. And so she remained standing, and she listened as he told her about Amanda Kershaw's phone, and the sex club, Chandler Knowles, and the words scrawled on Justin Chamberlain's legal pads, the words that had pierced Jonah's heart, if Clara was right about what she heard in his voice.

"I'm so sorry," she said, her voice choked with emotion for him, with the blow that had obviously knocked him for a terrible loop, and no wonder. *No wonder.*

All of these years, he'd tortured himself, and it'd all been a lie. A sick, dirty lie meant to cover other men's evil deeds.

"Jonah, it's not your fault."

He laughed, but it sounded more as though he were choking. "Isn't it though? Isn't it my *fault* that I was so damn full of myself that I couldn't see I was being used? What a *fucking* patsy. They must have laughed at me. God, they must have seen me as the biggest *joke* of all. Wasn't it my *fault* that my own brother couldn't trust me enough to shed light on the things he suspected?"

Clara paused, trying to organize her thoughts. All of this was coming as such a shock, and she hadn't even had a moment to think. Jonah had though. Here in the dark as he'd grieved and hidden and suffered all over again under the weight of things that were not his to carry.

"What will you do?" He had some proof . . . the phone, the club, though it sounded as if those girls were there willingly even if they had been coerced, their weaknesses exploited. Anyone who would have corroborated what he now knew was dead, or very close to it.

"I don't know. I haven't decided yet. Maybe nothing."

She didn't know what to say to make this better. She stepped away from the wall, reaching for him, but he moved away, into the center of the cabin or so it seemed. She was disoriented again, emotionally overwhelmed by the need to comfort, to soothe.

"Jonah?"

"You should go, Clara."

"Go? Jonah, you don't have to bear this alone. I'm here to help you through it. I know it must be devastating. I do. But we can . . . we can work through it together. If you'll let me."

"There's no future for us."

"What? *Why?* Jonah, I know you're hurting, but you've made so many strides. This doesn't have to change how far you've come, how far—"

Clara spun around, hearing a sound behind her and suddenly not knowing where he was, or if that had been him at all. Had he *left*? Had he left her there in the darkness? Her heart jumped, sweat breaking over her skin. She was alone in the middle of a dark room.

She called his name again, taking a few steps, reaching for a wall, *something*, but only grabbing empty nothingness.

"Jonah," she implored again, reaching for her flashlight, just wanting to aim it at the floor, to get her bearings. But when the light came on, a hand clasped her shoulder and she let out a small scream, instinctively sweeping the light up and directly into his uncovered face.

He'd been responding to her call, coming for her where she reached for him in the dark and now they both stood blinking at each other in the sudden light.

Oh God, what had she done? She cringed, the shock of her mistaken act of betrayal crashing over her. Jonah recovered from the sudden light at the same time she did, opening his eyes on her horrified expression. His gaze did a quick scan of her face, his own registering deep despair. Clara swore she saw his heart break right in front of her, and the stark pain in his eyes was like a blade to her heart.

"You promised," he said brokenly.

"Jonah," she whispered, reaching for him, taking in the face she'd longed to see forever. For a frozen moment, Clara stared, but *not* because she was horrified. She stared in the same way anyone who sees something different about a person seeks to understand and then put aside. And this wasn't just any person. This was Jonah, her beloved.

In one sweeping moment, she saw that the damage to the left side of his face did more to highlight his beauty than anything.

The bones on that side of his face were easier to see, the skin stretched over them the way it was, his features pulled downward in a perpetual frown. And because of that, the strong structure of his face, the masculine elegance of his creation, was all the more obvious.

And not only that, but the scars and disfiguration on the one side only served to highlight the stunning nature of the other.

He was beauty and pain, glory and suffering, vengeance and grace, and all things made stronger and more meaningful because they have an opposite.

Jonah let out an animal sound of hurt, of devastation, turning from the light, from whatever was on Clara's face that he'd surely misread.

"Get out!" he bellowed.

"Jonah, please. I didn't mean to do that. You must know—"

"Get out!" he yelled even louder, making Clara jump as a small whimper escaped her throat. "I don't *ever* want to see you again."

"I'm so sorry, please, Jonah. It was a mistake."

"*We* were a mistake." His back was to her now, his face down, still hidden though she'd already seen and accepted it. It'd only taken but a moment.

"We were . . . No, you know that's not true. We're magic." She reached for him but he stepped away.

He laughed, and it was an ugly sound full of hurt and the desire to inflict the same pain he was feeling.

"There's no magic, Clara." He turned back to her, lifting his face to use as proof of his statement. "There are no ghosts in the garden. The wall doesn't weep. The stone absorbs water when it rains and then releases it as it dries. Jesus Christ. It's not magic. It's just science," he ended sharply. And with that, he turned again, walking away from her.

The door slammed as he left her there, crying in the dark.

CHAPTER THIRTY-THREE

"Clara darlin' what's wrong?"

Clara stopped, turning toward Mrs. Guillot's gate. She hadn't seen the old woman because she'd been bent down, arranging several potted chrysanthemums near the front entrance.

"Oh, Mrs. Guillot, I'm sorry, I was lost in my own head."

"I can see that. It doesn't appear as if your thoughts are pleasant ones."

"No, Mrs. Guillot. I'm afraid they're not."

Mrs. Guillot's wrinkled forehead creased even more. "Things not going well with your masked gentleman?"

Despite herself, Clara smiled. *Masked gentleman.* But then her smile slipped as she recalled the way she'd accidentally exposed him, and then the last words he'd yelled at her before she'd raced from his property, out of the gate and into the street beyond.

She'd texted him another apology, a long message expressing her deep regret in the way she'd shined a light on him without his consent. But he hadn't written back, and the silence that rang in her ears, his ignoring of her, was getting louder by the day. She was finding it harder and harder to take full breaths.

"I made a mistake, Mrs. Guillot." Clara hesitated, wanting to tell the truth to the old woman—her friend—about who Jonah really was, about his scars, about the reasons he wore the mask, but she couldn't do it.

She didn't want to expose him any more than she already had, without his permission, even in any small way. "I . . . I hurt him. Deeply, I think. And he was already hurting." A tear ran out of her eye before she could catch it. "It was a mistake, but he can't forgive me."

"Nonsense."

"What?"

Mrs. Guillot made a clucking sound. "He *can* forgive you. You're a kind girl who made a mistake she regrets. Your heart is hurting just as much as his. He can forgive you," she repeated. "You just have to convince him."

Clara sniffled on a small laugh. "That might be the tough part. He was a lawyer once. A very good one. *He's* the convincing one. Not me."

"Even better. He'll *respond* to a good argument. But honey, you don't need the best presentation skills in the world to make him see the light. The *truth.* You just need to put the love I see in your eyes, behind your words. *Make* him listen to you. And if he still pushes you away, you know you did your very best, with every ounce of love in your heart. And *that* is where you will find your peace. He will have to find *his* peace on his own, in his way."

Clara stood straighter, feeling infused with the passion behind Mrs. Guillot's words. She was right. And she'd reminded Clara that she'd never been one to give up—not on anything.

Be wary of the man with two faces, the fortune teller had said. *He'll hurt you if you let him.*

Yes. *Yes.* Of course he would. Because broken people tended to break things, didn't they?

Clara's father had repeated part of the fortune teller's line. But then he'd added, *so don't let him,* because he believed in her that strongly. He always, *always* had and because of that belief—that deep, abounding, fatherly love—Clara had striven to make her dreams come true no matter the obstacles.

A shuddery breath went through Clara. She would *not* let him. She would fight for Jonah, and give him every reason to fight for himself, for *them.*

Clara leaned forward, and despite the short gate between them, she threw her arms around Mrs. Guillot. "I'm so lucky to know you," she whispered, kissing her on her soft cheek before pulling away.

Mrs. Guillot laughed. "I'm lucky too, darlin'. And I'm here whenever you need me."

Clara thanked her again and then headed toward her apartment, a new purposeful spring in her step.

Yes, Jonah had been a lawyer. He had argued for a living once upon a time. *So I have to do better,* she decided with conviction. She had to persuade him. She had to make him realize that she hadn't meant to hurt him and his scars didn't matter to her.

She'd been picturing him for the last four days, the way he'd looked illuminated by the light, the whole of his face revealed to her.

It'd taken a moment for her to merge the picture of the man he'd been, with the reality of his scarred and damaged face, but only a moment. He'd been beautiful to her and seeing him as he was hadn't diminished her love for him, not in the least.

Clara unlocked her apartment door, throwing her dance bag on her couch and heading for the shower.

Even if he forgave her for what she'd done, Jonah was so convinced he'd be rejected if he walked through the world, that he wasn't willing to budge. A good tactic for a lawyer who needed to exhibit passion and determination on the courtroom floor. A bad quality in a man who was *wrong* and needed to be willing to listen to someone else's sound reasoning.

After showering quickly and drying her hair, Clara called for a ride and then paced outside as she waited, going over the points she wanted to make.

She wiped her hands down the sides of her hips, nerves cascading through her. It would take audacity to show up at his house again after he'd thrown her out.

Fifteen minutes later she stood before his fence, traces of daylight fading to gloom, that hour that was easy to allow courage to melt into fear. Clara hesitated, taking one deep fortifying breath. Even the tall grass seemed to pause and hush, waiting to see what would happen when the wish collector realized the dauntless girl was back. At least . . . that's what Clara tried to tell herself she was . . . though it could be argued she was less dauntless than pushy and foolhardy.

So don't let him.

Okay. She brought her shoulders back. *I can do this.*

She knocked, and a few minutes later she heard a door close and the sounds of footsteps trudging toward her. Myrtle opened the gate and didn't look at all surprised to see her. "Hi, Clara." She opened the gate wider, allowing her entrance.

"Hi, Myrtle. I'm here to see Jonah. Though . . . he's not expecting me." She glanced to the side, fidgeting. "In fact, he'll probably be less than pleased to know I'm here."

"Well," she sighed, her eyes full of sadness. "I don't know that he can *get* any less pleased than he's been this past week, so I don't reckon that'll be an issue. He's out back again. Seems he lives out there these days. That or he's slinking through the halls of Windisle like some wounded animal. Do your worst, dear."

She'd attempted lightness, but Clara could see the pain in Myrtle's tightened features, the weariness around her eyes that was surely from the worry she'd been expending on Jonah's behalf.

Gratitude flooded Clara for the second time in less than an hour, and she wrapped her arms around Myrtle, hugging her tight. Myrtle returned the hug and then nudged her along, giving her a sad smile as Clara turned toward the place she figured Jonah would be.

She'd never walked the path through the slave cabins in the light of day and, though she had another burning purpose for being there, she couldn't help but to look around in wonder as she walked, seeing this place as it might have been a hundred and fifty years before as slaves came and went, walking this very same dirt path as they headed for the fields, or returned home at the end of a day of hard labor.

Sadness descended upon her, a desperate wish to change things she could not change for people she did not know. Things long past, people long gone. Except Angelina, perpetually trapped, and wishing to be set free in death as she had never been in life.

"Why are you here?"

Clara turned toward his voice with a small intake of breath. He stood against a gnarled tree next to a patch of wild violets, his stance casual at first, but she saw his hands clenched by his sides, knuckles white. And his face, his face was uncovered, the last of the day's dwindling sunlight finding him through a break in the trees.

She allowed herself a moment to look upon him as a whole. Uncovered. Bared to her. *Finally.* He had no idea how beautiful he was, scars be damned. He was *hers* and her love for him swelled in her chest so that she had to take a deep breath to keep from rushing to him.

Gossamer mist rose from the ground and lacy strands of moss draped from the trees, shifting gently in the breeze and creating a dreamlike quality to the woods around them. *His lair, indeed,* she thought, her heart skipping a beat. And God but she hoped he'd let her stay.

Clara stood taller, stealing herself. "I came to apologize again, not via text, but to your face. You don't have to accept it, but you can't ignore me this way."

He raised the brow on the uninjured half of his face. "No, you make it pretty tough to ignore you, even when I want to."

That hurt her, but she held her head high. "I wouldn't have had to come uninvited if you'd have answered any of my calls or texts."

"I didn't want to be pushed, Clara."

"Jonah." She moved toward him, reaching, and seemingly instinctively, he drew his face back, turning it. Her arm dropped by her side. "Please accept my apology. Please know that I would never do something to hurt you on purpose, or to break a promise."

He regarded her for a moment and then moved closer. "I saw the way you looked at me. That moment when you first saw me, told me everything I needed to know."

His voice sounded dull, dead, but a muscle ticked in his jaw, once and then again. He tilted his head. "You told me once that you pictured me as I was, because you had nothing else to go on. How do you feel now that you know *this* was the face that was above you as I fucked you in the dark?"

He was being crude in order to rattle her, to push her away. Okay then, she'd be honest. "Of course I pictured you as you were. I had nothing else to go on. Now I do. And I like what I see, every scar. Even *more* because it's *you.* Not as you were then, but as you are now. It only took me a moment to merge the two. But you, you haven't managed to do it over eight years."

Jonah laughed, and there was both a cruel edge to it and a note of desperation as though he were forcing himself to be cold, and it was costing him. "This"—he motioned toward his face—"is *really* what you want? You want to see *this* face looking down at you?"

God, why was that so hard to believe? His scars were extensive, yes. The burns he'd sustained made her cringe internally, not because they were ugly, but because she *wept* inside considering the pain he'd endured.

"Yes, actually. I never gave you any reason to think I didn't. You misread my reaction, Jonah, I told you that. And I think inside you know it or you wouldn't have been concerned about me pushing you into anything. I'm *here,* aren't I? Back again, willing to risk appearing a fool. You're the one pushing *me* away. Maybe *you* don't want to look at *me*. Maybe you enjoy picturing someone else. Maybe you *prefer* the darkness, Jonah, because you don't like what you see when you look at me in the light."

He stared at her, his body frozen, his expression momentarily baffled. "You think that?"

"I have no reason not to. I'm here, offering myself to you, and you're rejecting me. What else should I think?" She was bluffing. He'd only ever made her feel beautiful. But maybe turning the tables on him this way would make him see how ridiculous he was being. "Maybe you wouldn't have looked twice at me in your previous life. Maybe you're *settling* for me now because you think I'm all you can get, but you'd rather keep the lights off when you're with me."

"That's stupid."

"Is it?"

"Yes," he growled.

"Really? Were there many girls who stopped by your gate then? Lots of other choices?"

"Clara, stop. I see what you're doing."

"Do you? What am I doing? Telling the truth?"

"You know that's not true. You *know* I want you." His words were spoken harshly, that same muscle in his jaw ticking.

"Do you? You weren't ready to show your face, sure, but with the lights off, who were you seeing? One of those perfect society girls you used to date? The ones I saw when I looked you up? Were you picturing one of them, Jonah? The curvy redhead maybe or—"

"Stop it. I want you far more than I ever wanted any of them."

Present tense, Clara thought. Good. But not enough. "Prove it."

They stood staring at each other for a frozen moment and then another as Clara's heart sank in her chest. There were sounds around them, she was sure of it, but all she could hear was the rush of her own blood in her ears. She had thrown the ball into his court and now, if he wasn't going to respond, she was going to have to be willing to walk away. Jonah continued to watch her, still and tense. Unmoving.

Clara's shoulders dropped, though she lifted her chin. "For a man who used words for a living, your silence speaks volumes, counselor." Her voice emerged as barely more than a pained whisper though she knew he heard her by the clenching of his jaw. She paused for another beat and then with an aching heart, turned back onto the path that led out of the wooded area.

There was a loud exhale of breath and then sudden movement behind her and before she could turn back, Jonah's hand was on her arm, and he spun her toward him as he crushed his mouth to hers. *Yes, yes, yes*! Her heart thrilled, expanding with joy. He wasn't going to let her walk away. She reached up, wrapping her arms around him, gripping him to her. She'd *hoped* she would push him to touch her, to kiss her, for she knew he would turn away if she tried to take the lead, and he *needed* not only to be told but to *experience* the fact that she wanted him just as much with nothing between them.

She wanted all of him, and she wanted to *show* him. But she hadn't expected quite so much . . . hunger. He walked her backward until something touched her calves and a short grunt of fear burst from her as she fell backward into the unknown.

But his hands were on her, guiding her as she fell, her backside hitting something smooth and solid. A bench. Yes, she thought she remembered a wooden bench off to the side.

He was above her now, his mouth still devouring hers as he braced one knee next to her hips, holding the nape of her neck as she kissed him back just as fiercely.

He came over her and she lay back on a sound that was somewhere between a sigh and a plea. This kiss was born of desperation, of hurt, perhaps of a sprinkling of anger too, and she didn't care. All she cared about was that his lips were on hers and there was nothing between them anymore. She was sorry she'd hurt him, sorry he'd felt betrayed, but she was not sorry it had led to this. *Us. You and me. Face to face, skin to skin, heartbeat to heartbeat.*

"You like this, Clara?" he growled, lifting his face so she could look at it closely, pressing his hard body into hers.

She brought a finger up and ran it over the slope of his cheekbone, over the ridged skin of his jaw, her thumb running along the frown of his bottom lip.

"*Yes,*" she whispered, bringing her lips back to his.

For a moment he didn't kiss her back, but then all at once, his tongue lapped into her mouth and he let out a tortured groan, weaving his fingers into her hair and pulling her even closer as though attempting to meld their bodies.

Clara gripped him back, wrapping her legs around his hips and lifting herself toward him, a silent plea. He moaned and then pressed his groin to hers, pinning her there.

He nipped the skin of her throat and she pulled his hair, both of them panting as their mouths met and then moved to some other needy patch of skin: his ear, the base of her throat, his fingers as she sucked them into her hot mouth, and he made a raw sound of lust that shot straight between her legs in a warm rush of wetness.

He took a nipple in his mouth, pulling at it through the material of the sweater dress she was wearing, and she tipped her head back, gasping in pleasure.

She was delirious with it, delirious with him, as he brought his mouth back to hers, kissing her as he lifted her dress, lowering her underwear. And then she heard the sound of a button being unsnapped and the drag of a zipper and a few moments after that, he was pushing inside of her, the slickness of her arousal, easing the way.

"Oh, Jesus. Clara. Clara," he murmured. She ran her fingers through his hair, kissing the scarred side of his forehead. He paused, breathing harshly against her throat for a beat before beginning to move.

"Yes," she said again. "I like this. *You.*"

The mood between them changed, softened, and his movements became less frantic, his kiss slower as he glided steadily in and then out, the controlled strokes inflaming her and driving her pleasure higher . . . higher, until she tipped over the edge, crying out his name a moment before he shuddered inside of her.

He pulled away from her then, disengaging, not looking her in the eye as he fastened his pants and then dragged her underwear up her thighs and lowered her dress. He looked at her then and there was something in his gaze . . . possession maybe? But mixed with a sort of sorrow.

"Jonah."

He sat beside her on the bench as she sat up and for a moment they both stared into the trees, the shadows of dusk gathering.

She looked at him in profile, the damaged side of his face the only part she could see in that moment, and still he was beautiful. As beautiful as that photo she'd first gazed upon on the library monitor what seemed like a thousand years before. *More* beautiful maybe, because the scars she was looking at spoke of the fact that he'd tackled a man with a gun in his hand and a bomb strapped to his chest while everyone else was running away.

It spoke of his suffering, but ultimately of his heroism, his care and concern for others, his *soul,* and God, she hoped those scars would speak of his *triumph.*

"I would have looked twice at you," he said. "Then. Now. In any lifetime, and under the brightest of skies." His voice was low, soft. Sad. She took his hand in hers and he tilted his head, glancing down at their laced fingers. "I'm sorry for the things I said, for being cruel." He blew out a slow breath. "I do forgive you. But I can't live a life you want me to. Or one you deserve," he said softly. "Especially"—his words fell off as if he'd decided against saying whatever he'd been about to say—"especially the way it would be, Clara. You have no idea."

He turned his head then, showing her both sides of his face, the man he'd once been, and the one he was now. "Do you want people shuddering when we walk into a restaurant together? Staring? Whispering? Saying ugly things?"

"It's *you* who can't handle that, Jonah. Not me. You give those people too much importance and not enough to the ones who matter." She let go of his hand and ran her finger along the ridges of his damaged chin.

He lowered his eyes, so much shame still obvious in his drawing away from her. She wanted to weep for him. She wanted to shake him until he saw sense.

And it was suddenly clear to Clara why he still carried so much pain with him regarding his damaged face. He'd mentioned several times the way people had looked at him directly following the bombing, the horror in their gazes. He'd brushed it off, said he'd deserved it, but Clara realized now that those looks, the rejection that had come along with them when he had needed love and understanding so very much, had hurt him deep down in his heart and soul.

The scars he wore on the outside were only skin deep. It was the scars he'd sustained within that still pulled the tightest. They hadn't healed, not all of these years. Not only that, but he'd built a life on those internal scars, told himself a story about himself based on every flinch he'd received, every day since.

"Jonah," she whispered and he met her gaze. "It's *you* who doesn't realize that you should hold your head high and wear those scars like the courageous battle wounds they are. I would walk *proudly* into any restaurant with you. And you would keep your eyes on *me,* not anyone else. On me, Jonah. And who cares if people stare? Those scars you're so ashamed of are proof that you threw yourself at a madman while everyone else ran away."

"I told you, I didn't do that on purpose."

He was lying to himself, but fine, she wouldn't argue the point further if he wanted to insist running toward a madman holding a firearm was an instinctive act, something anyone would have done when no one else did. She would make a concession there for more important points.

"Was it an *accident* that you patrolled streets in order to make people feel safe? Did you do a dozen other good deeds that they spoke of on the news because you simply stumbled upon them? You helped a woman get surgery for her son when she was unable. Or was that done without thought as well?"

"No. But I was covered up. And throwing money at people isn't brave."

Clara released a frustrated sigh. God, this man was stubborn. And he was going to stubbornly hold on to the ridiculous lies he'd been subsisting on. Maybe even, in some sick way, they were comforting to him. An excuse. Rejecting them would mean he'd have to be willing to walk past that wall of his and out into the world again.

"No," she said, choosing to ignore his statement and instead answer the question she'd posed on her own. "You did it because those scars you're so ashamed of caused you to suffer, yes, but also to learn and to grow and to use your pain for good."

He stared off into the last of daylight fading beyond the horizon, his expression unmoved. "You should go. It's getting dark."

Clara's heart constricted, pain rising inside of her but she pushed off the feeling of desperation. Mrs. Guillot had been right. She would find peace in the knowledge that she'd given it her all, tried her very best to convince Jonah that she was not ashamed of him and that he must find a way to hold his own head high. But if, in the end, he insisted on pushing her away, it would be up to him to find his own peace. Without her. Because he would never accept his face before he accepted his soul.

Clara pressed her lips together, looking off in the same direction as him for a moment, her heart feeling as if it were cracking down the middle. "Have you decided what you're going to do about what Mr. Knowles told you? The phone . . ."

He was quiet for a moment before he finally said, "No. And I don't feel like talking about it."

That might have hurt Clara most of all. They'd been intimate, yes. He'd made love to her only minutes ago. But since they'd met, he'd been her friend, her deepest confidant, the person she talked everything through with. And she'd felt like she was that same person for him. And now to be shut out of his thoughts, his world, was like a blade to her heart. He'd said he forgave her, but maybe that wasn't completely true. "You can trust me, Jonah."

He let out a sound that was something between a laugh and a moan. "Maybe you shouldn't trust *me,* Clara. My own brother couldn't."

She watched him for a moment. Yes, that had to wound him deeply. Maybe he wouldn't talk to her, but she'd been thinking about the whole situation for several days now, and she had something to say to him about Justin. "Your brother—"

"Clara."

"No, Jonah, I'll leave because you want me to, but I'm going to say this first. I went through that folder your brother put together about the Chamberlain family history, each note he made, each thought he jotted down, and I feel like I gained insight on the kind of man he was. Just a little but enough to say this."

Clara took a deep breath. "Your brother should have shared what he knew with you, instead of being vague. But he didn't because he believed you would blow him off unless he had concrete evidence. Was he wrong?"

Jonah stared out at the trees, quiet for so many beats, Clara didn't think he'd answer her. "I don't know."

"You feel betrayed by everyone, and the rest of them deserve that and more. But your brother, Jonah, he had your best interests at heart. He was a man, like you, trying to make good choices, trying to do right by the people he loved, trying to be the opposite of your father who'd hurt him as he'd hurt you. His choices weren't always the right ones, but anything bad that happened because of them was not intentional. He wasn't perfect, and I think all of these years you've pretended he was. You've put him on a pedestal and created some sort of saintly caricature in your mind. He wasn't saintly. He was just a man. Just your brother. But I believe with all of my heart that he loved you, and he'd want the best for you now."

Clara stood and watched as Jonah's hand trembled and came up off of the bench where it had lain. He was going to reach for her. Hope ballooned and then burst when it dropped back onto the wood. His eyes remained downcast.

"I'm sorry," he finally said, and she could hear the regret in his tone, the sorrow. And it increased hers because it didn't have to be this way if only he'd see it. "I'm sorry I stole the magic of this place from you."

Clara regarded him, recalling his words. *There are no ghosts in the garden. The wall doesn't weep. The stone absorbs water when it rains and then releases it as it dries. Jesus Christ. It's not magic. It's just science.*

"You didn't steal anything from me, because you're wrong," she said, and it surprised her to hear the surety, the strength in her own voice, because she still felt so hollow inside, so desperate to convince him.

Jonah seemed to pause, tilting his head in that way of his to peer at her more closely from his good eye. He blinked in confusion as though he'd expected her to sound hurt and wasn't sure what to make of the reason she did not.

But she realized then, that his words, meant to be harsh, had only made her more confident in her conviction. "There *is* magic. Us. *We're* magic. Two lonely people who found each other despite the barricade between us. I felt your heart, Jonah, even through a wall made of rock. *We're* magic, but you're too blind to see it. Choose to continue hiding behind the wall if you want, but don't ever tell me there's no magic. You're the one who's chosen to shut it out."

Clara's gaze went to the cabins in front of her, outlined in the dim light. Again, she had that feeling that everything around her was stilled . . . hushed. *Waiting* for something that might or might not happen.

She envisioned them again, the men and women and children who had called this place home once upon a time.

She pictured Angelina herself, making her way from the grandeur of the big house to the dirt paths that led to the squalor of these small cabins.

She wondered if John had ever seen this place, if perhaps it was there where they'd met in secret and fallen in love. And her heart bled for all of it.

"They would have done anything to have the ability to leave this plantation together," she mused softly, to herself maybe as much as to the man sitting on the bench willing to watch her walk away. "To walk through the streets hand in hand, to *claim* their freedom." Her eyes moved to him. "And you, you dishonor them and yourself by staying locked away by choice."

Jonah didn't answer, but she could see in his posture, in the way his shoulders hunched, that he was suffering too. But if he wouldn't do anything about it, she couldn't force him to. She could only love him. And offer him grace. But this time, from afar.

"What would they say to you?" she asked before turning and walking away. It was her closing argument. She left him to answer the question on his own.

CHAPTER THIRTY-FOUR

The bar/restaurant was bright and crowded, the sounds of raucous chatter barely making its way to Jonah's ears where he stood against the building across the street.

He watched her hungrily as she laughed at something the male dancer he'd seen her dance with at the masquerade ball said. Jonah was unable to hear the sound from where he stood, but the sweet memory of it lived inside of his soul, and it wove through him then, causing him to suffer. Causing him to pine. Causing jealousy to rip a jagged path down his spine.

Why was that guy touching her? Did he think that because he was her dance partner, he was allowed to touch her anytime he wanted? As though he had some *right* to her body?

His hands fisted at his sides. Didn't the stupid bastard know she belonged to Jonah?

Only she didn't. His fists uncurled. She didn't belong to Jonah, because he'd pushed her away. He'd told her to leave, demanded she stay away. And then as though that hadn't been bad enough, he'd tried to steal the magic that brought her such joy. But she hadn't let him and wasn't that just like Clara? To hold on to something that held no basis in reality? *We're magic. Us.*

God, he was used to pain, or so he'd thought, but this was of a level he hadn't even known existed. He closed his eyes as a raw groan moved up his throat.

Why was he *doing* this to himself? To prove that he'd been right, that he could *never* offer her the life she deserved to live? The one she was living right then under the bright lights of the restaurant with a group of friends in a very public place.

She seemed to be enjoying more social activities lately. As she should. As a young, vibrant, beautiful woman like Clara was meant to do.

Clara wandered away from the group, peering out of the large glass window, and for a second he swore their eyes met. She *saw* him, he felt it, or even if she didn't, she still knew he was there. But she wouldn't come to him. He knew that as surely as he knew his own name. She's already done it twice—two times more than he deserved—and that was all he was going to get.

Clara looked away, smiling at something a girl said as she came up beside her, turning her back on Jonah.

Clara had fought for him, she really had. He'd recognized that, and it'd made his heart throb with love for her and his insides twist into a knot of fiery longing.

She thought she knew how it would be, but she didn't know. All eyes on him, whispering ugly words, clamoring to get pictures, to make insinuations, to publish the first shot of what Jonah Chamberlain had become. He knew. He would not put her through it. *Keep your eyes on me,* she'd said, but they'd make that impossible. Yes, he knew. He remembered well.

He was still trying to come to terms with the fact that he'd been used, lied to, manipulated. The knowledge was like a dagger lodged painfully in his heart. He'd thought . . . well, he'd thought there was a chance he could resume some sort of normal life. Clara had helped him believe it. But hell, maybe he didn't even want to be part of a world that operated that way.

Even if that's where Clara is?

Keep your eyes on me.

He could have asked her to keep coming to Windisle. He wouldn't have to wear a mask anymore, not now that she'd seen him and accepted him for what he was. Maybe he could even go to her sometimes in the dark of night. But what kind of life was that? And what kind of bastard would he be if he asked her to accept it?

Clara deserved spotlights, and candlelit parties, well-lit restaurants, and days washed in sunshine.

He turned away, pulling his scarf up and his hat down, ducking his head as he walked, promising he wouldn't follow her anymore. There was no point.

And yet he couldn't seem to help himself.

He followed her to rehearsal in the morning and home at night, his jaw clenching as he watched her ride that damn bus. How many months had it been? Hadn't she saved up enough for a decent down payment by now, for the love of Christ? What kind of pittance did the New Orleans Ballet pay their dancers anyway?

He would have left her alone, he told himself, if he didn't have to worry over her damn safety every day of the week.

He'd buy her a car if he thought she'd accept it, but he knew very well she wouldn't. And hadn't it been *him* who'd told her it wasn't brave to throw money at something?

Jonah wound up the music box she'd given him for his birthday, watching forlornly as the tiny dancer spun. He *had* resisted sneaking into the theater and watching her dance. He could put himself through a lot, but that amount of suffering felt un-survivable. He couldn't watch her dance and then walk away, return home to his lonely world behind Windisle's wall. He couldn't do it.

At night he dreamed he was atop a horse, its footfalls pounding the earth as they flew through the darkness. *Hurry, hurry. Don't let it be too late.* A river rose in the distance, its dark, shimmery path drawing him forward, his heart soaring. *I'm almost there.* And then a scream ripped through the night, causing his horse to rear up beneath him as he yelled, falling backward onto the hard ground. He rose, dust filling his lungs as he stumbled blearily, the iron of a gate flashing under the moonlight as the screeching wail continued. *Oh God, no, no. No—*

He woke up night after night, a yell on his own lips, his limbs shaking with the power of the dream.

He was barely sleeping.

The music in his hand came to a stop, the silence hanging heavy over Jonah, just before he heard what sounded like a slew of footsteps walking through the house below. *What the hell?*

There was a knock at Jonah's door, followed by Myrtle's head peeking in. "There are some men here to see you," she announced. "They have a couple of dogs with them that they tied up outside. One of the men has tattoos on his face, and they're asking to see you." The Brass Angels were at his house. Myrtle didn't sound surprised, which meant she wasn't. Which *meant* either she or Cecil were behind this.

Christ. "Tell them I'll be down in a minute."

She left the room, and Jonah eyed the mask sitting on top of his dresser. The men welcomed into his house right that second had never seen his face uncovered. But he stopped himself from reaching for it.

He didn't have to go out into the world and brave the stares, the whispers, the judgment of those he didn't know. But fuck he was weary of covering up. He was plain exhausted. And maybe he could at least brave being uncovered here, behind his own walls, in front of men who wore scars of their own, inside and out.

Jonah walked slowly to the living room where he heard them talking, heard Myrtle offer them a beverage before her footsteps retreated.

He entered, standing in the doorway, his heart thumping, waiting for them to turn their heads and get a look at him. Augustus turned first, raising one eyebrow. "Is that meant to be a dramatic entrance?"

"Who called you?"

"The old man."

Cecil. What was this? Calling in reinforcements? Some sort of intervention?

Jonah narrowed his eyes, turning to Ruben. "Hey man," Ruben said, exhibiting no reaction whatsoever to Jonah's scarred face, sitting down on the couch and bouncing on it slightly as if testing the springs. But Ruben had gang tattoos on his *face* so of course he wasn't going to be fazed by someone else's messed-up mug.

His gaze moved to Eddy who *was* staring, but not with horror, more with interest. "So that's what you look like," he finally said.

"Yeah. This is what I look like."

Eddy nodded. "It's better than the mask."

Jonah let out a humorless huff of breath.

"Kinda badass, actually," Ruben offered. But again, he had tattoos all over his *face*—amateur ones—so . . .

"Also," Eddy said, "my buddies, the ones who didn't make it home because a bomb blew up underneath them?" Grief passed over his young features, Jonah recognized it immediately for what it was, and it caused his heart to clench in sympathy for what he'd lost, the very obvious toll it'd taken. "If only they had come home with a few burns. If only." His two final words were spoken gruffly as though he'd had to force them out. *If only.* Jonah had far more than a "few burns," but he got the guy's point. Yeah, he was scarred, but he wasn't dead.

Jonah entered the room, leaning against the wall next to the fireplace. "Why'd you come?"

"Well," Augustus said, stepping forward, "other than the fact that your family's worried about you, so were we. We haven't seen you in weeks, and the old man said he thought you were planning on keeping it that way."

Your family. Jonah didn't bother to correct Augustus, not that there was really anything to correct. Cecil and Myrtle *were* family, perhaps not by blood, but something stronger. By loyalty. By love. However, Jonah didn't especially appreciate the old man's meddling at the moment. He'd been doing just fine skulking through the halls of his own home night after night, thank you very much.

"What else did the old man tell you?"

"That you were betrayed, lied to, used. That you're ashamed of your scars because you think they tell the story of your character."

Jonah huffed out a breath. That was a succinct summation. Seemed everyone had him figured out. He couldn't argue with it. Come to think of it, he hadn't put up much of an argument to the points Clara had made either. And he was supposed to be a great arguer?

Maybe because your arguments on this matter are weak, an inner voice chided.

"You didn't know what was going on, did you?"

Jonah shook his head slowly, understanding that Augustus was talking about the corruption within his firm. "No." The word was rough, grated. "I was blind."

"But now you see."

Jonah laughed though it was laced with pain. "Yeah, now I see. At least mostly. This eye doesn't work so well anymore." He offered an ironic tilt of his lips, turning his head slightly, indicating his damaged left eye, the skin pulled downward at the corner.

Augustus smiled. "Still better than being blind."

"I guess."

"I *know.*" He paused. "You have nothing to be ashamed about, man. You should tell your story, whatever it is. Out in the open."

"I don't think so. I have no interest in being dragged through the mud. Let them speculate."

"Maybe after you tell your side, yeah. Once that's out there, let them say what they say, Jonah. They're going to anyway. But what I know is that you helped a whole slew of people who might have the opportunity to travel a better path now because of you."

Something expanded in Jonah's chest. He wasn't sure if it was pain or pride. Maybe a mix of both. Clara had said basically the same thing to him. *You give those people too much importance and not enough to the ones who matter.* He expelled a breath. He did, he knew he did. He just didn't know how to let go of the shame.

Keep your eyes on me.

"What do you think about my face?" Ruben asked.

"He thinks it's butt ugly like the rest of us," Augustus said.

Ruben shot him a dirty look but then grinned. "Your mama didn't seem to mind last night."

"Man, do you even know how old I am? My mama's been dead for fifteen years, you sick gravedigger."

Despite himself, Jonah laughed.

Ruben's grin faded, his expression becoming serious after a moment. "It's not easy," Ruben said, sitting up on the couch and gesturing to his own marred face. "Wearing your mistakes and regrets on the outside where others can judge them. But, man, the problem is not that others judge you harshly, it's that you believe what they say."

Jonah sighed. All of his well-laid plans were beginning to crumble. He could feel it like a quaking inside. First Clara had chipped away at his long-held beliefs, creating so many cracks he was barely holding himself together, and now these men—these *friends* when he hadn't had friends in so long—were knocking over the few final sections of stability he'd managed to maintain.

So maybe his plans weren't so well laid after all.

He eyed Ruben for a minute, his eyes running over the rough, poorly drawn art that must tell a story, though he didn't know what. "You ever consider getting that removed?" he asked. "I've got the money if you need it, and I've sorta got this thing about granting wishes." He attempted a smile, but it felt shaky.

Ruben chuckled. "Nah. These tattoos remind me who I was, and who I've fought to become. They might not be pretty, but I'm proud of them." He paused. "Spend that wish granting on your woman. Or hell, better yet, spend one on yourself."

The men stood, Augustus patting him on his shoulder as he passed by, leaning in to say, "You have more friends than you realize, man. Think about that."

Jonah nodded, too overwhelmed to speak, too many thoughts and questions raging through him to begin to put in order.

Ruben gave him a fist bump and Eddy stopped on his way out. "If anyone understands the desire to end your own life, it's me. We met at the edge of a bridge, remember? You helped me believe that life is worth living again."

"You don't have to worry about that, Eddy. I'm not planning to end my life."

"Aren't you?" He looked right into Jonah's eyes. "Locking yourself back here, isn't that exactly what you're doing?" Eddy gave him one final meaningful look and then followed Augustus.

The men filed out, leaving him alone again. Jonah sank down on the couch. God, Eddy was right. He had come to Windisle to end his life. Not in the same way Angelina had, but for the same reasons—a complete lack of hope.

Angelina hadn't had the same opportunities he had to make a different choice. The reasons for her hopelessness had been deep and powerful and all-consuming. Unchangeable. Held in place by so many others.

What would they say to you? Clara had asked. And he suddenly knew, sitting right there in the quiet of Windisle where Angelina herself had once stood. *He knew.* She'd tell him to find a way to keep on living.

A sound in the hall right outside of the room caused Jonah to look up where Cecil was standing observing him silently, the expression on his face disapproving, the same way it'd been for the past couple of weeks.

"I suppose you've got your own piece of advice for me too, old man?"

"Yeah. Get your daggum shit together."

CHAPTER THIRTY-FIVE

Savannah Hammond read the last line of the article she'd just completed, saving the file and quickly composing an email to her boss before forwarding it on.

She sighed. A playoff between little league teams. God, the topic was so boring she'd almost fallen asleep trying to write the piece. So instead of focusing on the teams, cute though they were, she'd written the article to highlight the unbelievable behavior she'd witnessed from the parents.

Competitive didn't begin to cover it. Their antics were downright disgusting. Over a kids sport team? They were supposed to be adults and they acted like angry psychotics. Their kids were going to be on anxiety meds by the time they were twelve.

No doubt the article would get returned to her with a note to rewrite, but what the hell? It was worth a try. And at least writing it hadn't put her to sleep.

It was frustrating. She'd been working for the online newspaper for almost nine years now, and she was still writing junk articles that changed no one's life for the better.

Close to a decade, and she was little more than a cub reporter. Sometimes she felt like quitting. Maybe she wasn't cut out for the business. Only . . . she *was.* She felt it like a fire burning in her belly. If only she were given the right opportunity.

She thumbed the printout sitting on top of a pile of papers on her desk, the grainy garage photo catching her eye. The masked do-gooder. *Speaking of changing lives for the better.*

She'd tried to convince her boss to put her on the story of the unknown man who'd been making waves in New Orleans of late, but he'd said no. And Savannah knew the reason why. He considered her soft. He gave the exclusives to the cut-throat reporters, the ones who were willing to get up in the face of a murdered kid's mom, or shove a microphone at a shell-shocked husband who'd lost his wife in a house fire an hour before.

She was willing to go after a story with everything she had, but she refused to use other people's grief for headlines. It went against every moral fiber inside of her.

Her phone rang. "Savannah, line one," the receptionist said when she picked it up.

"Thanks, Shannon." She clicked over to line one. "Savannah Hammond."

"Ms. Hammond?"

Hadn't she just said that? "Yes? How can I help you?"

"Do you have a minute to meet with me?"

"Who is this?"

"Jonah Chamberlain." Savannah paused, the pen she'd been tapping against her desk stopping abruptly. *Jonah Chamberlain.* God, it'd been years since she'd heard his name.

In a flash it came back to her. The Murray Ridgley trial. She remembered it well. She'd been a new reporter when it'd all unfolded. She'd been assigned to park herself outside of the hospital and wait for the young, handsome lawyer to emerge. She'd been all but advised to get in his injured face and get the most grisly photo she could. Every news outlet in town had apparently given the same directive to their crew, because it had been a mob out there, day after day.

Truth be told, her heart had ached for him. He'd tried to tackle that maniac and taken a bomb to the face for his trouble. But no one was talking about that. They were focused on the fact that he'd defended Murray Ridgley and gotten him off so he could cause mayhem on the front of the courthouse steps. As if he'd intended for that to happen.

But ratings were always higher if there was a villain or a sideshow, so they'd assigned the role of villain to Jonah Chamberlain.

Savannah *hadn't* waited for Jonah Chamberlain to be wheeled outside. Instead, she'd sent him a sympathy card and written a letter about how sorry she was about what happened to him. He'd never read it, or so she'd thought, but she'd sent it all the same. A promise to herself, of sorts, that as tempting as it might be, she would never sell her soul to the devil for a story.

"Yes, I . . . I know who you are."

There was a beat of silence. "I'm in a car behind the building." He explained his exact location and she told him she'd be right down, replacing the phone receiver and standing immediately. *Jonah Chamberlain.* What could he want? And what would he look like after what had happened to him? No one *had* ever managed to get that highly sought-after photograph.

She spotted the car right away, an old Cadillac she thought only elderly people drove. It was parked in a side alley, behind a garbage dumpster and under the dim overhang of the building next door.

Savannah's footsteps slowed as it suddenly occurred to her that this might not be the safest situation to walk into alone. But she gathered her courage. She'd always relied on her instincts and those, along with the hesitant quality of Jonah Chamberlain's voice on the phone, told her that her safety was not at risk.

She walked to the passenger side door and pulled on the handle. It opened with a click that echoed in the empty alley and Savannah bent her head to peer inside.

The man she recognized as Jonah Chamberlain was sitting in the driver's seat, only his profile on display. Yes, it was him. His good looks were almost shocking in their classic perfection. But as he turned his head toward her, Savannah blinked. *Oh God.* The left side of his face, the side that had taken the full extent of the blast was scarred and stretched over his bones as though it'd melted that way.

Her heart lurched with sympathy for him, for the agonizing pain he'd obviously experienced. She slid inside of the car, turning her body so she was facing him.

"Hi."

"Hi." His hand, which had been resting on the steering wheel appeared to relax as he turned his body toward her as well. There was something . . . God, she used words for a living but none of the ones she'd become familiar with worked for this man. No, there was something beautifully *fierce* about him. Something that brought to mind ancient battles and warriors who walked through fire. A god who had fallen to earth and been scorched by the edge of a star. Lord, where were these descriptions coming from? Maybe she should have been a romance writer instead of a reporter. But geez, all she could think was that she was happily married. But if she wasn't . . .

Savannah cleared her throat, feeling awkward and sort of ridiculous. "This is a surprise."

He chuckled and it was full of something Savannah couldn't read. "Yeah." He paused for a moment, his expression becoming serious. "I want to thank you for that letter you sent me when I was in the hospital. It meant a lot."

She blinked at him. He *had* received it. He remembered. She nodded but before she could say anything, he picked up an envelope on his lap and handed it to her. There was a hard rectangular shape at the bottom.

"It's a phone."

"A phone? Whose phone?"

"How much of the Murray Ridgley trial do you remember?"

"Quite a bit."

He nodded. "Good." He paused, peering through the windshield for a weighted minute. "I want to reclaim my life." Jonah Chamberlain flinched slightly, the shadow of what looked like old hurt flitting across his dual face, seeming to settle on his scarred side as though that was where he carried pain and always would.

And then he told her what he knew as she blinked at him, the enormity of the information hitting her full force.

When he was finished laying out what could be the news story of the decade, full of corruption at the highest levels, he looked at her, his light brown eyes moving over her face, trying to determine if she really could be trusted perhaps.

"I need someone who has contacts . . . who will know the best way to go about exposing what I've just told you." He paused and the air in the car felt weighted. "Will you help me?"

Savannah chewed at her lip, her mind buzzing, already arranging and rearranging the best way to handle this information, the list of people she'd grown to trust over her lackluster career who might be able to help her.

She looked at the man sitting in front of her, the whirling thoughts in her mind slowing. This man had obviously lived with so much sitting upon his shoulders for so long. She wondered if, before now, he'd had anyone to help him bear the burdens he carried. Whether he had or not and for whatever his reasons, he'd chosen *her* and a feeling of deep honor caused her heart to constrict.

"Yes, Jonah. I'll help you."

CHAPTER THIRTY-SIX

He'd done it. He'd set the wheels in motion. *I want to reclaim my life.* Now what happened remained to be seen. Now what happened was in Savannah Hammond's hands. But peace settled inside of him, the same peace he'd felt as he'd driven out of that alley.

You have more friends than you realize, Augustus had said, and Jonah had chosen to trust him, bringing to mind not only those who had hurt and betrayed him, but those who had offered small tokens of kindness, of understanding.

He'd done what Clara had accused him of doing—he'd put too much credence in the judgments of those who didn't matter, and not enough in the ones who did.

Clara.

God, he owed her so much. His life maybe. She already had his heart.

Spend that wish granting on your woman, Ruben had told him. *Or hell, better yet, spend one on yourself.* The only thing Jonah wanted was her. Clara. And all right, he wanted to find the bravery, the *peace,* Ruben had obviously found to walk out into the world and claim his scars for the things they stood for. Regrets, yes, and shame, definitely. But maybe, *maybe,* the fact that he'd overcome and that he strived to do better, to *be* better. But the only one who could make that wish come true was Jonah himself.

Clara had been right. He needed to find his worth, to believe that it still existed. Eddy was right too, because he had given up on his own life.

Jonah had spent the last two days going over the words Clara had said when she'd shown up to fight for him, turning them over, letting them *in.*

Dance your heart out, he'd told Clara once upon a time. *For your father. It's what he would want.*

But he'd been a hypocrite, because instead of trying to live a life that would make his brother proud, he'd hidden himself away behind a damn wall. His brother hadn't trusted him because he'd seen Jonah as a replica of their father, and hell, wasn't that exactly what he'd been trying to be? And okay, the truth was, Jonah hadn't trusted his brother either. They'd both been so busy trying *not* to be their father, and trying to *be* their father, that neither one had figured out who they were as individuals. The sadness of that, the true regret, the wasted time, was a knife to Jonah's heart. But maybe it wasn't too late.

He wasn't perfect. And I think all of these years you've pretended he was. You've put him on a pedestal and created some sort of saintly caricature in your mind. He wasn't saintly. He was just a man. Just your brother. But I believe with all of my heart that he loved you and he'd want the best for you now.

Somehow, Clara's assertions had brought his brother closer to him. He felt more real in Jonah's heart, not that one-dimensional caricature he'd painted Justin as for so long because of his own guilt.

These last few days he'd been recalling the *real* Justin, his words, his spirit, his innate curiosity, and the sound of his laughter. And yes, his imperfections too. *God, he missed him so much.*

"All right, fucker, we both wasted a lot of time. Help me out now, would you?" Jonah murmured to himself, willing to believe in that magic Clara believed in so fervently that she'd been willing to fight for him even when he was unwilling to fight for himself.

Magic.

Wishes.

Spend that wish granting on your woman.

Clara wanted him to come out from behind his wall, but not just for her, for himself. And the truth of the matter was that Clara was a woman who rarely wished for things for herself. Clara was a woman who spent her wishes on others.

Help me help you, Angelina. The selfless wish that had brought Clara to him in the first place.

Jonah almost laughed. Leave it to Clara to wish for the one thing he could not grant.

You could try. The idea whispered through his mind, once and then again. *You could try.*

He stared out of the open window of the living room at the late afternoon sun, the heavy floral curtains fluttering in the breeze. November first was a cool, bright day and brought with it the scent of fall: rich earth, crisp leaves, and that slightly smoky tinge to the air, a much appreciated reprieve from the steamy New Orleans summer. Peace settled over Jonah. Inexplicable. Comforting. He let it, not casting it aside as he'd done in the past, believing he didn't deserve the feeling. He allowed it in, let it settle inside. Accepted the gift with a thankful sigh.

Jonah closed his eyes, leaning back in his chair, taking in a lungful of the fresh air.

Help me help you, Angelina.

Clara had come to Windisle to solve a mystery for two dead people who were supposedly trapped. Jonah wasn't sure if he believed in that. But what if there was a way to bring that magic back to Clara in a very real way? To *grant* her wish? What if there was a way to find the note?

Jonah lived on the same grounds where Angelina had lived and died. She'd been read the note inside of Windisle Manor, perhaps in the very same room where he now sat.

Jonah had a sudden inexplicably clear picture in his head of Angelina squeezing the paper tightly in her fist as she wept. Maybe it hadn't been destroyed long ago. *Maybe* she'd hidden it somewhere. Maybe it'd been moved to the attic in one of the dusty boxes or trunks that littered the space.

He'd told Clara he'd look for it, meaning to, but only to appease her, but then he never had. He had some making up to do with Clara and searching for the note was as good a place to start as any. Maybe it was under a floorboard in this very room. *Jesus, where do I even start?*

Jonah stood. He'd at least try. For Clara, he'd try. If it came to nothing, that was okay. At least he'd have his own effort to give to her when he left this house and sought her out. At least he'd have something small to present—a tiny gift for all of the things she'd given him. But he didn't want to think about that just yet—the seeking out. He was still working up to that part.

Okay then, where to begin?

Jonah turned his thoughts to the riddle of John and Angelina. The first question was, if they *did* linger, *why?* What did they want? Was it the curse that somehow kept them both there? *A drop of Angelina's blood being brought to the light.* The words the old priestess had said would *break* the curse. But what did it mean?

"All right, Justin, you want to prove to me you're still the same busybody I always knew? You always did love the story of John and Angelina. And you always loved a good mystery. So help me—"

The breeze gusted in, lifting the curtain and whipping it against the edge of the fireplace mantel where a knickknack rabbit rested. It fell to the floor with a sharp crack, but didn't break.

Jonah huffed out a breath, bending down and retrieving it, replacing it on the mantel. As he rose to his full height, his eyes met his own, his face inches from the mirror that hung over the fireplace. He stared at himself for the first time in a long while, but this time, he tried his hardest to see himself not through the lens of his own self-hatred, not through the stares of those who'd turned away, but from Clara's perspective. From Myrtle's and Cecil's and hell, even from the men who'd been to Windisle several days before, the men who'd become his friends, his *brothers,* and accepted him easily and without judgment.

You give those people too much importance and not enough to the ones who matter.

Jonah turned his face left, then right, then looked at himself full on. This was him now, and he needed to accept it. He'd never be the man he was before, but would he want to be? Yes and no, and he didn't get to have both.

He sighed, smoothing his fingers over the scars, remembering the look in Clara's eyes as she'd touched him with love. *With love.* Jonah blew out a breath, missing her so desperately it made his skin break out in goosebumps. He ran a hand through his thick, dark hair, staring into his own eyes, the left one pulled tight, the color cloudier than the other.

"God, I'm almost *too* handsome," he whispered, the way he used to do for his brother's benefit as he got ready for high school in the morning. It had annoyed Justin, and as his brother, it was Jonah's duty to do it regularly.

Humble too.

Jonah smiled, hearing in his head what had always been the exchange between the brothers. A private joke.

Jonah turned his face, looking at his profile from both sides, re-learning himself maybe. The thing he'd refused to do all of these years. Instead he'd used strangers' long-ago reactions as his mirror, as the thing that spoke of his worth. Or more precisely, the lack thereof.

Since the day his brother had died and Jonah's world ended, he hadn't wanted to look himself in the eyes, had avoided mirrors altogether. Only now . . . looking at himself didn't feel painful. In fact, he not only saw *himself* in the mirror—scars and all—but he saw his brother too. They'd looked so much alike.

"You both got those Chamberlain good looks," their mother had always said. And suddenly it seemed like something to be treasured that Jonah got to see a piece of his brother in himself—even if only on one side—every time he looked in the mirror.

And things . . . shifted. Jonah felt it inside, something clicking into place, and clearing some path that had been previously blocked.

He brought his fingertips to his jaw, his cheekbone, brushing his hair back, seeing the Chamberlain widow's peak.

Chamberlain.

Chamberlain.

A drop of her blood . . .

Jonah froze. No, it couldn't . . . Holy shit. *He* was a drop of her blood. Angelina's.

Her father, Robert Chamberlain, had been Jonah's sixth great-grandfather. They'd called her a Loreaux, but really, she'd been a *Chamberlain.* He had the same blood as Angelina running through his veins. In fact, he was the only one left who did. His father was dead, his brother was gone, his aunt Lynette hadn't had children. He was the last of the Chamberlain blood.

I'm the answer, he thought, shock and wonder crashing through him. *At least in part.*

That vague ticking feeling he'd shared with Clara intensified inside of him, but no, it wasn't ticking. It was *pounding.* Just like the pounding of hooves in that nightmare he couldn't seem to shake. *Hurry, hurry. Don't let it be too late.* He spun around, running his fingers through his hair, gripping his head.

A drop of her blood being brought to the light. It seemed to chant in Jonah's head along with the pounding of hooves on hard-packed earth, rising suddenly to overwhelm him, voices echoing somewhere in the recesses of his mind.

A drop of her blood being brought to the light.

A drop of her blood being brought to the light.

The light. What was the light? He'd always pictured it as some cosmic glow . . . a description of the afterlife. But what if . . . what if Clara had been right? What if the light was . . . the truth? What if John's family *had* lied to Angelina just as Clara surmised? And what if exposing that by finding the note was what would break the curse?

A drop of her blood being brought to the light.

Me *finding the truth.*

Oh God, that's why they had both stayed. John, cursed never to find true love—*his* true love, Angelina unless the curse was broken. And it could only be broken *there,* at

Windisle. And Angelina, knowing the truth once she'd passed on, had waited for John until they could be together again.

God, did he *believe* in the legend of John and Angelina? He didn't know. He wasn't sure. But he very suddenly couldn't let the idea go. It took hold, gripping Jonah, making him desperate to figure it out. He felt an energy that didn't seem to belong to him coursing through his blood, an urgency that spurred him on.

We're magic. Us.

Keep going, *yes.* The light . . . the light. *The truth.*

The wind had kicked up, the curtains whipping around the window, the wind chimes peeling as if with glee in the near distance. *The light, the truth, the light, the truth.*

The same knickknack rabbit fell off of the mantel again, this time shattering and propelling Jonah's body forward, out of the room.

She had gone to the garden and that's where his feet took him, through the front door, around the house and down the path to the fountain, long since broken and out of use. He walked around it, considering it from all angles, feeling frustrated and very suddenly silly. He sat against its base. Mist swirled in the air, painting the untended surroundings with a dreamy brush. What had overcome him? What had that been?

He closed his eyes and lifted his face to the sky. This was . . . no, this was for Clara. He'd gotten carried away because he wanted so badly to please her, to beg her forgiveness. *Help me help you.*

The wind had grown softer, ruffling Jonah's hair as if it were someone's soft touch. A hush descended and he felt a feather-light tickle against his hand and opened his eyes. An errant petal from a distant flower brushed over his knuckle before being picked up by the wind once more and landing on a stone rosette on the side of the fountain. Jonah stared at it, the crimson petal reminding him of a drop of blood against the sun-bleached stone.

He tilted his head, regarding the rosette upon which the petal had landed. Something about it seemed . . . crooked. He reached out slowly, his fingers pressing against the carved flower. *It's loose.*

His heart started pounding rapidly again as he turned so he was fully facing it and used both hands to pry it loose. It came out with a grating sound and he let out a surprised breath. There was a piece of paper inside, folded up so as to be small enough to fit behind the decorative carving.

With shaking hands, Jonah pried it out, unfolding the tattered paper, trying to control his heart rate. His whole body felt charged, a vibration rippling through his veins.

The light, the truth, the light, the truth.

As delicately as possible, he smoothed it out on his thigh, noticing that the bottom edge looked burned, as though it'd been pulled from a fire.

The slanted script, small formal letters mixed with large sweeping ones, was dark and rich and completely preserved. The amazement he felt at having found it was almost too much to comprehend.

The note. Oh dear lord, it's the note.

Jonah read it, each line, then again, his breath coming out in a loud gasp. Oh *Jesus.* John had not only loved Angelina, he had loved her so much he was willing to sacrifice everything for her. *Oh God.*

Jonah knew the truth. He was holding it in his hand.

The wind whipped up again, joy coursing through him that was so pure and strong, it was almost painful. It burst forth, leaving him breathless and in awe as if love itself had just moved through his body.

A charm of hummingbirds danced speedily by him, their iridescent wings fluttering against the scarred side of his face as he closed his eyes and drew back on a surprised inhale.

When he opened his eyes again, they were gone and the mist on the ground began to dissipate as the sun moved from behind a cloud.

"Did you see it?" Myrtle's voice rang out. "Oh Lordy, Lordy! Did you seem them?"

Jonah staggered to his feet, turning to Myrtle. "Who?" He felt dazed, almost drugged as he looked down at the piece of paper in his hand again, marveling at what he'd found.

"He picked her up. They were laughing and crying and he swung her right around, and they disappeared together into the mist. Oh Glory Be. I gotta sit down."

She reached a hand to her face, frowning as her hand fell away. "Where are my glasses? Oh Lordy I'm not wearing them." She glanced back to the place she'd come from, squinting into the quickly dissipating mist, facing Jonah again with a confused frown.

Jonah waved the note in his hand at Myrtle. "I have to go to her, Myr—" He suddenly paused. November first. It was Clara's opening night. Fuck, how had he forgotten? Because he'd made sure to. He hadn't *wanted* to picture her dancing so beautifully under those bright lights, knowing he couldn't be there.

"I have to tell her," he said. "Now. Right now. Will you drive me to the downtown theater? I don't want to waste time finding parking." *I don't want to be too late.*

Myrtle looked shocked. "The wonders of this day might never cease."

She grabbed Jonah's hand and practically dragged him out of the garden, apparently worried he might change his mind.

But he wasn't going to change his mind.

He was *not* going to be too late.

CHAPTER THIRTY-SEVEN

"Blast this traffic," Myrtle blurted, glancing at Jonah worriedly through her Coke-bottle glasses, the ones she'd thankfully stopped to put on before getting behind the wheel of a car.

He'd spent the first fifteen minutes of the drive attempting to calm his breathing. He rubbed his sweaty palms down his thighs, forcing himself to take large gulps of air. The happenings of the day seemed like a dream, or something that had happened in a story, not to him. But they had. They *had.*

Outside of the car, a parade passed by on a street that ran horizontally. They were only about ten minutes from the theater, but he was already late. The show was probably halfway over by now.

Streets were blocked off everywhere because of the parade, and unprepared, they'd gotten stuck in it.

"Day of the Dead," Myrtle mumbled.

"What?"

"The parade. They're celebrating the Day of the Dead."

"Huh." Jonah watched for a moment, anxious energy pumping through his veins. Day of the Dead. Of course it was.

He made a split-second decision, taking the mask from his pocket. "I'm going to get out here," he said. "I think it'll be quicker if I walk."

Myrtle glanced at the mask. "No, Jonah," she said, so much heartache in her voice. "Not that old thing."

"Don't worry, Myrtle. It's okay." Grabbing the handle, he opened the door. He began stepping out and then turned back to Myrtle, leaning toward her and grabbing her in a fierce hug before pulling back. "Thank you," he said, his voice hoarse with appreciation. "For the ride. For loving me. For never once abandoning me. For a thousand small things. Thank you."

Myrtle nodded, tears pricking her eyes. "You're my boy," she said.

Jonah grinned, slipping on the mask, and jumping out of the car. He ran toward the street the theater was on, mixing with the parade.

He tried to stick to the sidewalk, but got caught up in the crowd and before he knew it, was being pushed along, jostled, moving as if they were all one giant, symbiotic creature.

The sky overhead was dark now, the stars hidden behind the clouds, lights and swirling ribbons bursting into the air.

"This way, Jonah. Take my hand."

He gasped, whipping his head around, trying to see Justin, for it had been his voice he heard.

He felt his hand being pulled and lurched forward, through a space in the crowd, trying to see who was ahead of him but there were too many bodies, too much movement.

"Hurry up, slowpoke. She's waiting for you."

"Justin. Slow down. Let me see you."

Jonah heard his laughter, felt his hand being tugged again as he ran faster, zipping through spaces in the crowd he hadn't even realized were there until he was bursting through them. There were so many people.

Horns blew in his ear, the laughter and celebratory sounds rising and falling as he whizzed through. Music played somewhere nearby and faces moved quickly in and out of his vision. Some had makeup done to look like skulls, some bleak, done only in black and white, others vivid and colorful with climbing flowers and swirls of magenta, blue, yellow, and red.

"I love you, little brother. Live for me. Make me proud." Justin's voice was just a whisper now as if he had moved far ahead.

Jonah staggered very suddenly out of the throng, his chest heaving, turning quickly in a full circle. *No one was there,* yet his palm still felt warm.

He stilled, tears clogging his throat, wondering if he'd just imagined what had happened. Behind him the parade continued by. A little girl handed him a red rose as she passed, looking over her shoulder and smiling as she moved away.

Jonah turned toward the street. The theater was directly in front of him. He walked toward it, his attention briefly caught by a white man and a black woman who stood in a doorway laughing and kissing. As he passed, the woman saw him watching them and smiled shyly, pushing her boyfriend away teasingly. He laughed and took her hand and they turned in the other direction.

Jonah grinned, his heart filling with sudden joy as he turned, jogging across the street, the rose gripped in his hand.

"Sir, would you like a ticket?"

Jonah turned his head to see an older gentleman. The man's eyes widened as he saw Jonah was wearing a mask, but then he glanced back down the street to the parade, the surprise fading to understanding.

"Sorry, I thought you were here to see the show. It's half over but it's sold out. My wife's not feeling well and we have two seats near the front if you'd like to enjoy the second half. It's wonderful."

Shit, Jonah hadn't even thought about a ticket. "Actually, I am here for the show. Let me pay—"

"No. I'm just happy they're not going to waste." He glanced at Jonah's mask again as he handed him the tickets, perhaps wondering why he hadn't removed it yet. His wife pulled on her husband's arm and they moved away, down the street.

Jonah gave one of the tickets to a bored ticket taker, who didn't even glance up at him and entered the theater, the outer hall deserted except for a beautiful woman with long, dark curly hair to her waist standing behind a coffee counter.

There was a vase of white roses in front of her and Jonah hesitated but then turned, approaching her.

She took in his mask, but didn't comment on it, instead asking, "We sold out of baked goods during intermission, but there's still a cup or two of hot coffee if you'd like one?" She looked tired, but there was unmistakable pride shining from her eyes.

Jonah shook his head. "Can I buy one of those roses?"

She looked slightly confused, but plucked one from the vase, handing it to him. Jonah dug a twenty out of his pocket and threw it on the counter. "Thanks."

Jonah could hear the music from behind the doors in front of him and his heart thrummed in his chest, beckoning him forward. Toward Clara.

He pushed the doors to the darkened theater open, the music swelling as he ducked inside.

All eyes were cast on the stage as he took his seat and he only received a few second glances from the people directly around him. But then they turned their attention back to the performance and Jonah did as well.

He lost himself in the story, in the heart-squeezing beauty of Clara's dancing, in the pride he felt in her, soaring inside of him along with the musical notes.

Right then, he didn't love her for how she made him feel, or how she'd inspired him, or anything else that had to do with himself. For that moment in time, Jonah just loved her for *her,* for Clara, for the woman who had spent hour after hour practicing so resolutely that she danced like an angel. For her heart, for her mind, for all the ways she made the world a better place by being in it. He loved her purely, deeply, and with every fiber of his being.

Keep your eyes on me.

The show came to an end, Jonah's anxiety returning, flooding through his body and causing his heart to pound against his ribs.

The lights came on as the audience stood, bravos being flung into the air, whistles rising high above the crowd. Jonah focused on breathing, his eyes never leaving the swan who emerged with the other dancers, smiling that smile he hoped to see every day for the rest of his life. *Please. Please.*

The audience began sitting, those around him taking their seats and beginning to gather their things. But Jonah remained standing as the dancers began leaving the stage, the stage lights dimming.

Murmurs began, then whispers as the audience members noticed him standing there alone in his mask.

The swan, Clara, hesitated and then turned, her gaze locking with his, eyes growing wide. Her lips parted and she walked back toward the center of the stage, the other dancers stopping and turning their heads to watch her.

Jonah stood in the audience looking up at her, breathing heavily under the rubber of the mask, and Clara stood on stage, a singular spotlight on her as she peered back at him. Waiting.

Keep your eyes on me.

He heard the whispers now. They broke through his fear, his uncertainty.

Oh my God. It's the do-gooder. Have you heard of him?

That guy who goes around helping people?

What's he doing here?

I think he's here for her. The dancer.

Oh God, what would they think when he revealed himself?

Keep your eyes on me.

Jonah reached up and the whole auditorium seemed to still as he pulled the mask up and off, dropping it on the floor beside him as he took in a shuddery breath.

Clara grinned, putting her hands over her mouth as tears rolled down her cheeks.

There was a collective gasp in the theater as people took in his damaged face, but he didn't turn his gaze to any of them. He kept his eyes on her for another frozen moment as she walked to the edge of the stage, as close to him as she could get.

Who . . . who is he? He looks familiar somehow.

How do you think he got those scars?

I don't know. But this is one story I've gotta hear.

He saw flashes in his peripheral vision. People were taking pictures, recording this moment, documenting it for all time. *Keep your eyes on me.*

"Step on me!" one of the audience members said, and confused, Jonah finally broke eye contact with Clara to look at a guy who was offering Clara his back so she could step off the stage.

Clara laughed through her tears as several other men turned, beckoning her forward. She took the first step, the audience reaching their hands up to help her stay stable as she crowd-surfed toward him.

Jonah laughed, braving a glance at a woman next to him and seeing that instead of horror, she had a look of wonder on her face.

Clara drew nearer, and he held out his arms for her, grasping her as she slid down his body, tears still coursing down her cheeks, mixing with the heavy makeup she had on, several thick black trails marring her cheeks. She looked like a mess and he loved her so much it hurt.

He handed her both the white and red roses and she blinked, her face crumbling for a moment before she laughed with joy.

She brought her hands to his face, gripping him, the whole of him, and he leaned forward, their foreheads coming together gently. "I love you."

She sniffled, laughing, another black trail making its way down her face. "I love you too. My wish collector."

"I have so much to tell you, Clara. You won't even believe—"

She ran a thumb over his lips. "I *will* believe."

He smiled against her thumb. Of course she'd believe. She always had. In Angelina. In justice. In *him.*

Jonah kissed her as the flashes continued to blink around them, the audience standing again, the claps beginning slowly and then swelling into an ovation that this time, was for them.

For love.

For magic.

For impossible wishes that somehow came true.

CHAPTER THIRTY-EIGHT

Dear Angelina,

I am entrusting this letter to my friend and comrade, Timothy Mansfield, and know in all faith that he will read it to you and that you, my love, shall hear my voice and cast aside any doubts that my absence has created.

I love you, Angelina Loreaux. I love you with the whole of my heart and every ounce of my soul. Neither time, nor distance, nor a million smoke-filled battlefields stretched before me will ever deter me from returning to you and loving you until every last star falls from the sky.

I am risking greatly in the fight for your freedom—and for my own, for if you are not free to love me, my life is without meaning—a fight of which I cannot speak just yet.

But have faith, my love. Believe that the world ***can*** *change, and that indeed it* ***will*** *change.*

Your eternal love,
John

EPILOGUE

Twinkle lights sparkled in the trees around them, casting the rose garden in a romantic glow.

Jonah took Clara's hand in his as they walked the cobblestone path, the sweet, sultry fragrance of roses swirling in the evening air.

From the open balconies, voices and laughter could be heard, and Jonah's lips curved into a smile as he glanced toward the place that had once been his self-made prison and was now one of his greatest sources of pride.

He stopped and turned toward his wife, pulling her against him and smiling down into her lovely face.

"You get more beautiful by the day," he said, letting go of her waist and taking her hands so he could step back and look at her.

She laughed, moving from side to side so that her black, lace dress swirled around her legs. She looked as though she *felt* beautiful. Loved. As she should for she was both.

She moved forward, bringing her hand to his scarred cheek. "So do you," she murmured, kissing him softly. And then she smiled, that smile that lit up his entire world.

Inside Windisle, the event being hosted by the Historic Preservation Society was just getting started. Clara and Jonah had wanted a few moments to themselves before dinner, so they'd escaped to the garden.

It had been five years since Jonah had gifted Windisle to the society. He and Clara had both agreed it was the right thing to do to preserve history and all that had happened behind the weeping wall.

The society, thrilled with the gift, had worked tirelessly to bring Windisle back to its former glory. They'd made the necessary repairs to the house—including fixing the rotting slave cabins—using artisans and craftsmen dedicated to preserving and presenting the story of Windisle, one of the American South's most important legacy homes.

Not only were they interested in preserving the plantation, but also the stories of those who had lived there. The brand new gift shop on the first floor—opened only the year before—sold books about the Chamberlain family and also about the story of Angelina Loreaux and John Whitfield, a book that was already a bestseller in the shop and frequently sold out. Inside was the true tale of John and Angelina's love and the resulting tragedy, including a picture of the note that Jonah had found, the original now encased in glass in an upper room of the revitalized home. Their light, *their truth,* would forever shine for all of the world to see.

The society had researched Timothy Mansfield, the man mentioned in John's letter, and found that he was a Northern soldier well known as a spy who'd funneled information from Southern soldiers working in secret with the north.

They found many documents known to belong to him that referenced the initials JW and now were believed to stand for John Whitfield, a Southern soldier who had gone to great personal risk to deliver secret information to the North so that they might win the war and free the woman he loved.

If only she had known. If only . . .

Timothy Mansfield had been killed several weeks before Angelina took her own life. It was presumed that, among other things, he had been delivering John's mail home and that the letter to Angelina had been mistakenly included in correspondence to his family.

What had John done when he discovered that his friend had been killed? When he found out that his family betrayed him and lied to Angelina? Or feared that's what might happen? There was no way to know for spies kept few records of their missions or detours home. But Jonah couldn't get the sound of those thundering hoof beats from his dream out of his head whenever he considered it. *Don't be too late . . .*

And being in love himself, Jonah understood more than ever, why John had refused medical treatment when his life was at risk, instead hurrying to join Angelina and be given the chance to love her again.

The tragedy of it all—the ways in which different choices, alternate paths, might have changed the outcome—nearly took his breath.

The garden where Jonah and Clara stood—the very garden where it was said John and Angelina first met—had been re-invigorated as well, with new, elegant pathways, stunning rose bushes, other flowers that attracted birds and butterflies, and a repaired fountain that provided the calming sound of splashing water.

Jonah imagined it looked just as it had so long ago when John and Angelina walked through it, a love blossoming in both of their hearts that the world was not yet ready for.

The weeping wall had been repaired as well, the cracks and holes filled in with new mortar, the stone cleaned, sealed, and replaced where necessary. It no longer wept. Maybe it was because of the work that had been done to it, or maybe it was because it no longer had *reason* to weep. Maybe it was science, or perhaps as his wife liked to believe, it was simply magic.

As for Jonah's own story, the corruption scandal that Savannah Hammond had uncovered brilliantly, relying on her contacts both in journalism and the justice system to find evidence and seek out the truth, had rocked New Orleans to its core.

All of these years later, Jonah was still floored at how far-reaching it'd turned out to be, at the number of defense attorneys, prosecutors, judges, and businessmen in practically every corner of the community who had been involved.

They'd all been a part of the club Jonah had been witness to, all part of a network bent on keeping secrets for one another, operating on favors and bribes and who knew what else.

Savannah Hammond, who'd been kind to him once upon a time when he'd needed it desperately, had done a damn fine job with what he'd given her, and subsequently she'd won award after award for her stellar journalism work.

But as stations everywhere pontificated about the Murray Ridgley case and the things that had been uncovered on his victim's phone, Jonah had chosen not to listen.

He'd told his story to Savannah, discussed his role in the tragedy and the betrayal by those around him. His account was all on the record and that was all he needed.

Some might criticize the fact that he'd been blind to what was going on around him, others might hail him a hero, but he didn't care anymore what strangers said. The truth had been revealed, and he kept his gaze trained solely on his wife, and the other people who loved him and knew his heart.

He still patrolled with the Brass Angels on occasion, but he'd resumed his work as an attorney, sometimes taking pro bono cases from victims of crimes whom the men referred to him. He did it for his brother. He did it for himself. It was his small contribution to *justice.*

And every so often . . . he granted a wish. Or two.

"Jonah," Clara said, stopping and sitting on the edge of the fountain. Jonah had a flashback to her sitting that way another time as he'd watched her longingly from the shadows of the trees beyond.

He sat beside her, the lights of the fountain glowing softly behind them. He tilted his head as she pulled her lip between her teeth, her expression uncertain.

"What is it?"

"I've been thinking." She paused, using her finger to trace an invisible path over the stone on which they were sitting. She met his eyes. "What would you think if I opened a ballet studio?"

He frowned, taken off guard. She'd talked about doing that someday but . . . not yet. At twenty-seven, she still had years of performing ahead of her. "Won't that be a lot? With your practice schedule and—"

"I'd quit the ballet." She shrugged, giving him a small smile.

Quit the ballet? It was such a big part of her life. She'd moved swiftly up the ranks to principal ballerina, and Jonah loved to watch her dance. He still brought a red and white rose to every local performance, or had them delivered when she was traveling, and he'd expected that he would for years to come.

"But it's your dream."

"It was. And I lived it. To the hilt. But the truth is, I have a bigger dream." She put her hand on her flat stomach.

Jonah frowned, confused and then . . . *oh.* He released a breath. "You want a baby?"

She laughed softly, shrugging again. "I do. Very much. And good thing because we did."

"We did what?"

"Made a baby."

Jonah blinked at her, his eyes moving between her face and her hand still splayed over her stomach, realization dropping over him, along with a tingle of joy that buzzed beneath his ribcage. "How—?"

"That rainstorm . . ."

Yes, the rainstorm. The power had gone off for four days and there had been flooding everywhere. Clara hadn't been able to get out to refill her birth control and well . . . it had been dark and stormy and they'd lost themselves in each other, not leaving their small but beautiful, historic home in Uptown New Orleans for days. Jonah hadn't been able to help himself.

He ran a hand through his hair. "This is my fault."

Clara laughed. "It absolutely is." She grinned, clearly happy about the news and Jonah laughed too, standing and sweeping her into his arms, turning her around as he kissed her.

He leaned his forehead against hers and for a moment they just breathed together as Jonah digested the news.

So much happiness swirled within him—hope—but a thread of worry wove through him as well. "Will he or she—"

"Yes," Clara breathed, bringing her hand to his scarred cheek, reading his concern before he'd even voiced it. "This baby will be *proud* to have you for a father. Lucky and proud."

Jonah released a breath, keeping his eyes on her as he'd done so many times over the past five years.

He pulled his wife closer, taking a moment to glory in the feel of her, the knowledge that together, they'd created life. A miracle. God, but he would try to be the best father he could. A father like Clara had had, the man Jonah had only met briefly when he flew to Ohio with Clara the Christmas after he'd found John's letter. The man who had passed away only a few months after that, but whose legacy was a beautiful, loving woman who made the world a better place. In the end, what more could anyone hope for?

"We should get inside," Clara whispered, kissing him again before pulling away. "Dinner and the presentation will be starting. And Myrtle will be putting on her glasses to come looking for us."

Jonah nodded on a smile, lingering another few moments with the woman he loved in this place that always felt enchanted.

And then he took her hand as they turned toward the house where so many of the people they'd come to call family were waiting for them: Myrtle and Cecil of course, his brothers from the Brass Angels, Fabienne—who Clara had formed a close friendship with—and her husband, Alphonse, fellow dancers, Belinda and Roxanne, and Mrs. Guillot and her "gentlemen friend", Harry Rochefort.

Tonight they would be the first to see a piece of evidence given to the society, which had been found in an old attic by a distant relative of John Whitfield. Signed by Abraham Lincoln himself, John was applauded for his work for emancipation, for diligence in righting the wrong of slavery. *He was hailed a hero. Rightfully.*

Clara looked up and Jonah followed her gaze as two stars streaked across the sky, dancing over one another and leaving shimmering trails of light in their wake. The glittering glow faded slowly, disappearing into some distant place far beyond.

"Do you think they're up there?" Clara murmured.

Jonah glanced at her, his heart swelling with love for the woman he'd first fallen in love with through a wall of stone and who he now walked side by side with through the world.

He'd once been her wish collector, but she'd been the one to give him all of the things he'd never dared to dream of. *Happiness. Peace. Pride. A soul mate.*

"Yes," Jonah whispered, squeezing her hand. That night it was easy to believe in magic. That night, there was magic all around him.

Dear John,

My deepest gratitude for your service to the Republic of which you performed at great peril to your own life, and despite tragic personal loss. The information you obtained led to advancements in the war that resulted in numerous victories for the Union, and hope for every man, woman, and child whose freedom has been granted.

It is my profound belief that the path you chose is one that history will judge to be righteous.

Respectfully, your friend,
A. Lincoln

ACKNOWLEDGMENTS

So many wonderful, talented people helped me tell this story and my heart is overflowing with thankfulness that I get to call them mine.

To my editing team, Angela Smith, Marion Archer, and Karen Lawson—You three help me dig deeper, try harder, tweak, tighten, and polish until my story shines. What would I do without you? (Answer: flounder—*a lot.*).

Renita McKinney, words cannot express how much I value you. Thank you for your seal of approval—without it, I would not have published this book.

The utmost gratitude to my amazing team of beta readers: Stephanie Hockersmith, Korrie Kelley, Cat Bracht, and Stacey Hert. Thank you for encouraging, for suggesting, for answering a million questions, and for spending so many hours helping me to perfect my characters and my story.

And to Elena Eckmeyer. I love you more than Stouffers.

Thank you to Kimberly Brower, my agent/superhero.

To you, the reader, thank you for taking this journey with me. Without you, I wouldn't be able to make my dream job a career, and for that, I owe you the world.

Thank you to Mia's Mafia for your constant love and support and for always showing up.

To all the book bloggers who spend their precious time promoting the stories they love, and filling social media with beauty and positivity. You are my heroines!

This book began as a short story I wrote back in 2016 and then shelved. Since then, my husband has been pestering me to turn it into a full-length novel. So, here you go, my love. Without you, these characters would still be sitting on a dusty shelf. Their souls belong to you. Then again, so does mine.

ABOUT THE AUTHOR

Mia Sheridan is a *New York Times, USA Today,* and *Wall Street Journal* Bestselling author. Her passion is weaving true love stories about people destined to be together. Mia lives in Cincinnati, Ohio with her husband. They have four children here on earth and one in heaven. In addition to Dane's Storm, Leo, Leo's Chance, Stinger, Archer's Voice, Becoming Calder, Finding Eden, Kyland, Grayson's Vow, Midnight Lily, Ramsay, and Preston's Honor are also part of the Sign of Love collection.

The standalone romance novels, Most of All You, and More Than Words, published via Grand Central Publishing, are available online and in bookstores.

Mia can be found online at:

MiaSheridan.com
Twitter, @MSheridanAuthor
Instagram, @MiaSheridanAuthor
Facebook.com/MiaSheridanAuthor

CPSIA information can be obtained
at www.ICGtesting.com
Printed in the USA
LVHW042350140119
603949LV00009B/443/P